GW00982544

A MELODY OF TEARS:
Sorrows of Syria

by Anas A. Ismael

New Friends Publishing, LLC

A Melody of Tears:
Sorrows of Syria

This is a work of fiction.
A Melody of Tears is based in part on the
true life stories of some Syrians.
Certain characters and incidents are a product
of the author's imagination.
Any relationship to other persons living or dead
is purely coincidental.

ISBN-13: 978-1-940354-07-1

All rights reserved
Copyright © 2013 by Anas A. Ismael

No part of this book may be reproduced
in whole or in part by any means
without permission of the author.

Cover design by
Yazan
All rights reserved

Cover photo credit
REUTERS/Zain Karam

Published by
New Friends Publishing, LLC
Lake Havasu City, AZ

Visit New Friends Publishing's website at
www.newfriendspublishing.com

Printing history
First edition published in September 2013

Dedication

I dedicate this novel to everyone who lost his or her life fighting for freedom and liberty, whether in Syria or elsewhere around the world.

Acknowledgements

A special thank you to all those who helped me and encouraged me to write this novel particularly Bill, Birchmore, Yazan, Bryan, A. Faour, Sanabelle, Richard, May, Anne, and Kareema.

Table of Contents

Preface

More than 100,000 Syrians have been killed in what many now call the Syrian Genocide. Millions are wounded, homeless, and hungry. In spite of all that, the brave men and women of Syria have persevered in their great quest for freedom and liberty with minimal support from the outside world. *A Melody of Tears* is a love story that begins a few months prior to the Syrian Revolution. The background events of the story are a reality that most Syrians continue to live on a daily basis, and many of the characters are based on real people and their stories. Their names have been changed.

The sorrows of Syria are far from over and the final ending of the Syrian story is yet to be determined. After decades of cruel oppression, the people of Syria deserve a free and democratic country built on the principles of human rights and social equality.

Chapter 1

Routine

August 15, 2010
Deaths: 0

Routine is one of life's worst misfortunes. To wake before dawn and reluctantly rush to work, to merely pretend at being fully alert and interested, the plastic smile and artificial glow of the eyes become necessary makeup. Even in his dream, Waleed could hear the hospital's rusty front door squeaking in pain as he pried it open. Above the door hung a decade-old picture of Bashar Al-Assad, dictator of Syria. The picture's original white had yellowed, but no one dared change it for a newer one.

It was this last haunting image that stuck in Waleed's mind as he startled awake to the call of his mother's voice.

"Waleedo! *Yalla* [Come on]!" Her tone always sounded somehow shriller on Fridays, his only day off each week.

"*Sho*, Mama?" he yelled back. "What do you want?" The question was more rhetorical, for he knew already how the conversation would go.

"Don't yell when I talk to you! *Yalla*, go get ready for Friday prayer. How old are you? Do I still have to remind you of Friday prayer? What will you tell God on judgment day . . ." She went on and on.

"I'm up," he said as he rose and stepped to the bathroom. "Getting in the shower now." From the heat of the water that trickled over his outstretched hand, he could see that the government had cut neither the water nor the electricity in the past twenty-four hours. For a young man living in Homs, a dreary and tightly packed city in central Syria, this would be a rare treat, a warm shower.

His mom's voice shattered the peace the sensation delivered him. "Don't use all the hot water, Waleedo!"

He ignored her. Not only that, he used the expensive shampoo to wash himself instead of the cheap body soap. He smiled as he did so, as if imagining the reaction on his mom's face when she realized that the shampoo was out much sooner than she had calculated. He didn't really feel guilty about it, either. Call it his small shower rebellion. In the shower, no one's social or political norms applied. It was a place where he could sing out loud, draw funny pictures of the president on the accumulating vapor, and even dance naked. It was like the shower didn't belong to Syria's specific space-time-regime continuum. As long as the water was running and the door was locked, this was truly a free space where not even the Syrian secret police known as the Mukhabarat could reach him. If only the family could afford to allow him showers every day. The water and electricity bills had been crazy lately.

Free as he had felt, when he shut off the water, reality returned to him in an instant. Propelled by a deeply ingrained fear of government reprisal, he carefully wiped away all the drawings and words he had written about the president for fear that future vapor would return them in ghostly condensation. There was no way to know, after all, whether and when the Mukhabarat might feel compelled to enter his bathroom.

Back in his cramped bedroom, he slid into his clothes. They smelled fresh, for his mother had just washed and dried them the previous night. He finished dressing by putting on his white, round prayer hat. By now he felt better and much more alert.

"Good morning, Father," he said as he trundled down the stairs.

Waleed's father, Mohammad, a high school physics teacher who made a living out of giving private lessons to rich kids in and around the city, merely grunted in reply. Waleed knew him to favor mornings as brightly as he did.

"You were in there a long time," said Khalid, Waleed's oldest brother. He was a dour and secretly devout believer—hardly a positive trait in Syria.

"Mama will never let you hear the end of it if there is no hot water when we return," said Sami. With his quiet disposition, Waleed's other brother could not have been more different from Khalid, although he was never afraid to speak his mind. He was not shy about admitting to a distaste for soccer and sports in general. He was unembarrassed by his passion for the arts. He refused to be a doctor, a lawyer, or an engineer despite the tremendous family pressure that was applied on him. However, what alarmed his family was that sometimes Sami appeared to be unafraid of speaking openly about politics. His unpredictability was dangerous yet intriguing.

"Never mind the shower," Waleed said, shrugging off his brothers' stares as he moved toward the door, his father's hulking shadow leading the way.

Outside, the whole neighborhood shuffled together toward prayer under the burning August sun. The dwellings rose up on either side of the corridor as blockish multistory hives so sand-blown that they had nearly shed their concrete charm. In a few long blocks, these dreary structures gave way to a massive and startlingly green courtyard at the foot of an ornate, multi-domed mosque. Its domes gleamed in impeccable silver. Its twin spires towered as the highest points in the city. The buzz of the men filing toward it hung heavy in the air. There was an easy silence, which was not entirely due to a special devoutness among Syrians. Rather, it had something to do with the fact that the Mukhabarat so thoroughly monitored the Friday prayer sermons.

As he approached the impressive building with his family, Waleed was glad to see his friend Omar. The young man moved in his strangely nervous way toward the mosque. So intent was he to get inside that he didn't notice Waleed's approach.

"*Sho*, my friend," Waleed called out.

Omar turned, a confused look on his round but pleasant face. "Ah, Waleed. I didn't see you."

Waleed noted Omar's disheveled hair beneath his prayer hat, which stood cockeyed atop his head. His clothes appeared clean, but a healthy ring of dust had collected near his ankles. "You look how I feel."

"I feel fine." All the same, Omar looked down at his feet as if to examine himself.

"It was a joke," Waleed said with a chuckle.

The smile on Omar's face warmed him from within the same way the sun warmed him from above. He had known Omar since primary school. They had spent endless nights together during high school, studying for exams and completing projects. Omar had dedicated a lot of his time to helping Waleed through high school in both academic and non-academic ways. Waleed sometimes wondered if he would have ever made it to medical school without his good friend's support. They separated for six years during medical school, Omar securing his medical degree from the University of Damascus while Waleed matriculated to Aleppo. Their reunion came a year ago when they began residency training. Omar's secret plan had always been to complete his training, move to America, and drag Waleed with him, but destiny had other ideas.

Side by side, the two friends passed into the relative cool of the mosque, their families intermingling all around them. Sandwiched between his two brothers, Waleed came to kneel and await the imam's first prayer. Before him stretched a sea of men in white, their prayer caps like the breakers of waves in a storm.

The first sermon flew by while Waleed daydreamed. He pondered the usual stresses of his life, namely his job and his government. On the former, though this was supposed to be his day off, he could not stop thinking about the annoyance of his typical routine. He so disliked how the patients always got mad when he woke them too early, and how he couldn't respond in kind because it wasn't considered professional. Instead, every morning he had to put on a mask of compassion and beg their pardon, then keep pretending that he was excited about being a doctor; pretend he loved his coworkers; pretend he knew what he was doing all the time; pretend that two hundred dollars a month was enough money; and of course, pretend that he loved the way the government, who everyone had been trained to adore, managed the healthcare system. Adhering to that last one was of special importance, but to Waleed, as to most everyone, it came naturally. It was a show that every Syrian child must master in kindergarten and perfect before completing their schooling. Some people joked that this was one reason that Syrian drama and TV production had flourished in recent years. Everyone was so good at pretending.

Waleed glanced toward the *minbar* at the head of the human sea, where the imam continued to drone about something he wasn't following. He chanced a look at his brother Khalid, who kept his dark and serious eyes fixed on the prayer leader. Khalid seemed a true believer, and for him, it was not routine. Or maybe it was. There was no way to know. Only the Mukhabarat possessed such knowledge. Khalid had been unemployed for months in spite of graduating with a law degree from the University of Aleppo. It was there, in Aleppo, that Waleed and his older brother had really gotten to know each other well. For the first time in their lives, they found themselves outside their family routines and occupying two new roles. They were no longer brothers fighting over who should wash the dishes, but rather, two bachelors in a beautiful city glowing with joy—on the outside, at least. In this way, the two brothers had learned to love each other only when they realized that what really connected them was neither blood nor duty.

"Hasten to the remembrance of Allah," the imam said, snapping Waleed back to reality.

To his left, he heard Sami snicker as the imam began praising the Syrian president. Waleed turned to glare at him, reminding him with a look that the secret police were watching. Sami appeared unconcerned. This came as no surprise to Waleed. His brother was far more into arts and music than he was into acting. Such was his disinterest in the latter that many in the family feared he might not be safe in Syria much longer. Already there was talk of sending him away to America for his own sake.

"We seek refuge in Allah from the evils of our selves," the imam continued.

With that, Waleed drifted back into his daydreaming.

As a twenty-five-year-old internal medicine resident, he was just another actor in this four-decades-long drama that was Syrian compliance with the ruling party. From a distance, it appeared that he loved everything about his life: his job, his salary, and his government. But deep inside, deeper than he dared go, he was sick of it all. He was sick of merely existing. Every Friday morning, he followed this same routine, forcing himself out of bed so he could go to Friday prayer with his father and two brothers. He always made sure to shave his face especially well on these days so that the government agents at the mosque wouldn't think he was associated with a religious opposition group. In Syria, government agents were as much a part of life as hummus and tabbouleh. They were everywhere and nowhere. They were the eyes of a government that could see you even when you were changing your clothes. They could read your thoughts and interpret your dreams. Syrians said that everyone was a government agent until proven otherwise, but how do you prove someone otherwise? You don't.

The first sermon passed without Waleed catching further word. Not wanting to appear disinterested, he tried to tune in to the second sermon, finding that, as usual, it was about Gaza.

"What human being can do the things that were done to the children of Gaza?" the imam said. He was so far away that Waleed could not see his face. Through the heat of the room, the imam flickered like a white candle. His voice carried loudly all the same. "What human being could accept the cruel blockade on Gaza?"

The imam went on and on in this fashion. Ever since the war in Gaza had broken out several years ago, it had been the primary topic for religious leaders in Syria. It was featured in speeches by the president, the first lady, the media, the mosques, the TV shows. It was like this with most things. Every few years, one topic became the obsession of the Syrian media until it was hammered into everyone's minds. Before Gaza, it had been the war in Lebanon. The media had obsessed about it so much that everyone kept a Hezbollah flag in their apartments or their houses. Before that, it was the war in Iraq. It was always the same theme: a Western power conspiring against the Arabs, an Arab nation being victimized, and Syria standing as the only country to defy that Western imperialism. For this reason, the regime loved to refer to Syria as the "fortress of resistance." Oddly, sometimes after the media invested time and money projecting someone as a villain, they would change their minds about him and initiate a reverse propaganda campaign. It got confusing.

With a "Peace be upon you," the imam announced the prayer over.

As the congregation replied with a voice of its own, Waleed shook himself out of his reverie. The walls seemed to vibrate from the more than three hundred voices rising to the same call. Everyone rose at once, herding only vaguely toward the doors and talking like old friends. Some meant these shows of affection. Others merely put on faces to demonstrate their dedication to harmony under the gaze of the Mukhabarat that stood like sentinels along every wall.

Silently Waleed scanned the crowd for Omar. They had gotten separated in the scrum of men finding their places. After prayer, the challenge was to pick your way out of the building without running into ten people who knew you and wanted to chat. It was only Omar that Waleed wanted to see.

Alas, there would be no second meeting on this morning. Instead, Waleed dived into the small talk alongside his father and brothers. They greeted neighbors, friends, and social risers. It was a picturesque routine that the people of Syria, and Homs in particular, would soon dearly miss.

Chapter 2
Facebook

> *Facebook was one of many websites in Syria that the government would ban one day and allow the next. The decision whether to block or allow a website depended on a multitude of factors. For example, any political or religious website was blocked. Any site that "offended social norms" was blocked, except those which brought cash to the pockets of Rami Makhlouf, the president's cousin. All the profits from cell phones, internet services, and most communi-cation media went directly into Makhlouf's bank accounts. While his greed had certainly hurt most small business owners in the country, it had the benefit of liberalizing the use of cell phones and internet access, given the great profit they generated. Facebook was blocked and unblocked so many times that it seemed the government couldn't decide whether or not it was worth the profit. The main risk it posed was its ability to allow young Syrians to form groups and think freely with limited government restrictions. On the other hand, it allowed the Mukhabarat to easily collect voluntarily shared information about people who used the site. In a sense, Facebook is and was every intelligence agency's dream.*
> *—Syria: A History in Blood* by Celine Dubois

September 15, 2010
Deaths:0

One Thursday night in September, Waleed was up late trying out his new Facebook account. He sat in the small den in the corner of his house, the lights turned low because the rest of his family had retired to bed long ago. He was so enthralled with the images on the screen, so enamored with the way the light glowed warmly over his fingertips, that he hardly noticed the hour. There were three new notifications on his page. When he saw them, he felt as excited as a child getting ready to open his Christmas presents. Could it be a new friend request from someone who would change his life? Could it be a message from an old friend? Or perhaps an invitation to a secret group of people who were sick of the status quo?

His fantasies faded away quickly, as two of them were "likes" for his new profile picture. They weren't even from anyone special, really—just some random people he hardly knew.

The third notification, however, was a message from Sireen. Sireen represented one fifth of a larger circle of friends that Waleed shared with Omar. They were a nonpolitical group, of course, but they had long enjoyed each other's company. Her message read:

> *Hi, Waleed. Thanks for adding me on Facebook. I will be in the main library on Sunday. I'm trying to decide on a graduation thesis. Why don't you stop by?*

To this, Waleed replied:

> *Hey, Sireen. You are welcome. Why don't we meet at lunchtime at the falafel place near your college instead? I've spent the last six years of my life in libraries. I don't think I'll be of much use in helping you pick a graduation thesis. I don't know much Syrian history. We invented writing. Then the Romans occupied us, then the Turks, then the French, and then Hafez Al-Assad.*

To his surprise, she replied instantly. He did not expect her to be up at this time.

> *Are you crazy? Don't you know Facebook is watched? Don't talk politics here. They'll liquidate us both.*

Waleed sighed as he typed his reply:

> *Calm down. What did I say? I just mentioned his name, I didn't insult or anything. Why are you still up, anyway?*

> *I can't sleep.*

> *Why not? Are you worried about not finding a topic for your graduation thesis?*

There was a long pause as Waleed awaited her reply. He turned and glanced behind him to make sure no one in his family had sneaked in to read over his shoulder. Finally, her response came through:

> *No, not really. I have a few ideas in mind already. I'll*

probably do something related to the evolution of the modern Syrian dialect. I think I miss my family in Daraa.

Don't worry. Before you know it, it will be spring break. College time flies by fast. Why don't you hang out with some girls in your dorms?

My roommate isn't home this week. She went back to her family.

Sireen's roommate was a girl named Fatima, another member of the five friends along with Omar and Sireen. She was from a village close to Homs and was majoring in English literature. Her father was a rich businessman who treated her like a princess. She dyed her hair blond and always had a cloud of perfume exuding from her clothes. Her main objective in life was to find a rich husband. The edge of her ambitions was to live in a large house and drive expensive cars. She was fairly attractive to men, but was rarely impressed by any of them. She had gained notoriety for dumping her boyfriends days after starting to date them. But Sireen loved her, and that gave her a carte blanche to be in the group.

That Sireen cared for Fatima was no small thing, either, as she indicated in her continued response to Waleed:

To be honest, I don't get along with girls very well. I've been that way since I was a child. I just can't seem to enjoy the topics they like to talk about.

For the first time, Waleed glanced at the clock. He cared little that the time read 1:37 a.m., for here he saw an opportunity:

Well, if you want, I'm still up and I don't plan on going to sleep anytime soon.

Another long pause followed before Sireen returned:

I don't think I understand what you mean.

Nothing. I just thought that you might be feeling lonely and would want someone to be with you.

Someone like whom?

Waleed's heart began to beat quicker as he typed his reply:

Someone like me.

Another long pause, this one unbearable. Waleed found his fingers fidgeting over the keys, itching to type about a dozen different things at once to explain himself. He didn't mean to have been so presumptuous. Or had he?

Finally, the reply came through:

Are you suggesting that I sneak you into the girls' dormitory?

I don't know. If you want.

Thanks, but no thanks. I can't believe it! You guys know how to turn everything into an opportunity!

Waleed felt as if he might break into a cold sweat. He furrowed his brow as he typed.

No! That's absolutely not what I had in mind. I would just hate it if all the Jinn stories about the girl dorms were true and you happened to be alone when they showed up.

Don't worry, the Jinn are scared of me.

A smile broke over Waleed's lips, diffusing the tension he felt.

Good, because before you moved into the girls' dorms, people reported seeing Jinn there. They appeared in apartment 17 in the form of a little girl called Dalida.

Waleed! Don't joke about those things. You'll make me nervous. And how did you know I live in apartment 17?

Waleed chuckled under his breath.

I didn't know that. What does it matter, anyway? I thought you weren't scared of the Jinn. . .

I'm not. There is no such thing.

If you say so.

For the first time, the lateness began to close in on Waleed. He yawned broadly, leaning back in his chair as he waited to see where Sireen would take the conversation. Her message made him laugh, this time out loud:

So what happened to the girls who saw them?

No one knows. It was just one girl. She disappeared right before you moved in. She was extremely smart and beautiful. She used to study political science. She loved politics. Then one day she vanished and rumors spread that she used to deal with Jinn. I didn't believe them, but I'm just telling you.

Waleed . . .

Sho?

Now I'm scared. But no, you cannot come to my apartment alone.

Okay, I'll just go to sleep then.

No, don't! Please.

By now, Waleed had been beaming for so long that his cheeks began to hurt. He typed feverishly.

It's okay. Just keep all the lights on. I hear the Jinn are scared of light.

I have a solution. Come to my building and we'll go for a walk in the street until sunrise. Then I won't be scared.

I'm really tired. You'll be fine. I shouldn't have told you those stories.

Waleed!

The sensation of warmth began to spread over Waleed's chest as he teased her in reply:

What if someone sees us walking alone at night? What would people say?

Are you serious? I'm the one who should be worried about that, not you. Don't you know how our dumb male chauvinistic society works? Always blame the woman. Just come, please. I think I'm hearing things.

With a sigh, Waleed checked the clock once more. It was 2:00 a.m. The chances of being spotted at this hour seemed much smaller. Besides, he did want to see Sireen—more than he ever would have guessed.

> *All right, I'll be there in fifteen minutes. Do you need anything?*

> *Great! Bring some sunflower seeds and soft drinks with you.*

> *Any other orders, your highness?*

> *No thanks. See you soon.*

Five minutes later, Waleed was riding toward the college campus on his bicycle.

~~~

Homs was peacefully asleep in her diamond-sprinkled nightgown, beautiful as she had always been for thousands of years. Like the rest of Syria, she was ancient, calm, and wise, yet oblivious to the pain and tears that awaited her. This would not be the first time that Syria would witness the massacre of her children with her own eyes. Perhaps it wasn't oblivion, but wisdom. Perhaps she had survived enough invasions and destruction that she no longer had any fear. After all, countries don't die. Nations don't die. Only people do.

~~~

Sireen pulled her arms tightly around her waist as she waited for Waleed. The city had assumed a deathly silence. In the eerie stillness, every sound to her was the Jinn. She jumped at every movement, every motion she caught with her wide eyes.

She knew she shouldn't be so fearful. She was too old to be afraid of such things, after all. This was her last year of majoring in ancient history and English literature. She wondered what her parents would say about her jumpiness. Her father was a Damascene merchant and her mother a survivor of the Hama "events," a refugee who had fled to Damascus years ago. As government harassment of the natives of Damascus increased, her parents had moved to the more rural part of the city before Sireen was born, eventually settling in the neighboring province of Daraa. She had grown up there, and so she considered herself a Darawi in every way—save, of course, for her well-preserved Damascene accent. Her special area of interest was the Aramaic language. She loved to talk for hours and hours about how everything people knew about the history of the Syrian people was a lie. This was a dangerous red line she regularly crossed. She had an unshakeable belief that modern Syrian was not a dialect of Arabic, but rather a unique language that had its roots in the language of Jesus Christ. When she first moved to Homs, she had gotten in touch with Waleed's mother, and that was how they had met and later became good friends.

By the time Waleed appeared on his bicycle at the edge of the campus, she was overjoyed to see him. He looked surprised by the warmth and excitement with which she greeted him.

"Oh, Waleed," she said, running her hand gently over his arm. "I'm so embarrassed to have made you come all the way here." She felt thankful for the darkness, for she could feel the blush that bloomed over her cheeks.

"You should be embarrassed," he replied, his tone rich with sarcasm. "I mean, c'mon, Sireen. To be afraid of such superstitions at your age!"

Sireen smirked. "Can you for once be a gentleman with me?"

His laugh was rich and enchanting. "I didn't find sunflower seeds, so I got you some flowers instead." To her great surprise, he produced a handmade bouquet of jasmine he had been holding behind his back.

"*Shukran kteer* [Thank you so much]! That's so thoughtful of you." She clutched the flowers gently to her breast, holding them with both hands.

"So where do you want to go?" he asked, his eyes fixed on the flowers.

"I don't know," she said, twisting back and forth gently at the hips. "Let's just walk and talk. I feel so lonely."

Waleed shook his fist at the air playfully. "God curse loneliness. Why are you feeling lonely?"

Her eyes narrowed as she buried her face in the flowers. "All my girlfriends are either married or engaged or have kids, and I'm still sitting in my parents' house like pressed pickles."

With a gentle hand, Waleed slid a finger beneath her chin and brought her gaze up to meet his own. "First of all, you're not at your parents' house. Second of all, pickles are sour, not sweet like you."

Her heart raced at the look he gave her. She had been flirted with before, but rarely in such a serpentine manner. The smile at the corner of his mouth and the sharpness of his eyes clearly drove the point across. When again she felt her blush come to bloom, a broad smile swept away the seriousness in his face, and all tension disappeared. She could sense that he was joking about his affections, but then, there was something of significance in the way he looked at her.

"By the way," he said casually, "I was kidding about the sunflower seeds." He handed her a small bag from his pocket. "There you go."

For the first time, Sireen saw something in Waleed that she had never noticed before. He had always come across as a foolish and perhaps immature young man, but it seemed to her now that he was capable of complete command when he chose to assume it. He could be a gentleman when he wished, a brave man when he wished, and a mature man when he wished. He cared enough to come to her rescue in the middle of the night; he cared enough to bring her what she asked for; he cared enough to surprise her with things she *didn't* ask for; and yet, he covered it all with the crude mask of boyish playfulness. In other words, he was pretending to be someone much less substantial than he was.

All at once, it dawned on her. She could see how he really felt about her, though he tried to hide it. But instead of confronting him, she decided to play along.

As they walked aimlessly through the empty streets of Homs, their feet tracing twin winding lines over the dusty concrete, she kept looking at his black eyes, which sparkled under the moonlight. Though the silence seemed almost thicker along the edge of the campus, not only was she no longer scared, but she also felt safer than she had in a long time. They saw no cars or people as they wandered aimlessly from block to block. The scent of the jasmine danced beneath her nose, lending further calm to the moment. A bird flitted overhead, coming to roost atop a nearby apartment building, which she immediately recognized as Omar's.

"Where are we going?" she asked him.

"I figured we would take in the sights from Omar's roof."

She gave him an impish grin. "How will we get up there without Omar's key?"

He smirked in reply. "I have my ways."

After several clumsy tries, Waleed scaled the tall aluminum fence barring entry to the fire escape on the side of Omar's building. From inside, he unlocked the latch and swung open the door.

"After you, my lady," he said with feigned gallantry.

"My hero," Sireen said, chuckling as she took to the stairs.

After a five-story climb, Sireen stood beside Waleed atop a broad, flat roof overlooking much of the western side of the city. From the light of the full moon, she felt as if she could see nearly everything from here. In the distance was the mosque, lit as always with the floodlights that made its silver domes flicker and gleam. Up here, the stars were faintly visible despite the soft, incessant light of the city. From time to time, Waleed broke the silence with arbitrary topics, but all Sireen could hear was music and love songs.

"Are you listening to me?" he asked after a time.

"Huh?" she said, shaking her head. "Oh yeah . . . for sure. I'm listening."

"So do you agree that it's better for me to leave Syria?"

Her heart stopped in her chest. "What?" she said, sounding more frantic than she had intended. "No! Why do you want to leave Syria?"

"Sireen! What have I been saying for the past hour? I'm tired of this routine; tired of the lack of opportunities, the corruption, the silence, the fear."

"But leave Syria?" Her hands closed tighter around the jasmine. It had suddenly lost its pleasant smell. "And go where?"

"I don't know. The Arabian Gulf. America. Europe. *Anywhere.*"

"But they say that we make a better living in Syria."

He sighed, his broad shoulders slumping. "They say a lot of things, Soso. Don't believe all of what you hear."

In one moment, she wanted to reach out and take him into her arms. In another, she wanted to shove him away. "Why are we talking politics now?"

"We're not. Not every objection about anything in Syria is a political statement."

She shushed him anxiously. "Someone will hear you," she whispered. "Maybe you're not afraid of Jinn, but you should be afraid of the Mukhabarat."

"Where are they?" He shrugged and turned a little circle. "It's just me and you up here."

Despite herself, Sireen's eyes began to dart from place to place, reflexively searching the dark alleys and landings below. "They have eyes and ears everywhere. Can we change the subject now?" Just then, she noticed the huge poster of President Assad plastered on the wall of the building across the street. Assad seemed to stare up at them as he pointed his index finger.

Waleed gazed skyward. "Okay, I'm sorry. Hey, look, the sun is starting to come out!"

Instead of looking to the horizon, she focused on him. From his awed expression, it was as though he had never seen a sunrise before. The sky was still dark, the sunrise being delivered slowly like new life from the womb. Sireen was amazed at how hypnotized Waleed appeared to be as he eagerly waited for the sun to crest the horizon. He looked like a three-year-old child staring through the glass of a candy shop. Then his eyes lit up as the first rays of fresh sunlight reached his face. Only then did Sireen tear her gaze away and watch the horizon. She, too, found herself hypnotized as the darkness lifted away from Homs. The clock tower, which she could see vaguely from where they stood, began to weave a dress of gold for itself out of the newborn threads of light.

Breaking the silence with their harsh clattering, the cleaners appeared to give the old city its morning facelift. A cold breeze came by, forcing Sireen to move closer to Waleed, and then a little closer, until her head was touching his shoulder. In fact, just then, her ears were close enough to hear that Waleed was quietly talking to himself, or maybe he was singing. She held her breath so she could hear his soft whispers. What was he saying?

"If the people, one day, decide to live . . .
Then definitely, fate shall answer.
And definitely the night shall be lifted . . .
and definitely the chains will be broken . . . "

He went on reciting the famous Arabic poem, so quietly at first that only he could hear it, but then loud enough just for her to hear as well. She felt another shiver run down her spine, but this time not of cold. This time it was for fear of the possibility that the Mukhabarat could hear him. Even so, at her own risk, she stayed close to him and further laid her head on his shoulder. As he went on reciting the poem softly, she realized what he saw in the sunrise: hope.

Hope was also forbidden in Syria.

She eventually joined him in repeating the forbidden verses, but instead of just reciting them with him, she gave them a melody.

"And as I listened to the bombardment of thunder,
the music of the wind, and the beat of the rain,
I looked at Earth and asked, 'Mother, why do you hate
us humans?'
And she said, 'I bless the ambitious, and those who
dare to challenge danger.'"

When they had finished, she gave a deep sigh. "Waleed, who are you really?"

"Nobody, really."

"Good. Nobody is good, at least in this country and this time."

"Till when, Sireen? Till when?"

"Till everyone drinks coffee."

He scrunched up his face. "What? What coffee?"

"Until everyone decides to wake up at once."

"You think they will?"

She shook her head, then inhaled the fragrance of the jasmine. "No, I don't. They won't. Life is more precious than dignity and freedom and hope."

He shifted his weight to one side, easing away from her touch. "I thought you guys in Daraa were happy with the situation." By "the situation," she knew he meant "the Syrian regime."

"And I thought you guys in Homs were happy with the situation," she said defensively. "Everyone assumes that everyone else supports the situation. They say everyone who is unhappy with the situation was sent by Israel to weaken our national resolve. Honestly, I doubt all that. I think it's just their way of keeping us hypnotized so we won't see the reality that we don't have jobs, we don't have money, and we don't have the freedom to do anything."

"Look who's talking politics now," he said with a smile. "What if I were Mukhabarat?"

"Then you would be the sweetest Mukhabarat I ever met."

"Usually you only meet one in your lifetime," he said with a fading grin.

She leaned into him, wanting desperately to throw her arm around his waist. "Then I guess you're the first and last one I'll ever meet."

"Hey, you!" a voice interrupted from behind. They both leapt in shock, pulling away from one another and turning to see who had come to rob them of their peace.

Chapter 3
The Listeners

"Very mature of you, Omar," Sireen said through the laughter of everyone sitting at the lunch table. "You're acting like a high school girl."

"I wish I had captured the look on your faces when you saw me," Omar said, his puffy cheeks pulling back in a smile. "You were terrified."

Waleed couldn't help but smile as he noticed the way Sireen blushed, bringing even more light to the bright college cafeteria in which the five friends sat. She looked lovely on this day, the cacophony of other students in the background sounding like enchanting music as he watched her defend herself.

"What were you guys about to do when I interrupted, anyway?" Omar asked.

Sireen's blush became a scowl. "We were about to none of your business. I can't believe you were spying on us."

"I wasn't," Omar said with a defensive shrug. "You walked to my roof with your own legs."

"That was Waleed's brilliant idea."

With a smirk, Waleed placed a hand on his chest in a show of innocence. By now, the joke had grown somewhat tired, but he still appreciated the attention it brought to Sireen's hidden affections for him. It had been a month since the night Omar had caught them on the rooftop watching the sunrise. That had been the last sunrise Waleed had seen since then, and he suspected the same was true for Sireen. Things had become somewhat awkward since that day, as Omar had taken just about every opportunity to bring up the subject with everyone they met. Omar was one of the biggest fans of jokes in a town that enjoyed them a great deal. Jokes were an essential part of Homsi culture. They were to Homs what pizza was to Italy. There was nothing a Homsi loved more than making jokes about himself and spreading them all across Syria. The jokes always began with some variation of "Why did the Homsi . . ." as in, "Why did eighteen Homsis go to a movie? Because it said eighteen and over."

Waleed appreciated how central jokes were to the otherwise oppressed

Syrian culture, but in Homs, they were of special importance. In this city, no one cared where you hailed from or what religion you followed, as long as you had a good sense of humor, and more importantly, you knew how to take a good joke. Homsis were quite possibly Syria's kindest and most light-spirited people, and yet their fluffy exterior camouflaged a fierce, metallic interior—a ferocity which would soon be revealed.

In this way, perhaps no one was more Homsi than Omar. To him, everything was either funny or had the potential to be converted into a joke. Waleed was not in the least bit surprised that being discovered nearly cuddling with Sireen would serve as long-term fodder for his good friend. He only wished the little amateur comedian hadn't taken pictures of them on his cell phone before sneaking up from behind to startle them.

"So, tell me, Sireen," Omar said, "what are you willing to give me to delete those photos?"

Sireen pursed her lips. "I don't see the humor in anything you're saying, Omar. I mean, really. Can you please just die? Just drop dead. Stop consuming oxygen."

"Come on, Sireen," Omar said, reaching out to touch her forearm. "Could you really handle my death? How boring would your world be without me? Besides, I'm going to be a plastic surgeon one day. You do want that bump on your nose fixed, don't you?"

"*Ya Allah* [Oh, God]." Sireen threw her hands in the air as if exasperated. "You're so *heavy-blooded* [annoying]."

Waleed chuckled.

"All right, all right," Omar said. "I'm sorry. I'll be a gentleman."

"I don't know about that," Sireen said, cocking her head to one side. "You would need sex-change surgery before you qualified."

"Hey! Nice one. You're becoming more Homsi every day." Omar offered a victorious smile as he patted Waleed on the back.

"Why are you patting *me* on the back?" Waleed asked, his smile uncontrollable.

"I'm just saying she's becoming more Homsi. Your mom would rather you be with a Homsi girl, right?"

The heat rose in Waleed's face. "First of all, no. My mom is not Homsi herself. Second of all, I'm not looking right now. And third, Sireen and I are just friends."

"Oh, are we?" Sireen said.

Try though he may, Waleed could not ignore the appearance of the temper behind Sireen's eyes. "Of course we are, Soso."

"Soso? If we're just friends, you will call me Sireen."

Waleed groaned. "Could you stop acting like a college student? Let's all try pretending to be adults."

She glared at him. "I *am* a college student, *Doctor* Waleed. Maybe you should only hang out with doctors like yourself, if we're too immature for your taste."

"What's all this about?" Waleed looked from side to side as he tried to beat back his own blush. "You're embarrassing me and yourself."

"Do they not know?" Fatima yelled at Sireen in a surprisingly sharp and acrimonious tone.

Waleed had been so intent on the conversation that he had almost forgotten she was there at the table. She sat beside Azad, the final member of the group of five friends. Azad was a story in himself. His family had moved from the northern city of Amoda, seeking a better life in Homs. He spoke of tales of abuse and mistreatment of the northern Kurds by Syrian authorities. The government repeatedly claimed that they were cracking down on a Kurdish separatist conspiracy meant to divide Syria, but Waleed secretly believed Azad's version of the truth. Publically, of course, he pretended to think his friend overzealous, but inside, he sympathized with the Kurdish plight.

"There is nothing to know," Sireen replied to Fatima in a subdued voice. Quickly she pivoted. "So how was your vacation with your parents, Fatoom?"

"Never mind that. Where's your—"

"I lost it, okay?" Sireen interrupted. "No, they don't know. I told you I'm still not sure myself, so can you please respect my privacy? Now, how was your vacation?"

As the tension between the two women hung in the air, Waleed looked from one to the other. When he glanced at Omar, his old friend showed him a face so exasperated it almost made him laugh.

"It was fine," Fatima replied coolly.

This turn in the conversation left him puzzled. From the look of the other two men at the table, he wasn't alone.

"It was fun," Fatima added, her hands fidgeting. "My dad took us around in his new BMW. He let me drive it."

Fatima's and Sireen's families were both considerably richer than Waleed's. He never begrudged them this fact, for he had always felt comfortable in his home. He could not speak for Omar or Azad, however, for they had their own inclinations on the matter.

"Drive it?" Sireen said with a wrinkled nose. "When did you learn to drive, Fatoom?"

She shook her head. "I didn't. My dad just got me a license."

"*Wasta* [nepotism]?" Azad asked.

"No, not *wasta*. I just don't have time to take the dumb test, so my dad made me a license."

"All right," Azad said sarcastically. "And how is that not *wasta*?"

"Oh, can you stop it with your idealism? Call it whatever you want to call it. It's just a stupid license. It's not like I robbed a bank."

"It's all the same. If you can kill one person, you can kill a thousand."

"You would have done the same if you could, so please stop preaching."

Once more, Waleed could feel the tension starting to build around the table.

By now, it was almost as if it had spread to the nearby tables in the cafeteria as well. He sensed the eyes and ears tuning into their conversation, even as everyone pretended to go about their own business. He knew that Azad would have to tread carefully here or risk the whole scene boiling over.

Azad did not tread carefully. "I would rather starve to death than accept a *wasta*."

Fatima's face darkened. "Well then, you might very well starve to death, because that's the way the system runs. Take it or leave it."

With a flourish, Azad crossed his thick arms over his chest and arched his bushy eyebrows. "I would have loved to leave it. All I need is a passport, and I'm gone."

"What's stopping you?" Fatima asked with a sound of disgust.

Azad leaned forward and pointed to his face. "Maybe you've forgotten. I'm Kurdish."

Waleed clenched his jaw, because he could sense where Fatima would take things next. She had done it many times before, after all. He only hoped she wouldn't do it so loudly that the neighboring tables would overhear.

Fatima left him wanting. "Well, if you guys behaved yourselves and didn't try to break Syria apart, you wouldn't have been treated this way."

There was little Azad could say to this without causing a scene. Instead, the two friends glared at one another, each breathing heavily. Waleed shifted uncomfortably in his seat as he searched for something to say to diffuse the tension.

It was Omar who beat him to the punch. "Hey!" he shouted, his face quickly melting into a smile.

"It's okay, Omar," Azad offered. "Fatima's just repeating the propaganda like a parrot. It's funny that some people aren't even allowed to have a legal birth certificate, and others can get professional licenses without even getting tested."

"You are so unpatriotic!" Fatima said with obvious disgust. "Everyone is equal in Syria."

"You're right. In Syria, everyone is equal—equally *repressed*."

At this, Waleed couldn't stop himself from speaking. "Guys!" he said, waiting until all eyes turned to him. "Let me remind you that we're in a public place. Do you want us all to end up in our *aunt's house*?" The term was code for "political prison."

Indeed, it was almost as if the five friends hadn't noticed where they were. By now, the cafeteria was almost full of students. Most of the tables were packed with potential eavesdroppers, and more had formed a long queue to enter the dining hall. Only God knew who had been listening to them and for how long. Realizing what they had done, the friends remained silent for a few moments, waiting for someone to jump up and say, "I'm from the Mukhabarat. Why don't we all continue this chat in my office?"

"We love Bashar!" Omar yelled, as if speaking to any Mukhabarat out there.

Waleed's breath grew short. "Omar, what are you doing?"

"Confusing them," he said with a laugh. "We love Bashar, and there is only one person we love more than him . . ."

"Now what are you doing?"

". . . His father, Hafez! God keep them on our heads forever."

It seemed to Waleed that the entire crowd was shifting nervously. Some looked at them with genuine fear, as if this outburst would somehow fall back on them personally.

"Of course we love his father, Hafez," Azad said, joining the sarcastic choir. "It's so sad that he died. Do you know how he died, Fatoom?"

"Yeah, um . . . No. How?"

"You really don't know?"

"No, I don't think anyone knows."

"I do."

"Okay, then tell me, Mr. Sherlock Holmes."

Azad threw his head back, jutting out his chin. "Wasn't he the one who built modern Syria, as you guys say?"

"Yes, absolutely," Fatima said.

"Well, that's how he died."

Waleed drew a breath to express his confusion, but Fatima beat him to it.

"I don't understand," she said.

"It's simple," Azad said. "Don't you see? A block fell on his head while he was building modern Syria." Waleed thought he could see his friend's pupils slowly dilating. From his medical training, he assumed that this meant Azad's heart rate had climbed. He did not need a medical degree to realize that the same thing was happening in his own chest.

Silence followed. Fatima was clearly not amused.

"Homsi!" Omar said, pointing at Azad. Then he burst out laughing.

Slowly but surely, everyone else at the table joined in on the crime. Waleed thought that he heard several onlookers adding to the laughter, as well.

"You know, guys," Omar said, "I think we should all go home and pack our bags. We're all going to our *aunt's house* in the morning!" He elbowed Fatima. "Fatoom, we'll need your *wasta* to bail us out."

Fatima giggled. "Trust me, there is no *wasta* on Earth that can get someone out once he's in."

"Have you ordered yet, gentlemen?" a waiter asked, as if appearing from thin air. From the way his lips quivered beneath his thick mustache, Waleed could tell that he was annoyed. "I see you've been here for almost an hour and nobody has ordered yet."

"Thanks for reminding us," Waleed said. "We got lost in the conversation."

"I can tell. All right, let's go around the table for your orders."

Waleed ordered some hummus, tabbouleh, and a plate of *fattoush*, or bread salad, for the table.

"And one mixed barbeque for all of us," Omar added. "Pick the good kabob for us, will you?"

The waiter nodded as he wrote this down.

"And can we have a plate of grape leaves, as well?" Fatima asked.

"Your order will be right out," the waiter said, his tone deadly serious. "What about you, sir?" he asked of Azad.

"What about me?" Azad said with a frown. "I'll just eat with the rest."

"You know, sir, you look like someone I know. What's your name?"

"Azad El-Ayoobi."

The waiter gave a thoughtful look. "Yes. I know a few people from that family. They look like you."

Waleed felt uncomfortable about the way the waiter carried himself as he spoke to his friend. He wanted to say something, but what could he say?

"Really?" Azad said. "How do you know them?"

"I've worked here for a long time," the waiter said. "I know all the families of Homs."

Azad looked doubtful. "I see. It's interesting, since we're the only people from my family who live in Homs."

"Well," the waiter said, looking strangely embarrassed, "God creates forty lookalikes for each person." With that, he turned away and headed toward the kitchen.

Soon the food arrived. Everyone ate in silence. Something about the waiter's prying into Azad's life had unsettled Waleed, and he could sense that his friends shared the sensation. He spent the rest of the meal glancing from person to person in the cafeteria, looking for whispered exchanges or suspicious glances. By the time he had finished, he had concluded that he was just being paranoid. All the same, he made a point to remind himself that he couldn't allow his friends to speak this way in public ever again. What they had done was risky indeed, for thousands of men and women in Syria had lost their lives or their freedom due to conversations far more benign. In this place, one word could be the difference between life and death. Being identified as a potential threat would lead to a silent stalking from the Mukhabarat. The secret police would identify all of the target's contacts before slowly building to the inevitable climax. On a carefully selected night, at around dawn, to be precise, visitors would stop by the target's house and make him disappear forever.

Waleed shuddered as he wiped his mouth with a napkin. Sometimes the close friends or family members of the target also disappeared. No one ever knew what happened to those who were taken. Certainly there was torture, rape, and humiliation involved, but the exact details would never be revealed. Waleed imagined dingy basement rooms where the organs of the targets were removed and sold. He pictured prisons where the guards would test chemical agents on the taken. He suspected the regime of Nazi-like experimentation facilities, where prisoners would go for days without food or water, exposed to all the colors of torment. To everyone in Syria, this was by far a worse outcome than dying.

Pondering these images made Waleed feel sick to his stomach. He thought about what it would be like to be taken. Most of the time, people disappeared silently, but he remembered a neighbor of his who managed to scream as he was dragged into the streets. At first, Waleed had thought this was merely a mistake on the part of the secret police, but later he would learn that they had meant for this to happen. The Mukhabarat sometimes allowed for a public scene in an effort to deliver a message. Over the past decade, the frequency of these displays had dropped significantly, but this wasn't because the regime had changed its nature. Rather, the people had learned to submit.

This was a new generation to which Waleed belonged. He cringed every time he thought of the term "the Baath Generation." He had walked a long road to becoming one of the multitudes of "good citizens," starting on a steady diet of propaganda from kindergarten and following it all the way through graduate school. The propaganda machine had brainwashed his generation day and night.

Because he was so familiar with the regime's structure and tendencies, Waleed knew that there was a total of thirteen or fourteen Mukhabarat agencies. Each agency's only job was to detect any signs of opposition to the regime, no matter how small, and exterminate it before it turned into a threat. For that reason, paranoia was normal in Syria. If you were not paranoid, people thought you were crazy.

Azad was one of those crazy people. Had this been any other place under the thumb of a dictator, he might have been called brave, but by Syrian standards, he was insane. "An eye cannot resist a needle" was a Syrian saying that defined the general feeling of the country's citizens. Given the choice between living on your knees or dying on your feet, most people chose to live.

~~~

Back in front of the warm glow of his computer, Waleed clicked away at his keyboard, anticipating every new missive from Sireen. For the past month, she had become his outlet—his escape from the tedium of the everyday world and his fears about his safety and the safety of his friends. On this night, however, Sireen would bring him back to the pain of thinking about Azad.

Hey, Azad joined Facebook. He just added me.

Waleed groaned as he typed his reply.

Oh, Sireen. This cannot be a good thing! He's already attracting lots of bad attention from government agents.

I think it's a good thing. A few months ago, no one used Facebook, and now everyone I know has joined. I bet the government isn't happy with this.

Why wouldn't they be happy? Now they have a direct window to peak through at everyone in the country.

In that case, we shouldn't be chatting here. I bet you some lonely Mukhabarat agent is reading our conversation and getting a kick out of it. Let's watch a movie instead. How about Twilight?

Waleed sighed with relief, glad to have an outlet through which he might escape the realities of his own oppression—even if that outlet had to be a low-grade teen movie.

No, let's watch a vampire movie.

Twilight is a vampire movie, Homsi.

I know that, but I meant a real vampire movie.

If you mean Dracula, forget it. I won't watch a horror movie.

With a smirk, Waleed looked to the ceiling, thinking about how he might win her over to something a little more engaging. Then the solution hit him.

Okay, how about a vampire movie with Brad Pitt in it?

Sounds like a good deal to me. Brad Pitt could act in an Egyptian movie and I would still watch it.

I'll go buy it from my neighbor, Abo Shehab. He can get you any movie in the world just for 15 Liras.

Abo Shehab? Is that his real name?

No, it's his business name. He doesn't want to be caught stealing all those movies off the internet.

Tell him not to worry. No one cares about such things in this country. There is only one way to get in trouble. Anyways, bring it and let's go to Omar's roof. Hopefully he won't mind.

Waleed's heart skipped a beat at the thought. He had been thinking the same thing. It had been far too long since that romantic sunrise.

Omar's on call tonight. He's on his vascular surgery rotation, sitting around hoping that someone gets shot in their carotid artery so he can learn something.

Not in this city. The only thing people shoot here is birds. Tell him it's a skill he won't ever need.

You never know, Sireen. Life is full of surprises.

Chapter 4
Visitors of the Night

The ancient Citadel watches over the city of Homs as it has done for over four thousand years. Until the city was thrashed by recent violence, Homs was beautiful. She had grown more beautiful as she aged. Her people had changed little. They no longer spoke Aramaic like they did 2,000 years ago, and they wore jeans and T-shirts, yet they were the same. Their religious and political beliefs varied, yet they were the same. There was no way to determine whether a Homsi was Muslim or Christian without investigating. There was no way to determine whether a Homsi was rich or poor without investigating. They all used the same subtle variations of Syrian Arabic and the same minute deviations from the common Syrian cuisine.

For four decades, the regime worked relentlessly to break up this coherent social structure found in most Syrian cities, a structure thousands of years in the making. First, they created sectarianism, under which no one was considered Syrian anymore. If one was an Alawite, he received special privileges, unless he was opposed to the regime. Alawites make up about a tenth of the total Syrian population. For hundreds of years, they had mostly lived in the mountains and coastal areas, remaining fairly isolated from the "Syrian melting pot."

If one was Sunni, he faced discrimination, abuse, and harassment by the regime, with the exception of some solid regime loyalists. Sunnis represent mainstream Islam as practiced in most Muslim countries. They make up about seventy-five percent of the total Syrian population. Most of them speak Syrian Arabic, while others speak Kurdish.

Christians, Druze, and Ismailis make up the remainder of the population. They did not enjoy the same advantages and privileges as the Alawites, but they were also not subjected to the same level of harassment as the Sunni majority. The regime kept them in line by propagating fear of a Sunni takeover and of prophesized revenge against minorities.

To further divide the various communities, the government also championed the rhetoric of Pan-Arabism. The concept was simple: Arabs stand above all. To meet this effort, they wiped out thousands of years of Syrian history and pretended that Syria had seen its dawn with the birth of Arabism. The Kurds and Assyrians, who made up about a fifth of the population, were deprived of basic rights such as education, jobs, and even citizenship. The main obsession of Pan-Arabism was Israel. Believers thought Israel to be the root of all evil in the world. They taught that Israel worked as the direct cause of poverty and oppression in the entire Arab world and beyond.

This served the ruling elite well. Whenever the Syrians asked where their tax money went, the ruling body would blame the losses on preparation for a potential war with Israel. In reality, the money went to private banks overseas to line the pockets of the corrupt government elite.

—*Syria: A History in Blood* by Celine Dubois

October 31, 2010
Deaths: 0

It was 11:00 p.m. when Waleed felt his phone vibrate in his pocket. Along with Azad and Omar, he sat at a table in the middle of a bustling market crowd, the noise of the bartering around him drowning out all but his thoughts. When he answered the call, he had to strain to hear the voice on the other end of the line.

"Waleed, where are you?" It was Sireen.

"I'm in the vegetable market. Do you need anything?"

"What are you doing in the vegetable market so late at night?"

"Hanging out with the guys, having *arguileh* [hookah]. Come join us."

"I don't use *arguileh*. You shouldn't either, Doctor. How about I go on a long walk from the University City to the market? By then you'll be done with your smoke and we can go for a walk."

Waleed stuck his finger in his opposite ear to stifle the noise. Somewhere, someone was cooking shawarma. He could smell its inviting spices even over the acrid smoke he shared with his friends. "Are you insane? You want to walk all this distance alone and at night?"

"Come on, it's Homs, not Baghdad. What could happen to me? It's a boring city. Nothing ever happens here."

With a frustrated scoff, he pulled away from the phone. Omar gave him a knowing look. "All right, but meet me at Azad's instead. We're headed there soon. And promise to call me if anything goes wrong. I have a bad feeling about tonight."

"A woman's instinct?" she teased.

Waleed laughed. "You're becoming more Homsi every day. I should get back to the guys now. Stay safe."

Midnight crept up on them as they smoked their *arguileh* and talked about everything guys talk about. They dropped the volume of their voices whenever they talked about love and romance, speaking in hushed tones just beneath the din of the shrinking crowd—lower still when they talked politics or exchanged jokes about the regime. Even their laughter was silent, just in case someone was listening. By the time they finished and started heading for Azad's house, they had talked and smoked more than their fill.

"Anyone hungry?" Waleed asked as they stepped through the door to Azad's small but well-appointed home.

"I'll go prepare something for you guys," Omar responded as he headed to Azad's kitchen. "I'll make tea and cheese, and I think I saw *makdous* in the fridge earlier this afternoon."

Azad looked content with the idea as he took a seat in the easy chair in the darkened corner of the room. When he flipped on the lamp with its stained glass shade, his face came to light in soft blues and reds.

"I think we smoked enough," Waleed told him. "I can feel the cancer cells building in my lungs."

"You're such a doctor," Azad said with a wry smile. Then his expression changed. "Hey, weren't you waiting for Sireen? It's been a while, hasn't it?"

"You're right! What's taking her so long?" Waleed went to the window and peered out into the dimly lit street. "I told her I have a bad feeling about tonight."

"Well, whatever happens, I really hope it works out between the two of you. In fact, there's one way to know for sure."

Waleed turned away from the window, intrigued. "Oh yeah? What's that?"

"I'll read your coffee cup." Azad grinned as he called back to the kitchen. "Omar, do you mind making coffee instead of tea?"

Omar stuck his head in from the next room. "Mr. Azad, I'm a surgical resident, not your housekeeper. But fine, I'll make it."

Soon afterward, Omar returned with snacks and coffee. The men ate ravenously, Waleed realizing that he was even hungrier than he had thought. As soon as they were done, Azad told them to flip their empty coffee cups upside down.

"Why are we doing this?" Waleed asked, feeling somewhat annoyed by the exercise—in part because it seemed silly and in part because he was still worried about Sireen.

Azad threw his head back theatrically. "Because many fortunetellers use the stripes and patterns that form from the dregs of your coffee to predict the future."

"So you're going to predict my future now?" Waleed asked dryly.

Fervently Azad pointed at Waleed's cup. "Only if you stamp your thumb in the center of the cup."

Waleed did as he was told, bringing his thumb down in the center of the cup's bottom. "Like that?"

"Yeah, yeah," Azad said. "That's good. Now give me your cup." He smiled wickedly as Waleed handed it over. He raised one eyebrow as he examined the thick film that had collected in the bottom of the cup. "Now this is really unusual."

Leaning forward, Waleed peered into the cup to see what his friend was talking about.

"Do you see how the coffee patterns are so symmetrical?"

Waleed nodded.

"Exactly half of the cup is extremely black and the other half is white. What are the odds of that happening?"

"So what does that mean, fortuneteller?" Waleed asked as he sat back and crossed his arms over his chest.

"There is a sharp, straight line that carries you—a road, if you will—and it carries you from an area of extreme darkness to an area of light. I guess it could be taking you from the lonely bachelor's life to a happy marriage or something like that. I'm not sure." His eyes grew wide. "Oh, actually wait a second. The road never makes it to the white side of the cup! It stops suddenly. That must mean that you'll break up just before getting married! I'm sorry."

"Just what I needed to hear," Waleed said sarcastically. He held out his hand, letting it hang in the air between them. "Give me your cup."

Azad made a thumb print on the bottom of his coffee cup, then handed it over.

When Waleed looked inside, he feigned even deeper surprise than his friend had shown. "Oh, Azad! I've never seen anything like this before. Your coffee cup is black."

"Yes, it had coffee in it, genius."

Omar belted out a laugh.

"No," Waleed said adamantly. "There are no markings at all. It's just black. I wonder what that means . . ."

When Azad stood, Waleed showed him how the bottom of the cup was indeed caked in black film.

"It means that Omar needs to learn how to make proper coffee," Azad quipped.

They all laughed.

"Do mine next," Omar said excitedly. He sat up with his cup clutched in both hands, passing it to Azad, then Waleed, and back again. "Both of you read it."

Azad went first. "I see a man with two children. I guess you'll be a father of two. Then there's something on top of you. It looks like a wheel. I have no idea what that means."

At that, Omar awed derisively.

When it was his turn, Waleed stared into the cup for only a moment before he realized what he was looking at. It was the Greek letter *theta*, notorious for being an ancient symbol of death. "Yes, it's a wheel," he lied. "I don't know what it means, either. We should ask our neighbor Om Zaki. She knows everything, except how to knock on the door before entering someone's house."

They all laughed, a joyful moment that was broken by the ringing of Waleed's phone.

"Sireen!" he said with relief when he heard her voice. "It's you. What took you so long?"

"It's nothing to worry about, silly," she said. "I was just watching a show and got caught up."

"You were watching a show?" he asked, confused.

She ignored him. "You want to meet me at the park for a walk?"

Waleed looked to his friends, who had already dived into their own animated conversation. "All right, I'll be there in a minute. Bye." He explained that he was leaving, shook hands with his friends, and departed.

~~~

After everyone had left, Azad put on some music and went back to his bedroom. His parents and sister had gone to Amuda for a few days. Since childhood, he had wanted to study cosmology and astrophysics. The universe and its complexity had always intrigued him. In the hopes of meeting that goal, he had completed his high school training even though he was never officially recognized by the state as a student. He made a living by teaching his classmates the subjects they were weak in, even though he wasn't a registered student. Most of them went to college while he ended up moving with his father to Homs, where they both ran a fruit shop in the vegetable market at the Baba Amro neighborhood. In spite of that, he had spent the past six years educating himself about the universe. He would spend hours and hours quibbling with equations, shuffling variables, and then staring into the night sky with his homemade telescope before playing with a few more variables. His dream was to finally reach a substantial conclusion, publish it, and move to Europe or North America, where someone might actually appreciate his skills.

It was 3:00 a.m. when a strong knock on his door interrupted Azad's deep thoughts. From the frantic nature of the knock, it sounded like someone was scared and in danger. He rushed to the door, but then hesitated. What if this was a thief who knew that everyone had left and was trying to break in?

When the knocking stopped, Azad looked through the magic eye of the door and didn't see anyone. Flustered, he returned to his desk. He had not been sitting long when suddenly the knocking resumed, this time more aggressively. It wasn't knocking anymore. Someone was clearly trying to break in. Azad panicked and grabbed a knife as he dialed the police department.

"Hello! Someone is breaking into my house . . . yes . . . my name is Azad . . . . Azad Ayoobi."

The operator searched for his name for a few seconds, then hung up.

Confused and frightened, Azad called again, and as soon as he identified his name, they hung up.

The door was starting to crack under the impact of strong, repetitive pounding. Judging by the fracture lines that formed, he could tell they were using a large cylinder to break the door, maybe a tree trunk or something similar. This had to be the work of more than one person. Realizing he might be facing a gang, he put his knife aside and reached for the phone again. He was shocked to find that he had no phone service, and then the electricity went off. Azad was ready to wake up from this nightmare, because nothing made sense anymore.

The door cracked open, then splintered apart. As he expected, there were several men—five of them, he deduced on second count. Two were holding a large metal rod to break the door open. Two were dressed in black leather and the other three in military uniform.

"Azad Ayoobi?" one of the men in black asked.

"Yes, sir," Azad answered in a weak, trembling voice. His knees could barely hold him. His imagination was racing, as was his heart.

The man who had asked his name sat down in Azad's favorite chair as the other four kept silent. He lit a cigarette, the flame from his lighter cutting through the grim darkness.

"Sit down," the man commanded.

When Azad tried to grab a chair, one of the armed men fired a shot in his direction.

"Sit on the floor, you dog!" the soldier yelled.

It was then that Azad realized who the men were. They must have been the Mukhabarat. Their accent was clearly not Homsi. Without uttering a word, he lowered himself to the floor.

"Come closer," said the man on the chair.

Azad made to stand, but the man stopped him with a wave of his hand.

"No . . . crawl." A vicious, sadistic smile spread across the man's face. The others followed suit. They had the look of vampires who had just seen blood. "Don't worry; we'll be very democratic. This is a democracy, as you know."

Azad nodded.

The agent took a long drag from his cigarette. "When is your family coming back from Amuda?"

"I don't know, sir," Azad said, his concern shifting from himself to his family in an instant.

"Bu Somer, help him remember," the agent said to one of the soldiers.

The soldier, a hulking, barrel-chested man, moved toward him slowly. He came within a few feet before lashing out and kicking Azad in the face.

Azad tumbled backward, his face and then his elbows ringing out in pain as he caught himself on the hardwood floor. "I really don't know, sir," he said as the blood began to pour from his nose.

The soldier kicked him again, this time in the ribs. He rolled to his side, spitting blood onto the rug beneath the agent's feet. Even as Azad tried to collect himself, he felt the soldier's boot stomping on the side of his head. His vision began to blur. The only thing he heard above the sound of the soldier's boots against his blood-slicked skin was the solemn laughter of the soldiers.

"Enough, Bu Somer," the Mukhabarat agent said finally. He allowed Azad to roll onto his back.

Azad tried to sit up, but found that the pain prevented him from rising.

"When are your parents coming back?" the agent asked.

"In a week, sir," Azad mumbled, trying to ignore the pain.

The agent leaned forward in the chair, leering over Azad. "We heard that you're unhappy with the government, so we thought we'd come have a chat with you. We figured maybe you would have some suggestions for us."

"No, sir. I am happy."

"That's not what we were told."

"Whoever told you was lying, sir."

Another soldier came and kicked his face. "Don't talk without permission, you dog."

"Our sources don't lie," the agent continued. "So maybe you can tell us what you want. That way, we can make sure we do it right next time."

"Nothing, sir," he said, fear making his body go stiff.

"Are you with the Muslim Brotherhood?" the agent asked.

Quivering in fear and pain, Azad clutched his arms around his bare chest. "No, sir. Not at all."

"Who, then? Mossad?"

"No, sir. I swear."

"The Americans?"

"No, sir. I swear to God."

"The Lebanese? The March Fourteenth Alliance?"

"No, sir, not at all."

The agent, finally finished with his cigarette, leaned back, crossed one leg over his knee, and stamped the butt out on the wood of Azad's mother's end table. "Then only one group is left . . . the Kurdish Separatists."

"No, sir. I'm not a Separatist."

"Bu Somer." He looked to the first soldier, who pulled out an electric rod. "I heard you like physics, so we thought we'd do a physics experiment with you."

The soldier hit him with the electric rod. This was a different type of pain—the kind of pain that made Azad wish that they would just kill him and get it over with. Every sense that Azad possessed was bathed in white hot fire.

"So, the Kurdish Separatists?" the agent was asking by the time Azad regained his wits.

"No, sir," came the hollow reply. His voice was so weak and distant that, to Azad, it almost didn't sound like his own.

By the time the soldiers had finished kicking and prodding him with the rod again, he could feel little more than the pool of blood that had collected beneath him.

"The Kurdish Separatists?" the agent repeated.

Azad finally understood. They didn't want the truth. They wanted a confession. "Yes, sir," he said quickly.

"Okay, gentlemen," the agent said. "Stop. We need to talk."

The soldiers stepped back several paces and stood at attention.

"Unfortunately," the agent said as he reached for another cigarette, "this group to which you just admitted to owing your allegiance? They are considered an enemy of the state. You are under arrest."

The frightened sound that escaped Azad's broken lips was not voluntary.

"Oh, don't worry," the agent said, feigning sympathy. "We'll get you a great lawyer when you arrive at the prison . . . and we'll take good care of your parents and whore sister when they get back."

They dragged him into a large van. The last thing Azad saw before they pulled the black hood over his head was that the door was left open from the way they had broken it. He knew that the wind would keep blowing into the empty house until his family returned—if the Mukhabarat ever allowed them to return.

As they tossed him into the van and disappeared into the night, the city would remain drowned in silence. No one would know. No one would object. The Earth would keep revolving around the sun. The universe would keep expanding. It would be as if nothing had happened.

Chapter 5
Sail-less Journey

November 15, 2010
Deaths: 0

"She sat with fear in her eyes
Contemplating the upturned cup
She said, 'Do not be sad, my son
You are destined to fall in love.'
My son, he who sacrifices himself for his beloved,
Is a martyr

For long have I studied fortune-telling
But never have I read a cup like yours
For long have I studied fortune-telling
But never have I seen sorrows like yours
You are predestined to sail forever
Sailless, on the sea of love
Your life is forever destined
To be a book of tears . . ."

"Nicely done," Sireen said, clapping. "I love your style of reciting poetry."

Waleed felt warm as he took a mock bow before her. "Thank you, my lady. But it's really nothing to do with me. It's the beauty of Nizar Qabbani's poetry."

Sireen slid away from the tree trunk upon which she had been leaning and lay in the lush green grass at its base. Her lovely eyes narrowed into a squint as she gazed up at the bright yellow sky. "You know, he's probably the greatest Syrian of our time. I wish he were still alive. His ideas were so revolutionary."

Waleed paused and looked into the distance. He saw the sprawl of Homs reaching out like a twisted hand into the park that served as their frequent refuge. "You think they took him?" he asked, his voice softening.

She opened her eyes in a flash of gorgeous but troubled brown. "Azad? I wish I knew. He just vanished suddenly. Maybe he moved back to Amoda?"

The book tumbled from his hand, settling on the ground between them. He sat beside her. "I don't know. He wouldn't just move overnight without letting us know. I was with him the night he disappeared."

"I don't know," Sireen said, sounding cautious. "But I heard rumors."

Waleed pulled his knees close to his chest and wrapped his arms around them. "What rumors? What are they saying?"

Sireen sighed. "I didn't want to tell you because I knew you might get upset."

"Tell me," he urged.

"My roommate Fatima told me there's a rumor that Azad was receiving weapons from Kurdistan and arming the Kurds in Damascus. They were planning a large terrorist attack in Damascus. I don't know if it's true."

"Weapons? Kurdistan? This is a joke. This is the biggest Mexican soap opera I've seen in my life. It just proves that the Mukhabarat were the ones who took him. They always spread nonsensical rumors to justify their behavior." He fell back to lie beside her, exasperation washing over him.

Sireen made a face before rolling onto her side and propping herself up on her elbow. Her long black hair cascaded down over her slender arm. "What if it's true?"

Scoffing, Waleed began counting his points on his fingers. "If it's true, then what were the weapons he supposedly had access to? The tomatoes from his father's shop? Or did he use his interest in physics to design a nuclear reactor in his kitchen?" He tried not to sound irritated, but the more they spoke, the more difficult that became.

"I'm sorry, I'm just telling you what people are saying. Anyway, according to the rumors, he fled Syria and is now in Kurdistan."

Waleed sat up with a start. "The waiter!"

"What waiter?"

"That day in the cafeteria, a waiter came and asked Azad for his name. Only him. He must have been a Mukhabarat agent!"

Sireen's face lit up conspiratorially. "You're right! That must be the reason they took him. That makes a lot more sense than this Kurdistan story."

"I hope they kill him," Waleed said, startling Sireen into a gasp.

"Why would you say such a thing?"

"I would rather him die once than die several times a day. You have no idea what they do to prisoners—the kinds of torture they apply. It's beyond imagination." He felt tears gathering. He stopped in an effort to prevent himself from crying. "He's such a gentle guy. He won't survive in the dungeons of the Mukhabarat even for a week."

"God help his family," she said sadly. "They must be so heartbroken."

"I think they left Homs and went back to Amoda. I wish everything would change. I wish we could press the restart button for this country somehow."

Sireen furrowed her brow. "You're not dreaming about regime change, are you?"

Waleed simply sighed, not wanting to corrupt Sireen's innocence with his dangerous thoughts. She would certainly be safer the more naïve she remained.

That was all he cared about.

He slowly came to his feet and offered his hand to Sireen to help her up. Together they walked down to the street and headed for her dormitory.

After he had left her, he decided to continue walking alone. He went to the Baba Amro neighborhood, just in case Azad was there hiding out. To Waleed, the irony of the situation was striking. One sentence, one word, one letter was enough to kill or forever imprison a Syrian. Yet most people failed to see that they were all prisoners in a large, dark prison. That was why Nizar Qabbani, the poet, couldn't take it any longer; that was why he had fled the country he loved so much.

It was like everyone was under a powerful spell. Walking in the streets of Homs or Damascus or any other Syrian city was like traveling through an enchanted city where everyone failed to see the obvious, a place where everyone was captive and brainwashed through some sort of black magic, willingly supporting the world's worst government.

But what if, beneath that surface, deep inside, no one really wanted the status quo? What if everyone was just like Waleed, an in-the-closet opposition to the current regime? How large was this closet? What if there were millions of Syrians already in it? He sighed, realizing how useless these thoughts were. *It's not like a revolution would ever rock Assad's land*, he thought.

As he walked the streets, hands in his pockets, he realized how hard it was for a Syrian to forget who was in charge. The reminders were everywhere. There, just a few meters away from him, was a large poster of Bashar Al-Assad. The lower border of the poster read, *God, Syria, Bashar, and that's it.* Waleed was saddened by the thought that the walls of his city had become Assad's personal photo album. His pictures were everywhere—one in a suit, one in military uniform, one wearing the Arab Thoub, one with sunglasses on. His brother, Maher Al-Assad, the man who controlled the notorious Fourth Division of the army, also had a few pictures here and there. Of course, their father, Hafez, had pictures everywhere, as well. One poster featured his picture in black and white with the caption, *God bless your soul, our eternal leader.* Even some of Bashar's friends had their pictures up in the city. There were pictures of the Hezbollah leader, Nasrallah, and pictures of Iran's Ahmadinejad here and there.

Waleed shoved his hands in his pockets as he continued down the narrow roads of the Baba Amro neighborhood. *Maybe Azad did escape*, he tried to convince himself. *Maybe he's now living underground in hiding.* A few blocks later, he found himself standing outside Azad's house. His heart sank at the sight of the shattered door. Then it fluttered when he heard a sound. A light flickered for a moment within the doorway—a candle dancing just inside the landing. Someone was in there.

Waleed strode to the broken door and reached out to push it open, then hesitated as he heard music coming from inside the house, along with talking and laughter. The music was loud and festive, and the voices he heard clearly did not belong to men trying to hide from someone.

Instead of pushing open the door, Waleed leaned closer to peer through one of the cracks. The room was foggy with smoke from an *arguileh*. The smell of *arak*, a Mediterranean alcoholic beverage, was pungent. From the sound of it, the men were getting drunk. Waleed could also hear them stomping on the floor as if dancing. He suspected the dance was the *dabkeh*. There must have been three or more men inside that room. The laughter was loud and boisterous. The music's volume rose to the point that it was so loud the listeners had to have been trying to cover another noise. It was an unusual sound, this music. It was too rural for even a medium-sized city like Homs. It lacked an organized musical beat and had very few instruments. The lyrics were basically a word salad. The men were obviously outsiders to Homs. So what on Earth were they doing in this house? Waleed could hardly believe that none of the neighbors had objected.

A few minutes later, there came another twist: women's voices joined the chorus of men. One woman was laughing loudly to a clapping noise. She was complaining about the music and wanted to change it. As she made the change, there came a few seconds of silence broken only by a faint, low-pitched voice that sounded like crying. It was this that compelled Waleed to push the door open a few inches for a closer look.

The amount of smoke in the room was shocking. There were indeed three men sitting on the floor. One of them had an *arguileh* in his hand, and the others were drinking *arak*. There were two women, both wearing extremely short red skirts and tight tops. One was dancing in the center of the room, surrounded by the three men. The other one was huddled in a corner and trying to cover up her body as if forced to wear her skimpy clothes. She looked scared, helpless, and much younger than the other woman. She was quietly crying with her head buried behind her knees and her arms trying to cover her exposed legs. Everyone else in the room was in some kind of trance created by music, alcohol, and smoke.

When one of the men noticed the younger woman, he grabbed her leg and started dragging her toward the center of the room as she screamed helplessly. The man was too drunk to do anything more. He simply fell to the floor. The girl then stared toward the door as if she suddenly realized that this was her chance to escape. Waleed wasn't sure if she could see him.

The older woman looked at her with fire in her eyes. "Fairouz, go now! They're too drunk to know anything."

"But what if they beat you for letting me go?"

"They'll beat me anyway, darling. Please go. One day I'll escape, too."

"Come with me!"

"No, darling. They have my son. If I don't do what they want, they might hurt him. Don't worry about me, dear. One day I'll be free, too, I promise. *Yalla, habibti* [Come on, baby]."

The girl called Fairouz slowly made her way toward the door, then looked back one more time. "Samira, just come. This is your chance. We'll escape and start a new life. Your son has a God who will protect him from those bastards."

Waleed drew a breath, not wanting to make any noise to startle the women as they made their plans.

"Darling, you don't know the Mukhabarat," the older woman said. "You're too young. Your generation doesn't know anything about what they're capable of doing. Let the wings of your youth carry you out of this hell. Go, child! They'll wake up any minute. Go! Go now! God be with you!" With that, she began shoving Fairouz toward the door.

The girl nearly fell, but then picked herself up slowly and turned for her escape. She did not get far before she found Waleed standing in the doorway. She made a face as if preparing to scream, but he quickly covered her mouth with his hand. As she sucked fearful breath through her nose, he placed a finger on his lips, ordering her to be silent. "It's okay," he said into her ear. "I'm not going to hurt you." With that, he lowered his hand.

"What do you want from me?" she whispered.

"Nothing. If you don't mind me asking, why are you and all those people in my friend's house?"

Fairouz looked surprised. "I'm in the middle of running for my life. Do you mind staying out of my way now?"

"All right, I'm sorry." Waleed let her go and backed away. "I'll walk with you, then."

"Fine. Do whatever you want, but I'll be walking fast." She started to walk as Waleed followed her.

The night seemed somehow chillier as he tried to keep up. He didn't want to stare at her, but her revealing outfit made it difficult. Her legs were so long, and he couldn't remember the last time he had seen so much soft, feminine skin. "I'm Waleed. Who are you?"

"I'm none of your business."

"What are you doing in Azad's house?"

"You know Azad?" the girl said in a completely different tone. "Do you know anything about him? Where is he?"

"Who are you?"

"I'm Fairouz, his sister. I was with my parents and younger brother in Amoda for a month. When we came back, we found those thugs in our house. They had stolen everything of value and broken lots of things. When they saw us, they started beating my brother and we all tried to escape, but they kept me and forced my family to leave."

"They just left you with those thugs?"

"They told my parents that if they saw any of them in Homs, they would kill my younger brother. So they had to leave."

"Why? What did you guys do to them? Why would they target you, I mean?"

"I have no idea," she said as sadness came into her voice. "They stole our house, they kidnapped Azad, and they destroyed my father's store."

"And what about you? Did they hurt you?"

"Me?" she asked, clearly surprised. She stopped in her tracks, turning to look at him for a long moment before bursting into tears. "No, they didn't hurt me."

Waleed understood that she didn't want to talk about it. "So where are you going now?"

She began walking again, frantically this time. "I need to get back to Amoda, to my family."

"You need to get out of Homs fast. Once you're out, you can go wherever you want."

"We have relatives in Rokn El-Din in Damascus City."

"I don't think that's a good idea. They will search for you there, and you know how tight the security is in Damascus. They have eyes on every inch of that city. I've never run into a situation like this before. I thought this kind of harassment ended in the eighties. I guess it never did. People just learned how to appease the government."

She had the look of a lost animal, desperate and afraid. "What do you think I should do?"

He glanced down at his wristwatch. "About two hours from now, there will be a Homs-Hama bus. Take it. From there, find what bus route would get you to your parents the fastest."

"I don't know if I can plan that trip on my own."

Waleed reached out and gently grabbed her arm, easing her to a stop. "I know you're not prepared for this, but you have no choice. Just pull yourself together and do this right."

Her expression softened as the weight of what he was telling her settled in. "All right. I'm just scared."

"I know." Waleed reached into his pocket, producing his wallet. "Here, take five hundred Liras. It's all I have."

She gave him a doe-eyed look. "I can't accept your money."

"Just take it. Don't sleep tonight. We'll keep walking around, and then you can sleep on the bus."

Later, they found a shop that was still open. He bought her a black *abaya* so she could cover herself. They kept walking in narrow, dark alleys until 5:00 a.m. when the buses started running again. As she stepped onto the bus, Waleed doubted that he would ever see her or anyone from her family again.

"Take care," he said. "God be with you."

She started crying as if she had finally grasped the magnitude of the mess her life had become.

"There is no God but God," he reminded her.

With that, the doors closed between them and the bus took off into the unknown, bearing her away to a dark sea on a ship with no sails.

Chapter 6
Chaos Theory

At first glance, everything in the universe seems uniform and smooth, almost flawless. The sea waves hitting the shores of Latakia repeatedly for thousands of years, the ancient waterwheels of Hama rotating along the Asy River since the dawn of human civilization—these are matters of perfection.

However, no sea wave is identical to the one before it. Each rotation of the waterwheels is different from the one before. There is no predictability in anything around us. We are merely trying to make meaning out of chaos.

Fortunately, there might be some patterns within that very chaos. Edward Lorentz first proposed chaos theory in 1961. One of its main aspects is commonly referred to as the "butterfly effect." A small, seemingly irrelevant event such as a butterfly flapping its wings can alter events in such a way as to create a tornado in one place or prevent a tornado in another.

On December 17, 2010, one of the greatest examples of chaos theory came to light. The entire world watched on their TV screens as it unfolded into one of the major political events of the twenty-first century, blurring the lines between friends and enemies and mixing the colors of past and present.

It all began in a small Tunisian town called Sidi Bouzid. The instigator, Mr. Al-Bouazizi, was a simple street vendor struggling to make a living. Future generations will probably call him a revolutionary leader or a visionary, but the truth is that he was a simple young man frustrated with everything. He had grown used to police harassment on a regular basis, but when they confiscated his fruit cart, his only source of income, he was outraged. Forgetting that this was the Arab world, he went to complain to a municipal officer. There, the forty-five-year-old woman who served the post scolded him and slapped him.

Feelings of despair, injustice, and helplessness took over the young man. This dangerous mixture of feelings could kill an individual, but it could also create a revolution when it affected a number of people over a certain mysterious threshold. Bouazizi's pain was everyone's pain, and yet it was a pain expressed by no one. Arabs had become a group of hundreds of millions of butterflies that forgot how to fly—that is, until Bouazizi flapped his wings.

    Angered, frustrated, and helpless, Bouazizi lit himself on fire, igniting what later would be called the Arab Spring.

    —Syria: A History in Blood by Celine Dubois

December 17, 2010
Deaths: 0

<>

"A young Tunisian man set himself on fire after being slapped by an officer," Waleed read out loud. He sat at the computer desk, his brother Khalid pacing across the rug behind him.

"Why would he do that to himself?" Khalid wondered aloud.

"Hey, check this out! They have pictures of him on fire on Al Jazeera's website."

Waleed felt his brother's presence hovering over his shoulder. "It says that he's still alive!" his brother said. "The man sustained burns to ninety percent of his body, but is currently in the intensive care unit."

"Man," Waleed said. "That's even worse. Turn on the TV. Maybe there's more news about him."

To their surprise, there happened to be a news report about the very same man on Al Jazeera. The report was initially talking about the man's life and his current state of health. There had been no real response from the Tunisian authorities on the incident at that point.

"It's so random what makes it to TV," Waleed said, deep in thought. "I mean, a man burns himself and it's on Al Jazeera, but forty thousand were killed in Hama in the eighties and it wasn't on a single news channel."

Khalid placed his hand on Waleed's shoulder. "It's a different era, brother. Now there is satellite television, laptops, and the internet."

Waleed spun around in his chair. "Really? So you think if they wanted to repeat the massacres of Hama, they wouldn't be able to?"

"Well, there's no reason to do it now. The people who were killed were the last remaining true men in Syria. Now we're all just obedient slaves. Why should they do a massacre? Who wants to kill a good slave?"

He could scarcely believe it, but Waleed was listening to his normally devout brother spouting negativity about his government. "I know," he said when the shock had worn off. "You're right. But hypothetically speaking, let's imagine that one day some Homsi starts pumping nicotine into our water supply until all of Homs wakes up from the spell we're under and they decide to overthrow the government. Do you think they could do a Hama massacre here and now?"

Khalid shook his head fervently. "No way. They can't. The whole world is watching. They can't block the media like they did in the past. There is no Soviet Union to protect them. There are American troops in Iraq right on our border. And there is an international community watching. There is no way for the regime to kill us by the thousands anymore."

A strange silence hung in the air between them.

"You feel better now?" Khalid asked.

Waleed laughed, relieving himself of some of the tension. "Yes, I do. In fact, I'll go start an uprising right now."

"Boys, dinner is ready!" yelled their mother from the kitchen. "*Yalla*, Waleed. Prepare the dinner table. And Khalid, call your brother to come home. He's at Om Qassem's house, studying with her son."

"I'll set the table, Waleedo," Khalid suggested. "You go get Sami."

Waleed accepted the offer without complaint, for he hated setting the table. As he opened the front door to the house, he was surprised to find four policemen standing outside. A slow dread climbed up his spine. Had they heard his conversation with Khalid? Had they really read his thoughts? Did they have some spyware in their apartment that allowed them to eavesdrop?

Such was his fear that he could not speak. He simply stood in the doorway, petrified.

"Yes, we're looking for Waleed," one of the officers said.

"Looking for me?" Waleed managed. "What do you want from me?"

The lead agent feigned a look of distress. "Is this how you greet your officers? Have your parents not raised you properly?"

"Greet my officers?" Waleed breathed.

"Invite us inside, boy," the agent demanded.

Waleed startled, straightening up and turning for the door. "Hold on, please. My mother needs to get dressed for company, and then you can come in."

Their fake smiles faded into cold stares, the stares of animals hungry for a kill.

"We are not here for your whore mother," the lead agent said. "We are here for you, and we are coming in." All at once, they entered, pushing him to the floor as they passed.

"Oh my God!" his mother yelled. "Who are you people? Have you no shame, walking into a house with women without asking permission? Don't you have mothers or sisters?"

Before she could continue lecturing them, one of the men took out a gun and pointed it at her, shocking the entire house into silence. "Any more comments?" he asked, the gun still in his hand. "Good." Then he pointed the weapon at Waleed and stepped toward him. "I have one question for you, so give us what we need and we'll leave you alone. Am I making myself clear?"

Waleed's body had retreated into a cold kind of survival instinct. His limbs had gone rigid, but his mind was clearer than it had been in weeks. "Yes."

"You mean, 'yes, sir.'"

"Yes, sir," Waleed repeated.

"Good. Tell your mother to make us coffee."

Waleed looked to his mother, whose knees quivered visibly. "Mother, would you please make these men some coffee?" he asked politely.

Without a word, she turned for the kitchen. In a moment, Waleed could hear her banging around in there.

"So," the agent said with an air of pleasantry, "do you know why we're here?"

"No," Waleed said quickly before correcting himself. "No, sir."

"We're here to ask about a girl . . ."

"Which girl?"

The agent looked frightfully annoyed. "Don't interrupt me." He seemed to take great pleasure in the slowness with which he retrieved a cigarette and brought it to light. "Do you know a girl by the name of Fairouz?"

Waleed's heart pounded in his chest. It beat so rapidly that it lost its rhythm altogether, tumbling into chaos. Being a doctor, he began to wonder whether he had gone into some kind of atrial fibrillation. "No, sir," he lied. "I do not."

"Do you know someone by the name of Azad?"

His throat became dry. Even talking felt like a challenge. "Yes, sir."

"Were you close to him?"

"No, sir."

"How do you know him, then?"

"I used to buy vegetables from his store."

The agent took a puff of his smoke, blowing it into Waleed's face. "Where is he?"

"I don't know, sir."

"Where do you think he is?"

"At home?"

For a long while, the officer kept his dark eyes trained on Waleed as if studying him. His gaze was so transfixing that it eventually became all that Waleed could see. The details of the room fell away, then his brother and mother. Finally the soldiers disappeared, leaving only the agent's prodding eyes. He felt himself disappearing into them as if walking down a long, dark hallway.

"Okay," the agent said after a time, snapping Waleed from his trance. "It seems that you are useless." He looked from one side to the other before bending down over him. "You know, if I find out that anything you told me today was a lie, I will cut out your tongue. I promise." With that, he raised his arm high and slapped him hard. "That was just a reminder."

The men left without fanfare, disappearing as if they had never come. Waleed's mother quickly rushed to the door, locked it, knelt before it, and started reciting prayers. Khalid came to Waleed to check if he was okay. Waleed kept silent. He got up, washed his face, and returned to the living room to sit on the couch. He snatched up the remote control and turned on the television. He settled on the Al-Arabiya channel. There it was: another report about Bouazizi, the man who had burned himself because of a slap on his face. Suddenly, Waleed felt that he knew exactly what was going on in Bouazizi's mind: the shame, the humiliation, the anger, and the helplessness.

Finally, as his brother watched him with his mouth hanging open and his mother recited prayers, he felt compelled to speak. "It's all the same trash. We're all the same. We're all one system. I wish I could do what he did and burn myself in shame."

His mother came up out of her prayerful meditation. "Waleed, *habibi*, don't say that. It will be fine, darling."

"Nothing will ever be fine as long as we're ruled by those mafias."

"Waleed, enough politics! I don't want to lose you. You hear me? It was close today!"

He shrugged his shoulders and didn't bother replying. He knew this was an argument he could never win.

~~~

That night, thousands of young men and women in the Middle East and North Africa also knew exactly how Bouazizi felt and why he had done what he did. They understood the feelings and thoughts that had gone through his mind. They knew that they were all the same, that they were all prisoners under stagnant regimes that seemed immune to change.

Well, they knew wrong.

Chapter 7
Green Tunisia

January 14, 2011
Deaths: 0

"Green Tunisia, I have come to you as a lover
On my brow, a rose and a book
For I am the Damascene whose profession is passion
Whose singing turns the herbs green
A Damascene moon travels through my blood
Nightingales . . . and grain . . . and domes."

Waleed paused in his reading, the echo of his own racing thoughts drowning out the words of the great poet. He sat with Sireen in their favorite spot atop Omar's roof. In the distance over Homs, a storm appeared to be gathering.

"Don't stop, Waleed," Sireen said, blissfully unaware. "Nizar Qabbani takes me to another world. It's like he could read the future. Tell me the rest of it."

With his mind elsewhere and his heart not in it, Waleed complied.

"From Damascus, jasmine gets its whiteness
And fragrances perfume themselves with her scent
From Damascus, water begins . . . for wherever
You lean your head, a stream flows
And poetry is a sparrow spreading its wings
Over Sham . . . and a poet is a voyager."

When again Waleed paused, this time it was because he felt suddenly overcome. The tears that collected in the corners of his eyes, he did his best to hide.

"Isn't it amazing?" Sireen asked, unable to see Waleed's disquiet. "It's amazing how his favorite flower, the jasmine, was the symbol of Tunisia's revolution. If only he knew that Damascus simply sat and watched while the smell of freedom and jasmine perfumed Tunisia. Is there more to it?"

Waleed nodded, then cleared his throat and read.

"From Damascus, love begins . . . for our ancestors
Worshipped beauty, they dissolved it, and they melted away
From Damascus, horses begin their journey
And the stirrups are tightened for the great conquest
From Damascus, eternity begins . . . and with her
Languages remain and genealogies are preserved
And on her land, epochs materialize. "

"What a great poem!" Sireen said as she rested her head on Waleed's shoulder.

As many times as they had come to Omar's roof, this was the first time they had sat this close together. The last month had been one of magic and inspiration for many in the region. Millions of people had become believers in miracles and dreams come true. It all started on the seventeenth of December, after that first slap to Waleed's face. It was the slap that woke him up from a Matrix-like illusion into the ugly reality in which he lived. His mother prohibited any discussion of politics at home, and it was not safe to talk about it at work, so his only outlet was Sireen. Over the past month, she had listened to him talk for hours and hours about how much he hated the way the country was run, the way his hospital functioned, and even how much he hated Bashar Al-Assad.

A week after that day, Waleed and Sireen, along with the rest of Syria and the greater Arab world, collectively started tuning in to the bizarre events taking place in the small town of Sidi Bouzid in Tunisia. Shortly after the hospitalization of Bouazizi, his family embarked upon a public protest against government corruption. This was not only done under the light of day, it was done under the coverage of Al Jazeera and other major channels. The rough beatings that led to the deaths of some protestors fueled more protests until the entire city of Sidi Bouzid was crying out for freedom. This was an unprecedented event in the Arab world. An entire town was protesting against a ruling elite, against corruption, against injustice. Soon, young Tunisian activists realized the historic importance of this moment. Being technologically savvy and highly educated, young Tunisians quickly took the battle to cyberspace, the only space relatively uncontrolled by authoritarian regimes. Soon enough, there were Facebook pages and groups dedicated to helping organize and unify the protestors.

Waleed and Sireen had watched in awe as the protests spread from one city to the next and as their slogans became bolder and more daring. "The people want to overthrow the regime!" was the signature slogan of what was later known as the Tunisian Revolution. The television blaring in Waleed's living room showed hundreds of thousands of people all over Tunisia taking to the streets, chanting, "The people want to overthrow the regime!" The slogan was so daring that it left Waleed dropping his jaw right along with the entire Arab world. It was so outrageous to the Arab ear that it was akin to hearing a three-year-old talk about sex. People around the Arab world would smile and giggle every time they heard what the Tunisians were bluntly yelling in bright daylight. Like everyone he knew, Waleed was cautiously optimistic, but he didn't truly believe that it was possible to overthrow an Arab autocrat.

And yet, clashes between the protestors and the police kept escalating. Dozens of people died. Soon the protests reached Tunis, the capital city.

The rougher the policemen got in dealing with the protestors, the larger the protests grew. The reports Waleed read suggested that Ben Ali, the Tunisian dictator, soon realized that he was in trouble and began making compromises. He promised major reforms. He promised freedom of expression and freedom of press. He promised to wage a war on corruption and to create jobs. To Waleed's astonishment and delight, the people didn't buy any of those promises. The protests continued to spread. Soon they took control of many major squares in the capital city.

Finally, Ben Ali gave his third and last speech. "I understood you," was how he began. By the next day, January 14, 2011, Ben Ali was on a private jet, trying to escape Tunisia. Before he departed, he asked the Tunisian army to intervene and crush the protests, but when the army refused his orders, he could see that it was checkmate for him. He fled while he still could. The next day, celebrations across Tunisia were broadcast live on Al Jazeera and every other major TV channel around the world. It was one of those unforgettable TV moments when a Tunisian man ran through the streets of Tunis, shouting, "Ben Ali escaped! Ben Ali escaped! You did it, Tunisians!"

Waleed had wiped away the tears in his eyes as he watched the Tunisian miracle live on television. The tears gently made their way down his cheeks, healing the pain of the slap from the corrupt officer. As the protestors started chanting the Tunisian anthem, he had repeated it with them in a soft voice. "If the people one day decide to live, then definitely fate shall answer . . ."

"Are the Tunisians really free now, Waleed?" Sireen asked like a child questioning her father.

"Yes, they are. Who would have thought that it was possible to overthrow an Arab regime?"

"I know! I still can't believe this whole Tunisian Revolution took place because of one person!" Sireen lifted her head and looked excitedly at Waleed. "I wish Nizar Qabbani were alive. He would have written another poem to Tunisia called 'The Jasmine Revolution.' I'm so glad we lived to witness this moment in history."

"Me, too," Waleed agreed.

"But it's not like it's going to affect our lives in any way."

Waleed smiled wickedly. "You never know."

She laced her arm under his, causing his heart to pound as he stared out over the buzzing city he called home. "Oh, I know," she said. "Trust me. I know how pathetic our Syrian people are. They'll never do anything like that—not in a million years. Trust me."

"Well, that's what people said about Tunisians before their Jasmine Revolution, right?"

"I don't hear anyone even joking about the government around here. How do you expect such people to start a revolution? Maybe Azad was the only person who opposed the government, and they took him away."

A pain formed at the back of Waleed's throat, causing his eyes to water. "I miss him, Sireen."

"I know." She moved closer to him, returning her head to his shoulder. "May God protect him."

He gazed down at her, wanting desperately to look her in the eye. "Thank you for being there for me."

"Don't thank me," she said, glancing up at him for the briefest of moments before looking away. "I love every minute I spend with you."

"Do you like me?" The question came out flat and unexpected. It hung in the air like a foul smell as Waleed wished he could take it back.

"What? No!" she said quickly. "I mean . . . Yes!"

Waleed chuckled despite his discomfort. "Which is it, then? You don't like me?"

"No," she said awkwardly, turning her head away.

"Really? Then why are you blushing and avoiding eye contact?"

"I'm not," she insisted, her face growing redder every moment.

"Take a deep breath. I didn't mean to embarrass you, but I'm a doctor. I'm not dumb."

"Yes, you are. Dumb Homsi."

"Hey!" he said flirtatiously. "Don't be racist. I thought you liked Homsi guys."

~~~

When their gazes locked, Sireen felt lost in his eyes. They were dark and mysterious, as if they carried the ancient secrets of thousands of years. The moonlight reflected elegantly on his shoulders and hair. She could almost hear his heartbeat in that silent Syrian night. Then he extended his hand, offering it to her. Her heart nearly ran out of beats, but she couldn't make herself take it. He kept his hand extended toward her, as if not to admit that his offer had been rejected. Then he smiled and started reciting more Nizar poetry:

"I have no power to change your nature
my books are of no use to you
and my convictions do not convince you
nor does my fatherly council do you any good
you are the queen of anarchy, of madness, of belonging."

~~~

"You're bribing me with poetry?"

"I'm not bribing you with anything," he said, somewhat disappointed as he withdrew his hand.

Sireen slowly lifted her fingers and moved her hand toward his. He wrapped his hand around her fingertips, and then, motivated by his physician reflexes, slid his fingers around her wrist and felt the rhythm of her quickened pulse. Then their eyes locked again. Her blue eyes turned almost black from the darkness of the night and the dilation of her pupils.

After a moment, she withdrew her hand and leaned back on a sack of dried vegetables, gazing at the sky. Waleed looked around for another sack. When he found it, he dragged it next to her.

"What are you doing?" she asked.

"Nothing." He went to the other side of the roof and broke a small branch from the jasmine tree that had climbed its way over the building. Almost every building in the neighborhood had its own jasmine tree that had embraced its walls for decades. He placed the jasmine branch on her lap and said, "Take a deep breath. This is the smell of freedom, coming all the way from Tunisia."

"Thank you," she said, her voice subdued. "I love jasmine."

He took a seat beside her. "I've been reciting poetry for you all day. I want to hear you do it."

"No, I'm really not good at it."

"Come on. Do it for me."

"All right, but don't laugh at me."

"I won't."

Reluctantly she took the book from him and began to read.

"What do I tell him if he asks me
Whether I hate him or whether I love him,
What do I say if his fingertips begin
Brushing the night of my hair
And how could I allow him to get closer
Or allow his hands to sleep around my waist
Tomorrow, if he comes I will give him all his letters
And we'll feed the fire everything he wrote . . ."

"*We* wrote," Waleed corrected her.

"What?"

"The poem says, 'feed the fire everything we wrote,' not 'he wrote.'"

Sireen sighed. "It's not going to work out."

He frowned and turned to look at her. "What isn't going to work out?"

"Us."

A finger of fear caressed his mind. "Why not?"

She leaned away from him. "It's complicated, but we had better end whatever is happening between us."

Waleed shook his head in confusion. "This makes no sense. Am I doing something wrong?"

"No, you're not," she said, sounding regretful. "And I'm not. It's just destiny. It's not going to work out."

A sudden anger washed over him. Waleed rose to his knees. Behind Sireen, the city lights seemed to fade away. All he could see now was her resistant face. "What are you saying? How could you say that? Were you just messing with my feelings all this time?"

Her large eyes brimmed with tears. "No, I swear. I was just not thinking clearly. You're an amazing guy, but . . ."

"But what? Is there something I don't know?"

"There is. I'm sorry." As the sun started to make its appearance after a long night of slumber, a tear spilled over her cheek. "I'm sorry, Waleed. I'm so sorry." She repeated the words several more times as she stood, picked up her bag, and headed for the stairs.

"Let me walk you home," Waleed offered, a strange desperation gripping him. "It's not safe."

"It's Homs. There is no safer place. Besides, the sun is almost out. Thank you."

Waleed could not understand what was happening. He could see the love in her eyes and could almost hear her heart shattering slowly along with his. After she turned and left him, he stood near the edge of the roof, peeking down to see whether Sireen was really leaving or if she was going to change her mind and come back. A minute later, he saw her exit the building. She looked up in his direction, waved, and walked away swiftly.

Defeated, Waleed returned to his vegetable sack, sad Arabic love songs playing in his head. This was so strange. Had he misinterpreted all her moves for the past few months? Did she have someone else in her life? The chain of questions went on and on, until someone pressing lightly on his shoulders interrupted it.

"Waleed? What's the matter?"

Waleed looked up with a start, seeing that Omar had come to him. He held a steaming cup of coffee in one hand. "Nothing, brother."

"I didn't just meet you yesterday, you know. I know when something is bothering you."

"You know what's going on," Waleed said with a sigh. "Stop asking."

"You love her, and she doesn't love you?"

"I don't know for sure. She's been giving me all kinds of signals for months, but when I made a move, she turned me down."

Omar furrowed his brow and took a thoughtful sip of his coffee. "That's very strange. I totally agree. She wasn't very subtle, either. But you know how women are. She might change her mind tomorrow."

"I think there's someone else in her life."

"I doubt it. It doesn't seem like it."

"Yeah?"

"Yes. And even if there is, a thousand women would wish to be with you.

I'll find you the prettiest girl in all of Homs." Omar scrunched up his face and began speaking in a grandmotherly voice. "I want to see my grandkids before I die." When Waleed refused to laugh, he softened his expression and took a different tack. "No, this is not right. We need a serious intervention to cheer you up. Hold on, I'll be back."

He was gone for ten minutes before returning with the most unusual of things: two children and two large cages full of pigeons. Waleed wondered whether there would be a clown and a parade to follow, as well. He sat in puzzled disbelief as Omar placed the two cages on the floor and instructed the kids to introduce themselves.

"*Ana* [I am] Shadi," the first kid said, raising five fingers. "I'm five."

"Five in the eyes of the devil," Omar said, in reference to an old Syrian custom that it was rude to point your open palm at someone's face. "Don't point your five fingers at *Ammo* [Uncle] Waleed."

The younger kid slowly walked toward Waleed and extended his hand, waiting for him to shake it.

Waleed took it and gave it a gentle shake. "What's your name, *habibi*?"

"*Ana* Hod-Hod."

"Tell him your real name, Hod-Hod!" Omar lectured.

"Hadi."

"Tell him your full name."

"Hadi Ahmad Thaati."

"Thaati?" Waleed repeated.

"Saati! Saati!" Omar replied with disappointment before turning to Waleed. "They're my nephews. My sister's sons. Hadi here is two years old. Their father is from Damascus. They live in our same building."

Waleed wanted to interview the two-year-old a little more, but the boy had already lost interest in him as he ran toward the birdcages and started kicking the bars, laughing, and running around. He kept repeating that same pattern for at least five minutes, finding it more hilarious each time he did it.

"I didn't know you sold birds, Omar," Waleed said when he had lost interest in watching the child.

"These? No, I don't sell them. They're too intelligent to be sold. They are mail pigeons."

"Mail pigeons?"

"That's right. They can deliver letters and light objects from one place to another."

Waleed raised an eyebrow. "What? Whatever happened to normal mail or phone or email?"

"Nothing happened. It's my hobby. You have your hobbies. I mean, why do you memorize useless poetry?"

Waleed paused, trying to decide whether that was an insult that required a retort. He decided that he would let it slide. "So, what exactly can they do?"

"Is it six a.m. yet?"

"Yes, it's five after six. Why?"

"Golden Knight is awake now."

"Who? Golden what?"

Omar gave him an incredulous look. "Golden Knight. Are you deaf? It's my friend's secret name."

"What's his real name? And why does he have a secret name?"

"I'm not telling you his real name. We're a group of four pigeon lovers in and around the Baba Amro neighborhood. I'm actually the only one who is inside the neighborhood. The rest are scattered on the fringes. We all have secret names to make it more interesting. We make-believe that we're sending each other important messages. Yes, it's immature, but I don't care." He pointed excitedly to the sky, where a pigeon approached from afar. "Oh, look who just came! It's my F-16."

"F-16? You are crazy."

"She is one of my pigeons. I call her F-16. It looks like I just got mail." Even as he spoke the words, the pigeon flew over the roof and came to land on his hand. In a moment, it dropped to the floor and started stomping its claws with anger. It looked almost as if it was annoyed by all the visitors. Omar went down on his knees and grabbed the pigeon. He started rubbing its feathers before removing a small paper attached to its claw. It was a letter that Omar read aloud. "'Good morning. Did you hear the news from Tunisia?'" He smiled and asked Waleed, "Isn't it much safer than normal mail?"

Waleed was amazed. "If the Mukhabarat catch you, they'll kill you and your pigeons."

"Don't worry," he said with a wry grin. "I'm sure some of these pigeons already work for them."

"*Ammo* [Uncle], Leed!" Hod-Hod mumbled as he ran toward Waleed in fear of being attacked by the F-16.

Waleed lifted him up. "Go away, fat bird. Don't bother Hod-Hod."

"Faaat bird!" Hod-Hod yelled, waving his fist at the apathetic bird. Then he turned to Waleed and demanded to be put down. The moment his feet touched the floor, he ran at the poor bird.

"Hod-Hod!" Omar scolded. "Leave her alone, or I will give her your new basketball."

"No! No!" Hod-Hod said as he continued to chase the terrified pigeon.

His smile fading, Waleed straightened up and looked to his friend. "Omar, should I ask you, or should I ask the wolf?" It was a Syrian expression meaning, "Can I ask you for a favor?"

"Not the wolf, of course."

"Good man. I think I need a favor."

"Anything for you. A favor from me?"

"No, from your pigeons."

Chapter 8
Al Jazeera

> *Al Jazeera is perhaps one of the world's most controversial television channels. It probably has the largest margins of freedom of speech of any Arabic television channel, and for that reason, it holds greater influence on Arab public opinion than perhaps anything else. This particular channel placed a tremendous amount of power in the hands of the State of Qatar, a tiny member of the Arabian Gulf states.*
>
> *Almost all Arab governments had one thing in common: they all hated Al Jazeera. It became a problem for the Americans, as well, when it presented a very grim view of the war in Iraq. The Al Jazeera factor was crucial in toppling the Tunisian regime and in further encouraging the Egyptian protestors in Tahrir Square. Suddenly tiny Qatar found itself at the heart of the Arab Spring. In a way, Al Jazeera was both its gift and its curse.*
>
> *—Syria: A History in Blood* by Celine Dubois

February 5, 2011
Deaths: 0

It had been more than two weeks since Waleed and Sireen had last spoken. He had called her twice over that period, but she didn't pick up and he didn't want to appear too desperate, so he stopped calling. He thought about calling her roommate, Fatima, but then chose otherwise. It certainly helped that he had been on night float in the emergency department for the past few weeks; he barely had time to scratch his head. In addition to that, whatever free time he could manage, he spent watching Al Jazeera. The past week had been full of history-making live on television.

He learned that, inspired by the Tunisian uprising that had led to the collapse of the Tunisian regime, youth groups in Egypt had organized Facebook pages calling for protests throughout Egypt. This all began on January 25, a banner day of emergency department exhaustion for Waleed. That day, he watched bleary-eyed but enthralled as protestors started pouring into the streets of Suez, Alexandria, and most importantly, Cairo. The

Egyptians had learned an important lesson from the Tunisians about the vitality of occupying major squares. In Egypt, that space was Tahrir Square, located in the heart of Cairo. Hundreds of thousands of protestors poured into the square and occupied it in a matter of days. The freedom slogans of Tunisia had made their way here: "The people want to overthrow the regime." However, unlike little Tunisia, Egypt had major political weight in the Middle East, so it received a tremendous amount of world attention. CNN was there. The BBC was there. Fox was there. Alarabiya was there. France 24 was there. And most importantly, Al Jazeera was there.

It was the latter that Waleed tuned into every chance he got. The network covered the event, in all its intimate details, day and night. To Waleed, it felt almost like an astonishing reality show. He watched as Hosni Mubarak gave two speeches promising reforms and blaming the chaos on foreign elements and infiltrators.

Every day at work, it seemed that the uprising in Egypt was all anyone could talk about, provided they did so in hushed, private circles. Some of the colleagues Waleed spoke with thought that the regime in Egypt was too stable to overthrow, while others were almost certain of its collapse. He lay in the latter camp. From what he could see, the mobs kept growing in size every day. The police force became increasingly rougher in dealing with the protestors. They used water, rubber bullets, electric sticks, horses, camels, and every soft weapon they had at their disposal to disperse the mobs—all of it captured on television. No matter what they tried, they failed.

Waleed gasped at the sight of people being run over by cars and buses, people dragged into dark alleys and beaten to death. By the first week, dozens of people had been killed and hundreds injured, but hundreds of thousands were still determined to overthrow the regime. None of these deaths went unnoticed. The media was on top of it. Waleed took it all in.

It was exactly these things that he thought about as he stalked down the long, chaotic hallway of the emergency department, doctors and nurses conferring all around. A patient passed in the opposite direction, dragging his IV along beside him. Waleed was so lost in his thoughts that he had to leap to step out of the IV's way.

"Dr. Waleed," came the voice through the overhead speaker, "a call for you. Dr. Waleed."

"Not another admission!" Waleed mumbled to the bright-eyed resident doctor trailing him. "I'm dead tired."

"At least no trauma cases today," the resident said eagerly.

Waleed stopped to look directly at the young resident. "Are you kidding? I *want* some trauma cases. That's the only thing I can learn from the ED doctors." He left the resident slack-jawed, wondering whether it was a joke. Waleed found a phone on the wall at the end of the hall and answered the call announced over the speaker. "Hello, it's Waleed from the ED returning your call."

"Hello, Waleed from the ED returning my call."

He recognized the voice immediately. "Omar! Done with work?"

"Yes. Thanks for all the surgery admissions, jerk. A partial bowel obstruction admitted to us? Are you serious? You've really become an ED doctor."

"Oh, no," Waleed said glumly. "Am I really acting like an ED doctor?"

"Yes. You don't admit patients for observation to surgery; you dump it on internal medicine! Or are you trying to protect your kind?"

Waleed rubbed his temples with his free hand. "Man, the medicine people are overwhelmed. Just leave them alone."

"Anyways, I'm coming down to the ED. Let's have breakfast." Omar didn't wait for a reply before hanging up.

"Sharif," Waleed addressed the resident next to him, "I don't think ED doctors are dumb."

"Why, thank you, sir. That's a great compliment."

Waleed smirked. "It's just that the ED makes people dumb, even if they're smart. I just realized that."

Sharif groaned. "Why do I have to hear this from another medicine resident?"

A new patient walking in with her family caught Waleed's eye. He recognized one among the group as Fatima, Sireen's roommate. "Sharif, I think I'll see this admission, if it's all right with you."

"Praise the One who changes everything," Sharif said in surprise. "Okay, you've got it. This is the last patient we'll see this shift. The day team is almost here, so I'm going to head out. See you tonight. *Salam*." He grabbed his backpack and his stethoscope and headed out.

Waleed approached Fatima and her family. They seemed somewhat distressed. She was with her mother, father, and possibly an older brother. Her mother, who appeared to be in her early sixties, looked like the patient. Waleed could tell that she was breathing heavily. In fact, he could hear her wheezing with each breath. He could also tell that she was either having a bad asthma attack or a COPD exacerbation. It was surprising how quickly they were able to get a room in the ED, given that there were patients who had been waiting for hours and with seemingly more serious conditions. It didn't take Waleed long to realize that her brother was wearing a military uniform and was probably some big shot in the Syrian army. This would be more than enough to have his mother bumped up the waiting list.

Fatima looked happy to see him.

"Good morning," he said with a broad smile. "I'm Dr. Waleed."

"Bring the best doctor in the hospital," the brother said. "My mother is sick."

Waleed looked nervously at Fatima, who averted her gaze. "Well, that would be our chief, and he's not working today."

"He's what?" the brother said. He puffed out his chest, trying to look down on Waleed even though he was a full two inches shorter. "I don't care. Bring him here."

Fatima looked embarrassed. "Hussein! Spare us. I know Dr. Waleed. He's great."

With a placating smile, Waleed addressed the stocky, mustachioed Hussein. "I'd be happy to call the chief if you don't want me seeing your mother."

"No, Dr. Waleed," Fatima said, stepping between them. "My brother doesn't know you like I do. We would be happy if you could see her."

Looking like a kicked puppy, Hussein reluctantly stepped aside. Waleed took a brief medical history, then examined the patient. The problem was clear immediately.

"Madam," Waleed said gently, "it seems that your COPD is acting up. We'll have to start you on some steroids intravenously, and we'll give you some nebulizers. Hopefully you'll feel better after this. We have great nurses who will keep a close eye on you, but first we have to admit you to the hospital to stay overnight." With one last glance at the scowling, dubious-looking Hussein, he pardoned himself to leave. "It was a pleasure meeting you."

"Thank you so much, Waleed," Fatima said, following him into the hall. "Please don't mind my brother. He's a really sweet man, but you know the army changes people. He's a general. Hussein Sleiman is his name."

"I have not heard of him," Waleed said apologetically. "But I understand the tension when your mother is sick."

Fatima shifted her stance from one hip to the other and brushed her blond hair out of her eyes. "So, how have you been?"

"I'm doing all right. Busy with work and the news!"

"Oh yeah, we're all glued to the screen. It's a big slap in Israel's face."

"Israel? I'm talking about the Egyptian revolution."

"Yes, I mean I'm glad the Egyptians finally said enough is enough on their peace with Israel."

Waleed furrowed his brow. "I don't know where you heard that. All I heard was that they had had enough of the corruption and injustice."

"Of course that's a part of it. But you have to ask yourself why a revolution occurred in Egypt but not in Syria. It's because our leadership is in harmony with its people. The Egyptians want to be like us in confronting imperialism and Zionism."

Waleed recognized the sentiment immediately. His friend was parroting a recent interview with Bashar Al-Assad.

"Maybe," Waleed said, realizing that this discussion was no longer safe to continue.

Fatima demurred, batting her eyes. "Waleed, this is a crucial time. We have to keep our eyes open. There are enemies who want to harm our country from without and from within, and it's our duty to expose them."

"*Inshallah* [God willing]," he replied coldly.

Her expression changed considerably. Gone were the histrionics, replaced now with something akin to affection. "How is your friend Omar? I think I have a crush on him. Do you think we have a chance of being together?"

Waleed tried not to let the shock show on his face. "Would that be all right with your family?"

"What do you mean?" She did not look pleased with the reply. "Do you mean because we're from different religious sects?"

That was exactly what he meant, but realizing the tremendous awkwardness of the situation, he said, "No, silly! How am I supposed to know your religion? I don't even know his." Desperate for a change of topic, he blurted out a lie. "I think he likes you, too."

Fatima nodded smartly and held her hands behind her back. "Thank you for trusting me with this information. By the way, I hope you're not too upset about that other friend of yours, the Kurd."

"Which Kurd?" Waleed said with a more serious tone.

"What was his name? Azad or Mazad or something."

"What about him?"

"I think he's been arrested. He turned out to be a traitor."

Waleed's face suddenly flushed with anger. He could feel his heart pounding in his chest. "I heard."

"He admitted to being an agent for the Kurdish Separatists trying to break up Syria."

Waleed clenched his jaw, his fists, and even his toes in an attempt to restrain himself from saying something he might later regret. He suddenly became acutely aware of all the eyes and ears surrounding them in the hallway.

"You know what's funny?" she said, but Waleed remained silent. "I'm the one who busted him. From one word he said during our lunch last time, I knew he was a traitor. I told my brother about him, and they carried out an investigation and figured out that it's true. Now they're trying to uproot his entire network. It seems to be centered in Rokn El-Deen in Damascus."

It took every ounce of Waleed's strength not to speak.

"Keep your eyes open today," she went on. "Today is February fifth, the day of our supposed revolution. Some traitors on Facebook were calling for a revolt in Syria like the ones in Egypt and Tunisia."

"Really? How come no one heard?"

"For an obvious reason. Didn't you hear what President Dr. Bashar Al-Assad had to say? He said that we are not Tunisia and we are not Egypt. This wave will not touch Syria because our leadership listens closely to its people. Besides, we are the only country that stands up to America and the West."

"So, it's today?"

"It was supposed to start about an hour ago. A protest. I guess no one showed up." She burst out laughing.

"Well, Fatima, I hope your mother feels better soon. I need to get some work done."

Upon excusing himself, he ran to meet Omar. He was never happier to see his old friend.

"Omar! You won't believe this . . ."

Omar shrugged his round shoulders, clearly surprised at Waleed's insistence. "Believe what?"

"I just found Judas."

Chapter 9

Qays and Layla

I pass by these walls, the walls of Layla
And I kiss this wall and that wall
It's no love of the houses that has taken my heart
But of the one that dwells in those houses

Waleed wrote these words on a tiny letter that he hoped would make its way to his Layla, Sireen. They were the words that Qays ibn Al-Mulawwa had said to his beloved Layla during the Ummayad era. Damascus, being its capital, was the breathtaking hub of the world at the time. Back then, the culture saw that the lovers of Damascus would write each other poems and try to find creative ways to deliver those letters without being seen by the vigilant eye of society.

The story, as Waleed recalled it, was that Qays was a Bedouin who was so madly in love with Layla that he was known as Layla's Madman (*Majnon Layla*). As they grew up, word spread about the two lovers. To protect her reputation, the family banned Layla from seeing Qays.

Qays began wandering the deserts in desperation, until one day his father decided to take him to Mecca in search of a cure for his insanity. In time, Layla got married to another man, but her heart remained with her beloved. Soon after, she ended up succumbing to the sorrow and dying. When Qays heard the news, he lost whatever sanity he had left. He rushed to her grave and remained there for days before dying as well, buried in piles of his own poems. One of them read just as Waleed had written:

I pass by these walls, the walls of Layla
And I kiss this wall and that wall
It's no love of the houses that has taken my heart
But of the one that dwells in those houses

Those words traveled through time to make it from Qays's mouth to Waleed's ears. Soon they would travel through space to Sireen's window, carried on the wings of a white pigeon. This was the favor that Waleed had asked of Omar and his friend "Golden Knight." Together, they would train F-16 to carry out a very specific and classified mission: delivering a letter to Sireen's window. Waleed placed two red rose petals in the letter, rolled it, and secured it in a tiny envelope, which he attached to the pigeon's leg. He fed her well and patted her. He hugged her tight for a few seconds, as if it were her that he loved, then sent her flying away on a rainy February day.

The mission would be difficult, Waleed knew, but Omar assured him that nothing was impossible for F-16.

~~~

The bird went soaring through the wind and rain. She could sense that this was no ordinary letter she carried this time. The distance wasn't short, either. The recipient lived on the Homs University campus, which was between Baba Amro, where Omar lived, and Bab Sebaa, where Waleed lived. F-16 took off from the symbolic birthplace of their new love story, Omar's rooftop. She carried a tiny letter attached to her leg and a small jasmine necklace around her neck as she made her way over the quiet neighborhood of Baba Amro.

The rain was starting to slow, and a ray of sunshine peeked through the clouds every minute or so to encourage the little white pigeon to keep the mission alive. Many meters below her, she spotted Omar and his friend "Golden Knight" shaking hands and giving each other high fives like proud parents watching their child walk for the first time. In a way, the bird knew that what she was doing was illegal. She was a "communication medium" without Mukhabarat approval, but as long as Omar and the Golden Knight didn't care, she didn't care. On the street only a few meters below stood Waleed, holding little Shadi's hand, baby Hod-Hod perched on his shoulders.

~~~

"You see the bird, Hod-Hod?" Waleed asked, trying to distract the boy from pulling his hair.

"No! No! No!" Hod-Hod yelled as he smacked Waleed's head repeatedly.

"Thank God I'm not the one raising you, violent child." He hoped Hod-Hod wouldn't understand any of the words.

"Where's bird?"

"There," Waleed said as he pointed toward F-16. "You see it?"

"Oh! He gone?"

"Yeah, he's upset because you keep hitting *Ammo* Waleed."

"*Ammo*," Shadi said, pulling on Waleed's pant leg, "where is he going?"

"He's going to deliver a letter."

"To your wife?"

Waleed laughed. "No, not to my wife."

"To who?"

"To someone," Waleed replied, trying to end the unpredictable chain of questions that could erupt from the mouth of a five-year-old.

"Okay," the kid said, sounding unconvinced.

"Okay, guys, let's play a game where we watch the pigeon without talking." As Waleed shifted his weight, he added, "And may God keep your parents well so that no one else has to be stuck with you."

"What?"

"Nothing, *habibi*. I'm talking to myself."

Shadi made a puzzled face as he gazed up at Waleed. "My mom said only crazy people talk to themselves."

A sudden laugh erupted from Waleed's throat. "Okay, you're losing the game. Whoever talks more loses."

~~~

The pigeon could no longer see its cheering crowd. She resisted the temptations of the scattered fruit and vegetable shops across Baba Amro. She resisted the temptation to dive into some of Baba Amro's ice cream places and cafes at a time of day when the floor would be full of delicious crumbs from ice cream cones left behind by schoolchildren. She resisted the delectable smell of Abu Elias's kabob and shawarma as it sent columns of delightful smoke into the sky to tempt those birds of weak will. Not F-16.

~~~

Sireen was not looking forward to Valentine's Day. She wished she could spend the day with Waleed, but she knew better than to allow such a thing. She had misled him long enough, and she had to put an end to it. She just wanted this day to be finished. What a terrible idea this holiday was. It was a day to remind the lonely of their loneliness and those who had been hurt of what was hurting them. As she went to her window, she wondered what Waleed might be doing. She remembered the time she had seen him sleeping on the Hama-Homs bus. They had all gone on a trip that day: Fatima, Omar, Azad, Waleed, and her. They went to try the famous ice cream of Hama next to the beautiful ancient waterwheels of the Asy River. She couldn't stop staring at him while he slept peacefully. He had such a serious face when he was sleeping, with his eyebrows crossed and his lower lip touching his faint moustache, like a baby about to cry . . . a baby with a moustache. It was funny to watch. As she sank deeper into her thoughts, she noticed a beautiful white pigeon flying toward her.

To her surprise, the pigeon landed on her window. It looked exhausted as it breathed rapidly. Beside herself, Sireen started stroking the pigeon's feathers. She couldn't believe that it did not fly away at her touch. In a moment, she felt brave enough to carry the pigeon on her hand into the room. She crushed some biscuits that she had and spread them on her desk. The pigeon just kept staring at her. Then Sireen noticed the jasmine necklace and realized that this wasn't a regular pigeon. She noticed the small letter attached to the pigeon's leg. When she reached for it, she found that it was indeed a letter with her name on it. Sireen opened the letter and sniffed it; it smelled like pigeon.

Sireen's hands were almost shaking as she read the letter in amazement. The pigeon, clearly realizing that its mission was accomplished, celebrated with a delicious meal of biscuit crumbs.

When Sireen realized that the letter was from Waleed, her heart soared, then sank. What was he trying to do? How could she explain to him that this was a journey that needed to end? She knew what such a relationship could cost. It could prove to be a disaster for her, for her family, and most importantly, for Waleed. She held the letter close to her heart and closed her eyes in a desperate attempt to block the flow of tears and get a glimpse of what Waleed had written. Why had she allowed this to happen? Why had she made the first move to start a story that could lead to uncertainty at best? She could almost hear his laugh, smell his favorite cologne, and feel his touch. She tried to stop herself but couldn't. She reached for a pen and tried to explain her feelings in the words of Nizar Qabbani:

If you are my friend . . .
Help me . . . to leave you
Or if you are my lover . . .
Help me . . . so I can be healed of you . . .
Had I known . . .
How deep the sea was, I would not have sailed . . .
Had I known . . .
How things would end up, I would not have begun . . .

She rolled it and placed it back on the pigeon's leg. The bird appeared better rested after its heavy meal. Sireen went to the sink and got some water to offer. Sure enough, after a few sips from the bowl, the bird appeared ready for another mission.

Two hours passed. Sireen sat in a rocking chair she kept beside her window, watching the rooftops of Homs slowly becoming wetter with rain, listening to the occasional bombardment of thunder. Every time a pigeon flew by, she rushed to the window, her heart leaping. She had almost given up hope when a pigeon finally made its way to the window. Sireen rushed toward the exhausted pigeon and started massaging it and stroking its feathers. She had already prepared a bowl of water and some sunflower seeds, hoping the bird would like them. Then she reached for the letter attached to the pigeon's leg and started reading. The reply was also in the words of Nizar.

Come back to me . . . for the Earth has stopped
As if time has stopped making seconds
Come back to me . . . just the way you are
In the clear or in the rain
For, what is my life . . . without you in it?

The wind had grown stronger, and the pigeon was clearly not in the mood for more adventures. Sireen decided not to make it fly any more that day.

Instead, she passed the time pondering the letter and watching the bird bob happily at the sunflower seeds.

An hour later, her phone rang. It was Waleed, she knew. She took a deep breath and picked up the phone.

"How are you?" she said, trying to sound indifferent.

"How's my pigeon?"

She smiled. "She's a sweetheart."

"Her name is F-16."

Nervously she chewed on the nail of her little finger. "Why am I not surprised?"

"Sireen, I really want to talk to you."

"I know. The bird told me. But Waleed, it's not going to work. Please don't make this harder than it already is."

"It can't get harder than this!"

"Waleed, I think I should go now."

"No. You can't just go. You come and you talk to me. It's not fair. I need to understand."

"Waleed . . ."

"Let's meet after the sunset prayer in Baba Amro. I'll come pick you up, and we can go for some *kibbeh*."

She sighed, looking to the bird for support. The pigeon chewed thoughtfully on a seed. She nearly laughed. "I really don't think this is a good idea."

"You don't have to order *kibbeh*, then. You can order tabbouleh."

This time, she couldn't help herself. She laughed. "Pick me up after sunset prayer. But I can't stay long."

~~~

Around sunset, Waleed went to pray at one of the mosques of Baba Amro. For some reason, there was an unusual number of security officers in the mosque. Men in such uniforms never prayed, so their presence was always a bad omen. Given the general sense of discomfort at the mosque, everyone evacuated the building as soon as the prayer had ended. Waleed headed toward the university complex to pick up Sireen. Desperately he hoped to clear things up. As soon as he arrived, he gave her a call. She was ready and down in no time.

"Do you want us to just stay here and talk?" she asked.

"No, let's go on a walk to Baba Amro."

"That's a long walk."

"Well, we're going to have a long talk, then."

"All right. Let's do it."

Awkwardly, the two turned and made their way through the grassy campus to the boulevard beyond. The rain had subsided, but light gray clouds lingered overhead. Waleed was glad to have brought his bright yellow umbrella, though from the smell of the air, he wasn't sure he would need it. As they rounded the corner onto a street lined with market tables covered by a permanent roof, Waleed gathered his thoughts on how he might start. His ears rang with the catcalls of the merchants selling their various wares.

Waleed decided to be direct. "Sireen, you made me believe that you care about me and then you changed your mind. That's not fair."

She kept her eyes trained on the ground, as if watching her small, slender feet pass one before the other. "I do care about you."

"And when you care about someone, you cut them off from your life like that?"

"I cut you off *because* I care about you."

He couldn't help but come to a stop. "Listen to what you're saying. This makes my blood boil."

She slumped as she turned to face him. "Our relationship has no future. It's a beautiful illusion that will never be real."

"What are you saying? Why? What's the problem?"

"There is no problem." She stared off toward the horizon, as if debating whether to share what was on her mind. "Waleed, if you really love me, let go of me, please."

He stepped to her, trying to take her arms in his hands, but she backed away, leaving his embrace hanging in the damp air.

"I wish I could; trust me," he said. "I've been living in a toxic routine for so long, but I saw something pure in you. I saw something very special, very different. Let's just give this a chance, Sireen."

She turned away, her long, navy blue skirt wheeling with a flourish. "You don't understand."

"Explain to me!"

"I can't."

For a time, they stood in this way, Waleed standing behind the woman he loved as she hung her pretty head and kept her silence. When Waleed could take it no more, he returned to walking. She followed. As they made their way deeper into Baba Amro, something caught Waleed's attention.

Sireen saw it, too. "Do you see what I see?"

"I'm not sure," Waleed said. "This can't be real."

The two of them stood before a massive handwritten sign on the wall of a four-story apartment building. The red letters contrasted starkly with the soft white paint of the wall.

"Who could have written this?" Sireen said.

"Someone who wants to be killed by the Mukhabarat."

Sireen began to read. "'Put an end to corruption. Put an end to injustice. Put an end to evil. Let us bring down the regime of Bashar Al-Assad. Starting on March fifteenth, twenty-eleven.'"

"March fifteenth?" Waleed wondered.

"I guess it's the planned date for a Syrian Revolution, just like the one that was planned for February fifth. No one dared to show up to the protests."

"How do you know about it?"

"Oh, Fatima went on and on about how evil that movement was."

Waleed's heart leapt as Sireen's gaze lingered on him for a moment longer than usual. He wondered what she was thinking. Did she ponder the depth of what a revolution would mean? Or did she ponder the depth of the love she might share with him?

His thoughts were rudely interrupted by two police officers.

"Did you write this?" one of them demanded. His face was so fat as to seem all jowl. It didn't match his otherwise slender body.

"No, we didn't," Waleed replied, a sudden chill running up his spine.

"Then who did?" asked the other. This one had a sparse mustache and some of the fuzziest hair Waleed had ever seen. He could hardly believe the officer was allowed to remain in the service with such unkempt locks.

"I don't know," Waleed said. "We just saw it for the first time right now."

"Liar!" said the one with the mustache. Before Waleed could respond, the officer had produced his club and shoved Waleed to the ground.

As Sireen shrieked, the other officer began kicking Waleed in the groin. Searing pain rippled to his extremities and back again.

"Who wrote this?" he barked between kicks.

"I don't know," Waleed managed.

"He said he doesn't know," Sireen hollered.

"No one talked to you, whore!"

She stepped forward and pointed her finger in his face. "Let him go, or you will regret it!"

"How dare you talk to him like that!" the jowly officer said, snatching her by the shirt.

She pushed his hand aside, reached for her phone, and dialed a number. To Waleed's great relief, the officers let her make the call without further assault. She spoke quietly to someone before handing the phone over to the mustachioed officer.

"I'm sorry, sir," he was saying in a begging tone. "I'm sorry, sir. It won't happen again."

By the time the line clicked dead, both officers wore sober expressions.

"Madam, please forgive me," the officer said. "I didn't know you were the fiancée of General Hussein Sleiman. Please forgive us."

"I'm not the one you should apologize to."

Waleed remained on the ground in pain, but it wasn't the beating that hurt him; it was the news about Sireen's betrothal. He climbed to his feet, and without saying a word to anyone, staggered away into Baba Amro. He felt stupid, naïve, and misled. How had he misinterpreted all those signals and pushed aside all the warnings? What had made him so emotionally blind?

This must be what love does to us, he thought. *It distorts reality in every way to fit into the perfect square we believe exists. We reject, we deny, we project, and we use every defense mechanism known to man to fight an obvious truth until we wake abruptly and rudely.*

For Waleed, this was one of those moments. The feeling was awful. He was barely able to drag his feet through the streets. His heart beat slowly and heavily. He just wanted to get home and not talk to anyone. Even the trees and the pigeons of Baba Amro could feel his pain. The wind paused, the sun dimmed, and Waleed kept walking.

Chapter 10
Children of Daraa

In most countries around the world, adults have more rights than children. Adults can choose their representatives, while children can't. Adults get to make laws that govern both themselves and children, without the latter having a say. This was not the case in Syria. Both adults and children had the same rights. Neither adults nor children could choose their representatives, and neither group got to make laws and regulations. To make matters even more utopian, the Mukhabarat and police equally harassed both adults and children. In a way, there was no cutoff age at which someone crossed from childhood to adulthood. There was no meaning to the age of eighteen or twenty-one or thirty or forty. The only difference between children and adults was that children knew less about the ugliness of the Assad regime than their older counterparts.

Ladies, gentlemen, and children of all ages tuned in for the events of the Arab Spring as they unfolded on their TV screens. The slogans from Tunisia and Egypt were vivid in everyone's imagination. Another shocking event was the outbreak of mass protests in Libya. Qaddafi, who was already three-quarters crazy, went into full-blown madness at that scene. Within days, he declared full-fledged war against his own people.

Then, after a February school day, a group of elementary school children in the city of Daraa were walking home when a random thought crossed their minds. They started writing anti-regime graffiti on the walls of their school. Within days, the children were imprisoned and savagely beaten. The parents were outraged.

The city of Daraa began boiling with silent anger. It seemed that being a child in Syria didn't make you immune to the regime. The only way to immunity was absolute obedience and submission. The children of Daraa had to learn the lesson and set an example for children across Syria.

Adults stood on the sidewalks watching the children defy all norms. Adults stood on the sidewalks as the children were arrested and tortured. After all, this was Syria.

—*Syria: A History in Blood* by Celine Dubois

March 6, 2011
Deaths: 0

Waleed and Sireen hadn't spoken since he was beaten up by her fiancé's thugs. He felt so stupid for not realizing months earlier that she had been playing with his feelings. He hadn't been himself since the day he learned the news. He hadn't gone out with anyone or talked to anyone outside of work, save for Omar. He even avoided going to Friday prayer in his neighborhood mosque in Bab Sebaa, instead going to Omar's new mosque in Baba Amro to avoid running into any of the people who would want to start annoying conversations. But as the Arabic saying goes, "Many a vice turns out to be a virtue." For a change, Waleed now found more time to read, something he hadn't done in a long time. He had been reading more medicine from Harrison's, and more importantly, secretly going online and reading the updates from the Facebook page for "The Syrian Revolution 2011." He didn't dare join the page even under a fake name.

He was back to his old routine cycle of hospital, home, sleep, wake up, hospital. The only excitement in his life was watching the Arab Spring unfold in nearby countries and secretly imagining it happening in Syria. It was no longer safe to discuss this topic in public, especially since the Syrian regime was opposed to the Libyan revolution. Waleed only talked about it with Omar and with his brothers. It was quite difficult to get hold of Omar in the hospital these days because they had different schedules, so they mostly met after Friday prayer. Waleed started going to the mosque more often than just Fridays, as well, hoping to catch Omar so the two could grab a bite or simply have a chat.

~~~

"May God accept your prayer," Waleed told Omar as he met him on the fringe of the strangely small scrum of people outside the mosque in Baba Amro.

"From us and from you, brother," Omar said, smiling warmly. Then he gave a quizzical look. "Since when do you attend the evening prayer?"

Waleed inclined his head. "Since I decided to get closer to God."

"Ha ha! You just want to see me, don't you?"

"You're not helping reinforce my prayerful behavior."

"Ha! Sorry about that. I suppose you're right. I should encourage as many people as I can to pray the evening prayer in our mosque. Look how empty it is! On Fridays, half of Baba Amro is here, but for other prayers, it's almost empty."

Waleed leaned closer to his friend so he could speak in lower tones. "What's happening on March fifteenth?"

"Shhh," Omar said, looking around as if to ensure no one had heard. When he spoke again, it was in a whisper. "The revolution, buddy. It's coming to Syria."

"I really doubt that. Wasn't it planned for February fifth? No one showed up then. Why do you think they will now?"

Omar flashed a grave expression. "I don't just think; I know. Trust me. Last time, no one knew about it. That's why it failed. This time, everyone knows."

"I haven't heard about it on Al Jazeera or anything."

"Only because the media has refused to publicize it. Everyone is afraid of our dirty regime. But there's a large number of 'ghosts' spreading the message. How else did you find out about it? I never told you anything."

"I read about it on Facebook, and I saw it written on a random wall here in Baba Amro."

"Exactly. Tonight, there will be a large public awareness campaign across the nation."

Waleed gave a dubious look. "How is that possible?"

"You'll find out tonight if you're interested."

Suddenly the small crowd felt much larger around them, almost as if everyone had tuned in to their conversation at once. A quick glance from side to side showed that Waleed was merely being paranoid, but his unease remained all the same. "Omar, what are you doing? This could get you killed."

"Waleed, my brother, someone has to die for us to live."

"These people don't fear God. They know no morals or laws."

"And that's why it's time to put an end to them. Listen, I'm not going to force you to do anything you don't want to do. I love this country, and I am willing to take the risks."

"What's there to love about this country? People are only alive because of the lack of death."

"You're confusing things. This hell we're living in is not Syria. Those people around you are Syrians, sure, but they are under a spell. Syria has been a great nation since ancient times. This is just a shadow. It's an illusion. The government is not real; the regime is not real; and the people are not real."

Waleed sighed. "I have my doubts about what you say, but I hope you're right and I'm wrong."

Omar smiled and began walking away. "At midnight," he said over his shoulder, "I'll be on your favorite rooftop."

Waleed smiled back and shook his head. He was both intrigued and worried by Omar's risky behavior. He didn't want to be dragged into the fray just yet, but he knew deep inside that he was probably already a part of this.

As he left Baba Amro, he was surprised to see that the strange red writing had appeared on another wall. It read, *Down with Assad! Join us on March 15.*

It occurred to Waleed that if this was truly happening in a city as apathetic as Homs, it must be happening to an even larger degree in other cities. He smiled and walked quickly away, fearing someone might mistake him for the author of the words once more.

~~~

It was a cold, moonless midnight as Omar and Waleed stood on the rooftop, hunting for ghosts. It was not evil spirits they sought, but brave, selfless ones. All night, Omar had been acting in a manner unfamiliar to Waleed. He wore a sharp, serious look on his face. There was no joking or laughing. Waleed kept staring hard at the place where Omar had fixed his gaze. Suddenly, the ghost appeared. A man with blond hair and a covered face raised his right arm and flashed his cell phone light twice. To Waleed's chilling surprise, Omar raised his arm and flashed his cell phone once in reply. Waleed didn't say a word.

The ghost ran further away from Omar's building, ducking behind an alley wall before sticking his arm out and again flashing the light twice. Omar replied with another single flash. The ghost repositioned to a third place further up the street and did the same move. This time, Omar flashed his light three times. Then he reached into his pocket and gave Waleed a set of binoculars.

"Watch," he ordered.

Waleed obeyed silently, looking for the ghost with his binoculars. He was spraying something on the wall with graffiti: *Rise up for the sake of Daraa's children.* He lowered the binoculars and gave Omar a puzzled look. Then he peered through the binoculars once more, finding that the ghost had disappeared. About fifteen minutes later, a second ghost, this one with dark hair and a similarly covered face, appeared on the other side of the neighborhood. The same ritual took place.

"What is going on?" Waleed asked of his friend.

"The revolution is coming. That's what's going on."

Waleed lowered the binoculars. "That's crazy. Three people are not a revolution."

Omar raised one of his eyebrows. "Three people? You are about to be surprised, my friend."

"By what?"

"Tonight, and every night at one a.m., and until the real revolution begins, there will be symbolic rituals. It's spectacular."

"Where is it?"

"Right here. Just wait ten more minutes."

Indeed, ten minutes later, Waleed saw something that made his mind fly, as the Syrian saying goes. Omar produced a small homemade torch that he dipped in a bucket of cheap gasoline he kept near the corner of the roof. Then he lit it on fire. He went close to the edge of the roof and started waving the burning torch. A minute later, another lit torch appeared on a faraway rooftop. Then another. And another. By the time the clock on Waleed's cell phone struck 1:00 a.m., half of Baba Amro was lit up with torches on rooftops.

Omar's tears slowly moved down his cheeks, glowing as they reflected the firelight. "I've never seen this many freedom torches. You must be good luck, Waleed."

By 1:10, the lights had disappeared. What a remarkable sight it was. To Waleed, Omar's prophecy now seemed very real. Syria was silently boiling and ready to explode in a matter of days. Thirteen government agencies of secret police and Mukhabarat were oblivious to what Waleed had just seen. The ghosts, the torches, the writing all surprised him, but what surprised him most was Omar. Behind his friend's jokester mask was a brave, serious man with strong beliefs and convictions and perhaps the personality of a true leader. God only knew how many such people existed in Syria—people who were clowns during the day and revolutionaries at night.

From Omar, Waleed would learn that, over the next few days, several such symbolic gestures would take place in many Syrian cities. Freedom torches, freedom balloons, freedom kites, and even freedom Liras started to appear. The rituals were so brief and quick that messages seemed almost subliminal, with words such as *Revolution*, *March fifteenth*, *Change*, and *Hope*. The rituals lasted for only a few seconds, but every second of freedom seemed longer than an entire generation of repression. Relativity perhaps.

Chapter 11

Boiling Point

> *It is no secret that the Prophet Muhammad, peace be upon him, had a deep love for Syria and its people. He spoke so fondly of Syria that many believe it to be one of the holiest lands for Muslims after Mecca and Medina. Throughout the ages, that land was known for its honest merchants and its hospitable people. The drastic erosion of Syrian values and the corruption of its people over the course of fifty years shocked many Muslim scholars. Some began to wonder if the people of Syria had gone so far astray that they would not even bother to save their own children from the sadistic hands of the Assad regime. Was the hell of tyranny ever going to be hot enough to melt the chains of oppression and boil the blood of the oppressed?*
> —*Syria: A History in Blood* by Celine Dubois

March 15, 2011
Deaths: 0

It was Tuesday, and classes were still going on, but Sireen decided to take some time off and stay with her parents in Daraa. Skipping classes, staying up late, yet waking up early had become the characteristic hallmarks of Sireen's depression. On March 15, she got up early and went to the kitchen to make herself some coffee, a new habit she had picked up. She put on some Om Kalthoum music as she made her morning coffee.

> *"This world is a book, and you are its thoughts*
> *This world is an eye, and you are its sight*
> *This world is a sky, and you are its moon*
> *Will I see you tomorrow?"*

The song went on.

"All this for your fiancé, Soso?" her mother asked. She hovered over her with a knowing smile.

"Mother, please."

"What now, Sireen? What's wrong, *Inshallah*?"

"Mama, you know exactly what's wrong."

"Yes, I do. You are getting engaged to a man that every girl in Syria wishes to be with. He is very mature; he's financially stable; and he has a very prominent position. But of course you don't want that. *I've baked you and kneaded you*," she added, meaning, "I know you very well."

Sireen groaned and crossed her legs, inclining herself away from her mother. "I don't want to talk about this now. It seems that my happiness is not important at all in this matter."

"*Ya Elahi* [My God]!" Sireen's mother called out of the kitchen. "Sameer, come talk to your daughter. I can't handle her anymore. Get me my blood pressure pills, also. She raises my blood pressure, and my chest is hurting now." As always, she clutched at her chest, pretending to be in pain.

"Soso!" came the voice from upstairs. "Stop torturing your mother! If your mother dies angry with you, you won't even smell paradise no matter what you do." Sireen detected half a laugh in her father's words.

"May the name of God bless my heart," her mother said, fanning herself. "Why are you mentioning me dying now? You'll bring bad luck to the house with your choice of words. Who else spoiled her but you? I told you to let me raise my daughter the way I wanted to, but no, you had to spoil her."

Her father appeared, trundling down the stairs. He was a thin, wiry man with a pleasant face that always seemed to hold a smile. He wore a simple flannel shirt and a pair of jeans slightly too short for him. The room lit up whenever he entered.

"What's the matter now?" he asked. "What's all this about?"

Sireen's mother stopped fanning herself and shook her head. "Look at your daughter. I don't care anymore. She doesn't have to get married if she doesn't want to." She gave her daughter an incredulous gaze. "You're welcome to stay with us forever and help me with the house." As she spoke the words, she really hammed up the chest pain.

"Baba, I don't want him," Sireen pled to her father. "I don't want him. I hate the way he looks and I hate the way he talks. I don't want him."

Her father placed his hand gently on her shoulder. "Soso, *habibti* [my love], we gave them our word. This is not a game, darling. Besides, he loves you very much. He always gets you presents and compliments your beautiful blue eyes, which you got from your father, I might mention." He opened his eyes wide and smiled.

"But, Baba! I changed my mind." She pulled away from his touch. "Tell them we've cancelled it."

He looked genuinely hurt. "I wish I could do that, Soso. It's really not an option now."

"What do you mean it's not an option? We just call them and tell them we changed our mind."

"If we piss off those people, it could get ugly. You should have said something before things got this far."

"What do you mean? Are you saying I have no choice?"

"Yes, Soso. That's what I'm saying. We agreed and you agreed when they first asked two years ago. If we get them upset now, they could hurt us. He's a big man in the army. You understand me, don't you?"

"I understand," she said as she felt the tears rush to her eyes.

Her father hugged her tight and began rubbing her hair. "Don't cry, *habibti*. Don't cry. He'll be a good husband. He'll take good care of you. I know he will."

Sireen sniffled away her sorrows. "Okay, Baba."

"May God look after you, daughter. *Yalla*, you should apologize to your mother. Then we'll all have lunch and watch television."

Reluctantly, Sireen did as her father bid. The moment she apologized, her mother stopped fanning herself and clutching at her chest. It was true that Sireen had agreed to get engaged to Hussein when he proposed. At the time, he presented himself as a mature, caring man, and Sireen would have settled for anyone in those days. Back then her father, who had always provided well for his family, was drowning in debt, and Hussein wasn't only rich, but could also use his connections to absolve her father of his financial obligations. Sireen's father had always been an honorable man who hated bending the rules, but in Syria, there were no rules, so how could you bend that which didn't exist? It used to be that the old merchants of Damascus would never sign written contracts because a merchant's verbal agreement was enough. But during the Assad era, even contracts had become meaningless. It was a different time and a different nation. People joked that even the plants and animals were corrupted under the rule of the Baath party in reference to the increase in deforestation.

It was interesting to Sireen to see her mother so adamant about her need to marry her betrothed, for her mother had initially been uncomfortable with the idea of marrying her daughter to a non-Sunni man. Sireen supposed that it was only a few grams of gold later before it became less of an issue for her mother.

The fact remained that Sireen could sense her fiancé's shallowness. Hussein was clearly attracted to her—so much so that they hardly talked about anything except how beautiful he thought she was. It was flattering the first few times it happened, but eventually, she had gotten tired of hearing it. The compliments became so nauseating that the moment she had gained an opportunity to move to Homs, she had seized it to get away from him, if even for a while. Hussein had resisted the idea at first, but when his sister Fatima took Sireen's side, the balance tipped in her favor. Sireen thought that all she needed was a break from him in order to fall in love with him the way everyone said she would, but then Waleed had appeared and scattered all her cards.

"Sireen, come here for a second," her father's voice called, disrupting her thoughts.

"What's the matter?" she asked, rising from the kitchen counter to join her father in the living room. She found him sitting in front of the television. With the way his body was inclined on the couch, it was clear that he was spellbound by whatever blared on the news. "Is something happening today?"

"Well, some people were calling for a day of rage in Syria today, sort of like in Tunisia and Egypt."

"Is there anything on the news about it?"

"No, not really. What are they saying on the internet?"

"Hold on," Sireen said, hurrying to the computer terminal in the corner of the room. "Let me check."

"Okay check, but be careful, darling. Don't go into any opposition websites. They might be monitored. They'll take you to jail."

"Don't worry," she said with a sarcastic smile. "My fiancé won't let that happen." She clicked a few keys, navigating to her favorite site. From the first image that roiled onto the screen, she could see that something big was happening. "Baba, there are demonstrations!"

He sat up with a start. "What? Where?"

"In Damascus," she said with a broad grin. "There are demonstrations in Syria!"

He leapt to his feet and came to look over her shoulder. "No way, darling. You must be mistaken."

"No. I'm sure. Here's the video." She clicked the mouse and brought a loud, chaotic video to life. Thousands of demonstrators had taken to the streets in a familiar city. "This is in Damascus!"

"In the capital! This is unbelievable. Those kids are crazy. They'll all get killed."

"Those kids are heroes, Baba."

"*Dead* heroes, darling. What are they saying in the demonstrations?"

Sireen turned up the volume. "God, Syria, and freedom only."

"What else?"

She strained to listen for more. "The Syrian people cannot be humiliated." She continued to Facebook. "Look, Baba! They're saying on Facebook that there are protests in other cities."

Her father looked suddenly troubled. "Shh!" he said, his eyes becoming shifty.

"What? There are reports of small protests in Hama, Homs, and even here in Daraa."

"Shh!" he said again as he sprang toward the front door.

"Oh my God," Sireen said softly. "I hear it, too."

Sireen and her father stood side by side near the door, which her father opened wide. Neither spoke. The dusty wind of Daraa was blowing softer than it usually did. The birds had toned down their voices. There was a voice coming from afar. It wasn't that of a crying child or an arguing couple. It was a rhythmic song that kept getting stronger and less chaotic every minute. It seemed to be coming from the Omari mosque just a few blocks away from Sireen's house. The rhythm seemed familiar, yet so alien. Then it became clear enough to hear across the area surrounding the mosque.

"God, Syria, and freedom only!"

The words kept repeating in an infinite, rhythmic pattern like the heartbeats of a lover. Then another sound rudely interrupted the lullaby: gunshots. Dozens of gunshots. And then silence. The dream was over.

Sireen stood in the doorway of their old house. Her father went back into the living room without saying a word. The wind started blowing again, and the birds returned to their cacophony. She took a few steps closer to the street, ignoring her father's orders to get back into the house. She wondered what had just happened. She experienced flashbacks to all her conversations with Waleed on the rooftop back in Homs. She wished he were here to witness this event. It might seem utterly insignificant to most, but it probably would have captured Waleed the way it captured her.

~~~

She found herself walking the ancient streets of Daraa toward the Omari mosque. The ancient city she called home dated back to the Canaanites, once so prominent in the Middle East. Omar Ibn El-Khattab, one of the Prophet Muhammad's companions, had passed through Daraa and built the ancient mosque of Daraa, known as the Omari mosque.

The closer she came to her destination, the more she found that the city was still boiling in silent anger. It was no surprise that a small mob had broken out into protest near the Omari mosque. Or was it? After all, this was Syria, where "no voice is louder than that of the battlefield," as Hafez Al-Assad put it. To Sireen, this meant that, whenever an opposing viewpoint got loud enough, Assad would create a battlefield to suppress it. His strategy had worked for decades. Unlike major cities like Damascus and Aleppo, Daraa had a relatively weak Mukhabarat apparatus and police force. However, today was different.

In defiance of all her instincts, Sireen kept walking toward the Omari mosque. Its signature light tower loomed high in the cloudy sky like the very finger of God. The wind was strong enough that her long black hair was pulling back on her head, telling her not to proceed. When she got close enough to the mosque, it looked almost as if she had just walked into Assad's residence. Against the backdrop of the mosque's varied stone walls, there stood a huge number of security officers, policemen, and of course Mukhabarat. At least eight men and two women were being beaten and arrested on the flat gray concrete just outside the walls. The police insulted them vulgarly, kicked them, and beat them with electric sticks. Sireen was shocked by the sight of the young men and women screaming for help as they were pushed into a large black vehicle.

The small protest had vanished by the time she arrived. Then an eleventh guy, looking as if he was just passing by, was also arrested and beaten. The sight sent chills down Sireen's spine. She quickly repositioned herself behind a huge olive tree and peeked through its leaves to get a view of what was going on. The mosque was empty, and everyone was pouring out of the square. As people began to leave, an elderly gentleman passed her way. His forehead showed prominent wrinkles, but the look he wore did not mix with those age lines. His eyes were flaring with rage.

~~~

And so it happened that March 15 passed without any huge protests against the regime, but it did create a wave of silent anger. Hence, it rightfully earned its name: "The Day of Rage." The Day of Rage was no ordinary Tuesday; it was the end of one era and the beginning of another.

Chapter 12

Friday of Dignity

> *Few things are more precious than a man's dignity. Humiliating a friend can end a friendship, and humiliating a lover can end the deepest of love. Many are willing to give up wealth or take unnecessary risks to avoid being humiliated, but when it comes to choosing between life and dignity, most would choose life. After all, no one wants to die. The desire to live is deeply engineered in the human genome to ensure the survival of our species.*
>
> *It is that very principle that became the antithesis of the principles of the newborn revolution in Daraa. The conditions had slowly ripened, and the stars aligned perfectly. Everyone in Syria was talking about the small protests that took place on March 15.*
>
> *Even though all the participants had vanished and the regime had erased all evidence of the events, videos remained, and witnesses continued to talk. To make matters worse for the regime, all those videos made their way onto the internet for millions of Syrians to see. That was just the spark—a spark probably too small to start any major uprising in any Syrian city except Daraa, which had been silently boiling for weeks after the kidnap and abuse of its children. All it needed was a spark. That spark was provided on March 15.*
>
> *Three days later, the city was on fire, declaring the true beginning of Syria's revolution.*
> —*Syria: A History in Blood* by Celine Dubois

March 18, 2011
Deaths: 5

It was a beautiful spring morning. Life had returned to relative normalcy, but most people merely went about their routines as a ruse, for they all felt that something about that day was going to be like no other day.

Sireen put on a long white dress, and for the first time wore a white head cover like a good Muslim girl. She also wore her sunglasses to make it harder to identify her. She was about to commit the worst crime imaginable in Syria—worse than murder and robbery.

She left the house early in the morning before anyone in her family could see her dressed in this suspicious manner. She had read the safety precautions on Facebook multiple times, yet she had never felt this scared. She shook in fear. This was the fear of everything: the government, the Mukhabarat, her family, her fiancé, her career, her life. Everything was on the line, and yet a mysterious power was pushing her to do this.

A thought hidden somewhere in her mind suddenly surfaced and overrode all other thoughts. Perhaps it wasn't even a full thought, but rather a word: *dignity*. The name "Friday of Dignity" captivated her and many others in Daraa. As she left the house, a chill rippled down her spine, and she darted into a nearby shop, where she bought gloves as an extra precaution. She didn't want any of her fingerprints left behind.

She slowly walked to the Omari mosque in the heart of the city of Daraa. It was packed like never before. People were praying in the streets hours before the true onset of the Friday prayer sermon. Everyone was well disguised. Everyone knew that this was no ordinary prayer. She looked around to make sure no one recognized her, but the truth was that everyone was busy concealing their own identities.

To her surprise, her old childhood friend, Nicole, was there. Nicole had done a poor job of disguising herself. The oddest thing about seeing her here was that she was a practicing Christian. What was she doing there in the mosque, and during the Friday prayer? And why was she wearing a head covering? A cold stream of wind set the already quiet audience into utter silence. A few minutes later, the imam declared the beginning of the Friday sermon. Judging from the crowd, an outsider might have expected him to be talking about the approaching end of the world or judgment day. Everyone knew that this was not going to be a usual prayer. The number of people kept doubling by the minute to cover an area much larger than the dimensions of the mosque.

Soon afterward, a small group of late guests joined in and started pushing their way to the front. They were dressed in normal clothes, but everyone knew who they were. They were the party spoilers, the Mukhabarat. The second sermon had started at that time, and hardly anyone was listening. Even the imam himself was too busy looking around in disbelief as he spoke.

"The Prophet Muhammad, peace be upon him, said, 'Muslims are like one body of a person; if the eye is sore, the whole body aches, and if the head aches, the whole body aches.'" Even as he said the words, the secret police shoved their way toward him.

For the first time in a long time, Sireen found herself overcome with chills from something an imam had said. Outwardly, he spoke about a commonly quoted passage from the Prophet, but inwardly, she knew he was speaking of revolution.

"Each of us should strengthen our belief in Allah," the imam continued, his shrill voice rising above the growing murmur of the crowd. "We must renew our vow to follow only His law."

The imam ended the second sermon in a way that made it seem he wasn't entirely finished. But by then, he was very much under the glare of the Mukhabarat. "*Allahu Akbar*," the imam said slowly.

Everyone knelt down before the greatness of God. He went on reciting verses from the Quran and continuing with the typical Friday prayer rituals. "Peace be upon you and the mercy of God . . . Peace be upon you and the mercy of God." With this, he declared the end of the prayer.

By then, Sireen had joined everyone on her knees in an act of humility before God. But unlike usual, there was no rush to get up and run back home before the traffic jam. Everyone remained seated, breathing slowly and heavily in synchronized breaths.

"God!" came the cry from somewhere in the crowd.

"Syria!" came the call from another direction.

"Freedom!" said another person as if trying to guess a secret word.

"Freedom! Freedom!" several men started shouting.

"Freedom!" Nicole yelled.

Sireen remained silent, for her voice failed her.

Everyone remained seated, most of them quiet, except for a few sporadic shouts. One man then got up from among the crowd, produced a large gun, and pointed it toward the sky. "Stay seated like dogs!" he yelled before sending a few shots into the sky. That did the trick. Everyone stood at once, including Sireen.

"God, Syria, freedom only!"

"God, Syria, freedom only!"

The Mukhabarat stood in shock for a moment, then started shooting into the sky. When they finally stopped, a hush fell over the crowd.

One of the policemen, a short but well-muscled thug in a beret, strode forward. "All of you clear out!" he barked. "Unless you disperse, we will begin shooting directly in ten, nine, eight . . ."

Suddenly and out of the stress of the moment, a new slogan was born. "Death is better than humiliation!" one person yelled.

Then hundreds started repeating it: "Death, death, death . . . not humiliation."

"Death, death, death . . . not humiliation!" Sireen yelled at the top of her lungs. It was the strangest feeling—a powerful mix of fear and joy. Little did she know how addictive and infectious that feeling was. The more shots the Mukhabarat fired into the air, the more cohesive the crowd grew. Soon the police realized the scope of the issue and withdrew to call for reinforcements.

Sireen followed as the crowd marched into the streets of Daraa, calling for freedom and dignity. "Freedom, freedom, freedom!" echoed through the entire city. It was like an antidote that woke people up from an ancient spell as hundreds more started pouring into the streets to form perhaps the largest protest in Syrian history. There were men, women, and children. There were rich and poor and people of all walks of life. In a matter of minutes, Sireen started to see signs appearing out of nowhere. There were signs that called for freedom of speech, social equality, and justice for the kidnapped children of Daraa. By the time the reinforcements came, the crowd had grown to several thousand.

Dozens of men dressed in black, typical for the Mukhabarat, stood in front of the crowd and pointed their guns at the protestors. Sireen stood her ground with all the rest.

"Peaceful, peaceful, we are peaceful!" the protesters chanted. They raised their arms high and started waving them to show that they were unarmed. At the same time, they kept their arms moving to show that they refused to surrender. "Peaceful, peaceful!" Sireen chanted along with the crowd.

The response came quickly. "Shoot!" one of the guards in black bellowed.

Sireen ducked as bullets began tearing into her brethren. Dozens of people near her were shot. They fell to the ground with such force that Sireen could scarcely believe what was happening. The crowd broke into chaos as everyone started running in different directions. Sireen ran for her life, not stopping until she reached her front door and barreled inside. In the landing, she took off her white scarf and gloves, then strolled into the house as if nothing had happened.

"Sireen, where were you?" her mother scolded. "My heart was melting with worry!"

Ignoring her mother, Sireen went right to her room.

"I'm talking to you!" her mother called after her. "Where were you? Are you deaf?"

With the tears already falling down her face, Sireen locked her door. No matter how she tried, she couldn't shake the image that had made her run. She had seen a bullet go into a little boy's arm. As much as she wanted to stop and help, she had to ignore him and keep running for her own life. She wondered now how many people had been shot and whether any of them was someone she knew. She wished she had a crystal ball to give her some answers, but instead, she decided to log on to her new Facebook account under the name "White Dove."

There she found news about new protests in multiple Syrian cities. Shockingly, there were videos already posted of the Daraa protest. She watched them to make sure she wasn't in the videos. Fortunately, she wasn't. She felt somewhat relieved. Soon there was news that five people had died, four of them in Daraa. Dozens were injured throughout the country.

~~~

Within hours, Daraa and the rest of Syria were back to the usual abnormal silence. It was all like a dream. Many doubted it had ever happened. The videos that had been circulating on the net were never played on most major media outlets. This wasn't a big story from their point of view. Considering the history of the Syrian regime, newsmen and newswomen the world over knew that it was only a matter of time before Assad's lackeys proved themselves more than capable of handling a few mobs. Some commentators referred to the protests as "firecrackers," meaning that they would fade away as soon as they had started.

They were wrong. The very next day, larger crowds participated in the funeral of Syria's first "martyrs." Soon the funeral turned into a large anti-government protest. The Mukhabarat and regular police force arrived and again shot at the protestors, injuring dozens and killing several. Everyone ran for their lives. Assad spread a police force across Daraa to prevent the collapse of the regime strongholds in that city. Warnings were issued that there would be no mercy in dealing with protestors. Hundreds were imprisoned after capture on the streets and in their homes.

The following day proved an important day in shaping the collective vision of the revolutionaries. On that day, and after weeks of bloody violence in Libya, NATO declared the beginning of Operation Unified Protector. The unstated goal of the operation was to tip the balance in favor of Libya's revolutionaries, helping them topple the regime of Moammar Gadhafi, one of the most brutal dictators in the Arab world. Roughly 2,000 to 3,000 civilians had already been killed in Libya, and Gadhafi had declared war on his own people.

Gadhafi, like Assad, was not going to take no for an answer. His plan was to use overwhelming force to quell the Libyan uprising. It was all going according to plan until France, under the leadership of Nicolas Sarkozy and his foreign minister Alan Juppe, pushed for a NATO intervention in Libya. Britain was quick to respond to the French plans. The Russians and Chinese were strongly opposed to them. Germany was not interested. The US appeared to have few ideas about how to proceed. The country was under tremendous pressure from groups within its own borders and from its European allies to lead a multinational effort in Libya.

The people of Syria, both the government and the people, heard the message loud and clear. The Syrian government hoped that the regime in power in Libya would destroy NATO's mission, just as the Iraqis had done. The people of Syria knew that a Hama-style massacre was no longer possible in this day and age. The Soviet Union that had previously given the political cover to such operations was gone. It was no longer possible to hide such atrocities from public view. Most people believed that there was no way the world would sit by and watch mass genocide take place in Syria, if it were to come to that.

They were wrong.

The protests that day were the largest yet in Daraa, despite the increased security precautions. At least one hundred thousand Darawis had assembled in the streets, throwing the entire city into the arms of revolution. Videos poured through YouTube and Facebook. There was no more doubt that the Arab Spring had reached Syria. The regime responded to the calls for freedom and reform with more live bullets, this time killing at least ten more people, including a ten-year-old child. The city was infuriated. Hundreds of thousands took to the streets and occupied all major squares surrounding government headquarters. The protest organizers insisted that the protests remain peaceful, and so they did, in spite of the building rage.

~~~

"Where do you think you're going?" Sireen's mother yelled.

"Mother, please," she fired back. "You know where I'm going."

Her diminutive mother stood with hands on hips, trying and failing to look threatening. "You will not leave this house. Am I clear? And what's that in your hand?"

Sireen looked down at what she held as if seeing it for the first time. "It's a sign, Mother. It says, 'Dear soldier, if you are happy with your life, shoot me.'"

"You think this sign will protect you? You think they won't shoot you?" She began to pace and fume. "And I will tell you, if they don't shoot you today, your fiancé surely will. You are insane."

"Mama, it happened in Egypt and Tunisia. The army joined the people. It could happen here."

The older woman stopped pacing and turned to look her daughter square in the eyes. "You don't understand, do you? Those Mukhabarat will shoot and rape and steal. They are cruel and sadistic." She returned to her telltale pawing at her chest. "Why are you doing this to me? My heart can only take so much."

"I am doing what you should have done years ago," Sireen said, never sounding more authoritative as she took her sign and stepped to the door. "Forgive me." With that, she fused into the mass of protestors filing by on the street. This time, she did not bother trying to hide her identity. She knew she could get killed, but for some reason, that seemed small compared to the magnitude of the moment. She joined her fellow protestors in marching silently for miles. Eventually she chimed in along with them as they broke into their new favorite slogan: "Death, death, death . . . not humiliation."

She yelled again and again in defiance as soldiers started appearing on the edges of the crowd. It looked to her like an entire brigade awaited them up ahead.

"Peaceful! Peaceful!" the protestors yelled.

"Fire!" called a voice from behind a large rifle.

Time seemed to slow as Sireen set her eyes on the man who had given the order. She recognized him somehow. The man was not particularly attractive, but with his face contorted in such animalistic cruelty, he looked to her something less than human. Even though only a blink of an eye had passed, she felt as if she had many minutes to study his curling lips, his bared teeth, his fiery eyes. *How do I know him?* she wondered. Inside, she knew. But her brain was in denial.

The moment time returned to its normal pace, she heard the bullets shuddering past in all directions. Some soldiers had fired; others had refused.

As she watched the familiar man turn toward one of the latter and crack him in the face with the butt of his gun, she saw two people fall to their knees out of the corners of her eyes. They had taken bullets, one of them from the familiar man's own gun. Sireen flashed her sign at the hesitant brigade as their ruthless general prepared himself to call another volley.

"Fire!" the familiar man repeated.

You know, said a voice inside her. *You know who he is.*

But she shook it away.

This time, perhaps spurred on by the sight of their bleeding comrade, none of the men refused to follow the command. At least twenty people fell to the ground either dead or wounded, but still Sireen, along with the rest of the crowd, held her ground.

"God is greater!" she found herself shouting with the others. Her heart was beating faster than a durbakke drum. Her hands were numb and her breath was getting shorter and shorter. When she looked down, she saw blood running on the streets beneath her feet. Her mind reeled at the sight of it, causing her to lose her bearings.

The familiar general put down his gun, stalked to the top of a sandbag barricade his men had constructed, and started addressing the audience through large speakers set up on either side of the square. "Today, we have shown mercy in dealing with you," he said, his voice oily in its authority. "We could have easily wiped you all out, but we didn't. Make no mistake, we are not afraid to do so. If you think anyone will stop us, you are wrong. If you are waiting for NATO to come and save you, the wait will be long. I will give you three minutes to disperse before we call for more backup."

Silence hung in the air only for a moment. Sireen felt lost in it, for something terrible had occurred to her.

"Death, death, death . . . not humiliation!" the angry crowd responded.

Sireen did not repeat the chant this time. She was silent in shock. It wasn't the general's words that shocked her, nor was it his hollow threat—it was his voice. All at once, she realized that this was her fiancé. It was that same voice that had told her many times how beautiful she was and how much he loved her. She had heard him yell and threaten before. She used to call him "evil" in tones of mockery. But now she heard a quality she had never heard before: true evil. It was the voice of a murderer, a cold-blooded murderer.

"Fire!" Hussein repeated.

Gunshots, screams, crying.

"Death!"

"Fire!"

Screams.

Sireen's knees could no longer bear her weight. *What have I done with my life?* she thought. *What have my parents pushed me into with this madman?* No matter what happened this day, she knew she would have to spend the rest of her life with a heartless murderer. Though the tumult still raged, she could no longer hear anything but her thoughts. She could hear her mother telling her how Hussein was her best option and how most girls would kill to be in her shoes. She could hear his sister Fatima bragging about how her father took over someone else's company by threatening him. She could hear Waleed reciting his poetry from a rooftop in Homs. She could smell the jasmine in the air. She could almost see his dark eyes. How could she have left him and sold her soul to the devil?

Suddenly she was pulled back into reality as a young protester started shaking her hard and yelling, "Cover your face! Cover your face!"

"Huh? What?" she said.

A strong explosive sound came out of nowhere, sending a white cloud spiraling rapidly over the crowd. Panic erupted just as Sireen, along with the crowd, realized that it was tear gas. Everywhere Sireen turned, she saw coughing, choking, crying, and screaming. Strangely, no one moved.

More gunshots.

No one moved.

The smell was worse than anything Sireen had ever experienced. She could feel her throat getting tighter, her breathing getting heavier, but none of that mattered. She realized that she had no desire to move. When she and her brethren said that they would rather die than be humiliated, they meant it. And so she and the others held steady in the midst of the tear gas and live bullets. The gas began suffocating Sireen. Such was her pain that she nearly ran, but at the last moment, a strong wind arrived to clear the horror away. Following the wind came a thundering noise from above like the wrath of God. She looked up to see three helicopters hovering over the crowd. Her heart stopped. She instinctively grabbed the arm of the protestor next to her.

"It's okay," he told her. "Don't cry."

"It's the tear gas," she said, forcing a smile. "I am not afraid."

The protestor on her other side reached out and held her hand. Soon enough, everyone was holding hands and standing tight as a chain, a chain not of slavery, but of freedom. The helicopters kept hovering lower and lower until Sireen was able to see the people inside. She spotted cameramen filming from the bay doors. From the look of them, they appeared to be filming not for television, but rather to identify the protestors so the Mukhabarat could hunt them down later. At the same time, several protestors lifted their cell phones high in the air and started filming. Sireen supposed that these were the protest organizers, men and women who wanted to make sure their efforts and the killing was documented and later distributed on the internet.

A few minutes later, the helicopters left.

"Fire!" the orders came back. This time the rate of shooting escalated.

That did the trick. Chaos reigned. People started running for their lives.

"Fire!"

Sireen was getting more and more delirious. She didn't run away. Instead, she started running toward the blockade. "Stop!" she screamed. "Stop, please.

You're killing people." She kept making her way towards the front lines, oblivious to the live bullets.

"Fire!"

The man in front of Sireen fell to the ground, blood pumping from his neck and pooling onto the street. Sireen, guided by a certitude she didn't know she had, kept approaching the blockade. Something spurred her on—a feeling that if she could just get to the wall, she might be able to stop the madness. Long gone was her memory of Hussein leading these monsters. She was carried forward only by the instinct that told her that her salvation lay ahead, not behind.

"Stop!" came the voice, sounding surprised. "Hold your fire!"

Though the crowd roared all around her, a strange calm fell around Sireen.

"All of you hold your fire!"

"What happened, sir?" someone else said.

Sireen looked up, spotting that familiar face again.

"I'm going to arrest this girl," it said.

"It's not safe for you to go alone into the crowd, sir."

"You say the lie and then you believe it? You know that none of those people are armed. Just stay where you are."

The familiar man began to climb over the boundary. *Hussein,* she realized. It all came flooding back to her mind. *My fiancé. He is the general killing my people.*

The moment her mind returned to her, so too did the rage. With anger in her heart, she advanced on Hussein. Before she could get to him, she felt something bump into her foot. She looked down and barely had time to register that it was a grenade rolling around at her feet before a cloud of white smoke enveloped her, knocking her to her knees. She writhed and gasped for a clean breath of air, but it was no use. Hussein had disappeared. The protest had disappeared. All of Syria and all of death had disappeared. All that remained was the white, choking cloud.

As her sight faded from white to red and then black, Sireen knew the pain of drowning.

Chapter 13
Eggplants and Zucchini

March 25, 2011
Deaths: 85

"Come on! The time is upon us, Omar!"

Waleed watched as his friend traced a broad red marker over the bottom right corner of a placard. "Just five more minutes."

"Come on, come on!" Waleed said. "It's the Friday of Glory. We have to show people that all their misconceptions about Homs are just misconceptions."

Omar turned to level an annoyed gaze on his friend. "Go finish preparing your signs before you rouse me."

"They are done."

"All right, all right." He finished tracing the final loop in his latest slogan. "I'm ready. Show me the signs you've made."

Waleed flashed one of his favorite signs.

"God, Syria, freedom only," Omar read. He gave him an incredulous look. "Seriously? That's so last week. I need *ideas*. What was the new slogan in Daraa?"

"Death, not humiliation," Waleed said, feeling disappointed that he hadn't been cleverer in his friend's eyes.

"Yes," Omar said thoughtfully. "Make several signs that say that."

Waleed furrowed his brow. "Why don't you make them? My signs are done."

"Look how long it takes me to get them right," Omar said, pointing to his lone finished sign among a pile of discarded ones. "If I don't go slow, my handwriting looks like the squiggles of hens."

The cool breeze of the afternoon washed over Waleed as he laughed. Looking out from the rooftop, he could sense that Homs was ready to burst. It made him happy for the first time since he could remember. "How about some signs related to the martyrs of Daraa?"

"Yes," Omar said, raising a finger. "Can you think of anything, Waleedo?"

"All the slogans we ever learned were praising Bashar. 'Our blood, our souls are yours, Bashar.' Not the best thing for the occasion."

"Let's give them a taste of their own medicine. Our blood, our souls are yours, Daraa!"

Waleed brightened up. "I love it! I'll make a few signs related to that. This will make those bastards lose sleep tonight."

As Waleed turned, Omar reached out to grab his arm and hold him back. "Also, don't forget to make many flags so we can distribute them to the guys."

"I know," Waleed said, hanging his head. "I will do it even though I hate this flag so much. It reminds me of the regime. But whatever. I'll also make some Tunisian flags as a reminder that our goal is to overthrow the regime."

"Yes, and some Libyan flags while you're at it—a reminder that the world is watching and will interfere if it gets too bloody."

"All right."

Omar looked suddenly serious. "I'd better call Golden Knight. He makes the best flags."

"You know," Waleed said, shifting his weight to one side, "I've been thinking. I need a code name, too. Can you think of one?"

"Pink Panther," Omar said with a wry grin.

Waleed chuffed. "Save that name for your mother."

"Leave my mother alone, and let's get back to work. I'll try to make more signs related to Daraa and its martyrs."

With a nod, Waleed turned once more to get back to work, but once again, his friend reached out and stopped him.

"Have you checked on Sireen lately, Waleed?"

A strange doubt came to Waleed's mind. "No. Why should I check on her?"

"Isn't she in Daraa?"

"Not that I know of. Her family lives there, but we haven't spoken in a while." His mood became suddenly sour. "Besides, she's engaged to someone in the army. Fatima's brother. She's probably pro-regime now."

"Well, I don't know about that, but she is in Daraa. I'm pretty sure. I have my sources."

"Then don't ask me if she's doing all right. Ask your sources. She's fine, I'm sure." He batted a dismissive hand. "Let me get back to work, Omar."

"Wait," Omar said, stopping him again. "You do realize that we could die today, right?"

Waleed sighed. "Omar, stop this talk. We will protest, and we will not let them shoot us. You hear me?" By the time he had finished, he realized that he was holding his friend by the collar. He didn't mean to fly into such an anger. Awkwardly he let his grip loosen.

"Yes, I hear you," Omar said, doubt in his voice.

With his anger replaced by sudden affection, Waleed pulled his friend into a tight embrace. He almost broke into tears, but stopped short.

Omar returned the hug. "It's our destiny to fight for our country. Our fathers have failed us, and now is our chance. We cannot fail the coming generations." He backed away and kissed Waleed on the cheek. "Get back to work now. Today, many cities will join Daraa, and Homs has got to be one of them."

The two friends worked in silence, Waleed pondering the plan all the while. The plan was to meet up with ten more volunteers before prayer, and then have everything ready for a large protest to follow the close of the second sermon. Many of the volunteers were regular worshippers at the mosque, but some had actually never been to a mosque before. Some of them were leftists; some were Christian; and some were non-practicing Muslims. The mosque was the only place in Syria where all those people were allowed to meet without drawing too much suspicion. Under the emergency law—a law that had been in place for decades—gatherings were strictly prohibited in all of Syria. The only loophole in that law was the mosque. Over time, the regime had felt less and less threatened by mosque gatherings as more of the religious elite were handpicked by the regime itself.

Having finished a sign, Waleed stood to eye his work carefully. He admired the curve of his lettering in spelling out the slogan. A quick glance at Omar suggested that his friend had been right: his penmanship was poor by comparison. Waleed smiled as he returned to his work.

In truth, both Muslim and Christian religious leaders were among the most pro-regime elements—ironic, given the radically secular nature of the regime. This wasn't religious freedom after the American or Canadian model, where everyone was free to worship however they pleased. It wasn't like the secular French or Turkish model, either. This was fanatically secular. It was so secular that being religious in certain places of the country could lead to one's execution. The Assad regime was the Taliban of secularism. Entire towns and cities had been subjected to genocide and siege for being viewed as too conservative. With all forms of political opposition prohibited, many in the country started expressing their dissent by becoming secretly conservative. Sunnis gradually grew more Sunni; Christians more Christian; and the Alawites became more radicalized. The regime used that to its advantage by creating much division and mistrust among the different components of Syrian society. It made every group believe that some other group was about to attack and destroy them. Mistrust was everywhere, and that helped the regime provide a false sense of security and stability.

"When we meet new activists," Omar said, breaking Waleed's train of thought, "try not to use our real names. If one of us gets caught, they will torture him until he gives all the names he knows. Not knowing real names will help protect us all."

"Where are we going to meet before prayer?"

"At the apartment complex of Golden Knight."

Waleed smiled. "You mean I'm finally going to get to meet the pigeon guy?"

"The one and only," Omar said with a nod. "This place must be kept a secret. We will only meet there on rare occasions. After today, nearly all of the planning and organizing we'll do through the internet. So please keep your big mouth sealed about the location. I know that a bean can't go wet in your mouth," he added, meaning, "You talk a lot."

"All right, all right," Waleed said with a groan. "I got it." He brightened up as he remembered something. "Hey, I made those masks." He pulled one out of his duffel, showing it to Omar. It was a simple blue mask of terrycloth, but inside, he had secured a petal of onion with tape. "They're surgical masks with onion inside. They'll protect from tear gas."

"Don't worry about the tear gas. Just avoid the bullets, brother."

When they were finished with their preparations, the two friends placed their signs and flags and masks inside large garbage bags. Together they walked a few blocks to their meeting place. Waleed saw that it was a very old house—ancient perhaps—on the outskirts of the Baba Amro neighborhood. The structure's most telling feature was that it was camouflaged by large green grapevines. Given its low profile, it seemed perfect for the mission. Waleed could feel his heart pounding as he entered the house behind Omar.

A tall blond guy stood on the other side of the door. "*Salam!*" he said in a voice just above a whisper. "Come on in, guys. Everyone's here."

Everyone quickly introduced themselves by their code names. There was a total of about ten activists. Waleed was surprised to see that three of them were women. Judging by their code names, they came from different corners of the political and religious spectrum. They had only two things in common. They were all young, and they all had the same goal: the liberation of Syria. The blond who had greeted them at the door took the lead as the meeting came to order.

"Brothers and sisters," he began, "I salute your courage and your love for freedom. We have lived in poverty and injustice for four decades now. Everything has been robbed from us; our money, our bread, our history, our human rights, and our dignity." He puffed out his chest as he let the thought sink in. "But there is one thing Assad's cronies do not own: the future."

A murmur of approval rippled from the gathering.

"It is up to us to create a better future for our children," the blond continued. "We are not starting a revolution here; the revolution has already begun in Daraa. We are merely joining it. There have been small protests in many cities across the country. Daraa is in a state of complete uprising, and not just Daraa City, but the entire province has joined the revolution. Hundreds of thousands. There will be protests today in Homs, and that is no secret. Our job is not to create protests. Those come out of the vacuum. Our job is to organize them." The leader turned from one young man to one of the young women, nodding to each in turn. "Brother Spartan Fighter and sister Syrian Dignity will be videotaping as much of the protests as they can on their cell phone cameras. Abu Shehab will help in uploading them to the internet this time. Later he will teach you all how to do it yourselves." He pointed to Omar and then Waleed. "The rest of us will be carrying and distributing signs and banners. Try to avoid any political or religious symbols. This is a revolution for all Syrians. We don't want to exclude anyone."

When Omar nodded at Waleed, he reached for the bag of signs and held it up as if in offering.

"We'll split up into three teams," the leader continued. "Each team will head to a different mosque. I wish you all the best of luck. And please, stay safe. God, Syria, freedom only!"

Everyone quietly repeated the words after him before leaving the house in groups of twos and threes. Another guy joined Waleed and Omar. It appeared that Omar knew him from before, but Waleed had never met him before this night and could not recall his code name. When asked, the guy reintroduced himself as Abu Thayer.

The three protest organizers walked for half a kilometer with silence on their side. Waleed felt drowned in his ideas, dreams, and fears. After a time, Abu Thayer reached into a small bag he carried and handed masks to Omar and Waleed. "Here," he said. "I saturated them with onion in case we get attacked by tear gas."

Waleed raised an eyebrow at Omar, who smiled and said, "Thank you, brother. I think I'm fine without it."

Waleed agreed, but didn't want to embarrass the guy. "I will take one," he said.

In his bag, Abu Thayer also had a small first aid kit, water, and some sandwiches. Waleed suspected that he was expecting an Egyptian-style protest. He must have anticipated that the crowds would chant, and then the police would attack with tear gas or maybe rubber bullets, in the worst case. He really was naïve, Waleed thought, or perhaps just hopeful. But then, the closer they got to the mosque, the more fearful he appeared.

"Our children and grandchildren will be very proud of us," Omar said, trying to reassure Abu Thayer.

"Yeah?" the frightened young man said.

"Yeah! We are the generation that everyone has been waiting for. The promised generation."

"I hope so."

Omar clapped his hand to the young man's shoulder. "Don't hope so, *know* so. Now we're a small group of guys. Soon it will be all of Homs and all of Syria."

Waleed wasn't sure he believed that, and from Abu Thayer's expression, it appeared that he didn't either. But it was too late to back out now. Seeing the doubt in his friends' eyes, Omar tried another approach.

"What do you guys want to eat after the protest?" he asked.

Despite himself, Waleed smiled.

"Anything, anything," Abu Thayer mumbled.

"No, what are you craving? I promise to cook it for you."

"Stuffed eggplants and zucchini."

Omar lolled his head. "Are you serious? You're going to make me stuff eggplants? Fine, for the sake of your eyes, I will. I promise. They'll be ready before dinner."

At that, Abu Thayer smiled and seemed to loosen up. "And grape leaves?"

"Yes, sir. And stuffed green pepper?"

"Green pepper? I never heard of that getting stuffed."

"I can stuff anything," Omar said, his tone light and jocular.

Waleed could think of many ways to interpret the statement, but decided to think of it as Omar bragging on his cooking skills.

"Abu Thayer," Waleed said, pausing, "I want you to know something." He offered his hand for his new friend to shake. "I'm Waleed."

Omar gave him a nasty frown for not using his code name, but Waleed went on.

"I trust you, and I'm okay with you knowing my real name. We should be friends from now on."

"Thank you," Abu Thayer said, looking touched. "I'm Rami."

"Great to meet you, brother Rami."

"We're here," Omar interrupted, looking like he half-expected them to start exchanging phone numbers and home addresses. "What time does the sermon begin?"

"Usually it starts at a quarter to noon," Waleed said, checking his watch. "We're fifteen minutes early."

"Well, it seems we're fifteen minutes late," Omar replied as it became apparent that the mosque was already full and people were pouring into the streets.

A broad smile spread across Omar's and Rami's faces. Waleed found himself following their lead.

"Remember," Omar said, interrupting the moment of joy, "at the end of the prayer, don't start saying any slogans until everyone is outside the mosque. Otherwise they'll lock us in. Waleed, give the posters you made to as many people as you can. I will be trying to videotape the event. Now let's scatter. And if you need me, use the code names!" Omar kissed each of them on the cheeks. "You'll be fine, and we'll all have dinner tonight."

Emboldened by his friend's parting words, Waleed picked through the ever growing crowd. It seemed to him that at least ten thousand people had gathered in and around the mosque by the time the prayer began. As the imam started by reading verses from the Quran, a wave of spirituality swept over the audience. Waleed had seen this movie before. He had watched the videos from Daraa and Banias. He could sense that everyone knew that soon there would be a protest, and that soon there would be gunshots and death. There were men, women, and children present here, he realized. They all knew what they were here for, and yet Waleed wondered whether any of them knew exactly why they were doing it.

The closer the prayer came to its end, the deeper became the feeling that everyone had gone into a trance-like state. This was Waleed's first such experience. Never had he participated in something voluntarily where one of the possible outcomes was his death. He couldn't stop thinking of the thugs who had broken into his house and beaten him. He couldn't stop imagining those who had kidnapped Azad, or the man who had taken Sireen from him. This situation had to end, and if people had to die in the process, so be it. Before he could chase his thoughts any further, the prayer was over.

To Waleed, it appeared that the regime had implanted people to reverse the course of the protest. Ten or twenty men stood up at once at the end of the prayer and started yelling, "Our blood, our souls are for you, Bashar!" The more they repeated it, the more furious the crowd grew. The planted men had managed to effectively transform the dominant feeling among the crowd from fear of confrontation to a burning desire for confrontation.

"Our blood, our souls are for you, Daraa!" some young men responded.

Within five minutes, perhaps ten thousand people were chanting the new slogan. Waleed was screaming it at the top of his lungs as he started distributing his posters randomly. He had no idea where Omar was, but he was certain he was filming this with great joy. Wheeling around, he spotted his new friend Rami. The young organizer was not nearly as afraid as he had been earlier. He climbed an olive tree and sat on one of its large branches, chanting with a look on his face that bordered on euphoria.

Waleed imagined that it would be difficult for someone who didn't live in Syria to understand the utter joy in yelling out one's deepest, most feared feelings at the top of one's lungs—and in public, no less. Indeed, it was the closest thing to ecstasy he had ever felt.

Soon a large group of men in uniforms arrived. They warned the crowd that they had ten minutes to disperse, or they would be killed. Waleed, as with everyone, listened but did not really hear them. The people were eager to defy the authorities, and the authorities were eager to punish the people.

And so it came to pass.

As if manifested by prophecy, the uniformed men opened fire on the protesters. Immediately Waleed experienced a mixture of unusual smells: gunpowder, tear gas, and blood. Some men and women were screaming; many were still chanting. But no one was silent.

"We are peaceful!" some started calling out, but it was no use.

Waleed had never felt so scared before. He started running toward Rami's olive tree, pushing and shoving through the people that jostled through his path. Through the sea of chaos, he found not Rami, but Omar heading toward that same olive tree. Omar held his cell phone high, videotaping as much of the event as he could manage.

"Get down from the tree!" Omar yelled from a distance.

"I can't!" Rami hollered. "Wait till the stampede calms down."

For the first time, Waleed realized that his old friend looked frantic. "Get down from the tree!" Omar screamed. "It's all right if you break something! Just jump."

Rami drew a long breath to reply. "All right, but—"

Waleed never heard the rest as gunfire rang out.

"Rami!" Omar yelled. "Rami!"

What was going on? What was happening? Waleed was stuck in the middle of a group of people as he tried to push his way out toward Rami and Omar. By the time Waleed reached him, Omar was on his knees, sweating profusely, his eyes flushed with tears as he performed chest compressions on a body lying on the ground. Soon enough, Waleed could tell that it was no one else but Rami, drowning in his own blood.

"They shot him!" Omar said hysterically as he pressed on Rami's chest. "They shot him! In his right lung."

Waleed turned, guided by instinct. "I'll go call an ambulance. You try to stop the bleeding and continue to do CPR." He reached for his cell phone and tried dialing the familiar number. "We have someone who was shot," he bellowed into the phone when he thought he heard someone pick up. "I think a policeman or a soldier shot him. Hello? Hello! Are you there?"

"Stop wasting time," Omar said above the noise. "They won't help us. They were probably given instructions by the government not to help wounded protestors." He continued with the chest compressions. "Give him two rescue breaths, then keep holding pressure to his bleeding site. I'll continue chest compressions."

Falling to his knees, Waleed did as his friend asked. "Wait!" he said, holding a hand out to Omar. "I feel a pulse. I think he's breathing on his own, too."

Just as the word escaped Waleed's lips, Rami opened his eyes. Slowly and audibly he began to breathe. Waleed kept firm pressure on his bleeding chest.

"I'm hurt," Rami said.

"You're talking, at least," Omar exclaimed, the tears pouring over his cheeks. "Don't talk, my friend. I need you to stay calm. We'll take you somewhere safe."

Rami began to shiver. "I'm going to die, right?"

"No!" Omar said, sounding almost furious. "No one will die. You're going home with me. I'll take care of you. You're having stuffed eggplants for dinner."

"Why did they shoot me?"

"Rami, *habibi*, I need you to save your energy and not talk," Omar said, gently brushing the wounded man's hair. He flashed a pair of determined eyes at Waleed. "We must move him out of here before they find us."

"He needs blood immediately," Waleed said. "We have to take him to the hospital. I'll get his arms and hold pressure. You get his legs, and we'll rush to the hospital."

They did just that. They carried the young man on their shoulders and kept running toward the nearest emergency department, which was at least twenty minutes away on foot. They didn't want to risk waiting for a cab.

"Omar, I'm hurting," Rami kept saying.

"I know. I'll give you pain medicines soon. You won't feel a thing." As he ran, carrying Rami by the legs, Omar bowed his head and kissed the wounded man on his knee. "We need to make it soon so I can prepare your dinner on time."

"Omar!" Waleed cried. "Your arm!"

"Shh! It's nothing."

It wasn't nothing. Waleed could see that his friend had been shot in his left arm, just above the wrist. Blood gushed in intermittent waves, leaving long swaths on the ground as they ran.

"*Habibi*, are you with me?" Omar said to Rami. "Check his radial pulse!" he begged of Waleed.

"I don't feel a pulse," Waleed said. "Oh God!"

"Put him on the ground!"

Quickly the men laid Rami on the cobblestone street. Waleed was acutely aware of all the running that was happening around them. Feet tramped on the ground in all directions, beating a path away from the bloodbath that was Homs's first protest.

"I still don't feel a pulse," Waleed bleated.

"Resume chest compressions!" Omar barked. "What are you waiting for?"

"I don't think he's breathing."

"Just do your chest compressions! I'll give him rescue breaths."

They kept at it for at least twenty minutes. Omar was incapable of doing much due to his injury, and Waleed was exhausted.

"I don't think we're going to get a pulse," Waleed said finally.

In the distance, the gunfire rippled now and again, punctuating the screams and chanting with the clarion call of death. Waleed watched as a mother, her breast covered in blood, dragged her limp child away from the fighting. Somewhere to the south, an explosion rang out. An eerie silence followed, broken by the sound of thousands and thousands of feet beating against the concrete.

"I don't think you need to be moving your mouth!" Omar said, his tears causing his voice to quaver. "We'll get a pulse. Then we're almost at the hospital."

"He's been pulseless and without oxygen for half an hour now!"

"I don't care," Omar yelled, his face dripping blood, sweat, and tears.

"He's dead, Omar. He's dead!"

Omar seemed incapable of holding eye contact. "No, he's still warm. He just moved his arm, I saw it."

Waleed burst out crying as he let go of Rami and placed his hands on Omar's shoulders.

"Fine!" Omar yelled, pulling away from Waleed's grasp. "I'll do the chest compressions." But Omar did nothing. He merely stared down at Rami's body, a glassy, reticent look washing over him.

He was a doctor, after all, Waleed supposed.

"Rami, please forgive me. I beg you."

Chapter 14
Hope

April 1, 2011
Deaths: 200

As her life abruptly changed in the course of a day, and as her priorities wildly reshuffled, Sireen was surprised to realize that all she could think of was one Homsi boy. Oh, how she missed him! How she regretted not simply grabbing his hand that day and eloping to a faraway place. She wished that she could travel to a place where no one could find them—not her family, not her fiancé, and not the Mukhabarat. An island in the middle of the ocean, perhaps.

In the end, as she fought for life, it was thoughts of his eyes, his smile, and his poetry that saved her.

As she lay in a strange bed in a house not her own, she reached to the dusty nightstand and grabbed her phone. Scrolling through her picture gallery, she found a photo of Waleed that she had taken several months ago. A wide, boyish smile spread across his face. She could almost remember the smell of his cologne that day: Very Irresistible by Givenchy. With a sad smile, she held the phone close to her heart and closed her eyes.

"Are you awake, miss?" a man's voice asked.

She could no longer recognize all these new voices. "Yes, I am awake. Who is it?" She opened her eyes and looked to the door, which her caller had opened halfway. He stood just behind it and out of sight.

"Yousef. Miss, my mother says breakfast is ready . . . if you don't mind joining us before the tea and cheese get cold."

"All right," Sireen said, sitting up and sliding her bare feet onto the cold hardwood floor. "I will brush my teeth and join you."

"Thank you, miss. I also have those clean towels for you. They're for my sister, but she washed them last night for you."

"I appreciate that." She crossed the floor and opened the door to greet the man who had roused her. Yousef was a rail-thin man dressed in a simple robe of white terrycloth. He held a short stack of fluffy white towels. From the way he averted his large brown eyes, she could tell that he was uncomfortable to be near her when she wore only a borrowed set of pajamas. "Can you call me Sireen instead of 'Miss'? You're older than me, I think."

"Sireen," he repeated, blushing. "Here are your towels. I will go help my sisters set up the table."

She quickly went to the bathroom to wash her face and brush her teeth. Her face looked ten years older. She had a bruise on her left cheek, but she wasn't sure why. Her hair was in terrible condition, as she no longer had the luxury of washing it every day. That one protest in Daraa had changed her life more than she could have imagined. From what she learned later, after she had passed out, a protestor had carried her to safety. An army general demanded that they hand her over to him, but the protestors refused. They formed a large human wall to allow the man who was carrying her to escape. She cried for days when she learned that at least five people died in the process of saving her life. She really didn't think she was worth the lives of five men.

Her rescuer took her home to his family in Daraa. His mother and sisters washed her face and sprinkled flower water over her. The mother then put Sireen's head on her lap and started combing her hair and reciting verses from the Quran. Eventually Sireen woke to find four strange women staring at her and rejoicing at her awakening. She was terrified.

"Don't be scared, darling," the mother said. "We're normal people. We're not Mukhabarat. God, may He be praised, has willed that you be saved from death and torture. I am Om Yousef, and those are my daughters, Julnar and Jumana and Jamilah. I don't know if you remember my son, Yousef."

"Mama, let her catch her breath!" one of the daughters said. "Can't you see how her face is yellow? Let her rest."

Sireen remained quiet at the time, feeling completely disoriented and confused. It took her a few hours to get her mind back together and talk to her hosts. After that, she politely introduced herself to the women and asked them how she had ended up in their house. She learned that Yousef had risked his life trying to save her, and had sustained a gunshot wound to his left leg. Yousef's mother was not at all bitter or even upset at Sireen for bringing this mischief to her son. She said that if the free men of Syria didn't protect its women, they should shave their moustaches and write on their doors, "Sorry, there are no men in this house." She was a very old-fashioned woman who was clearly more attached to her son than anything else in the world. The family overall was a conservative family, and all the women wore *hijabs*, or head coverings. The family was very poor. They made a living by sewing clothes, table covers, and curtains.

Later, Sireen would learn that Yousef, who was twenty-nine, ran a small shop where he sold fabrics, curtains, and clothes made by his mother and sisters. They made enough money to put food on the table and to have meat once a week. In this way, they were much better off than many people in Daraa. Sireen tried not to notice that Yousef was an extremely attractive young man. He was tall and tan with dark hair and black eyes. He had a faint beard and moustache and an overall strong build. He would never allow himself to sit with Sireen in the same room unless one of his sisters was with him or the door was wide open. The only interactions she had had with him were related to the breakfast being ready or dinner being set. Every morning at around 4:00 a.m., Sireen heard his alarm clock going off. He woke up to pray the dawn prayer and recite verses from the Quran with a surprisingly beautiful voice. Sireen listened to him until he was done, and then went back to sleep. She felt indebted to him and wasn't sure how to express those feelings without embarrassing him or herself.

Om Yousef's voice interrupted her daydreaming as she lay in bed. "Sireen, *habibti*, come have breakfast."

"Yes, *Khale* [Aunt], I'm on my way," she hollered as she put on some borrowed slippers and headed to the living room.

"*Ahla w Sahla* [Greetings]!" Om Yousef exclaimed. "You look beautiful today. Come sit next to me."

Sireen took a seat beside her hostess on the rickety wooden bench alongside the breakfast table. In turn, she greeted Om Yousef's daughters, trying not to let her eyes linger too long on Yousef as he sat across the table from her. "*Khale,* Om Yousef, I don't know how to thank you for your hospitality."

"Just eat your food before it gets cold." She nodded at the food. "Say, 'In the name of God the most benevolent, the most merciful,' and start eating."

The prayer came quickly to Sireen's lips. "I think when I am finished with this delightful breakfast, I will walk home to my family on the other side of Daraa. I don't know how I can ever thank you."

Om Yousef inclined her head, her wrinkled eyes narrowing. "You don't need to thank us for anything. It's our duty. Yousef will walk you home today, and if you want to stay with us, our home is your home."

"No, no, there's no need. He doesn't need to walk on his crutches halfway across the city with me. Let his leg heal."

"Of course he will walk you home. What would people say? You've been with us for so long that you're like any of my daughters. Yousef would never let them walk around the city alone. Yousef, say something."

For the first time, Yousef looked up from his plate. He wore a beautifully benevolent expression. "You know what I'll say, Mother. Miss Sireen can't be alone until her foot steps on her father's doorstep."

Sireen tried to ignore the way her heart skipped. "I swear there is no need. Don't bother yourselves."

"Your bothering is comfort, Miss Sireen," Yousef replied, a blush washing over his cheeks.

Before Sireen could respond in kind, Om Yousef rose with a flourish. "All right, let me pack some sandwiches for the way. And, Sireen, don't forget us! You will have to visit us again. Maybe we can meet your parents, God keep them for you."

Sireen set down her spoon and finished chewing her *fatteh*, a mixture of yogurt, steamed chickpeas, and flatbread. "Of course. I really don't know how to thank you all for everything." She had to fight back tears as she spoke the words. Then she went ahead and hugged and kissed Om Yousef and her daughters. She considered doing the same for Yousef, but stopped herself at the last moment.

When the parting greetings were made, Sireen followed Yousef to the door. He had slung over his shoulder the small bag his mother had packed, but apart from the sandwiches and waters, he brought no further provision. He wore a simple robe and a white knitted *taqiya* [hat] that had begun to yellow.

"Thank you all for everything," Sireen said as she waved to the women of the house. "Please come visit me."

"May safety accompany you," they replied, waving back.

Sireen and Yousef walked a half-meter apart as they made their way up the street. Given its recent tumult, the city was eerily silent.

"So where's your house?" Yousef asked awkwardly after they had crossed a couple of deserted blocks.

"Near the Omari mosque."

"All right," he said with a sigh. "We'll have to take some side routes, because I can't be seen by the security forces."

"Why not?"

He looked down at his crutches. He was so graceful in the way he walked with them that Sireen had almost forgotten he had them. "Because I have a leg injury. They will know I was in a protest and take me." He laughed.

Sireen wasn't sure how that was funny, but smiled anyway. "My parents must be extremely worried. I feel so badly."

"I'm sure they are." He stopped suddenly, squinting his eyes as he looked toward the rooftops. "Let's go left. There's a sniper at the top of that building." He nodded in the direction he was looking. "You see him? The idiot's sunglasses are reflecting the light."

Reflexively, Sireen's hand went to her heart. "A sniper?"

"Over the past few days, they've deployed snipers on rooftops throughout Daraa to prevent protests. This is in addition to multiple checkpoints, of course."

"Checkpoints? I feel like I'm in Iraq or something."

Yousef shrugged. "It has to get worse before it gets better."

In silence, they continued on for another block, Sireen chewing on the thought of how this revolution would progress. It was an improbably humid morning for early spring. She felt glad that they were making this journey before the sun got too high. The humidity mixed with the acrid smell of stale gunpowder that still seemed to hang over the city following the protests. For as long as it had taken her to recover, she hadn't expected to find so much evidence of war, but then she supposed that perhaps her protest hadn't been the last.

"How's your leg, by the way?" she asked. "I feel so bad that you're walking with me."

"It's better now. I didn't go to the hospital because the Mukhabarat are all over the hospitals looking for wounded protestors to arrest. My sister Jamila helped with it."

"I thought she worked in making clothes."

"She does, but she's also a licensed nurse."

Sireen wrinkled her nose. "She has a college degree?"

"Yes, she does. Why are you surprised?" Yousef sounded somewhat angry. "We all do. Jumana has a major in chemistry and Julnar has a degree in art and music. I have a major in history. Did you think we were illiterate?"

"I'm very sorry. I didn't mean that."

"It's all right," he said, sounding calmer. "We hide it well."

"I'm majoring in history, too. I'm doing a double major, actually."

"Geography?" he asked with a childlike smile.

"English literature."

"When do you graduate?"

"I was supposed to graduate this year, but I missed so many days this semester that I think I'll take a leave of absence this year and maybe graduate next year."

He pursed his lips as he took a long stride with his crutches. "*Inshallah.* You know, we are living the greatest moment in Syrian history right now."

"That's a big statement, my friend. Syria is ten thousand years old. There were lots of historic events."

"But Syrians haven't truly ruled themselves since even before the Roman era. If the revolution succeeds, this will be the first time the Syrians have ruled themselves in a long time."

She had been so lost in her thoughts and in her compelling company that, when she looked ahead, she was surprised to see that they had already come to her street. She wasn't sure what she had expected to see, but it rather surprised her to find that nothing had changed. "Yousef, my house is at the end of this road. You don't have to walk all the way there."

"I promised Mother to take you to the doorstep."

"All right." She stopped for a moment. "Yousef?"

He too came to a stop, but he did not turn to face her. Instead, he stared down at his wounded leg. "*His eyes*?" he asked, meaning, "Anything for you."

"What do you need?"

"How come you work in a shop and not in the field you love?"

He appeared to ponder the question for a long while before shrugging. "Look around you. There are doctors who sell things on the street; there are teachers who work as cleaners; there are religious scholars who sell falafel. And they ask why we need to revolt. Look around you. Five percent of the country owns everything. We have nothing but our chains. We are strangers in our own land. The regime thinks they even own us. They look at us as slaves. Syria must wake up before the Syrian people become a myth like many other old nations before them."

Lost in the thoughts he had given her, she started walking once more. They passed the home of one of her favorite neighbors. She adored the arched entryway of this large home, along with its signature thatched balcony. Most homes in the neighborhood, and Daraa at large, featured such balconies, but this neighbor's looked somehow older and more ornate than anyone else's. Coupled with the recent work the neighbor had done to the stone façade, the house looked like the perfect marriage of the old Syria and the new. Beside it stood a long row of courtyard houses, their flat faces dotted with wood-framed windows and intermittent sandstone bricks of green and yellow. The intricate latticework over each window was the only thing that separated one house from the next in its look.

Just beyond these courtyard homes stood Sireen's. As the only house in the neighborhood with a cobblestone courtyard out front, she had to admit that it looked the most palatial. Her mother kept the space looking lively with well-pruned olive trees and long, low flowerpots. Looming two stories above the courtyard was Sireen's favorite space in the house: a tall, open-air balcony crowned by red brick arches. In her eyes, this was the best place in the world to read, particularly when the sun was rising and she had a morning cup of coffee steaming on the little glass mosaic end table beside her rocking chair.

"This is my house." She pointed ahead before they reached it. "It sounds noisy for some reason. My whole family must be here."

"Sireen," Yousef said, pausing and holding out a hand. "Slow down. There's a military truck behind your house."

Her heart sank. "My . . . my *friend* works in the military." She was not sure why she called Hussein a friend, for he was surely no friend to her.

Yousef remained suspicious. He slowly approached the house while stretching his arm to prevent Sireen from advancing before him. She watched as he carefully plodded a path through the courtyard to peer into one of the front windows. When she could take it no more, she followed after him, and despite the aggravated look he gave her, she peered in as he had. There in her living room she saw two soldiers in addition to an older man and woman. She was relieved to discover that neither of the soldiers was Hussein.

"Do you know those soldiers?" he whispered.

"I've never seen them before. Should I go in?"

"Just wait a little bit," he ordered as both of them ducked away from the window.

Crouched beneath the glass, Sireen was surprised to find that she could hear the conversation inside the living room. A man's voice dominated the exchange at first.

"You're really lucky, you know," the man said. "We never do this house arrest nonsense. This isn't Europe. But it's general Hussein's orders. Otherwise you would have been thrown into a dark dungeon and tortured until you told us where your daughter is."

Sireen felt a painful lump form at the back of her throat at the thought that she had caused so much trouble for her family.

"I should have Hussein throw *you* into a dungeon," her mother replied boldly. "I told you I don't know where my daughter is, and I told Hussein that she wasn't participating in any protest. She is kidnapped for sure, and you should be trying to find her. You are useless."

The breath stopped in Sireen's chest as she strained to listen.

"Woman, shut your mouth before I lose my temper."

"Lose your temper, then. I heard the general's orders very well. We're his second family, you know. He will have you killed if you even touch a hair on my head."

"Really? Why are you under house arrest, then, if he cares about you so much?"

Her mother scoffed. "It's protocol."

A painfully long silence followed before the soldier spoke again. "If I can prove that you or your daughter are members of the opposition, I won't need to worry about General Hussein's orders. We have clear orders from the president himself to kill all those who oppose."

"Well, don't hold your breath. We are not opposition. Good luck finding evidence."

Sireen was shocked at her mother's audaciousness. From the look in Yousef's pretty eyes, she could tell that he felt the same way.

"Let's go back," Yousef whispered.

"Back where? I can't leave my parents."

"You're coming back home with me."

"That's ridiculous!" she said, her voice rising to a yell. "I'm going inside to see what's happening."

He reached for her, but she slipped from his grasp, heading for the door. She pushed the door open and stood at the entryway. The first thing she saw when her eyes adjusted to the light was her mother's shocked expression. It was as if she had just seen a ghost. Her father wore the same look. The two soldiers glanced at each other in confusion. Before they had a chance to say a word, Sireen's mother yelled out, "Mariam! How are you, darling? We still haven't found Sireen, unfortunately, but the police promised to find her soon."

Sireen stood confused. "What?"

"Yes, I know it's hard to believe. It seems she is somewhere away from here, outside of the entire city of Daraa. If she were inside Daraa, they would have found her by now."

The hints finally occurred to Sireen, but she had missed her parents so much that she didn't care if she broke character. She started crying as she rushed to her mother and gave her a tight hug. Her mother remained unemotional as she whispered into her ear.

"Get out of Daraa. Go back to Homs." Then she slowly pushed her away and spoke with a loud voice. "Okay, Mariam. You keep your chin up. Say hello to your mother for me. Take care." Sireen could see that, deep inside, her mother was weeping, but she stayed cool to prevent arousing any suspicion.

Under the watchful gaze of the soldiers, Sireen slowly returned to the courtyard, where she found Yousef waiting for her beside the window.

"Let's get you back home," he said.

On the way back, Sireen kept sobbing. They didn't speak a word to one another. She realized how serious the situation was. For a second, she wished she hadn't been involved with all this revolution stuff, but it was too late now. She knew that she would probably never be able to go back to her normal life again. She might as well give up on going back to college or even living with her family . . . unless . . . unless the regime collapsed.

An unexpected new confidence came to her as she realized that the only way to retreat now was to push forward. There was hope in continuing this revolution—not a lot of it, but at least enough to keep her from entirely collapsing under the weight of despair.

Then, from across a distance, she heard the chants of a nearby protest. It was like the sound of a river running across a barren desert. Sireen wiped away her tears, took a deep breath, and looked at Yousef.

"Are you going in?" she said. "Because I am."

Chapter 15

Clock Square

Many involved in the Syrian Diaspora could not understand what had gotten into their brethren in the homeland. What had happened to those passive, indifferent youths? Who had given birth to this fearless generation? Did they really get their genes from Hafez Assad's generation—the generation that had surrendered the land and the sea and forgotten the ancient connection to the old country? The land was lost. The old beating heart of Damascus was taken by infarction brought on by smoke and fire. The older generation stood idle as the regime loyalists besieged and annihilated 12,000-year-old Hama. Their only saving grace was that they, the generation of surrender, had given rise to the most extraordinary Syrian generation since the dawn of writing.

As the uprising grew, the older generation was taken by shock, as if suddenly realizing that what was once their responsibility had become the burden of their children. In this way, they were cursed to watch in painful silence as their children died before their eyes. Confrontation seemed inevitable between the old mind and the new mind, for the contrast was stark.

April 18 was a special day in Homs. While most cities were still starting to mobilize larger protests in support of the city of Daraa, Homs had already moved well beyond that point. Homs was getting ready to stage the first large sit-in in its long history. There were no previous videos of a sit-in protest there. Tens of thousands of people poured from all corners of the city and gathered around the old clock in a square known as Clock Square. Young people from neighboring villages poured into the city, as well. The entire university campus turned out. The scene was shocking for the protestors, for the bystanders, and of course, for Assad.

—*Syria: A History in Blood* by Celine Dubois

April 18, 2011
Deaths: 390

The news Waleed read about Daraa was getting more and more alarming every day. On Facebook, there were rumors that a full siege was underway, and potentially a Hama-style massacre against the unarmed citizens of the city. Some posters suggested that the memory of the Hama massacre of 1982 was being resurrected as government media started using sharp language against Daraa reminiscent of the language it used against Hama at the time. The regime media was repeating stories about "armed gangs," "infiltrators," "Zionist agents," and "Islamic terrorists" day and night.

The protest movement grew like wildfire in spite of all that. The largest picture of Bashar Al-Assad at the entrance of Homs was set on fire. His father's statues were being destroyed across the country. Waleed learned that there was some degree of protest in every city—not so much in Damascus and Aleppo at that point, but Homs was certainly ready to lead the revolution.

Waleed and Omar continued to be actively involved in organizing protests, but there was a growing feeling that protests alone weren't going to cut it. It was time to move to the second phase of peaceful resistance: public sit-ins. If there was anything to learn from the revolutions in Tunisia and Egypt, it was the power of sit-ins and occupying public squares. Waleed joined the young men and women of Homs, particularly its university students, in starting a not-so-secret campaign calling for the people of Homs City and its surrounding villages to participate in a large sit-in at Clock Square, a beautiful, open square in the center of the city, a public place renowned for its central column topped by a cubic clock with a face on all four sides. The sit-in would call for democracy in Syria, an end to the murder in Daraa, and the release of a student prisoner called Tal Al-Malohi.

A young Homsi girl in her early twenties, she was arrested while still in high school, long before any mention of the revolution. Her crime was that she was no longer able to see the violations of human dignity all around her without being affected by them, so she had published her thoughts on her blog, using mild but only thinly veiled protest poems to call on the people to rise up and fight for their rights. One day, those poems made their way to a Mukhabarat office. Tal was arrested before her eighteenth birthday. Something about children, more than any other group, intimidated Bashar Al-Assad. The arrest of Tal and the children of Daraa was only the tip of the iceberg.

"Waleed, are you scared?" Omar asked as the two of them sat on his rooftop, enjoying some morning coffee.

"Just a little. I'm more excited than scared. This will be the first ever sit-in in modern Syrian history. I feel like this will be a success. The protests have been growing in size daily, and I think the villages might join, as well."

"Do you have your posters and flags?"

Waleed patted the satchel lying beside him on the rooftop. "Yep. I made several posters about Syrian unity, and then I made a few about Daraa and Tal. We should try to head there early so I can put some posters on the clock itself."

"And the flags?"

"Do I really have to print the Syrian flags?" Waleed complained. "I don't feel any connection to that flag. It reminds me of the regime. I mean, I don't mind it, but I'm not going to print any."

"That's fine." Omar set his coffee cup aside and got to his feet. "Let's head to the mosque. After prayer, we'll walk to Clock Square." Making a face, he reached down and grabbed a poster at the bottom of the stack of posters Waleed had made. "What is this?"

Waleed felt his blush warm his cheeks. "That's nothing. It's just a drawing I was playing with. You can throw it away."

"'Sireen, I miss you,'" Omar read. "Do you really still think of her?"

"I don't know, Omar," Waleed said with a sigh. "She disappeared from my life so suddenly. In the end, I knew nothing about her—only that she's engaged and is probably with her fiancé. But I've checked; no one has seen her in college or even in Homs. I think she could have gone back to Daraa. I worry about her safety."

Omar placed a hand on Waleed's shoulder. "Don't worry. She's safe, I'm sure. She's probably just sitting at home, mildly bothered by the noise of the bombing around the revolutionary neighborhoods. She might even be a supporter of the regime."

"No!" Waleed snapped. "I'm telling you, she isn't, Omar. I just need some time to forget about her. I really thought she was the one for me."

The two friends spent some time looking awkwardly at the ground beneath their feet. Waleed felt sorry for going off on his friend.

"Anyway," he said, trying to break the uncomfortable silence, "let's get back to business. We've got a country to save."

~~~

Waleed was not surprised by how full they found the mosque. By now, it seemed that everyone in the city had become familiar with the routine. At first, everyone—whether Muslim or non-Muslim, conservative, liberal, or even communist—would gather in the mosques. After that, they would wait for a signal from protest organizers like Omar and Waleed before quickly heading out to the streets. If the protests were large enough, crowds of new people would join in as the protest washed through the neighborhoods like a river carrying away years of shame. State media had once reported that most of those protestors were young men and women on drugs and hallucinogens they acquired from America and Arabian Gulf countries. While that claim was generally viewed as ridiculous at best, there was one thing true about it: it seemed that the young men and women of Syria, and especially Homs, were indeed intoxicated and addicted to those euphoric doses of freedom.

It was on the back of this freedom wave that Waleed followed the protestors from the mosque, through the buzzing streets of Homs, and toward the central Clock Square.

"Omar, do you see what I see?" Waleed asked, looking out across the masses gathered around the four-sided clock.

"Just look at them!" Omar said triumphantly. "Everyone is here, not just the city of Homs—the whole province is here." Tears came to his eyes. "I wish Rami was here, too."

"He is here. Our martyrs are always with us, my friend. Have some faith."

When the clock struck 6:00 p.m., Omar's lips parted into a joyful smile. "I feel like I'm in heaven."

The sun began to descend toward the horizon. *Slogans, chants, and a cool spring breeze*, Waleed thought. *What more could a protester ask for?* When he looked to Omar, he saw that he had produced his cell phone and had already begun recording.

The protestors' chanting grew more dissonant. "With my blood and with my soul, I will release Tal Al-Malohi!" some chanted. "The people want to topple the regime!" others yelled. Many called out for an end to the military operation in Daraa.

Then a stirring piece of news trickled back through the crowd, reaching Waleed's ears. It seemed that Maher Al-Assad, Bashar's notorious brother, was on the way with an army brigade to surround the protesters.

"He's giving us until midnight to evacuate the area or die," someone said.

Waleed's fear lasted only a moment. Long before Maher would arrive, the sweet taste of freedom had snuck into the hearts of all the protestors present. Waleed could feel it: Homs was forever awakened from its deep slumber.

Over a loudspeaker, a nearby mosque announced the start of the sunset prayer, ignoring all warnings from the regime. From his vantage atop a stone planting box along the edge of the square, Waleed could see that people had started praying in the streets by the tens of thousands. From the way they packed each block from corner to corner, he suspected that the numbers truly reached the hundreds of thousands, all told. Some were praying on rooftops, some on balconies. Waleed knew that some would be praying their very last prayer. He could hear the murmuring all around him. It seemed that everyone could sense that this would be the climax of all spiritual experiences. Waleed prayed as they prayed: for God's salvation and protection from the coming massacre.

When the prayer had ended, Waleed joined the people as they resumed their revolutionary slogans. Night had arrived, and the streetlights added to the beauty of Clock Square. People started climbing over the clock, singing and chanting as they climbed. Others distributed free snacks and water. Of course, many were busy videotaping the event. The more time went by, the more creative the young men and women became. Waleed spotted posters reading, *Goodbye, Bashar* and *Goodnight, Bashar*. On the base of the clock tower, other protestors had posted placards reading, *The Syrian people are one*; *Thank you, Daraa*; and *Homs, the land of peace*. It seemed to Waleed that hundreds of other posters were born from the crowd every minute.

Time flew by, and soon it was almost dawn. The deadline to evacuate had long passed, but nothing had happened. Waleed chose to view this fact as a point of hope. Along with the multitudes, he decided to stay in Clock Square and sleep there in the sleeping bag he had brought. In this way, he would rest right under the eyes of time and its clock.

"Aren't you going to sleep?" Waleed asked of Omar as he set up his sleeping bag just on the edge of a scrum of people already dozing.

"No," Omar said softly. "You sleep. I'll watch over you. I just want to keep watching this amazing moment in our history."

"All right, keep watching. I'm exhausted." Waleed battled through a prodigious yawn. "Wake me up if they start shooting at us," he added sarcastically.

Omar nodded, but did not smile. Within the next hour, most of the protestors had gone to sleep in what looked like a huge slumber party, but no matter how he tried, Waleed could not join them. He was too intoxicated with the sweet taste of freedom. It was almost dawn, but not quite yet, when Waleed opened his eyes to find that he had actually dozed for a time. The square was still quiet, a blanket of peace covering the young men and women sleeping around the clock. Waleed stared up at the birds in the surrounding trees, many of them asleep, as well. They reminded him of Omar's pigeons. Before he could get back to sleep, he noticed an unusual flock of birds moving toward Clock Square from a distance. He was alarmed, since it was too early in the day for such a migration. He quickly got up and watched in the direction from which they had come. He had a bad feeling about this, and he was right. Within minutes, hundreds of regime forces started pouring into the area, surrounding the sleeping protestors from all directions.

"Get up! Get up!" Waleed shouted at Omar.

When his friend had woken, the two of them started running around, poking people.

"They're here," Waleed said as he tried to hide the overwhelming fear that was taking over his thoughts.

"They're here!" Omar hollered as thousands of people started climbing to their feet. Everyone huddled close, holding hands. Some quietly prayed. Others touched the clock as if it would transfer to them some hidden powers. Many just stared toward the sky, hoping for a savior to drop from the heavens, sent either by God or by NATO.

The savior never came.

There was fear, for sure, and Waleed saw quiet tears everywhere, but there was no panic.

"Peaceful, peaceful, we are peaceful!" the protestors started chanting to the armed men. Many waved branches of olives, jasmine flowers, and flags.

Waleed kept his eyes trained on the soldiers, who remained quiet as they shuffled around to form some sort of configuration known only to them.

"This doesn't look good," Omar said flatly.

"No kidding," Waleed replied. "This might be it, my friend. This might be the end."

Omar reached out and clasped Waleed's hand. "It's not the end. It's the beginning."

"I want you to know that I love you, Omar," Waleed said, looking his friend in the eye. "More than my own brothers."

"Stop being scared," Omar said with an almost divine serenity. "Just don't let go of my hand." He stuck out his slight jaw as far as it would go. "You will die, but not today. I promise you, I'll protect you with my soul. If they're going to shoot you, they will need bullets that can penetrate through me first."

"Don't talk like that," Waleed insisted. "You're far more important to the revolution than I am."

Omar shook his head dismissively. "I was important in the beginning, but look around you now. Every one of these people is here because they're willing to die for their country. The men, the women, the children. We're all equally important."

Indeed, every person in Clock Square that night would become a leader in the revolution. A few young women broke out in a quiet, reassuring song: "Paradise, oh paradise . . . Our homeland is paradise . . . Our beloved homeland has a kind heart . . . Everything in it is paradise . . . Even its sand is paradise."

As Waleed watched in awe, the women started distributing dozens, perhaps hundreds, of small candles to the people in Clock Square. Over the next couple of minutes, the small candles joined with the light of the predawn moon in illuminating the square. By the time a candle reached Waleed, his voice had joined the melody of the soft revolutionary songs. He watched with a smile as a group of college students took out a large bag of sweets and started throwing candies over the protestors. When Waleed asked one of them why he was doing it, the young man said that they hoped the candy would calm the people while also letting the soldiers know that this protest had only peaceful intent. The attempt was not an utter failure, as many of the younger children became preoccupied with collecting sweets off the ground instead of thinking about their imminent doom.

Through the solemn song, Waleed startled as the soldiers fired ten warning shots into the air. The people did not stop singing and chanting. One of the soldiers called on a loudspeaker for everyone to evacuate the square before the clock struck on the next minute. In a panic, many started fleeing the square while others remained, determined to stay. Waleed fell into the latter camp, along with Omar and perhaps five thousand other men and women.

The chanting and singing continued, growing louder with every passing second, but strangely, the only thing Waleed could hear was the ticking of the clock high above him. It was as if he was counting the seconds until the peace would shatter.

The moment the clock struck the next minute, the crowd seemed to draw a collective breath of anticipation. The chanting and singing hushed all at once. "Fire!" came the order. Bullets began lancing into the protestors from all four corners. Blood poured over the square like a hundred open faucets.

"This is it, Omar!" Waleed said, clenching his friend's hand as he shook in fear.

"Open your eyes, brother," Omar said calmly. "And look at *them*," he added, pointing to the blockade of soldiers. "Look at the fear in their eyes. They're more afraid of us than we are of them." A tear trickled over his cheek as he shoved Waleed behind him to protect him from stray bullets.

~~~

"Fire!" the orders came again.

"No, sir!" one of the soldiers yelled. "Stop firing!"

"Are you defying my orders, soldier?"

"No, sir, but I can't shoot them."

"Shoot them or be shot like them," the general ordered as another more loyal soldier pointed his gun at his comrade.

When the soldier still refused, he was shot on the spot. Another soldier, a young man with doubts of his own, turned and bolted from the scene, disappearing into the night. The shooting then resumed, but this time it was worse—so bad as to force hundreds to start fleeing for their lives.

~~~

"Don't desert us!" Omar called out to one person who ran.

"We will leave now," the man yelled back, "but we will return when they're gone. I promise."

Waleed was heartened when he saw that at least three thousand people remained in the square in defiance of all natural laws. He could not tell how many people had run and how many had died, but there were bodies everywhere. Blood sluiced over the square, and yet the people remained, anchored by an inexplicable courage.

An equal dread crept up Waleed's spine as the next order came over the loudspeaker.

"Call in the tanks!" The general's voice became manic. "All you remaining bastards will be killed. It's too late to escape now."

The sound of the tanks preceded the sight of them. The rumble was so deep and penetrating that Waleed could feel it in his chest. The ominous rumble grew so loud that he could scarcely hear himself think, let alone keep up with the latest chants. He watched in terror as the wall of soldiers parted to make way for a pair of tanks just ahead, and still more to the left and right. He braced for them to fire, but nothing could have prepared him for the hellish noise of their terrible canons.

When his ears finally stopped ringing, he heard Omar hollering at him.

"Waleed! It's time to leave!"

He was not sure what made him speak the words, but Waleed had never felt more determined in his life. "No, we stay here or we die here."

Ignoring him, Omar grabbed Waleed's arm and started running. The moment his feet began beating against the ground, Waleed understood that his friend had the right of it. There was no point in fighting tanks. The two protestors ran aimlessly through the chaotic mob as snipers, soldiers, and tanks surrounded the area. Before Waleed knew what was happening, he felt Omar shove him to the ground. Immediately he felt a great soft weight fall over him. Then came a harrowing thud. A warm, wet sensation crept over Waleed's back.

Chapter 16
Via Dolorosa

The protest chants against Al-Assad's regime became a mounting choir from Daraa and its neighboring towns, spreading to every province like a blazing fire threatening to burn the thrones and crowns. The echoes of freedom reached the suburbs of Damascus, and the movement there grew robust. The dense core of the revolutionary movement proved to be very resilient, a golden core that could not rust.

The regime hastily declared the protestors to be armed terrorist groups supported by the United States and Israel. Bashar seemed to believe that the world didn't care about the fate of the Syrian nation, and that no outsider would even try to end his gloomy reign of grief and sorrow. He sent down orders to the police and armed forces to shoot and kill anyone seen protesting. Give Bashar some credit: he was right about the world at large. The world remained blind to every dying child and deaf to every widow's plea.

On April 22, the revolutionaries gave that Friday the name of "Good Friday." The name couldn't have been more appropriate, as each protestor marched down the streets of his city or village, walking his own Via Dolorosa, not knowing whether he would be the one on the cross this time. The regime, outraged by the wit of the protestors, slaughtered more people on that particular day than any since the beginning of the uprising. Nonetheless, every time Assad thought that he had at long last pinned the revolution to its cross, it would resurrect from the dead the following day

Hundreds of civilians were shot dead. The remainder were herded into a public square and forced to lie on the ground to form what looked like a giant human carpet. The soldiers then started marching over the bodies of the people while hitting them with electric rods and chanting slogans praising Bashar Al-Assad. "I am a human being, not an animal!" yelled a man from Bayadah as the soldiers marched. Every drop of blood shed, every attempt to humiliate the people, was converted into a stem cell of honor and courage and planted into the ill heart of Syria.

Faced with this terrifying problem, the regime needed a more permanent solution to stab the uprising and the country in its

heart. This solution would become the siege of Daraa.
—Syria: A History in Blood by Celine Dubois

April 25, 2011
Deaths: 570

"Sireen, wake up, wake up," Yousef called from behind the door.

"It's too early, Yousef," she said as she slowly got out of bed and went to the bathroom to wash her face. When she turned on the faucet, nothing happened. "Why is there no water?"

Yousef looked strangely happy. "There's no water, no electricity, and no phone service."

She felt suddenly less groggy. She ran to the living room, where she found Yousef's family gathered around the coffee table. Yousef's cousin Luma was there with her husband and baby twins, as well. Contrary to Yousef's lighthearted expression, they all wore concerned looks. Together they gathered around the breakfast table, said a prayer, and started to eat quietly.

"We are about to be invaded," Yousef said in a soft yet commanding voice. "Some of our friends who have infiltrated the Mukhabarat say there is a large military operation underway. The hope is that the world will intervene before it becomes another Hama-style massacre. The next few days will be difficult, but we have to be patient. We'll need to be conservative when using whatever food and water resources we have."

"When is the attack supposed to happen?" Om Yousef asked her son, her voice remarkably calm.

"Today, Mother," Yousef replied. "Today."

Indeed, as if he was reading from a book of prophecy, the sound of shelling began.

"We'll all need to stay inside the house today," he said, looking first to Sireen and then to the baby twins. "I will go and buy the essentials, especially milk."

"No, darling," his mother said. "May God bless you, don't leave the house now. It's not safe."

Sireen marveled at the brave look that crossed Yousef's face. "Mother, I have to go," he said firmly as he reached for his mother's hand and kissed it. "I'll be fine. This part of the city will probably be safe today."

"I'm going with you!" Sireen exclaimed.

"No, you're not," he responded with a firm frown.

She felt a sudden surge of anger. "Don't tell me what to do," she hollered, but her protest was silenced by the frightening sounds of shelling in a distant neighborhood.

The shelling then intensified, sounding as if it were inching ever closer.

Before she could stop him, Yousef grabbed some money and headed out, slamming the door shut tightly behind him. Sireen, undeterred, opened the door and followed him. She trailed as he ran to a nearby store, but was frustrated to find that it was already closed. Together they ran to the next street, and the next. Everything was closed. Up to that point, Sireen had followed him quietly, but at last she spoke. "Here! There's a small shop that's open."

He remained silent as he strode toward the shop.

~~~

Om Yousef joined the rest of her family in anxiously waiting, reciting verses from the Quran, praying, and softly crying. She was so worried about Yousef and Sireen. A few minutes later, she was overjoyed by the sound of heavy knocking on the door.

"Julnar," she said to her daughter, "open the door. It must be them."

The girl rushed to the door, but before she could open it, it was pushed open from outside. To Om Yousef, the scene was too familiar, even though she had never seen it before. Four men wearing army uniforms and one dressed in black leather shoved their way inside and immediately dispersed across the living room, pointing their guns and rifles at everyone in turn.

What polite guests! she thought wryly.

The man in black leather moved toward Luma's husband. "Let's do this the easy way," he said calmly. "Give us any money and jewelry you have in this house. Then you come with us. Do this, and we leave the women and children unharmed. If you resist, everyone will die, even those two." He pointed his gun at the baby twins, causing them to burst out crying.

"Don't hurt them, please," Om Yousef begged. "We're all one people. We're all Syrian." She approached him, her arms outstretched as if to embrace him. The man responded by pushing her violently to the floor and removing her head cover.

Her daughters screamed in protest.

"What do you think you're doing?" Jumana, the youngest, cried out.

"Take the man, and take this woman with the long tongue," the man in black ordered two of his soldiers. Then, as Om Yousef felt herself yanked to her feet, he pointed to the other two. "And you two go search the house. If you meet any resistance, shoot to kill."

Not a piece of furniture was left undestroyed. Not a drawer was left unopened. The men looted the entire house, even the kitchen. They stole all the milk, honey, and even olive oil. Then they shot the water tank from the bottom to make sure no water was left behind. Luma tried to beg for her husband's freedom, but the men attacked her, beating her, insulting her, and ripping off her clothes in front of her husband. Om Yousef watched as he painfully maintained his calm to prevent a massacre from taking place. Her legs went weak as the soldiers blindfolded and handcuffed Jumana and Luma's husband, dragging them out of the house and throwing them into a large van with many other people. Om Yousef trailed behind, wondering why her daughter had replaced her in the wagon.

Then, just as quickly as they had appeared, the men vanished to find their next victims. Om Yousef returned to the house, hollowed out with misery. There she found the remaining women lying on the floor, weeping in shock and horror. She couldn't fully believe what had just happened. It was like a nightmare that would end any minute, but the end would never come.

~~~

Upon returning from the store, Sireen and Yousef entered a vandalized house with four weeping women. Sireen could hardly contain her sorrow at the sight.

"Who did this?" Yousef roared with rage.

No one replied.

"I said, who did this?" he repeated.

Heavy shelling and screaming interrupted him.

"Where is Jumana?" he yelled as he punched the wall in anger. "Where is she?"

Om Yousef burst into tears, but said nothing. Sireen stepped aside as Yousef plowed through the doorway and ran into the street with no clear aim. The house next to theirs was open. Sireen followed behind as he cautiously walked inside. He stood in the doorway for a long while. In time, Sireen worked up the courage to come up behind him and peer inside. There, she saw four dead bodies on the floor. It was a husband, a wife, and two little girls. The house had been vandalized and robbed. The scene overwhelmed her. Yousef pressed his back against the wall in shock. Sireen tried to catch his eyes, but he seemed not to notice her there.

Without a word, he ran to the next house. She followed. There, they found a family of six, two of them dead and the others in a wailing frenzy. The next three houses were no better. The following two had collapsed due to heavy shelling. Yousef toppled to his knees, speechless, powerless.

"Yousef!" Sireen called in a soft voice.

He didn't answer. He merely shifted around on the ground.

"Yousef, are you all right?" Sireen said as she knelt down and started shaking him.

He closed his eyes and whispered, "Leave me alone."

"No, I won't leave you alone."

"Go back home. It's not safe."

"Nowhere is safe," she replied, standing when a moment of clarity came to her. She felt as if she had finally found an answer she had been seeking for years. She left Yousef on the ground, walking with purpose.

"Why are you leaving me?"

"I've got something to do," Sireen said as she stalked quickly away.

Her outrage gripping her from within, Sireen had decided all at once that she would make a deal with the devil himself. She was no longer thinking of herself or even her family, but if anyone could stop this madness, it would be Hussein. *Maybe this whole war is happening because he is mad at me,* she thought. *This is just his bloody way of expressing it.*

Of course she knew that the truth was far from this flight of fancy. But that did not deter her. She marched for at least four miles, through the ruined streets of Daraa, taking random turns and twists in the hopes of finding some sign to guide her. Finally, she reached an area on the outskirts of the city, where her family used to live when they were much poorer. She walked past the old playground she had loved as a child. The slides were full of bullet holes now, but the swings were still functional. Despite all the gunfire and destruction around her, she couldn't resist the urge to sit on her favorite pink swing. It looked rustier now, and for some odd reason, more intimidating. She propelled herself on the swing and closed her eyes. She could remember how her father used to push her gently on Friday evenings on this same swing. She kept flying higher with each pass, feeling her black hair flowing back and forth, her tears sliding down her face. She remembered well that once the swing reached its maximum altitude, she would be able to see over the walls of her elementary school. This was a skill crucial to learn for all students who escaped school during recess and wanted to know if classes had resumed. Once there were no kids in the playground, it meant that it was time to climb over the school wall and run back to class before someone noticed.

A breeze brushed against her cheeks, indicating that she had reached her destination. She opened her eyes to peek over her school wall, and was stunned by what she saw. It appeared that recess was not over. There were hundreds of people in the playground. The swing went back down and up again. Hundreds of men and women sat on the ground of the schoolyard. Dozens of soldiers and Mukhabarat agents stalked between them. The swing went down and back up. It seemed to Sireen that these people were hostages. They were all blindfolded, their hands tied behind their backs. Over the next few swings, Sireen tried to estimate the number of hostages. There were at least three hundred.

This time, when the swing went down and up, she saw that a soldier was pointing his rifle right at her face. Faster than her reflexes reacted, he shot at her. She fell backward off the swing. Her hair was buried in the sand, and her skirt ripped from the ankle to the knee. The bullet had missed her by a wide margin, but she was in pain from the fall. She knew that someone would be looking for her soon, so she got up and ran toward the school wall, hugging close to the barrier as she made her way around to the western side. There, on the far end of the wall, she was able to remove one loose brick and peek inside. Only a select few of her classmates growing up had known about this trick.

Inside, she saw people being beaten by electric rods. There was blood everywhere. One man hung by his neck from the basketball pole. There were three dead bodies inside the soccer net. The soldiers stepped over the prisoners and savagely beat them. She looked from face to face, but could not find her fiancé among the soldiers.

Undeterred, she cautiously made her way to the backyard of the school, hoping to hide there for some time. She found the yard full of people, as well, but here it was different. The prisoners were arranged into standing lines, and among the soldiers she spotted a familiar face: her fiancé himself.

She wasn't sure why, but the mere sight of him made her feel more determined to remain in hiding. She watched as the soldiers lined the prisoners up in five long queues. At the front of each queue stood a soldier next to a huge hole the size of a small room. She didn't recall ever seeing such a hole before. The soldiers must have dug it up recently. But why?

"Whom do you worship?" the nearest soldier asked a young man as he pointed a gun to his head.

"I worship God, sir," the man replied in a trembling voice.

"I'm going to shoot you," the soldier said, laughing. "Can God save you?"

His comrades burst out laughing.

"I don't know, sir," the prisoner said.

"Well, let's test the theory," the soldier said, shooting the man in the head.

When the man dropped to the ground, the soldier kicked his lifeless body into the hole.

Sireen's heart stopped beating. Her lungs stopped breathing. When she saw the joy on her fiancé's face, she wanted to throw up. He was enjoying himself.

"Next!" ordered the soldier as a terrified woman fell to her knees, begging for her life.

"I have three kids, sir," she pled. "They have no one else but me."

"So you think you deserve to live?" the soldier mocked as he pointed the gun at her head.

"Please, sir. I beg you."

"You beg me? I don't see how you're begging me." He laughed along with the other soldiers and their general.

"What do you want me to do, sir?" the woman asked, her hands folded before her.

"Why don't you start by cleaning my shoes?" the soldier said. "They're pretty dirty."

The woman gathered cloth from the hem of her long dress and reached for his shoes.

He kicked her hand away. "With your tongue, you whore."

"Sir?" the woman asked in surprise, her body shaking in fear.

Sireen felt a new wave of nausea rise in her throat as the soldier turned to look incredulously at his fellow tormentors.

"Are you deaf? I said with your tongue. Do you want to live or not?"

The woman burst out crying as she did as she was ordered.

"So, is this the dignity that you're fighting for?" the soldier mocked. "Clean it well, daughter of a whore."

With every passing second, Sireen felt more desperately sorry for this poor woman. Just when she thought she could take no more of the sight of it, the woman stopped licking the soldier's boot.

"Why did you stop?" the soldier yelled. "Did I tell you to stop?"

"No, sir."

"Then get back to what you were doing before I blow off your head."

"No, sir," she said as she climbed to her feet.

The soldier grinned hungrily. "You idiot. Your whole life is in my hands."

"No, sir," she repeated robotically.

The soldier looked outraged. He slapped her right cheek. "Say that there is no God but Bashar."

She turned the other cheek, her face covered in mud and tears. "There is no God but God, sir."

Sireen's heart soared, courage returning to her as if roused by a trumpet call.

The soldier slapped the prisoner again. "Well, go meet your God, then." He readied his weapon to shoot.

Sireen could no longer watch this horror from afar. She ran toward the men, crying and yelling, "What are you doing, you monsters!"

"Should I shoot, sir?" she heard one soldier ask the general.

"Tell them, Hussein!" she screamed. "Should they shoot?"

Hussein's mouth hung open.

"Sir?" another soldier said. "Should I shoot this crazy woman?"

"Your mom is a crazy woman, you coward," Sireen replied.

"Sir, I'm going to shoot."

"No, stop," Hussein ordered as he slowly closed the distance between him and Sireen. As she continued shouting insults, he grabbed her by the arm and dragged her away from his men. "Where have you been?"

She steeled up her jaw. "I've been with those people you're killing, you criminal."

Hussein's tension seemed to loosen. He shook his head at her. "Sireen, this is beyond you. This is a matter of national security. You need to go home now."

"Killing an unarmed woman, a mother of three, and humiliating her is a matter of security? To hell with that security!"

"Don't test my patience," Hussein said through gritted, yellow teeth. "I am already fuming from your adolescent behavior."

She ripped her wrist from his grasp. Somewhere far behind, a shell landed, kicking up a massive explosion. "Shoot me, then. You must be an expert at shooting women by now."

"Shut up!" he barked, slapping her so hard that her vision went red and she fell to the ground.

Despite the pain, Sireen started laughing. "I knew you were no different than the rest of them. I can't believe I almost married you. You're a man with no honor and no soul."

"Salman, tie her down," Hussein ordered of one of his men. "And make sure to tie her mouth."

"Yes, Salman," Sireen mocked. "Tie down your boss's fiancée. He loves it when other men touch his woman. Don't you see the horns on his head?" she said, indicating that he had no honor.

"Shut your mouth!" Hussein screamed, his fury etched on his face. "I know all about your lover boy in Homs. You thought you could make a mockery out of me? I'll teach you how to honor your future husband. Just wait till this mission is done. I will drink of his blood and throw his body to the dogs. I promise you."

It was all Sireen could do to keep herself from quivering in misery and fear. It was as if the man before her had transformed into the devil himself.

"Everyone back to work," he ordered his men. "Amjad, seal the deal for this woman."

Even as one soldier came to tie up Sireen, the soldier called Amjad got ready to shoot the prisoner who had licked his boots. Sireen braced for the horrible sound of his gun, but then something remarkable happened.

"Drop your weapon, coward," came the voice.

Sireen opened her eyes to see that one of the other soldiers was holding his gun at Amjad's head.

"Don't point your weapon at another soldier!" Hussein ordered as the rest of his men turned their own weapons on the defiant soldier. "I repeat, drop your weapon, now."

A few seconds later, another of the ten soldiers turned his gun on Amjad. "Let her go," he said through gritted teeth.

Hussein softened his voice, sounding almost afraid. "Let the woman go, Amjad. And let's all not lose track of why we're doing this. We're saving our country from an American-Israeli plot to destroy it."

So freed, the woman quickly ran to Sireen and sat next to her. She was shaking in fear. Sireen, her hands now tied and her mouth bound, tried to smile at her to give her some reassurance.

"The woman is gone," Hussein continued. "So both of you put down your weapons."

The two soldiers who had nearly defected lowered their weapons. Seconds later, they were riddled with enough bullets to kill dozens of people.

"Let this be a lesson to all traitors," Hussein said. "It will be our way or the grave." He pointed to the line of prisoners. "Now get back to work. No more goofing around."

The killing progressed at a much faster rate. Sireen watched in horror as the hole of death slowly filled with the bodies of men and women, young and old, adults as well as children. Sireen and her new friend sat crying like two frightened babies.

Just when Sireen thought she could take no more, the woman untied her mouth. "Let's get out of here, darling."

Sireen nodded in agreement as the woman untied her hands. They stood quietly and tried to sneak away. They made it only a few steps before a soldier noticed and asked whether to shoot them.

"No. Just tie them down again," Hussein ordered. He stood over Sireen, his eyes dark and yet adoring at the same time. "You know that I can't hurt you, but I can surely hurt this friend of yours if you don't behave, my love." He looked at his soldier again. "Put them somewhere far from here. I think they've seen enough."

"Yes, sir."

The soldier dragged them away to a spot far from the slaughter machine. Sireen could not see their surroundings due to the smoke from the shelling, but she felt the cold concrete of the wall pressed against her back and saw the flashes of light from the bombings overhead.

Then the voice of a soldier cut through the haze. "Let's have some fun, ladies." He grabbed Sireen's arm and started kissing her neck.

She kicked him in the stomach, but he spun her around and pushed her face first against the wall. His lips were wet against her bare skin as he squeezed her close to him. She could feel his manhood pressing into her from behind.

"Get off of me, you bastard!" she yelled.

He ignored her.

"She said to get off of her, you bastard!" A man's voice yelled from behind them. Sireen had trouble placing the voice at first, but then she realized that it was Yousef. She wrenched her neck to look back just in time for him to emerge from the dusty fog.

"Who are you?" the soldier asked, pointing his gun.

Yousef kicked the gun out of the soldier's hand so quickly that Sireen hardly saw him move. The soldier panicked as he scrambled for his gun skittering across the concrete.

"Run away now!" Yousef ordered.

"No, I'm not leaving you."

"I said leave!" he repeated in an intimidating voice.

Gripped by fear and worry, Sireen pulled the other woman to her feet. The two of them ran until they reached a small forest and disappeared inside. From behind, Sireen heard five gunshots and that same soldier's voice yelling, "You dog!" She screamed when she realized that Yousef had been shot and probably killed. She collapsed to the ground, not sure whether she was sobbing or screaming. Her new friend held her tight and began reciting verses from the Quran. They both wept and cried all night. No one found them, not even the angel of death.

Chapter 17
Ghosts

Hafez Assad, the previous dictator of Syria, was perhaps one of the most ruthless tyrants of the twentieth century. He, and others like him, seemed to fit under a unique personality disorder of their own, with its unique cluster of symptoms. To a man, they were possessed of a highly inflated sense of self-importance, to the degree of feeling that they were somehow supernatural or divine. In spite of that, they were highly paranoid, suspecting that anything could turn out to be a conspiracy against them. If they believed that a woman in a certain village was plotting against them, they would destroy the entire village just in case someone else like her lived there. In addition, they always found a race of people to pin all the world's woes on, whether it was the Jews, the Bosnians, or the Syrians.

Hafez Assad came from an extremely impoverished and uneducated family in Qordaha, a tiny Alawite village near the Syrian coast. Centuries of occupation by foreign powers had significantly weakened the Syrian identity. With Hafez being the mastermind, a group of Alawite generals performed a military coup over the government, making Hafez Assad the president of Syria. The high ranks of the army were replaced almost entirely by loyalists.

Assad's plan had one big weakness that he recognized, however: demographics. Over the next few years, there was a mass migration of the Alawites from more peripheral villages and into the heart of Damascus and other cities. This process was accompanied by a mass migration of Sunni Syrians to the countryside and Christian Syrians to the West. The very urbanized Jews of Syria disappeared in the process. Assad's dream of a "corrected Syria," as he called it, was becoming more real than he had ever thought possible. The once impoverished Alawites suddenly became Syria's most powerful group.

The regime also established semi-autonomous Baathist militias known as the Shabeeha, or ghost-like figures. They were allowed to form gangs that specialized in drug trade, human trafficking, and the theft of historical artifacts. In return, the regime would summon these ghosts to "deal with" any political dissident.

Over the next few weeks of the Daraa siege, with the ghosts entering the fray, outcomes became ever crueler. The dead were dumped into mass graves, men and women alike. The city died a thousand deaths. The fortunate died from a bullet or a bomb. The sick and young starved to death.

Hundreds of protestors gathered medications, milk, and canned foods and began smuggling them into the city of Daraa. One of these people was a thirteen-year-old boy by the name of Hamza Al-Khateeb, who was brutally tortured and mutilated. He was shot repeatedly in nonfatal fashion; his genitals were severed; and he was left to die slowly and painfully over two weeks. Hamza became an important symbol of the Syrian revolution, as new revolutionary hotspots began rising outside of Daraa.

—*Syria: A History in Blood* by Celine Dubois

May 20, 2011
Deaths: 1,150

When Omar's mother answered the door of her home, she warned Waleed in a whisper to expect to find his friend in poor spirits. But Waleed could not have prepared himself to see the usually boisterous Omar so downtrodden.

"Omar, how are you?" Waleed asked as he entered his friend's dimly lit living room. Omar sat at a small tea table of decorative wrought iron in the corner beside the computer room, his shoulders slumped and his lips slack. His eyes looked glassy and distant. He did not appear interested in the coffee his mother had left for him.

"I'm all right," he said, his voice cracking from what sounded like exhaustion. "Have a seat, my friend."

Waleed nodded to the sling Omar wore. "How's your arm?"

"I think it's better now. I probably can't go to work anytime soon, though."

"Does it still hurt?"

Omar failed to hide his wince as he brushed his hand against the bandages. "No, not really. The guys from the hospital are smuggling Oxycodon for me. It's just very dangerous to go back to work with an injury like this. If any *Shabeeha* see me, they'll know I got shot in a protest and they'll finish the job."

"Omar, I'm sorry."

"Don't be sorry. I would rather lose an arm than see you dead."

Waleed knew that his friend was in a lot more pain than he was letting on.

"Can I at least help with some costs since you're not getting paid?"

"No!" Omar shook his head adamantly. "Are you paying me for my service?"

"No, I swear, but you're not working, and I know your family depends on you for income. Let me at least take care of the kids' expenses until you get better."

Omar batted at the air. "Waleed, I said no. Besides, why are you sitting at home like a wife? Shouldn't you be getting ready for Friday prayer?"

"I was thinking of sitting this one out," Waleed said with a sigh. "Next Friday, hopefully we'll both be able to go together again."

For the first time, Omar showed signs of excitement. It was only a flash, but even that flash made Waleed feel better about his friend's state of mind. "What are they calling this Friday, by the way? I haven't been able to use my laptop much."

"It's called Azadi Friday."

"What's Azadi?"

"It's the Kurdish word for freedom. They're hoping to persuade the Kurds to be more heavily involved in the revolution."

"You think it'll work?"

"I think it'll help. The Kurds hate the regime more than we do."

With that, Omar slid away from the table. His movements were awkward and jerky, as he still seemed unaccustomed to moving with only the aid of one hand. Waleed followed his friend to the door. When they arrived there, Omar bent down for his shoes, but then stopped short.

"If you don't mind," he said, his voice strained from the pain, "can you help me put on my shoes?"

"You'll have to tell me where you're going first."

"We're going to my roof, you and me. Maybe we can get a glimpse of the protests. They always pass by my building." He nodded to the decorative cabinet bench beside the door. "I put my socks in the first drawer."

"Any other orders?" Waleed asked as he grabbed the socks and started putting them on Omar's feet.

"These aren't my socks!" Omar said in protest. "Look at them. They're different colors!"

"It's okay," Waleed said, reaching for Omar's shoes. "No one is going to see you."

"You know, after this accident, I decided to always keep saline bags and a full surgical kit at home, just in case." When his shoes were on, Omar came to his feet. "Okay, now get some carrots and a knife so we can snack while watching the protest."

"Fine, fine. You did save my life. I just didn't realize how high the cost would be."

Omar smiled wickedly. "This is only the beginning."

Waleed grabbed a knife, a bunch of carrots, and his laptop, and they both took the stairs that led to the roof. As they ascended, Waleed thought about the time he'd last snuck up to this rooftop with Sireen. It had been quite a while. Too long. In fact, it seemed almost like it had happened in a different lifetime. Yet the memories were scattered everywhere. Whenever he tried to forget, the jasmine tree would remind him. The caged pigeons remembered, too.

The tree called to him, so when they reached the roof, Waleed went to the edge and grabbed a few jasmine flowers, taking in their scent. The memories flooded his mind as he started kissing the petals. She was really gone, he realized. She wouldn't come back. She hadn't even sent him a letter or called him once. The moment of sorrow this caused him seemed to stretch on forever.

At the sound of the first voices rising in protest, he pulled himself together and sat next to Omar. Then, reflexively, he opened his laptop and logged on to Facebook. He was surprised to find a new message in his inbox. His heart leapt when he saw that it was from Sireen.

Waleed,
You may not want to hear from me at this time, and I understand that. I have misled you. I hurt your feelings. I don't expect to be your friend again, let alone more than your friend, but I want you to forgive me. Every day, I see death twenty times, and He looks me in the eyes and says, "It's not your turn yet." One day, it will be my turn, and I don't want to die knowing that I have hurt someone as pure and honest as you.

Waleed, I've seen more in the past few weeks of my life than most people see in their lifetimes. I saw people on the streets calling to be freed from slavery, and I joined them. That's all we did; we sang songs of freedom and called for liberty. I saw hundreds of people shot before my eyes. I've seen more blood and fire than a seasoned soldier. I saw houses being shelled and entire families massacred in cold blood. I became a refugee in my own right. I moved in with a family who offered me safe haven. Most of them have died. Only two girls remain from that family. The others were either murdered or died due to the lack of everything. There is no food, no water, no electricity, no medicines. There are no doctors, as they're either killed or kidnapped.

I was told that our house has been destroyed, as well, and I have no idea where my parents might be. I know they're alive; I feel it. The city is burning and its population is dying. There is nothing left here in Daraa. Even the trees and rocks are destroyed. No one can enter or leave without risking their life. I know I will die soon, too. I've been trying to send you this message for weeks, but there is no internet connection except in random places close to the Jordanian border.

Waleed, forgive me for all that I have done and said and for what I'm about to say now. I want you to know that I never misled you. I love you, I've always loved you, and I never lied to you. I was in an arranged engagement with a criminal from the armed forces. I thought he was a good man, but he turned out to be the devil.

I have to go now. The ground is shaking, and I think there are tanks approaching the area. Please promise me that you won't give up the cause. Daraa has decided to die so that Syria can live.

From Daraa, with love,
Sireen

"Waleed, come help me set up the camera so I can record the protests."

"I'm coming," Waleed replied, still in a state of disbelief.

"What's the matter? You look like you've seen a Jinni."

"I have," he started, but before he could continue, a soft breeze carrying the voices of freedom seekers interrupted him. "They're here."

"*Yalla* quickly. Set the camera for me. Remember, I can only use one hand." Omar guided Waleed on how to set up the camera so that it was high enough to get a good view, yet low enough to avoid being seen by snipers on rooftops.

Thousands of people, mostly young from what Waleed could see, started pouring into the streets of the Baba Amro neighborhood. "The people want to overthrow the regime!" they clearly stated. As always, the protests started joyfully and full of satire in what had become a weekly carnival. There were flowers and balloons everywhere. Different colored posters highlighted different messages. The crowd would start with singing and humming in a disarrayed fashion, then slowly unite under a popular song calling for freedom and liberty. Slowly protest leaders would emerge and start organizing the chants and slogans. It wasn't difficult to identify those leaders, making them the snipers' favorites every time. People with cameras or large posters were also attractive targets for snipers.

"Omar, get down!" Waleed said, ducking behind the low lip of the rooftop. "I see snipers."

"I've survived two shots, don't worry. Those snipers are retarded."

"Get down!" Waleed repeated as he forced his friend to his knees.

"Fine, fine. Am I still getting a good view with my camera?"

"Yes! It's not as good, but it's good enough."

"Where are the snipers?" Omar asked.

Waleed slowly peeked his head over the edge. "There's one on the rooftop right next to us, and I can see at least two more on nearby roofs."

"Are they shooting?"

"Omar, your arm got shot, not your ears. Do you hear any shooting?"

"No."

"Okay, then no. But hey, watch! He's getting his rifle ready. I guess he's waiting for something. In fact, now I see three others, and they're all in a position, ready to shoot."

"Those bastards!" Omar exclaimed as he squeezed the knife in his hand.

Waleed eyed the knife. "What if I threw your knife at the nearby sniper? It might save a few lives from his evil."

"Absolutely not."

"Why not?"

Omar fixed him with a steady gaze. "This is what the regime wants. Our revolution is a peaceful revolution—white like snow and peaceful like a dove."

"So it's better to let them shoot at us with no cost?"

"It's not going to be easy. It's going to be a long and painful road, but that's the power of our message. When people see that we're peaceful and the regime is violent, they will join our cause."

"You know that's not what they did in Libya."

"But that's what they did in Tunisia and Egypt."

"They got lucky! That's not how revolutions work!"

"Waleed, if you want to throw the knife, then go ahead and start you own violent movement, but don't say you're part of this revolution. We're a peaceful movement. You think I didn't have the urge to kill someone when I held Rami dead in my arms? He was much more than a friend to me, but I pushed those feelings away for the greater good of the cause."

A sudden anger came to Waleed at the thought that his friend was accusing him of being incapable of sticking to the peaceful revolution. To cool down, he listened to the protestors for a time.

"Shame, oh shame!" the crowd started singing. "Shooting unarmed people, oh shame."

"You see?" Omar said, looking at Waleed with a victorious stare.

The crowd went on chanting that popular song before blending into Homs's favorite revolutionary song:

"Homs, land of peace . . .
You've got the courage of revolutionaries.
You've got the fire of free men . . .
You gave birth to Martyrs.
Your pulse gave rise to the Waleed . . .
Victorious and free.
By God, by God . . ."

Then one would raise the call for Muslim prayer on a loudspeaker, and another would ring a bell resembling the Christian call for prayer in a sign of national unity. Waleed could sense that the crowd's morale was high. The atmosphere was that of young children running around in a circus. The snipers were all holding their positions and their fire, apparently waiting for some invisible signal.

"The people want to overthrow the regime!" the crowd chanted.

That was the magic word. The killer rain of bullets started falling from the rooftops and onto the protestors in the streets. The message was simple: anyone who thought of overthrowing the regime would be shot. Then came the voice of an army officer yelling, "Soldier, start shooting at the terrorists immediately!"

Apparently one of the soldiers was not obeying orders to shoot at his own people.

"Soldier, you have ten seconds to follow orders or be shot."

Omar quickly changed the angle of his camera toward the defiant soldier. Waleed watched over his shoulder as his friend zoomed in as much as possible. The image was blurry, but the soldier was clearly struggling to make a decision as he anxiously shuffled his rifle toward his face and away from it.

"Waleed," Omar whispered, "are you still good at baseball?"

"Sure," Waleed said with a curious smile.

"You see that soldier on the rooftop next to us?"

Waleed nodded.

"He's looking away. Throw the carrot at him."

"Throw the carrot?" Waleed asked in disbelief. "I'd rather throw the knife."

Omar glared at him. "You're not understanding me. Throw the carrot. This will create a distraction that will hopefully allow the good soldier over here to defect."

"This is so silly," Waleed said as he gathered a carrot in his right hand and prepared to throw. "Why don't we just use one of your pigeons as a distraction?"

"Over my dead body you'll touch my pigeons. Just do it."

Waleed squeezed the large carrot he held, lifted one knee up slightly, fixed his imaginary baseball cap, and threw the carrot toward the back of the soldier's head. He scored a direct hit. The soldier immediately panicked, started shooting in all directions, then picked up a loudspeaker.

"Sir, someone is attacking me," he shouted.

"Try to identify the source, soldier," the officer replied, sounding worried.

Waleed and Omar glued themselves to the floor, holding their breath in unison. The soldier kept shooting randomly, eventually hitting their roof with a few shots so aimless that he clearly didn't see them.

"It must have been some stupid kid," the officer said. "Get back to mission."

The only sound now was the protest as Waleed strained to listen for further orders from the officer.

"Soldiers, one of you is missing," the officer said finally. "That idiot who wouldn't shoot. Shoot him as soon as you see him!"

Waleed and Omar smiled, giving each other a high-five as they lay prone on the rooftop.

"What will happen to him now?" Waleed whispered.

"You don't have to whisper," Omar said. "There's thousands of people yelling and people shooting. As for our friend the defector, here's what happens to him now: he stops killing people!"

"But can't he protect people by shooting at those who shoot them?"

"We're a peaceful movement!"

"God, fine!" Waleed yielded.

The two young men rolled over onto their backs. Waleed could see that Omar was straining to look at his camera, probably checking to make sure it was still collecting decent images.

"Omar, I want to talk to you about Sireen . . ."

"Now? Can't this wait till we're not glued to the floor and within kissing distance of each other? People are getting killed down there."

"No. I have to tell you. She sent me a Facebook message. She's stuck in Daraa. It sounds like things are much worse there than here. There's shelling everywhere. The people are starving to death under the siege. She also said she loves me."

Omar grumbled. "I don't trust this girl. Maybe she's Mukhabarat."

"And maybe you are, and maybe I am. The bottom line is that I believe her and want to help her."

"Great," Omar said with a wry look. "Are you going to save her using your helicopter or your armored tank?"

"Keep mocking. I love her, and now I know she loves me. I'm not going to waste this chance. I'm going to find her."

"You're insane. Listen to yourself." Omar rose slowly to peer over the edge of the roof. "The shooting has stopped for now. Let's run downstairs and upload the videos on YouTube before they start shooting again."

Waleed helped Omar get up, and they ran madly downstairs before a random bullet could find its way to them.

~~~

The soldiers never resumed the shooting that day; they must have been terrified of the idea of more defections. The *Shabeeha* groups finally awakened from their slumber. Thousands of armed civilians were brought from the loyalist villages and scattered across Syria. That day in Homs, the *Shabeeha* took over the killing and shooting until the protesters dispersed. Two changes were slowly becoming the new status quo in Syria. First, the revolution was certainly growing in size and resilience. Second, the sectarian monster known as the *Shabeeha* was taking on a life of its own, becoming more hateful and murderous with each sunrise. The monster that had been locked up in a faraway place would be resurrected for the first time since 1982.

Chapter 18
1982

<>

Everyone in Syria knew the year 1982 very well. Everyone in Syria who had witnessed the events of that year was changed forever. Not only people, but also the entire structure of a city changed, and the meaning of being Syrian changed forever. That year, Syria, the historically rebellious country that had challenged entire empires, was forced into submission—not mere surrender, but complete submission. That year had an impact on the collective consciousness of the Syrian nation that no other event had.

One witness to the carnage was a young woman named Sabah. It was February 2, 1982, and the place was none else but Hama.

For several months, the city had been under a devastating siege. Nothing was allowed in or out. Tanks and government forces had shut the city from the world entirely. There was no electricity, water, or basic food necessities. It was the Muslim holy month of Ramadan, and people would fast all day and have nothing to eat or drink at sunset. The city had been under heavy shelling for weeks. Entire neighborhoods were destroyed; hospitals were bombed; and the city was in a state of chaos. By February 2, all forms of normal life had ceased to exist. Just when the people of Hama thought their nightmare was over, it turned out that it had just begun.

Sabah was twenty-two. She had fallen in love with a man from Damascus while she was getting her physics degree at Damascus University. Loay was his name. After graduation, she explained to him that she wanted to go back to visit her family in Hama and tell them about him. However, with checkpoints everywhere, curfews, and a killer siege, she was still stuck in Hama six months later. Normally this would have been a blessing for her, but not under those circumstances.

One of the main points of conflict between Sabah and Loay was that she insisted that he should move back with her to Hama. As one of the oldest cities in the world, Hama used to be a little heaven on Earth. With the beautiful Assy River running through its green hills, and with its ancient norias turning like guardians of time, it had the sweet smell of the past and boomed with life and joy. Children in Hama were envied by kids everywhere in the country. Not only did they get to play with the norias all the time, they also had the luxury of having the best sweets and desserts ever made by man. The ice creams and delicious cheeses made in Hama were a major tourist attraction for Syrians around the country. It was every kid's dream to take a picture of himself holding a cone of Hamwi ice cream or its most famous *halawet jibin* [sweet cheese] while standing next to a noria. The norias dated back to the forty-eighth century B.C., and many ancient myths warned that one day they would be floating on rivers of blood.

That night in 1982, Sabah and her family fled the heavy shelling on the neighborhood and went to hide in a shelter. Their neighborhood was completely erased, and almost everyone they knew had been buried in their own homes. Sabah then left the shelter against her parents' will and went back to see what had happened to their building. She found that there was no building, only stones mixed with blood and flesh. This would be the least of the horrors she would see that day.

While she was gone, the army swept into the city and found the civilian shelter. Everyone in the shelter was executed: her mother, her father, her brother and two sisters. Sabah could have been one of those, but it was her destiny to live on. She started running through her city, crying and shaking in fear. She ran toward the soccer stadium, where she found at least three hundred bodies that had been tossed into a massive pile. She tried to seek refuge in a mosque, but there were soldiers there that had taken dozens of men hostage.

They locked the mosque with dozens of men inside and set it on fire. Sabah watched from the relative safety of a darkened alley across the street. Several norias were destroyed as thousands of dead bodies were dumped into the unsuspecting Assy River, turning it red like wine.

Before Sabah knew what was happening, a soldier spotted her, grabbed her, and locked her up in a van full of civilians and soldiers. Every few minutes, the van would stop and a different soldier would execute a few civilians. Sabah slowly came to realize that this was like a training session for the soldiers before they arrived at the large massacre areas.

"Your turn," one soldier said to the next as he handed Sabah to him.

When the van stopped, the soldier dragged her down the street and pulled her behind a tree. In one moment, her entire life flashed before her eyes. More than anything, she wished that there was a way she could communicate with Loay before she died.

"I have orders to kill you," the soldier said.

"Please, don't," she said through her tears.

"It's up to me whether you live or die."

"Please, don't kill me."

"Fine," he said, a strange smile parting his lips. "You look like a good girl. How about I make you a deal?" Wickedly, he stripped her of her clothes.

Forty thousand people were killed in a city with a population of just over three hundred thousand. The rest were taken prisoner. Only a lucky few were able to flee. Sabah fled to nearby Salamiyeh, where an Ismaili family sheltered her. Word spread that the regime was targeting the survivors of the Hama massacres, and so Sabah changed her name to Sarah and tried to keep a low profile. About a year later, she fled to Damascus to find her beloved Loay. She was told that he had gone to Hama during the massacre, looking for a girl, and never came back. Ever since, even the mention of Hama or a massacre was punishable by death, and people would only refer to the worst crime in Syrian history as "the Events."

Sarah eventually married a Homsi man and settled in Homs, and for almost thirty years, she had avoided even the mention of her beloved city, Hama, until that day. . .

~~~

"Sarah, are you sure you want to watch this?" her husband Mohammad asked. He hugged her as her eyes flooded with tears, then kissed her on her cheek. "It's okay. This had to happen."

"I can't believe it," she said as the couple watched Al Jazeera broadcasting images from Hama taken by individuals on the streets. "I'm so proud of them. Look at them!" Hama had grown in size and population over the years, and almost half a million had gathered in Hama's main square known as Assy Square. That was the first time in over thirty years that Hama had come back to life, like a phoenix rising from the ashes. It was astonishing that a generation born out of the massacre was willing to stand on its feet against the regime. Large silk banners decorated the norias, the river, and the square. There, not only was Hama reborn, but the revolution took a new life that day.

Sarah watched as a young man named Ibrahim Al-Qashoosh stood in front of the hundreds of thousands of Hamwis and millions of Syrians behind their televisions and computers and began to sing what became the song of the revolution:

"Yalla, leave, Bashar
Come on, leave, Bashar
Bashar, you're a liar
And you can't give speeches
Freedom is at our doorsteps
Come on, leave, Bashar
Bashar, damn you
And damn anyone who supports you
We can't look at your face anymore
Come on, leave, Bashar
Bashar, stop pacing
Your blood will be spilled in Hama
Your sins won't be forgiven
Come on, leave Bashar . . ."

The song went on as the tears poured down Sarah's face. She could hear the voices of her dead parents, her sisters, and her childhood friends. She could see their spirits hovering over the crowds. Hama had come back from the dead; this was nothing short of a miracle. She grabbed her husband's hand and closed her eyes as memories of Loay came back to her. She had never loved anyone the way she had loved him, but she had wanted to forget and start a new life. God had given her three beautiful boys, and that had become her life.

She got up from the couch and went to her jewelry box. Inside, she kept all the jewelry that she had accumulated over the years, including her diamond and Turquoise engagement ring. There was also a small drawer she had kept locked for decades. She felt it was time to open it. As she slid the drawer open, she reached for an old picture older than her eldest son. It was her, and she was holding her father's hand. In her other hand, she held a Hamwi ice cream cone. A large, beautiful noria loomed in the background. The picture was taken in Assy Square years before Hama died, and decades before it came back to life. She was somewhat soothed by the background music that her son Sami was playing on his guitar.

Someone knocked on the door. She quickly put the picture back into hiding, wiped away her tears, and rushed to the door.

"Khalid, *ahlain* [welcome], darling!" she said, hugging and kissing her eldest son.

"How are you, Mother?" Khalid asked with a terse nod. Without waiting for an answer, he turned to Mohammad. "How are you, Father?"

"We're fine. How have you been? How are things in Damascus?"

"Damascus is simmering. Qadam and Qaboon and several other neighborhoods are having a massive protest movement. Al-Midan is practically out of government control in spite of all the killing and arrests. But it's not like Homs! What's happening here?"

Mohammad turned and swept his hand toward the living room, inviting his son to sit down. Sarah rushed to make some tea, but did her best not to make so much noise that she could not hear the conversation from the kitchen.

"It seems that Homs has made up its mind never to go back to slavery at any cost," Mohammad said.

"Any cost?"

"Yes, son. Even if they bury the city alive, they won't be able to rule over us again. Homsis are very stubborn."

"Khalid?" Sarah called from the kitchen, interrupting the men. "How's your brother?"

"He's fine, I think. Isn't he here?"

Sarah set the teapot down on the boiler, her heart racing as she entered the living room. "What? I thought he went to stay with you in Damascus to do some kind of training."

"He visited me for a week only, and then said he was going back to Homs."

Sarah sat on the edge of the sofa and covered her mouth with her hand, a deathly feeling creeping up her spine. "Mohammad," she said, her eyes welling over with tears.

"It's fine," Mohammad said, but she had known him long enough to see when he was lying. "There's just some confusion. We'll figure it out."

"You mean Waleed isn't here?" Khalid asked, arching an eyebrow.

A moment of silence and brainstorming followed.

"Omar!" Sarah suggested, relieved by the thought. "Call Omar."

She watched nervously as Khalid reached for his phone and did as his mother suggested.

"Hello, Omar," he said after a few seconds. "I'm fine, how about yourself? . . . Yes, I just got back today. I'll tell you all about Damascus later. Omar, do you know where Waleed might be? . . . No, he's not in Damascus . . . You don't know?"

"Give me the phone," Sarah ordered, and when her son ignored her, she grabbed the phone from his hand.

"Where is Waleed, Omar?"

There was a long pause. "I'm sorry, ma'am. I just don't know."

"Don't say you don't know. I know that you two tell each other everything."

"What can I say?"

A sudden fury rose in Sarah's chest. "*My heart is boiling*, don't you understand?"

No reply.

"Give me your mother. Omar, give me your mother." The tears came to her then, falling over her cheeks in urgent streaks.

"Hello, Om Omar," she said when the familiar voice greeted her. "How are you, darling?"

"As well as can be expected, I suppose."

"Om Omar, for God's sake, I need your help. My son has disappeared." She fought back a sudden sob. "Omar won't tell me where he is."

"Well, I can assure you that I will press Omar further to see if he has anything to say about this."

"Thank you, darling."

"I will call you when I know more."

A long sigh of relief escaped Sarah's lips. "I'll be waiting."

When she returned Khalid's phone to him, he was glaring at her. "Mother, you're really making a *dome out of a pimple*. I'm sure he doesn't know, and I'm sure Waleed is somewhere safe. It's not like Homs is safe anyway."

She ignored her son and remained silent, drowned in her own thoughts and memories. A few minutes later, the phone rang. It was Omar's mother again. Sarah snatched the phone from Khalid and answered.

"How are you, Om Omar?"

"I should be asking that of you," came the worried reply.

"I'm calm. Just tell me what you know, please. Do you know where he is?"

"It took some doing, but I got Omar to admit that your son is traveling to Daraa."

"Why Daraa?" There was a moment of painful silence as Sarah started getting agitated and anxious. "Om Omar, please ask your son."

She never could have anticipated the answer.

"Thank you so much, Om Omar. Come visit us soon. Bye."

"Mohammad!" Sarah called as she sat on the sofa and started weeping.

"What's the matter, darling? Don't stress yourself like that."

"Stress myself? Didn't you hear the conversation? Your son is on his way to Daraa! What have I done, God, to deserve this? Haven't I been through enough in my life?"

"Why is he going to Daraa?"

"For a girl. Your son, of course, wants to be the hero and fight the entire Syrian army and Mukhabarat to save her. He couldn't care less about how this will make us feel or about his future or about anything." She pressed her hands to her face, weeping into them.

"He'll be fine, Sarah. Calm yourself."

"No, he won't. No, he won't. You don't know those people like I know them. Their hearts are filled with hatred. You don't know anything. You didn't live through Hama. None of you did. I did!"

"Darling, it's not 1982 anymore. Times have changed. It's the twenty-first century. Governments can't commit genocide anymore without consequences."

"Oh yeah? Who's going to stop them?"

"Darling, the civilized world will intervene. The Americans, the Europeans, Turkey, many Arab countries. Syria is not an island. Besides, the Soviet Union is gone now. There is no one to sponsor world massacres and dictators."

Sarah pulled away from her husband, turning her back on him as she moved down to the other side of the sofa. Such was her anguish that when she caught a glimpse of Khalid still sitting in the recliner, it startled her to remember that her eldest son was still with them.

"You're too simplistic," Sarah continued. "He wanted to participate in protests and risk his life. I said okay. He wanted to secretly organize things with his revolutionary friends. I said okay. Now he's throwing himself in the middle of a war zone, and he doesn't even carry a stone to defend himself."

"Mom," Khalid said, sounding exasperated, "it's a peaceful revolution. I'm sure the regime will be gone before he even reaches Daraa. Relax."

"The regime will be gone? What regime? You think those gangsters and killers will give up their billions that easily? You think a few protests here and there will wake up their hidden conscience? You don't understand. You just don't."

"What do you want us to do, Mom? Just accept living in slavery forever? Have our children born into slavery like you had yours?"

"Don't talk to your mother like that," Mohammad barked. "You don't understand what you're talking about. Our time was different. There was no international community, there was no media, and no one even knew about what happened in 1982 until months after it was over."

"You really think so, Mohammad?" she asked, turning to look at him skeptically. "Trust me, they knew everything. Everyone knew. Everyone heard our screams and pleas. You can't hide something that large. But we don't have blond hair and blue eyes, so no one cared. We don't bleed oil or gas, so no one cared. And no one cares now. Syrians will protest for months and maybe more. They'll be shot by the dozens and maybe even hundreds every day. This battle is larger than you can imagine." She closed her eyes as she started getting flashbacks from a conversation she had had with her father years ago when she was still idealistic and optimistic.

"The larger the peaceful movement grows," she recited to her son, quoting her father, "the more savage they will become, and the more hatred and envy they will unleash. Soon, everyone will be forced to carry arms to defend themselves." She opened her eyes to see that his head hung low. "At that point, they will not hesitate to use their tanks and airplanes and even their chemical weapons to kill what can be killed. And if you think that anyone will come to the rescue, know that you are very wrong. There is no oil in Syria, so there is no money here. Just know that this will be the largest fight since the dawn of Syria, and if you think you're ready for it, then may God be on your side."

When she had finished, she stormed up the stairs to her room and locked the door. She sat down with tears flooding her memories. Fate was indeed ironic. Loay had died trying to save her from the savagery of the regime, and now her son was doing the same for a woman he loved. Despite the parallel, Sarah was desperate to stop her son.

With nothing left to do, she went down on her knees and prayed. "*Ya Rabbi* [Oh Lord], I beg you, keep my boy in your eyes and keep yourself in his heart and mind. *Ya Rabbi*, I've been through sorrows that no soul can bear, and I've seen evil that no human eyes have seen. Don't let my boy go through what I have endured. If you believe that those kids are up to this fight, please support them with all your might. Don't let the atrocities of Hama be repeated. *Ya Rabbi*, we have put up with poverty, humiliation, and injustice to protect our children's lives, and our children have decided to give up their lives voluntarily. If we were wrong in our judgment, please forgive us and have mercy on us and on our children. Amen."

Chapter 19

The Gold Cross

Being the birthplace of Christ's mother tongue, it was natural for Syria to have one of the most crucial roles in spreading the Christian message early on. More than seventy saints and five popes had come from Syria. In the entire world, only fifteen thousand people speak the Western Aramaic tongue of Jesus. All of them live in three villages in Syria: Maloula, Bakha, and Jabiddin. Those are the last Samurais of the tongue of Christ. In that sense, the answer for those who ask, "What would Jesus have done about Syria?" becomes a no-brainer. He would have pushed principal ahead of politics and economics.

It had been a while since the world had seen such leaders. It had been years since American president Ronald Reagan stood before the Soviet "evil empire" and demanded that they tear down the Berlin Wall. But times had changed, and the West had adopted a new policy of leading from behind. To pacifists, this was a stance long overdue, but to the more helpless countries in the world, leading from behind was little more than an oxymoron that gave the West an excuse to avoid any responsibility on the world stage.

For months, the world simply ignored the daily slaughter in Syria. Europe was drowned in its financial crisis and couldn't be bothered. The Arab world, secretly hoping to bury the Arab Spring in Syria, kept silent. Russia, China, and Iran were actively supporting the Syrian regime in its genocide. America, meanwhile, wished the people of Syria good luck and gave them an ice-cold shoulder. And while everybody led from behind, the unarmed civilians of Syria were pushed to the front lines against a vicious army equipped with everything from air power to chemical weapons.

Meanwhile, the anti-regime protests had reached an unprecedented magnitude. For the first time, the collective number of people participating had reached the millions. Hama was essentially liberated. The atmosphere in the city was that of an everlasting carnival, much like the way the city had been decades ago. American Ambassador Robert Ford visited the city during one of its routine demonstrations. He was greeted with

roses and olive branches, and he attested to the people's claim that there was indeed no armed rebellion in the city, but simply a peaceful movement demanding change.
    —*Syria: A History in Blood* by Celine Dubois

September 9, 2011
Deaths: 3,300

<>

Waleed rode the protest wave across the country, hoping it would carry him to his beloved. He had been slowly shifting locations while trying to be careful not to show up on any government radar. His strategy was to keep a low profile and move in slow but fixed steps toward Daraa. Getting to Damascus was not a big challenge, but moving from the city to rural Damascus was a different story. Rural Damascus had become a main opposition stronghold, as it had been historically. It was the main site from which the resistance movement operated against the French in the past, and the Romans before them. Rural Damascus was indeed the true keeper of the Gates of Damascus. As Waleed shuffled between the rural towns, he tried to reunite with Sireen in cyberspace whenever internet was available.

By late July, he had safely reached the town of Daraya. He told some of the locals about his quest, and a middle-aged man named Loay invited him to stay at his apartment. Like many Damascene, rising prices, unemployment, and government harassment had pushed Loay out of the capital and into the suburbs. He provided Waleed with everything he needed during his stay, from food to internet. Waleed told him about his quest to find love in the war-torn city of Daraa. Loay shared his stories, as well. He told Waleed that he had never married after losing the woman he loved during the Hama massacre of 1982. He had never found love again, and he therefore strongly encouraged Waleed to risk everything he had to reunite with his beloved.

That day, Waleed was lucky enough to be able to talk to Sireen on Skype. He thought she looked older, more exhausted, and yet more passionate than ever, but then, so did he whenever he looked in the mirror. He read her poetry at her request, but it wasn't Nizar's or Motanabbi's. It was his own.

"The shine in your eyes,
Like angels of the morning
Stealing my heart into heaven

When my heartbeats rise
With a touch of your fingers
My soul reaches cloud number seven . . ."

He started his first attempt at reading his own poetry as he watched Sireen's tears dance lovingly over her eyes. When he had finished, she told him about the horror, pain, and courage she had seen in Daraa. She shared with him stories about the family of a man named Yousef, about her missing parents, and about what she had witnessed at the Omari mosque. They both kissed the camera and promised each other to stay alive another day.

Meanwhile, the news was that the way back to Homs had become just as dangerous as the way forward to Daraa. Waleed had no option but to keep pushing forward toward the heart of Daraa. The Assad regime had declared war on Latakia, Hama, and Der El-Zor in defiance of warnings from Turkey and the United States not to attack Hama, given its historical symbolism. Waleed read about a siege similar to that of Daraa falling over Hama, heavy weapons running the shelling. The city succumbed to heavy bombing as tanks took control of Assy Square and occupied both cities. Hundreds died in the process.

In bits and pieces, Waleed learned that a tight siege formed around the cities, particularly Hama. Many had called Hama "a red line" that would lead to aid from the West, but they were wrong. The Syrian navy launched a full military operation against the beaches and resorts of the coastal city of Latakia. Der-el-Zor to the east paid a similar price as Russia, and Iran encouraged their ally to do all he could to crush the rebellion. Government forces continued pounding the cities, hoping to buoy the regime on the rising tide of blood. There were a few condemnations here and there, but no one wanted to be part of this mess. The Syrians were on their own.

In spite of that, the protest movement continued to grow and spread undeterred. It was notable how fired up rural Damascus had become. As Waleed traveled those areas, it was almost impossible to find one town there that wasn't sympathetic to the cause of the revolution. It was time to keep moving. Waleed said his goodbyes to Loay and pushed on toward the defiant suburbs of Daraa. Avoiding snipers, checkpoints, and vigilant soldiers had become a part of his new daily routine.

Life in the suburbs had become a living nightmare. Everything fragmented more and more as time went on, like a sheet of glass under a hailstorm. Towns were disconnected from their main cities, neighborhoods were separated by checkpoints, and roads were often blocked at multiple sites. Buying bread had become a daily risk the brave had to take. Water and electricity were scarce in areas deemed unfriendly to the regime in Damascus. The deeper Waleed went in his journey, the more dangerous it became, and the more skills and support he needed from his surroundings. Moving closer to Daraa City was a painful task. Almost every big building had three things in common: a water tank that had been shot from below, broken windows, and a sniper on nearly every rooftop.

Waleed's main strategy was to stay alive, travel by way of short night journeys, and use Skype whenever internet was available. By mid-August, he finally reached the town of Jasem, named after Jasem, son of Aram, son of Sham, son of Noah. This town was a fountain of revolutionaries thirty kilometers north of Daraa. Hundreds of its men and women had died trying to break the siege on Daraa. It was apparent to all the locals that Waleed was not from the area, as he persistently failed at mastering the Horani Syrian accent of the area. Horan, meaning "the dark land" or "the cave land" in Aramaic, was the southern area of Syria bordering Jordan and Israel. It was given this name after the color of its fertile soil. The locals believed that it was the blood of its martyrs that gave their soil its distinctive color. They were very supportive of Waleed's exodus, but somewhat cautious just in case he turned out to be a government spy. He finally met three young men who offered him safe haven, and more importantly, internet access.

~~~

"Sireen, can you hear me?" he asked over Skype.

Her eyes lit up like fire. "Yes, I can, but I need to keep my voice down. I think there might be some Shabeeha nearby. Tell me, how are you?"

"I'm almost there, Sireen. Hang on. We'll meet again soon."

"I still don't understand why you're doing this. A part of me can't wait to see you, but a part of me thinks this is a stupid idea."

"I'm doing this because I love you." He smiled. "So there's two stupid ideas for you."

"And what do I do if you get killed on the way?"

"I won't. I didn't come this far to die."

"If only it was that easy, Waleed. You really haven't seen what I've seen. Suppose you make it here alive. Then what? It's even more dangerous inside the city."

"Once I find you, I'll get you out of there, and we'll get back to Homs."

"And what if we die on the way back?"

"Then at least we die together."

She looked at him with sad but resolute eyes. "The internet connection here has been terrible. We used to be able to get some connection from Jordan, but even that is scarce. I think they shut it down or something."

"Maybe. No one wants us to succeed, darling. It would send a strong message to all the oppressed people of the world. Our freedom is a threat."

"Is there anyone on our side at all?"

"Perhaps some Gulf countries. Turkey, I think. Maybe France and Britain. No one knows for sure. What I do know is that a lot of countries are against us."

"It's terrible here, Waleed. The situation is catastrophic. Food and water have run out. Nothing is abundant but death. Everything is dying. People I know are dying. People I grew up with—*real* people. People are just waiting for their turn to die."

"One day we'll look back at this and be grateful it happened. I promise.

Forget about that for now, darling. We need to focus on . . ." Waleed stopped as the internet connection died. "Sireen . . . Sireen . . . can you hear me? Damn this internet!"

"You want to eat something, brother?" asked Jaffar, one of the three men hosting him.

He turned back to see his new friend with the scraggly beard wearing a quizzical look. "I would really appreciate that, Jaffar."

"I'm sorry we don't have much variety, but we've got yogurt and green olives."

"That is more than enough," Waleed said, trying to sound happy despite his disappointment about the loss of the internet connection. "I am so grateful."

Jaffar gave a thoughtful nod. "Eli is preparing tea for us, as well." He stepped aside. "Oh look. Here comes the tea."

Eli entered the small breakfast room where Waleed was sitting. Waleed cleared his laptop off the table as Eli passed around the small glasses of tea, Jaffar set the table, and Noah arrived with some fresh bread.

"So, what do you guys think of the course of the revolution so far?" Waleed asked, trying to get his mind unstuck from the lost vision of Sireen.

"It's stunning," Jaffar said as he tore himself a slice of the bread. "I never thought we'd make it this far."

"But we're still miles away from our goal," Waleed said sadly.

"We are indeed," Jaffar agreed, "but at least we have a goal now. Right, Eli?"

"Yes," Eli said in a low-pitched voice. "At least the people finally drank some Nescafe."

"Nescafe?" Waleed wondered.

"Yes, Doctor," Eli said with a wink. "I mean they're waking up from sleep at last."

Waleed chuckled. "More like waking up from the dead. They're getting CPR, I would say."

"CPR?" Eli asked, his pencil-thin eyebrow raised.

"You know," Waleed said, mimicking the action with his hands. "Chest compressions . . . breathing . . . never mind."

Jaffar seemed suddenly fixated on the cross Eli wore from a chain around his neck. It was large and golden, an eye-catching symbol indeed. "Eli, can I ask you a question?"

"I know what you're going to ask," Eli said.

"So go ahead and answer if you don't mind."

Eli shrugged. "The Christians are divided. There are Christian *Shabeeha* just like there are Sunni and Alawite *Shabeeha*, but I believe most of us deep inside support this revolution. How could we not? Jesus Christ was the ultimate rebel. But most of us are afraid of the regime's retribution if we say otherwise. So when people think that Christians are supporters of the regime, I get angry. What's the largest group of people subjected to exile in this country? It's us, the Christians."

"Don't you fear the alternative?" Jaffar asked as Waleed helped himself to some of the aromatic tea.

"It's hard to imagine a worse alternative than mass murder. You know, we were all Syrian thousands of years before I was Christian and you were Muslim. This fight is a fight for all of Syria. Yes, our cross is going to be large and our path of suffering will be long, but Syria will resurrect from the dead."

"Why are you so silent, Noah?" Jaffar asked.

Waleed looked at his third host wide-eyed.

"Shhh!" Noah replied, killing the conversation.

"What's the matter?" Eli asked.

"Someone's here," he said, and soon enough, everyone understood what he was talking about.

The footsteps were faint to Waleed's ears at first, but then there was an unmistakable shuffling coming from the landing just outside the front door. It sounded like a small group of men readying to break down the door.

"Eli, take any laptops, posters, everything to the closet," Noah ordered. "Jaffar, hide your friend."

The guys rushed to follow the orders as Waleed struggled to determine what they wanted from him. Before long, he found himself shoved into the closet with all the valuables. It was dark inside, but through the wooden slats, he could see and hear everything going on in the kitchen and the edge of the living room beyond.

It wasn't a minute later that the door crashed open under a heavy blow. Waleed held his breath as his three hosts fell silent and eight armed men in military uniforms stormed the apartment with their guns and rifles pointing in every direction.

"Stand with your arms up, you dogs," one of them yelled.

The three men followed the command without saying a word.

"What are your names?" asked another of the armed men. From his tenor and his uniform, this one appeared to be their commander.

"Jaffar."

"Noah."

"Eli."

"Eli?" the commander mocked.

"Yes, sir."

"What kind of whore-son's name is that?"

Waleed gritted his teeth, hoping that Eli would know enough to remain silent, lest he agitate them. To his relief, Eli kept his mouth shut.

"Is that a cross on your neck?"

"Yes, sir."

"Is it made of gold?"

"Yes, sir."

"Give it to me. I can use it to buy some *arak*."

Waleed tensed, straining to listen. Eli didn't move.

"Are you deaf? Give me the damn cross."

Slowly Eli reached for the cross around his neck. Waleed wondered at the significance of the trinket. Perhaps it was a family heirloom. Perhaps it was something dearer to him than gold or even the faith that it represented. Waleed's guess proved correct when Eli refused to remove the necklace.

The commander was clearly getting angry. He pointed his gun at Eli and yelled, "You know I can just shoot you and take it." He moved closer to his unflinching target as if to appraise the cross with a more careful eye. "Nice. And it bears inscriptions."

"It says, *Yeshu' Msheeho*," Eli said defiantly, meaning "Jesus Christ" in Aramaic.

An expression of disgust came to the commander. "Damn you and your Msheeho. What language is this? Is it Hebrew, whore-son?"

"No, sir. It's Aramaic. Old Syrian. The tongue of the Messiah."

"What the hell is that? There is no language in Syria except Arabic, you dog. Now give me the damn thing."

Eli ignored the orders. "I can't. You can have my watch instead."

Meanwhile Waleed, who had taken to clutching his laptop, noticed that the internet signal light had come back on. He tried hard to resist the urge, but ultimately he muted his computer and logged on to Skype. His heart quickened when he saw that Sireen was online. Sure enough, she replied when he called her. From the self-portrait window, Waleed could see that the image his laptop projected was simply his face surrounded by darkness. Sireen, meanwhile, was clearly bewildered, but it seemed to Waleed that she understood why he had called and was not speaking. They just stared at each other, exchanging foolish and anxious smiles.

"This is the last time I'm going to order you to give me the damn gold," the soldier said.

"Give it to him," Noah urged.

"So, you are their leader," the commander said.

Waleed tore his eyes away from the laptop just in time to see the commander bearing down on Noah. He glanced at his men and ordered them to take Noah away. Two of them knocked Noah to the ground and began pulling him away by his legs.

"I'm no one's leader!" Noah yelled as his head dragged along the floor.

Waleed's heart went out to him, but there was nothing he could do but stare down at the ghostly, distant image of Sireen and dream of a better day.

~~~

Noah sputtered and hissed as his captors tied his feet to the back of the truck, forcing his face to the ground. One man moved closer and put his foot over his head.

"Where are the weapons?" the man asked.

"There are no weapons!" Noah replied defiantly. "You know that more than anyone."

Noah winced as the man stomped hard on his head. "Don't talk back to me!"

"You asked a question," Noah said, the fear and disbelief running like ice in his veins.

"All right, that's it. Take this man on a tour. That will help him think."

Silence followed, the only sound the men's footsteps tracing away from him. Noah forced his eyes shut as tightly as they would go as the truck's engine roared to life. He knew what would come next, and the helplessness he felt was enough to make him lose all sense of resistance. His muscles went slack and his breathing slowed. This would be the end of him, he knew, and he was ready. Let them drag him through the streets like a tin can. He would not scream.

The resolve left him the moment he felt his body dragged roughly over the pavement. The pain shot through him from below, rock and dirt and solid stone carving into him like a billion dull molars. He screamed. His body bounced and rollicked over the pavement as the truck picked up speed. He felt himself roll as the truck reached the corner and made the turn. As the rough terrain abraded his skin, he pled not for help, but for death to take him. When death refused, he begged his captors.

"Stop!" he cried. "Please!"

Three times around the block, he could no longer feel his face. It was like his head was covered in a thick wet blanket. He could not see. Blood trickled down his throat, stealing his wind and his sense of surroundings. All he knew was the rumble of the truck and the way his body bounced.

~~~

"Stop it!" came the voice from outside the house.

Waleed snapped away from his laptop. He gently opened the closet door just enough to peer around the corner and see through the front door. The soldiers had pulled Eli and Jaffar out to the street, as well, so they could see what had become of Noah.

"Are you talking to me, *Msheeho*?" the commander mocked.

"Sir, there are no weapons," Eli said. "No one has weapons. If we did, we would have used them a long time ago."

Waleed sucked in a breath as the commander stepped closer to Eli.

"Is that so?" the commander said.

"Yes, sir."

"All right. Would you like me to crucify you, like they did to your *Msheeho*?"

"No, sir. I'm just explaining to you."

"I'm not stupid, you know," the commander said.

Before Eli could answer, the rapport of gunfire crackled through the night. Waleed tumbled back into the closet, realizing that the soldier had shot Eli in the head. In his panic, he kicked the closet door shut, the noise carrying through the house in a loud echo. Waleed braced himself, holding his breath as he waited to learn if he had been found out.

"What's in that closet?" someone asked.

"My cat," Jaffar replied, sounding hesitant.

"You know, if you're lying, I will shoot you twelve times. I promise. Why twelve? It's the number of men that had intercourse with your mother before you were born. What's in the closet?"

"My cat, sir."

The officer aimed at the closet door and shot three times. The first bullet missed Waleed. On the laptop, Sireen's eyes opened wide. The second bullet missed Waleed. Sireen started talking frantically, not realizing she was on mute. The third bullet hit Waleed's chest. Blood splashed everywhere, covering the keyboard and the screen. From the self-portrait, Waleed knew that Sireen could see only red.

"Say goodbye to your cat," Waleed heard from outside. "I don't think it has that many lives left."

"It has eight left," Jaffar replied in a crazy burst of defiance.

"You want me to kill you, too?" the commander threatened.

Waleed couldn't hear the reply over his own wheezing breaths.

"I won't," the commander hollered. "Instead, I will leave you alive so that you can go and tell your filthy people about what happened today so they learn not to mess with us. Tell them they need to be very afraid, for we are not afraid to crush them."

With that, the men left the apartment just as suddenly as they had come.

Waleed pushed the closet door open with his foot. He was covered in his own blood, confused, and struggling to breathe. He held his laptop with one hand and tried to stop his own bleeding with the other. He started talking to himself. Jaffar rushed to him and sat him down.

"They shot me, Jaffar."

"It will be fine," he said in a soft, reassuring voice. He took the laptop away from Waleed, looking surprised to find a crying girl staring at him. He looked at her and said, "He will be fine," then closed the laptop. He took his shirt off, ripped it, and wrapped it around Waleed's shoulder tightly. He grabbed Waleed's other hand and told him to press it tightly.

~~~

Jaffar left the house and shut the door behind him. There was a trail of blood from the door stretching all the way to the military truck, which was still visible in the distance. He ran toward them, his tears trailing behind.

"Stop, please! You're killing him."

He managed to get the attention of the soldiers, who found this amusing. They started driving faster and then slowing down to watch Jaffar chase after them.

"Please! This is inhumane. Stop."

They started shooting at the ground to scare him, but he kept running forward. His vision was getting blurry, perhaps due to dehydration or maybe because his eyes were flooded with tears.

"You took everyone else away from me. He's all I've got left. Let him go." He jumped and grabbed Noah's hands.

~~~

Waleed lay on the floor, feeling lightheaded and smiling like a child, with Sireen on the other end of the screen trying to hide her tears. He was still bleeding. He touched the screen with his hand, and Sireen did the same, weeping.

"Darling, don't move a lot," she was saying. "And keep pressing the wound tight. May God paralyze those who did this to you."

"It will be fine. It's just my shoulder." His tongue felt thick and uncooperative.

"They need to take you to a field hospital. Don't go to a real hospital. They might arrest you."

"Sireen . . ." he said as he closed his eyes, feeling weak.

"Waleed! Waleed!" she yelled. He didn't reply. The last thing he heard was the sound of her sobbing.

~~~

The soldiers were getting a great kick out of dragging Noah through the streets of the town and dragging Jaffar along with him as he kept holding his hands tightly. Jaffar slowly pushed himself under Noah by wrapping his arms and legs around his friend's nearly dead body. Their heartbeats united; their blood was mixed; their pain was shared.

"I'm here," Jaffar whispered to Noah. "I won't leave you."

Noah moaned in acknowledgment and in pain.

"God! There is no God but you! Don't abandon us!" Jaffar yelled before he lost consciousness.

The light went from Noah's eyes, as well.

Waleed bled on the floor, unconscious.

Eli was dead, his golden cross stolen.

But Syria's path of suffering had only just begun.

Chapter 20

Russia's Roulette

The sad irony of the Syrian humanitarian crisis was that, whenever the cries out of Syria got louder, the world simply turned the background noise up to avoid hearing it. Some changes did happen internationally, particularly after the savage assault on Hama and the occupation of its public squares by military tanks. The Arabian Gulf countries, especially Qatar and Saudi Arabia, expressed their solidarity with the people of Syria and as a result, the two main Arabic news networks, Al Jazeera and Al Arabiya, took a clearly pro-revolution stance. Syrian activists celebrated the milestone of finally breaking the "media siege" which the regime had imposed.

As more images started pouring out of Syria and getting broadcast on regional and international screens, many new voices began demanding that something be done about it. French president Nicolas Sarkozy and his foreign minister Alain Juppé showed the most interest among the Western countries. Meanwhile, the Russians, sensing the weak American stance on the issue (and not wanting to lose their last ally in the Middle East) were determined to stop any Libya-style intervention in Syria. This was perhaps one of Russia's biggest strategic gambles.

A UN Security Council resolution called for the immediate halt to attacks on civilians, allowing the peaceful assembly of protestors in Syria. Millions of people in Syria and the sympathetic Middle East watched as the votes were cast. Most felt a harsh slap in the face when Russia vetoed the resolution, and China, doing what it does best, copied the Russian action. The honeymoon that Russia had enjoyed with the Arab street, mostly due to its positions on the Israeli-Palestinian conflict, was over. The more images poured out of Syria, the more Russia found itself isolated internationally.

The love affair between the Russians and the Assad dynasty stretched back about half a century, when Syria was a pivotal ally for the Soviet Union during the Cold War. The Russians set up a strategic naval base in the Syrian coastal city of Tartus, from which they helped the Syrian regime establish the world's fourth *largest supply of chemical weapons.*

While the big powers slowly played the dirty game of politics, death and misery rapidly approached the individual men and women of Syria.

—*Syria: A History in Blood* by Celine Dubois

October 4, 2011
Deaths: 3,900

It was hours later. Maybe days or years. It was almost impossible to tell, things were so blurry. It felt like being in a dream, except that it wasn't. There was a laptop. There were soldiers laughing hysterically like hyenas around their prey. His hands and feet were bound with something sharp and painful. He bled from more places than he could count. His pain was tremendous. The laptop screen stared right in his face, the eye of its camera unblinking. It was all too confusing.

He wrenched his eyes open to find that he lay in an open space on a hilltop of some sort. He could see the clear blue sky and could smell the refreshing breeze of southern Syria mixed with tears, blood, and gunpowder. From a distance, he could hear music—not the artificial music made by singers and musicians; this was more natural. This was the music of autumn leaves, migrating birds, sand blowing over the dunes, and even the thrum of Earth's magnetic field. Young men and women joined this ancient Syrian song: "How beautiful freedom is! How beautiful freedom is!" the protestors chanted from far away. "Assad lost his legitimacy." They started rhythmically banging spoons and plates, since most of them could not afford real musical instruments. "With bowls and plates, we will remove the insane man! Down with the Assad regime!"

Bullets.

Silence.

Chants.

Bullets.

Autumn's leaves.

What a melody! Noah thought.

The song helped him pull away from the dreamlike state in which he found himself. As he started joining the real world, the first thing he noticed was that every inch of his body was in severe pain. He closed his eyes firmly, biting his lips from the agony. He discovered that the only things he could move were his head and neck. *Am I paralyzed?* he wondered.

On closer inspection, he realized that he was not lying, but rather standing upright inside a large hole filled with sand up to the level of his neck. His entire body was buried. *But why would they bury me?* he thought, horrified. *I'm not dead.* "I'm alive!" he managed to yell in panic.

"He woke up, sir," came the voice.

"All right, start recording," was the reply. "Our main character is ready." In a moment, there was the shadow of a large man standing over him, blotting out the sun. "What's your name, boy?"

"Noah."

"Noah, what?"

"Noah Al-Hor."

"I was told you are the leader of a terrorist cell."

"No, sir, I'm not." Noah squinted from the sun. "I'm a graphic designer."

"Do you want to live?"

"Yes, sir."

"I know that you have been making anti-regime posters and websites. Your life is in my hands. You know that, right?"

"No, sir." He hacked and spit when the wind blew a gust of sand into his mouth. "It's in God's hands."

Even through the glint of the sun, Noah could see that the officer was shocked. "Do you not understand where you are? You are buried. You are dead. I will finish burying you right now, and there is nothing your God can do about it but watch."

"I will die when it's my time to go, sir."

In the background, the protestors started chanting a strange slogan: "No fly zone! No fly zone! No fly zone!"

"You hear those traitors?" the shadow asked. "They want a no fly zone over Syria. They want foreign powers to come and invade our country."

"They want to be saved from you," Noah said, steeling up his jaw. "You are murderers."

"I don't understand your confidence," the shadow said, sounding almost remorseful as he placed his boot over Noah's head and began to press. "No one is coming to save you. No one! Not the Americans, not the Europeans, not the Arabs, not the Turks. You will remain prone before us until the end of time, and no one will stop us. No foreign troops will dare come here."

Noah winced as he pulled away from the pressure of his captor's heavy boot. "What about the Russians, the Iranians, and Hezbollah? Are those Syrian? Aren't they foreign troops who are here helping you kill Syrians?"

"Damn your God!"

A tear trickled over Noah's cheek. "Why are you doing this? We are all Syrian. This country is large enough for all of us."

"This is Assad's country. It's him or no one. He is your God. You understand?" The pressure from the boot redoubled. "Say that there is no God but Assad."

Noah whimpered, but did not relent. "There is no God but God."

The boot receded. "Smack him with the shovels until his hair turns red."

The soldiers followed the orders so quickly that Noah did not even have time to scream in protest. They hit him again and again until the blood was washing over his eyes, choking him and making everything run red. His head rang with every blow, but he did not lose consciousness.

"Okay, stop. I want him awake for this."

Through it all, Noah remained aware that the camera was still running. He would not give this man what he wanted.

"Say that there is no God but Assad, and there is no prophet but the Baath Party."

Noah spit. "There is no God but God, and his prophet is Mohammad."

The shadow disappeared, the sun pouring in from behind, warming Noah as the music of his surroundings stirred.

"Bury him. Show him who has the power to kill the living and raise the dead."

The soldiers obeyed. They started covering him with sand slowly until the light went out and the air grew thin. As hopeless as he was, Noah knew that he could still be heard through the earth. "God is great!" he hollered with his dying breath. "There is no God but God! God is great!"

"Go meet your God in hell," came the reply. "This is the fate of those who don't admit that Assad is their God."

~~~

"Let him go! This is not human."

Only a few seconds passed before the soldier who dared utter these words over the captive's grave was riddled with bullets. In the background, other soldiers began peppering rounds into the protestors, as well.

"Any other objections?" the leader asked as his captive moaned and screamed from suffocation.

None of the soldiers spoke. The captive lost his breath. The protestors were silent. Even the leaves stopped singing.

Then one of the soldiers started jumping and dancing on the sand where the captive was buried. The leader laughed along with his loyal soldiers, cracking up so hard it hurt. One of the soldiers wasn't so amused. With tears in his eyes, he grabbed his rifle and started running madly. His former comrades fired dozens of shots in his direction, but he escaped, disappearing below the hill.

"We'll get him later," the leader assured them. "It's all right." He patted his belly as he looked down at the mound that used to be his captive. "Let's go eat. We'll be moving into Daraa City tomorrow. There are thousands of people waiting to be buried there, too."

~~~

Meanwhile in Daraa, Sireen was trying to pull herself together from the shock of seeing her beloved's blood covering the computer screen. She felt responsible, for a part of her had always known that this journey would end in a disaster of some sort. Disasters had become too common in Syria not to expect one.

She plugged in her headset and carried her laptop in her arms like it was a precious child. In this way, she started walking the roads of Daraa long past curfew. She listened to music as she walked through the dangerous neighborhoods, singing along. The wind cooled her tears as they raced down her face. All around, she saw destruction, death, and roofless homes. A curious child peeked out at her through a large hole in his bedroom wall. She waved to him. He couldn't wave back, for his right hand had been amputated. She cried harder at the sight.

She passed a family of three children and a woman who appeared to be their mother. Nothing was left of their home but a wall. God only knew how many people they had lost and who would take care of them now. They were clearly starving. The baby's wailing suggested hunger pangs. In all of Daraa, there was no baby formula left. The siege was tighter than the stones of Baalbak. Sireen knew that she couldn't do anything to help these children, so she just turned the music up.

She kept walking, her laptop clutched delicately between her arms, her face soaked in tears. She wasn't sure where she was heading, but she followed a familiar path she had taken numerous times before. She could almost see her footsteps engraved in the stone. They used to be much smaller, faster, and happier, these footsteps. But what happens to them when you feel that the whole world has abandoned you? Sireen had changed so much in the past six months. Everyone had changed. Everything had changed.

Soon she realized where her feet were taking her when she found herself in her parents' neighborhood. She hadn't been there for some time, mostly because she was scared that her so-called "fiancé" had posted men on the lookout for her there. Memories flooded her mind as she shuffled closer to her house. She wanted to see her parents now more than ever. She wanted to make sure they were fine. She wanted to throw herself into her father's arms and weep.

As she came close enough to see her parents' house, her tears returned. It was like a thunderbolt had struck from the sky straight into her heart. The house was gone. In its place was rubble. The living room, her bedroom, and the kitchen had been reduced to pieces of broken masonry and bricks.

She stood in place, so harrowed that even the sky was moved and heavy rain began to pour. Young, thirsty children ran into the streets, carrying pots and bowls to fill with heavenly water. The siege had taken their usual water supply from them in an attempt to kill the revolution through dehydration. The children left the containers to fill and quickly ran back home to avoid the snipers. Not Sireen. She closed her laptop and kept it under her arm as she fixed her gaze on the ground. Her dress and her hair were soaked in rainwater, but her heart was too awash in sorrow for her to notice.

She slowly dragged herself to the site where her house once stood, placed the laptop on the ground, and fell to her knees with clenched fists. She stared into the eye of heaven and yelled, "Why? What have we done to deserve this?"

She started digging through the rubble, looking for everything and nothing in particular. She found an old doll she remembered from her childhood. She pulled it close to her chest as she synchronized her tears with those of the sky.

She kept digging. When she found a tattered kite, she understood that she had found her bedroom. As she examined the broken kite, she began to softly sing the song she used to sing when flying it as a child. It was a Fairouz song that she sang in Lebanese Arabic as delirium seized her mind. "*Teeri ya tayara teeri* . . . Fly away, kite . . . of sticks and paper . . . make me a little girl again . . . on the roof of our neighbor . . . Let time forget about me . . . Let time forget about me . . . on the roof of our neighbor."

A few minutes later, an intense determination surged through her. She began throwing away the bricks and stones insanely until she could see the remains of her bedroom couch. She removed as much debris from the couch as she could before lying down on it with her doll, kite, and laptop clutched to her chest.

She had never felt so hopeless and confused. She didn't care that she was out on the streets during curfew. She wasn't worried about any snipers in the distance that might shoot at her. Perhaps she wanted it.

She fired up her laptop once more, surprised to see it still working in the rain, and put her headset on so she could listen to old love songs. If a sniper wanted to take her now, let it be with a song she used to share with Waleed ringing in her ears.

The cool breeze, soft music, and memories of the past were enough to sedate her into a state of stupor. She only vaguely heard the two warning shots that landed near her couch. She simply turned up the music and ignored the shooter. She remained in her trance-like state, listening to music under the rain, oblivious to her surroundings. Memories of the past and hopes for the future had merged into a dreamy present. Soon she began to fly, her hair streaming behind her. She felt that she was weightless and soaring through the narrow streets of Daraa like a ghost. A few seconds later, she opened her eyes to realize that she was indeed flying. She was at least one meter above the ground, and the buildings were soaring behind her. She wasn't bothered by the illogic of the situation. She rolled her head to the other side and noticed a man's chest, his arms firmly carrying her as he ran from one neighborhood to the other. In the background, she could hear the rain, and of course the sounds of bullets. Finally, the man slowed to a stop.

"Baba?" she asked, snapping out of her reverie to find that she had been carried into a covered alley sandwiched between two apartment complexes that had somehow escaped the shelling. It was dark and dank in this place. Somewhere behind, she could hear the sound of the rain pouring through a hole in the ceiling and pooling at the far end of the alley.

"*La* [No]. Why were you outside during curfew hours?" the man asked in a warm voice. "You know they don't care if you're a woman. They'll still shoot you."

"I know this voice," she said as she squeezed her savior's hand. "I know this voice very well, but it's impossible. I thought you died."

The man removed the scarf coving his face. "It's me, Yousef," he said with a beautiful smile.

"Yousef?" she said in disbelief. "But I saw them shoot you."

"You might have heard a gunshot, but it was I who shot that guard. Then I disappeared."

"Why did you disappear like that?"

He looked ashamed as he let her down to carry her own weight. "I was afraid."

"I'm sure they were looking for you."

"No, it wasn't them I was afraid of. They don't scare me."

"Then who were you afraid of?"

"I was afraid of being accused of spoiling the peaceful revolution after shooting a *Shabeeh* in self-defense."

"You probably shouldn't have done it. We want our revolution to stay pure as snow."

"I'm sorry," he said with a sarcastic smile. "Next time I will let them shoot me."

She furrowed her brow at the weapon slung over his shoulder. "I see that you have a rifle. If you really want to keep the revolution peaceful, you would get rid of the weapon."

Yousef steeled up his brow. "Never. Don't worry, I won't intervene in the revolution, but we'll keep whatever little weapons we have for the right moment."

"We?" she asked, her heart skipping. "Who's we?"

"Those who care about the people of Syria more than anything, and those willing to die protecting you."

"Yousef, people die in revolutions, but this is a peaceful movement. We've got this. We don't need arms. Soon the international community will get mobilized and put an end to this. Have some patience."

"We have a lot of patience. We will not get involved unless you allow us to." Yousef held up a finger for silence when a call came through on his phone. "*Salam*, this is Yousef." He paused to listen. "Where did you find them? What part of the town of Jasem?"

Sireen's eyes glowed as she took a step toward him. "What's happening? Tell me, please."

"Hold on," Yousef said into the phone before turning his pretty eyes on Sireen. "They found two guys who were injured by the *Shabeeha* in Jasem. They're trying to help them."

Hope fluttered in Sireen's heart. Waleed was in Jasem. Could it be possible? "This could be Waleed. Ask them how they are."

"How is their status now?" he asked into the phone. The pause was unbearably long. "He says one of them is stable, but the other might not make it. They're being treated at a secret field hospital in the city. One of them is a local, and one is not from the town. That man's name is Waleed." Yousef was silent for some time before replying into the phone, "Make sure the surgeon is safe. He's the only one remaining in town. Get some men ready for Tuesday. We're heading to Homs to get some medicines and milk from donors to smuggle into Daraa."

"Who needs a surgeon?" Sireen asked. "The local or Waleed?"

"The local," Yousef said, but something about the way he looked away from her suggested that it was a lie. "Waleed is a common name. We don't know that it's him—"

"It's him," she said. "I know it is. Waleed is from Homs. Can you have your friends take him with them?"

"Yes, if he's healthy enough by Tuesday."

Sireen swooned, suddenly feeling entirely grateful for Yousef, his rifle, and the men who would band together with him in this way. "Thank you."

"Don't worry." He hung his head sheepishly. "I would do anything for you. You know that."

"Can I ask you one more favor?"

"Anything."

"Can I go with them to Homs, too?"

He bit his lip as the rain trickled down from his thick beard. "You really love him."

"Yes."

"All right," he said, sighing. "So be it, then. It's safer for you to be out of Daraa anyway."

"Yousef."

"Yes?"

"I'm sorry about what happened to your family."

He nodded. "So am I. The tax of freedom has been very high on our nation. It's the will of God. I accept his will."

"I haven't heard anything about my parents. Our house is completely destroyed."

"Oh, I'm so silly," Yousef said, smacking his forehead. "I forgot to tell you."

Sireen strained to find some hope in her friend's tone. "You know where they are?"

"I do," he said with a broad smile. "We helped a large group of civilians from your neighborhood cross into Jordan. I'm almost certain your parents were with them. They are safe now. They went to a refugee camp in Jordan called Al-Za'atary."

Her balance left her momentarily. She broke her fall by placing a hand on Yousef's shoulder. "Oh, thank God. Thank God. Thank you, Yousef."

"Here," he said, sliding out of his jacket. "Put this on."

Sireen felt warm and protected for the first time in weeks. She smiled.

From the alley, they entered an old, neglected building. The apartments were tiny. The paint peeled from the walls.

"I'm sorry, my princess," Yousef said mournfully. "I know this is far beneath your level."

"No, not at all. I'm a tough girl now."

"If I could, I would have placed you in a castle like you deserve, but this is all we have now. You will stay in this apartment. My sister is staying in it, too. She'll be delighted to see you."

"You're not staying with us?"

"No, my princess. Come on. That wouldn't be acceptable in the eyes of God."

"Where will you go?"

"I will stay with one of the men from my group. Don't worry about me. I will check on you every day, but from a distance. Then on Tuesday, at about three in the morning, some of my friends will come to get you out of Daraa."

"I won't see you again?"

"Of course you will. I will always be around you, and whenever you're in danger, I will appear out of thin air like a genie. As long as I am alive, nothing can hurt you. I promise."

Sireen laughed. "Indeed, you are a genie."

"Goodbye, my princess."

Yousef waved and disappeared back into the alley. Sireen was left wondering what was going on in Yousef's head. Was he like that with everyone, or was he falling in love with her? Did he not know that her heart was with someone else? She hated the idea of hurting her savior one day. She really cared about him a great deal, but not in the same way she cared about Waleed. She missed Waleed more than she missed clean water, electricity, and even quiet nights. Her heart beat faster as she hoped for Tuesday to arrive sooner. She didn't miss only Waleed; she was also ecstatic to see Homs again. It was, after all, the city where she had first fallen in love, staying up late at night under the jasmine trees and grape vines, spotting the central clock from random rooftops. Had Homs changed? Rumor had it that the city had taken over the torch of the revolution after the destruction of Daraa. Had it been destroyed, too? Did death haunt every house and corner of the city, as well? *Hopefully not*, she thought. She desperately wanted a break from this misery, from the smell of death and the sight of dying children and weeping mothers.

~~~

Three days later, at three in the morning, four men arrived, as promised. Sireen quietly joined them. They climbed into an old blue Toyota and began their exodus.

"Where are the others?" she asked the driver. He was a gruff-looking man with jet black hair, a strong chin, and a bulbous nose.

"They are already in Daraya, in rural Damascus, waiting for us." He turned his hardened gaze on her for a moment. "Miss, if you don't mind, we will be driving very fast. We need to be in Homs as early as possible. If you're scared, please let me know."

"I'm a tough girl," she said, throwing her head back. "Don't worry about me."

"Brother Yousef told us to take good care of you. It seems he has a great deal of respect for you."

Sireen remained silent, forcing her apparently shy companions into silence, as well. She leaned against the window and stared at Daraa, guilt-stricken as the car drove away. This was the guilt of abandoning someone you love at a moment of need because you feel powerless to help them. "I'll come back to you, I promise," she whispered to the city.

In no time, she had fallen asleep. In some circumstances, she might not have allowed herself to do such a thing in the presence of men, but from the way her companions leaned away from her—so vehemently that she might as well have been radioactive—she knew that she need not fear their advances. They practically sat in each other's laps not to bother her.

After two hours of sweet sleep, the car suddenly stopped. Sireen opened her eyes and saw a gray car slowly roll up to park next to theirs. She looked through the window and saw a dark, ghostly figure in the adjacent car. It was the most beautiful ghost she had ever seen. Her eyes opened wide, and her heart began to race. She rolled down the window and whispered, "Waleed?"

"Miss, please keep it down," the driver said.

"Is this them?" she asked.

"Yes it is, Miss, but please stay in the car. We can't blow our cover."

Ignoring the driver, Sireen swung the car door open and ran down toward the other car. As she drew closer, she saw that Waleed was leaning against the window, apparently sleeping. A thousand thoughts ran through her mind, and a thousand feelings stirred her heart as she ran to him. She cried and laughed at the same time when she became certain that this was, in fact, him. This was his hair, his neck, and his T-shirt. She stopped next to the car and knocked on the window, ready to see the surprised look on his face. He didn't turn to her. She knocked again, harder this time. He remained asleep. She laughed nervously and started hitting the window with all her strength.

The driver rolled down the window. "Madam, get back to your car. What are you doing?"

"He's not answering me!" she yelled nervously. "Is he all right?"

A guy came from behind, grabbed her by the waist, and started pulling her back. "Miss, please calm down."

Sireen pushed his hands aside and walked back to her car. From the passenger seat, she stared at Waleed through the window. The two cars drove side by side the rest of the way, Sireen's eyes ever fixated on her beloved during the journey.

The shine in your eyes
Like angels of the morning
Stealing my heart into heaven

When my heartbeats rise
With a touch of your fingers
My soul reaches cloud number seven

She recited the words to herself as dawn arrived. While the morning sun rose from its slumber, sleep landed in Sireen's eyes. She leaned her head against the rim of the open window, her hair falling against the door. The two cars continued to drive. The sun kept rising. A new day was born from the womb of the night.

Chapter 21
Flag of Independence

The ocean of blood was quickly rising. Fatigue, anger, and desperation could be found everywhere. Yet against all bets and against all odds, they persisted. Their perseverance was surprising. However, under certain circumstances, even diamonds can fracture. Suddenly there were different voices, different approaches, and disarray—until the great uniter was born. Green as the dreams of the emeralds, black as their sorrow, white like the jasmines of Damascus, and sprinkled with the foretelling stars of a better tomorrow, it was a symbol, a symbol that would turn the Syrians into a nation that would never again be torn.

Under the French mandate, Greater Syria was essentially divided into five states, and the "mandate flag" of Syria had already become a symbol detested by most Syrians. A different "independence flag" was secretly circulating among the revolutionaries. It was composed of three parallel bands. The lowest was black, the middle was white, and the top was green. Each represented an era of Syrian history. Along the middle white band were three little red stars representing various regions of the country.

After Syria achieved independence, the flag survived for seventeen more years, until the Baathists came to power and created a series of flags ending in the two-starred "Arab Unity Flag," which would become one of the most hated symbols of oppression in Syrian history. It was this very flag that kept haunting the Syrians on the streets.

With every Friday, the two-starred flag was progressively less noticeable. An online referendum was held, and the independence flag that had united Syrians under the French occupation was selected as the new symbol of the revolution—and by a wide margin. The psychological impact was tremendous and mysterious.

—*Syria: A History in Blood* by Celine Dubois

December 9, 2011
Deaths: 5,100

"We're out of green fabric, Aunt Sarah," Sireen said with a smile to Waleed's mother. "I don't mind donating my green dress to the revolution."

"No, *habibti*," Sarah said, her eyes narrowing pleasantly. "You don't have to. Om Omar is sending us more fabric with her son. It should be enough to make flags for this Friday. What are they calling this Friday, my dear?"

"It's called 'the Friday of the dignity strike.'"

Sireen stopped what she was doing when Sarah pointed at her stitching with an open hand.

"Darling, cut the stripes a little straighter. Also, your red stars are too large. Make them smaller, like mine."

"All right, I will." Sireen rooted around in the pile she had made on the table, finding a smaller star. "Is this one better?"

"*Teslameely* [May God keep you safe]!" Sarah said, beaming. "That's perfect. Ah, Sireen. I always wanted to have a daughter to bring to me memories of my youth, but God's will was that I live in a house with four men. No objection to God's will."

"Well, from now on, I'm your daughter," Sireen said with a big grin that quickly faded into sadness.

"What's the matter, my dear? You miss your mother, don't you?"

"Yes, *Khale* [Aunt]. I miss my parents so much, and I'm worried about them. They have no phones, no internet connection, and the only way I get in touch with them is through regular mail."

"I'm surprised they even have access to that over at that miserable camp in Jordan."

"Oh, they don't. A guy who helps smuggle refugees out of the country transports letters back and forth between us. It's just hard, *Khale*." Unbidden, Sireen started crying. "I haven't heard from them in a month. I don't know if they're alive or . . .'"

Sarah shushed her. "Happy words. Keep your faith in God strong." She came around the table and hugged Sireen before patting her hair. "This is our destiny, my dear. This is what's written for us. Your mother and I know this well. We used to be young girls in Hama, that once beautiful city. We looked evil in the eye, and we smelled the rotten smell of death. We lost everything. We lost everyone we loved. She's the only other survivor I know." Her voice changed, and warm tears appeared like ghosts from the past.

"*Khale*, I'm sorry."

"No, don't be sorry. I just want you to be ready for the worst, my dear. Your generation made a choice, against our advice. Now it's too late to change that decision. So you need to be strong, and we have no choice but to support you. My generation, we weren't cowards like you guys claim. We were simply paralyzed by the magnitude of the horrors we saw." She dried her tears, cleared her throat, and went on. "Both your mother and I were young, beautiful women, just like you. We were both in love. She loved a Hamwi, and I loved a Shami from rural Damascus. Don't you dare tell anyone. Our husbands would divorce us." She smiled.

"Of course I won't," Sireen said dutifully. "What happened to those men?"

"They probably died in the massacre of 1982. Everyone died then."

Sireen hugged her tight, trying to comfort her.

"Then I met Abu Khalid," Sarah went on. "He's been a great husband and father and everything I ever needed."

With a nod, Sireen wiped away a tear with the back of her hand. "I'll go make coffee for both of us. When I return, we'll only talk about happy things. Enough sorrow. Deal?"

As Sireen rose from the low coffee table and made her way over the woven rug toward the kitchen, she heard a heavy knock on the door.

"It must be our neighbor, Om Zaki," Sarah offered.

"Should I open the door for her?"

"Yes, please do before she breaks a bone. She's pretty old. Be warned, she's a crazy woman."

Sireen opened the door and found an old, frail lady standing there. She had dark blue eyes to go with her blue dress and a black head cover. She carried what looked like a torch of burning *bakhour*, or chips of wood covered with fragrant oils. After a pause, Sireen was the first to speak. "Good morning. Please come in."

"And who are you?" the old woman asked rather rudely.

"Sireen."

"Sireen who?"

"Om Zaki!" Sarah called from the living room. "Leave the girl alone. Come on in. Your mother-in-law loves you. We were just making coffee."

"My mother-in-law is long dead, ya Om Khalid." The old woman pointed at the floor. "Oh no!"

Sireen rushed back to take a look, but wasn't sure why the strange old woman was pointing to a shoe.

"My daughter, are you dumb?" Om Zaki said. "The sole of the shoe is pointing toward the sky. Don't you know this is terrible luck? Fix it. I don't want to touch them."

Bewildered, Sireen bent down and returned the shoe to its rightful orientation. As she went to the kitchen to make coffee, she thought about how she had underestimated the eeriness of this woman. At least if she busied herself with the coffee, she could avoid the arrows of her further comments.

"So who is this pretty lady?" Om Zaki whispered in a voice so loud Sireen could hear it from the kitchen.

"My relative, from Daraa."

"Daraa? She sounded Damascene to me. Is she still single?"

Sireen's heart skipped.

"Yes, Om Zaki. She is. Why?"

"How do you keep a single lady like her in a house full of single young men? What do you want people to say about her? Oh God, have mercy."

"People can say whatever they want. She is staying with me, and my sons are well-mannered men."

"Of course, of course. How about I protect her honor and marry her to my youngest son Hani?"

Sireen stifled a scoff.

"Om Zaki, leave the girl alone. She has two college degrees. Why would she marry your son?"

"What's wrong with my son? Maybe he's not educated, but he's a real man. He'll take care of her."

Sireen rolled her eyes and sighed. The coffee was ready. She brought three steaming cups with her. As they drank coffee, the conversation kept getting more awkward. Eventually, Sireen simply shut off her brain and stopped listening.

"Are you deaf, darling?" Om Zaki asked her after a time. "I said let me see your coffee cup."

"Oh, sorry," Sireen said, picking up her cup. "I wasn't paying attention. Here you go."

"Mashalla, your hands are so beautiful. You should always wear a blue bead to protect you from the evil eye."

More and more, Sireen just wanted this visit to be over.

Om Zaki stared into Sireen's empty cup. She squinted her old blue eyes and then opened them in shock, as if she had seen a ghost emerge from the cup. "Oh, darling . . . oh, darling," she said as she covered her mouth with her hand.

"What's wrong?" Sarah asked.

The old woman gave her a foreboding gaze. "This cup is not normal at all."

"What do you see? Tell us."

"I see a wedding dress . . . a long, beautiful wedding dress. You see it, Om Khalid?" She pushed the cup close to Sarah's face.

"That one?" Sarah said, wrinkling her nose. "But I don't see a face on it."

"Yes. There is no bride ; just a dress. It must be a sad, sad wedding. I don't understand why." Her eyes grew dark. "Maybe you'll marry someone you don't love." She paused as if to let the thought sink in. "Or maybe you'll get close to marriage and then it won't work. I don't understand it. My knowledge is limited, my dear. Or maybe you fall in sin!"

"Om Zaki!" Sarah yelled.

Sireen felt relieved to know that at least someone was on her side in this madness. The conversation had made her so uncomfortable that she kept looking back over her shoulder to make sure no one was listening.

"Okay, maybe not that last one, but it's very strange. Next to the white dress, I see fog. There is a huge mass of fog approaching her. You see it, darling?" She pointed the cup at Sireen, who didn't care to look. "You see those little black dots in it? They're not good. It's some kind of evil fog that is approaching you. Oh, in the name of God most gracious, most merciful. Please never walk in the fog. Something bad will happen. My dear, happiness is not written for you. I see tears, a thousand tears and more. "

"Om Zaki, enough," Sarah said. "You scared the girl. Look how her color turned yellow."

Sireen shook her head as if to deny it, but she did feel a little piqued.

"Om Khalid, I must break this cup. It's full of bad fortunes."

Sarah came to her feet with her hands outstretched. "No! Don't you dare. Give it to me."

Om Zaki wasn't going to change her ways on this day. She threw the cup against the wall. As the porcelain shattered, the old woman began reciting something to herself and blowing the Bakhour smoke around Sireen, who was terrified by the show. "All right, neighbors," she said when she was finished. "I must go now. I need to spread the Bakhour around in every apartment in the building."

With that, she walked out as if nothing had happened.

Sarah burst out laughing. "Don't believe a word she said, Sireen. She's got Alzheimer's. She's a crazy woman."

Sireen didn't need to be told not to believe her, and yet a part of her was still feeling apprehensive about the remote possibility that the woman knew what she was talking about.

"I'll go prepare some *fatteh* and *fattoush*," Sarah said as she made her way to the kitchen. "Go wake up the men so they can get ready for prayer. Don't go into their room, though. It's true that people do talk."

"I don't think anyone wants to go into that room," she said, and they both laughed.

Here in Sarah's small home, this was the first time Sireen had felt safe and protected in a long while. She had lost her college seat after her roommate, Fatima, had reported her revolutionary tendencies to the dean. After her rescue by Yousef and his men, Sireen found herself staying under this roof at Sarah's insistence. Indeed, her hostess had come to treat her like a long-lost daughter. The two of them stayed comfortably in one bedroom while all the men in the house squeezed into the other. There was Waleed, his father, his two brothers, and his new friend Jaffar, all sharing that tight space. There was no choice, of course, because resources were limited, but the culture that kept unmarried men and women apart was unwavering. This was the new normal in most Syrian homes. Everyone looked after everyone else because they knew that they could be the next group of people looking for a safer shelter and a warm bowl of soup.

For the first few weeks, Omar had also been sleeping over to help treat and take care of Waleed's and Jaffar's wounds. Waleed recovered fairly quickly, and for the past week had been able to walk around and even use his right arm. Omar advised him to walk as much as possible to prevent blood clots from forming in his veins. Jaffar, on the other hand, grew very ill, as his wounds were infected. Omar had smuggled in some intravenous antibiotics, and eventually was able to say that Jaffar's condition had stabilized and that he should start improving soon. This was when Omar took his leave, for his skills were better used elsewhere.

Initially, Sarah was so furious at Waleed for his actions that she refused to talk to him at all for the whole first week. But of course she moved on, like mothers always do.

Sireen had been keeping herself busy with revolutionary activism. Every Friday, she helped prepare posters, flags, and colorful balloons. She had also been helping Omar set up an underground hospital facility to aid the wounded that were denied treatment at government hospitals. The job Omar had taken on was truly massive, and it put him at tremendous risk to his own life. He was eager for Waleed to get better and start helping him, as well. Waleed had only recently begun to feel strong enough to join and help organize protests. Until then, he had spent most of his time at home reading and reciting Nizar Qabbani's poems and attempting to write his own. This left him and Sireen plenty of time to catch up on stories of the adventures they had once thought were impossible. Sireen cried for hours as she spoke of the massacres, the siege, and the deaths of people she dearly loved. They talked about Waleed's insane journey to Daraa and all the fascinating people he had met on the way. More importantly, they realized how much they had missed each other, and how grateful they were to be together once again.

After Friday prayer, Waleed, his two brothers, and Sireen joined hundreds of thousands of protestors in what had become a tradition as Syrian as tabbouleh and stuffed grape leaves. Almost everyone in the square carried his or her own homemade independence flag. Sireen was given the honor of releasing dozens of white, helium-filled balloons into the air as a symbol for the people to join the dignity strike and the civil disobedience campaign.

For the first time in weeks, Homs was once again the heart of the revolution. Daraa was withering under siege and Hama was still in shock from the bloody military campaign that had taken the wind out of its sails. Der-el-Zor was still under continuous bombing, as was most of rural Damascus. The capital itself saw significant progress in revolutionary activity, but far from what was needed to reach a critical mass. Aleppo, meanwhile, was in a deep slumber, which infuriated Syrians throughout the country.

"Are you sure you want to come with me?" Sireen asked as she tied the independence flag around Waleed's neck.

"I think I've had a long enough vacation," Waleed said with a wry smile. "We need to spread awareness about the strike as much as possible." He took one last look at the mirror. "How do I look?"

Sireen laughed. He did look rather comical with his unkempt hair and a flag wrapped around his neck. "Who cares? It's two in the morning. No one is going to see you."

"That's not true. Someone very important to me is going to see me; someone who I love more than anything in the world."

As he looked deeply into her eyes, she turned away, feeling herself blush. He moved closer and placed his hand in the doorway so that his shoulder almost touched her face.

"Someone I took a shot for and would do it a hundred times again if I had to," he added quietly. "Do you know how you can tell which person is most important to you in the world?"

Sireen looked up and dived into his soft eyes. "No, tell me."

"You go out on the streets of Syria and you get shot. At that moment when the bullet hits you, and before you fall or even feel the pain, time freezes for a second. You feel that your soul floats over your body and soars into the sky just high enough to see that thing which is most important to you once more before your soul leaves your body for good. That last thing I saw before I passed out was you."

Sireen sealed her lips and her eyes tightly, shedding a few silent tears. "Let's go," she finally managed. "It's getting late."

She felt Waleed following behind her.

~~~

They walked wordlessly side by side for several blocks until she finally said, "This looks like a good place. Give me a poster, please."

He handed her a poster bearing a large white flower, a symbol of peaceful resistance. Under the flower, it read, *Join the strike for dignity and freedom. May God keep you, keep yourself at home.* They glued a few posters in the neighborhood before heading out again to find another place.

"The compliance with the strike has been impressive so far," Waleed said, wishing they could instead be talking about the moment they had shared in his house just before they left.

"So I hear," she said, seeming uncomfortable somehow. Did she struggle with her feelings for him, as he for her? "Homs, Hama, Daraa almost full compliance. I don't know about Damascus and Aleppo."

"Large portions of the capital have been compliant with the strike. I was impressed by Damascus. The *Shabeeha* have been completely destroying and vandalizing all the shops that comply with the strike, yet Damascus has done fairly well."

"What about Aleppo? When are they planning to stand up for themselves?"

"I don't think Aleppo will ever get up." He smirked. "Not even if you gave it Viagra."

"Waleed!" Sireen scolded, but with that, the tension was broken. She laughed so sweetly. "I hope you're wrong. It just doesn't make sense. In the eighties, Aleppo was the only city that stood up for Hama. What happened to them? I don't know if civil disobedience will get us anywhere without a strong participation from Aleppo. They are the commercial center, after all."

"It's all right. It will all work out in the end."

Waleed moved closer to Sireen as the two of them strode through the chilly and wrecked streets. He could feel eyes peering out broken windows to watch them, but they saw very few other people outside the ruined homes.

"But what if it doesn't?" she said. "What if this whole peaceful movement is a waste of time, and more importantly, a terrible waste of innocent lives?"

"What are you saying? You want us to go back home and wait for the regime to hunt us down one at a time like ducks?"

"No! I'm saying what if the movement should stop being peaceful?"

A sigh came to Waleed's lips. "That's exactly what they want. They want to drag us into violence so they can use their full might to destroy us."

"They are already using the army to destroy us! Why are we losing our best men and women without even a fight? Waleed, maybe we should all support the Free Syrian Army and stop this wishful thinking." She sounded angry as she glued this latest poster to the wall.

Waleed watched her for a moment, unsure of how to proceed. "The Free Syrian Army is tiny. They hardly have any weapons. Our fathers liberated Syria from the French through civil disobedience. We can do the same."

"Those were the French! They were civilized people, not savage Baathists! You don't know how bad things got in Daraa. Those people don't understand strikes and protests. They will keep killing us by the hundreds until no one is left to protest."

Finding a barren wall still mostly standing, Waleed pasted up his own poster, carefully smoothing out the wrinkles. "We don't live in a jungle, Sireen. The international community won't sit and watch a genocide take place. It's just not possible."

"Oh really? What about the Holocaust? What about Rwanda? What about Hama?"

He gave her his most certain look. "My dear, the world has changed."

"I sure hope so," she said with a sigh. "Hand me over some more posters, if you don't mind."

"Don't put it here," Waleed said, staring down at the mud puddle beside the bench at which Sireen pointed. "It's not clean. There is *shmento* [cement]."

Sireen burst out laughing.

Waleed was puzzled. "What's funny?"

"*Shmento*," she replied with a wide grin.

"How is that funny?" he asked, laughing without really knowing why.

"Oh, nothing. It's just something random. It's not funny, in fact."

"No, tell me." He took this moment of lightheartedness as an excuse to put his arm around her waist. He adored her all the more for the polite and gentle way she pushed his arm aside.

"It was my graduation thesis, which I was working on before they expelled me."

"Your graduation thesis was about construction material?"

"No! It was about the Aramaic origins of modern spoken Syrian."

"What? That's insane. I don't speak any Aramaic. I don't think anyone does anymore."

"Not true." She raised an eyebrow as she glued another poster. "First of all, there are several small villages in Syria where they still speak Aramaic as their first language. They still use the same exact dialect that was used thousands of years ago in this land. Secondly, hundreds of Aramaic words and a lot of the grammar are things you use every day."

"So what's so funny about *shmento*?"

She gave a half-smile. "How do you say 'nobody'?"

"*Ma hada.*"

"Aramaic. What's the fourth month of the year?"

"*Neesan,*" he said, amused.

"Aramaic. How do you say inside and outside?"

"*Jowa w barra.*"

"Both Aramaic. The list goes on and on, not to mention that every single Syrian city and village has an Aramaic name."

"Wow. This is really interesting. After the revolution, we should spend our honeymoon in Maloola and learn Aramaic."

"Our what?" Sireen said, appearing startled.

Waleed's heart quickened in his chest when he realized what he had said. "Oh, I mean . . ." he stuttered. "I mean . . . do you need more posters?"

"Yes, please," she said with an odd smile.

The momentary pleasure this brought him was fleeting, for it was interrupted by a harsh voice from behind. "Hey you! What are you doing?"

~~~

They turned around to find a large army car pulling up behind them. Sireen blanched at the sight of the large assault rifle the soldier in the trailer wheeled around on them.

"Put your hands up in the air," the passenger said through the loudspeaker.

They followed the commands with looks of shock on their faces. Sireen looked around, but she couldn't see too far because it had become foggy. The street ahead had silently dressed itself in a long sheet of fog. Sireen felt as if her heart would beat out of her chest.

The passenger rolled down his window. "What do you have in your hands?"

"Posters," Sireen managed to say.

"Let me see them," he demanded.

Sireen's hands began to shake as she handed him the poster. She knew that as soon as he read what was in them, he would kill them both on the spot. She moved closer to Waleed and held his hand. He put his arm around her. She didn't resist this time. When the passenger, a middle-aged man with a sharp glare, was done staring at the poster, he took his gun out and pointed it right at Sireen. For a second, she felt that her soul had left her body and had begun gliding through the streets of the city. The city wasn't Homs, though; it was Daraa.

Then she glimpsed a man's face. He smiled at her handsomely and whispered, "I won't let them hurt you."

The man wasn't Waleed. This realization worried her more than the gun pointed at her face. She squeezed Waleed's hand tightly and quickly brought herself back to the real world.

"What's this poster?" the passenger asked her.

"It's nothing, as you can see," she said with surprising confidence. She was further relieved to see that the man was holding the poster upside down. He was probably illiterate, she realized. "My grandmother died, and this is to inform people of when the funeral is taking place."

"Oh yes, I figured," he said as he put his gun away. "What sect are you two from?"

"Umm . . . we're . . . we're Christians," she lied. "Don't you see the flower of Christ on the poster?"

"Oh yes, I've seen it before on churches. What's your name, beautiful?"

"I'm . . . umm . . . My name is Christina."

"What a lovely name," he said, biting his lip. "Come closer. Don't worry. What's your last name, Christana?" Without waiting for a reply, he reached out to touch her hair.

Waleed's hand tightened over hers, but she pinched him to signify that she had this under control.

"It's Christina," she corrected. "My last name is Saleebo." She pushed her hair back playfully and away from his grasp.

"Saleebo? Never heard that before."

"It's Aramaic. You know Saleeb, the cross of Christ?" She was just making things up now, having no idea what she was talking about when it came to Christian symbols.

"Who's the mute guy next to you?"

"Oh, I'm Wa—" Waleed began to say.

"He's my brother George," she interrupted, saving the day. "What's your name?"

"I'm Asef. You know, like the great Asef Shawkat?" He grinned as he made reference to one of the most vicious people in the Syrian regime, Assad's relative and head of the Mukhabarat.

"Of course," Sireen said pleasantly. "Well, Asef, it was great to meet you. We need to go back and prepare for the funeral. Stop by sometime for a chat. You want my phone number?"

"No, it's all right." He inclined his head in a show of bravado. "I can look you up from your name. I'll find out more about you than you ever wanted me to know, Christina Saleebo." He laughed.

"Good. I'll be waiting." She smiled coquettishly, grabbed Waleed by the hand, and began to walk away.

She had forgotten that Waleed wore a huge independence flag around his neck. Somehow it had flown around to his back.

"Hey, wait!" the soldier yelled. "Come back, you two!"

She almost fainted at the realization of what had happened. "Yes?" she asked, trying to found flirtatious despite her sudden anxiety.

"You be quiet," the passenger said. He leveled a deadly stare at Waleed. "What's that on your back?"

"Oh, this?" Waleed said as he removed the flag.

"Yes, what's that flag? I've seen it before."

"You seriously don't know what that flag is?" Sireen interrupted again.

"No, but I've seen it before, and I have a bad feeling about it."

"Don't be silly. It's the flag of the Russian . . ." She paused when she realized that he was not amused.

"I'm not stupid. This is not the Russian flag." He appeared agitated.

"Of course it's not the Russian flag. It's the flag of the veto. You know, the veto that saved us from an international meddling in our affairs."

"Veto? That's in Russia, right?"

"Yes, exactly. I'm impressed that our armed forces are so educated!"

He held out his hand impatiently. "All right, then. Give me that flag. I want it."

"Sure!" she said, handing it to him before grabbing Waleed by the hand.

"The veto flag . . ." he said in a stern voice. "I'll show you my veto flag." He reached for a gun and pointed it at Sireen. "You manipulative whore."

~~~

"Don't you dare call her that!" Waleed yelled, putting himself in front of Sireen and closer to the gun. He had never done something like this for anyone before, nor did he ever think the day would come when he would have to. He remembered when Omar had taken a bullet for him. He had never realized how much Omar cared about him before this moment. He could feel his heart rhythm convert into a sinus tachycardia, beating perhaps two hundred beats a minute. His lips were dry, his breathing was heavy, and the bitter winter wind penetrated his clothes and skin all the way to the marrow of his bones. As his heart accelerated, time began to slow. He could almost feel his soul dissociate from reality. Perhaps this was nature's way of placating those facing imminent death.

The gun slowly drifted upward and aimed at Waleed's head.

"Now!" Sireen's voice pierced through the serenity of the moment.

Now what? he wondered. *What is she saying?*

"Waleed, now!" she ordered. "Blow yourself up!"

How was he supposed to blow himself up? He had no explosives. His thought process had entered a deep freeze. Even so, he obeyed, reaching for his belt and pulling on it to see if the atoms in his body would somehow split and blow up the entire city.

"Now!" she repeated. "Blow yourself up!"

"What are you doing?" the officer yelled in panic. "Have you gone mad?" He put the gun away, pressed his hands to the driver's steering wheel, and motioned for him to put his foot to the gas pedal. The truck tore away into the fog at incredible speed.

~~~

Not a word was spoken afterward. Waleed collapsed to his knees. Sireen knelt beside him. The two held hands and stared at each other in great appreciation. The fog thickened around them, a blanket of haze covering them so that they could barely see one another. Sireen smiled at the thought that Om Zaki had almost been right about the fog, but there was no wedding dress and no true tragedy—just fog.

"Let's get out of here," Waleed said at last.

Chapter 22

Protocol of Death

What makes the potion of liberty and jeopardy such an alluring blend? What makes us want to find silver linings in clouds and geometric patterns among random stars? Why do we have the delusion that the world is on our side and the universe is our friend? That innate sense of cosmic justice, which feeds the idea that somehow good will triumph at the end, has been locked on one of our chromosomes since the time of epic battles and ancient gods. Perhaps it once presented an evolutionary advantage, or perhaps . . . good really wins in the end if we wait long enough.

The living situation in Homs had gotten considerably worse over the previous month. Every house in Homs turned into a temple full of candles, packed with visitors and loud with prayers. Electricity had become a delicacy, and water transformed into a precious chemical. People were beginning to use ancient water wells that hadn't been used since Thomas Edison invented the light bulb. Food and medical products were becoming more expensive by the day. Gasoline was less attainable than gold, and even the filthy coal suddenly found itself more valuable than black opal. Talks of a Daraa-like siege haunted the city as tens of thousands of troops were suspiciously amassing around the borders.

The regime's massacres during the Muslim holy month of Ramadan created waves of outrage in the Middle Eastern street, placing tremendous pressure on Arab governments to act, given the lack of a Western desire to intervene. Thus, the Arab League protocol was born. This protocol called for an immediate halt to all government violence against civilians. On the outside, it appeared to be a reasonable protocol. In reality, it was only a way to give the regime a new license to kill. Egypt's Nabil Al-Araby was head of the Arab League at the time. He chose Ahmad Al-Dabi as head of the Arab observers' team. Of all the people in the Arab world, he picked Mr. Al-Dabi, a Sudanese general who was accused of grave war crimes against civilians in Darfur. The message was clear to the people of Syria: no one is on your side.

In fact, the rate of killing and the use of heavy weaponry

increased dramatically after the implantation of the protocol, which later became known as the "protocol of death." The Syrians soon learned to be very, very careful what they wished for.

—*Syria: A History in Blood* by Celine Dubois

January 24, 2012
Deaths: 6,000

<>

"Do you hear that?" Waleed yelled. "I think the water's back!"

"I hear it," Omar said. "I hear it! Fill up as many bottles as you can, and wash all our medical equipment while we can."

Waleed took pride in following his friend's command. Over the past few weeks, he, Omar, and Omar's crew had made great advances in setting up an underground hospital in the neighborhood of Baba Amro and many smaller satellite clinics around the city. Those were mostly run by resident doctors expelled from hospitals for aiding victims of regime violence. Those residents soon made their way to the very top of the regime's hit list. To be seen treating someone outside the government hospital setting meant an immediate execution by government forces. Nurses, ambulance drivers, and medical students who did not abide by the rules faced a similar fate. The main problem with these efforts was the severe shortage of resources and medical products. Many pro-revolution doctors and nurses were asked to stay at government hospitals and help smuggle supplies. Being medically cost-effective was not only crucial, but failure to do so was fatal.

"The water tastes strange," Waleed warned his friend. "And its color is not entirely clear."

"Why don't you go analyze a specimen under a microscope?" Omar suggested. "Ola, God bless her, smuggled one for us from the medical school."

"All right. I'll do that. My brother Khalid and Sireen will be joining us soon. See if you have any tasks for them when they get here."

Waleed went to the adjacent room, where he found a microscope of a quality that impressed him. *Ola did a good job*, he thought. He spread the sample on a glass slide and took a look under the lens. The water was certainly not clear. He applied a gram stain to the sample to look for bacteria and was shocked to see hundreds of gram-positive and gram-negative bacteria in pairs, chains, and clusters. He applied several other stains and found all kinds of bacteria and even some parasites. From what he saw, the point was clear: the regime was trying to poison the people of Homs. *How did they manage to get all those different pathogens, and in such large quantities?* he wondered. Then it dawned on him.

"Omar!" he hollered. "This is a disaster. Come at once!"

"What happened? What's the matter?" Omar looked concerned as he entered the room.

"The drinking water! They mixed it with sewage!"

"Oh Lord! Are you sure of this?" He rushed to take a look through the microscope. "Oh God! This is a catastrophe. Those bastards!" He stepped back and smashed his fist into the table.

"What can we do now? The water has been out for four days, and everyone will rush to drink from it as soon as they know it's back."

"Where are those damned observers? Why don't they observe this instead of spending their time at five-star hotels sleeping with the regime's whores?" Omar smashed the table again and again. "We need to inform as many people as we can of this, and as soon as possible."

"*Salam*," came the lovely voice. "Why do you guys look like you've seen a ghost?" Sireen entered with Khalid in tow.

"Sireen, Khalid," Waleed said. "The drinking water is contaminated. I don't know if this is just in Baba Amro or the entire city, but we need to warn people right away. They're trying to poison all of us." Waleed tried and failed to hide the grim look on his face. He sat down and pressed his fist against his forehead. He reached for his cell phone to make a call, but found that there was no service. "Of course they shut down the phone service, and electricity has been down for days. They wouldn't want it so that anyone can be warned."

"We have to go warn people house by house," Khalid suggested. "There's no other way."

When no one replied, he kept after them.

"We're four, and we'll ask people to pass the message along before it's too late." He was interrupted by a heavy knock on the door. "Good, now we're five," he joked as he went to open the door to find a young boy panting for breath. "What's the matter?"

"*Ammo* [Uncle], where's Dr. Omar?" the boy said. "We need him right away. Assad's men shot my father in his neck. I need him right now, please." He began to cry.

Omar pushed past Khalid, looking only briefly back at Waleed as if to silently ask for his help. "I'm Doctor Omar. I'm coming with you right away. Don't worry." Omar grabbed his medical equipment, medications, and drips and moved closer to the boy. "*Habibi* [Darling], your arm is bleeding. Did you get shot, too?"

The boy cried harder. "Yes, but I'm all right. My father is in danger. Please save him. My mom has already been martyred, and my older brother. He's all we have left. Please save him." He reached for his right arm in pain as he begged.

"Waleed, I need your help with this one. Carry the kid and stop his bleeding while we run to find his father. I can't do this on my own." He looked at Khalid and Sireen. "You guys have to deal with the water crisis. You can do it on your own. I'm sure dozens of young revolutionaries will help you."

"Don't worry," Khalid reassured. "We got this."

Waleed stepped forward to gather the child and carry him into the makeshift hospital as the others left the house.

~~~

"We can do this," Khalid told Sireen as they performed the world's grimmest high-five.

Sireen felt her adrenaline pumping through her veins as she scanned the rooftops in the broken neighborhood before her. She imagined all the mothers and children in the neighborhood drinking feverishly from their poisoned taps. "All right, where do we begin?"

"I'll stay in Baba Amro. You go to our neighborhood and ask my brother Sami to help you spread the message."

Not a single minute was wasted as they both began their assigned missions. There were large protests expected on that day, which meant that dozens of people would be shot and would require underground medical attention. The last thing Omar's hospital needed was dozens of cases of poisoning added on top of that. It would completely overwhelm them.

~~~

Sireen was indeed feeling overwhelmed, as her hours of sleep had diminished dramatically. She had been eating and drinking just enough to keep herself alive, but not even close to satiety. Showering, electricity, and lighting had all become luxuries. She forgot how it felt to be warm during those freezing winter nights. She hadn't heard from her parents in months. She even forgot to notice that she had come down with the flu and had been feverish for a day. What's a flu when everyone around is bleeding and dying? What's a flu when people are being starved and poisoned?

She pushed it aside and ran back home to warn Waleed's family about the contaminated water. The way home was like a journey through hell—not because of the hungry kids on the streets searching through trash cans, and not because of the weeping mothers and sobbing lovers, but because she knew what they didn't know. She knew that the worst was yet to come. She knew that Homs would soon be another Daraa, and she also knew exactly what that meant. She had developed the skill of turning off her peripheral vision and blocking her ears whenever she walked in the streets. There was nothing she could do to save all those lives. She had no armies under her command like the observing West, and neither did she have a surplus of wheat and cheese reserved for the cattle. She was just one person with the flu.

"*Khale, Khale*, I'm hungry!" an eight-year-old girl said as she ran up to Sireen. She spoke the words with a soft voice resonating with shame and regret. She was clearly reluctant to ask for help.

Sireen just looked at her and remained silent.

"They killed my parents last month," the girl said. "I'm not from here. I don't have any other relatives in Homs. Can I have a piece of bread only?"

Without saying a word, Sireen knelt down and pressed the girl close to her chest. During the embrace, they held a detailed but silent conversation where they exchanged burdens. Sireen then got up, held her hand, and walked the girl home with her.

By the time they reached Waleed's building, she had learned that the little girl's name was Atargatis, and like Sireen, was nicknamed "Soso" by her mother. She was eight and a half years old. Her parents were activists from the neighboring city of Salamiyeh, a stronghold of secular opposition. It had historically been the religious capital of Ismaili Islam, the only religious minority that was staunchly anti-regime. The regime punished them with a systematic policy of impoverishment, neglect, and harassment of activists.

When they reached the building, something didn't seem quite right. People were leaving the building anxiously. Two men had been shot nearby and were being rushed to underground clinics. Sireen and her new friend pushed through the crowd and went upstairs to Waleed's apartment. She introduced the little girl to Sarah and related her story. She also warned them about the contaminated water. They offered the girl a sugar sandwich, some green olives, and a bottle of canned orange juice. They, too, were running out of food and water. Little Soso was delighted to have them. She hugged Sarah and thanked her when she was done eating.

"I think I'll keep her," Sarah told Sireen. "I always wanted a little girl. What kind of name is Atargatis? Is it Ismaili?"

"No, it's ancient Syrian," Sireen said. "I'll tell you all about it later. It's a fascinating story in Syrian mythology, a story the Baath Party has blocked from our curriculum. For now, though, I have to take Sami and go warn the people not to drink the water."

Sami was ready. She realized for the first time that she had never really done anything with Waleed's younger brother. They hadn't even had a full conversation. He was a quiet person, very discreet. He was shorter than his two brothers, softer, and clearly less interested in talking to her. Perhaps he thought she was shallow, or maybe it was just his nature. He had blue eyes like his mother and pale white skin like no one else in the family. His black, silky hair was long enough to cover his eyes, making him even murkier. He carried a bag of medical supplies with him as he signaled to Sireen that they should head out.

"Bye, Soso," Sireen said to the girl. "*Khale* Om Khalid will take good care of you."

The two knocked on every door in the building, warning all their neighbors not to drink any water no matter how thirsty they got. Then they went to the next building and the one after. In some instances, it was too late, as some were already showing signs of serious gastroenteritis. Sami distributed Flagyl and Ciprofloxacin like candy, as his brother had taught him to do in the early days of the revolution. Sireen would tell the afflicted to find one of the underground clinics if their symptoms did not resolve.

"Don't go to government hospitals," she said. "They will only let you die."

The stories coming out of government hospitals were shocking. Physicians were killed for helping opposition patients after being reported by loyalist nurses. Certain *Shabeeha* nurses were known to inject patients with multiple doses of potassium chloride until their hearts stopped. The wounded were allowed to bleed to death; the ill were left untreated; and those who were fine were stabbed and tortured with surgical equipment.

"We have told enough people who can pass the message along," Sireen said to Sami. "We need to go back to the clinic, since no one else is there. Don't you agree?"

"Sure," he said without looking at her.

She couldn't understand why he couldn't trust her like everyone else did. She smiled at him, but he looked away. Was he that cold with everyone, or was it just with her? Was he shy of women?

"I hear you're into art?" she said, trying to stir some conversation as they pressed on through the streets.

"Graphic design," he replied stoically.

"You think we'll win this revolution?"

"Yes," he said.

Yes? That's it? She was annoyed by his brief responses. She was simply unable to predict the way thoughts were deflected through the circuits of his brain before he produced such noncommittal answers. She gave up at last, and they walked all the way to the clinic without saying another word.

~~~

Sarah was startled by heavy knocking on her door. She rushed to the bedroom to cover her hair and woke her husband. There was no one else at home but the two of them and the little girl. The knocking grew heavier and then turned into forceful pounding. Before she and Muhammad could reach the door, it broke open. Sarah tumbled back onto the sofa as a vaguely familiar man charged inside. It did not take her long to realize that this was Hussein, the ex-fiancé that Sireen had told her so much about. He entered with four other armed men dressed in Syrian military clothes.

"Where is she?" he yelled at Sarah.

"Where's who, son?" she asked politely. "Can we help you with something?" She kept her head held high, covering her fear.

"Where's that whore? Where is she? Sireen and her little boyfriend."

"Son, I don't know who you're talking about. We don't have any Sireens in this house. This is my only daughter." She pointed to the little girl. "Can I make you some tea?"

Hussein was furious. He pushed Sarah to the floor and lifted the little girl in the air. "I have men capable of doing anything. Don't test us. Perhaps I need to refresh your memory." He smiled at one of his men and tossed the little girl in the air for him. He caught her.

"She's just a little girl," Muhammad said. "Keep her out of this, sir."

"Shut up, old man," replied the soldier who was holding Atargatis. She began to cry quietly as she looked to Sarah for help.

Sarah looked on hopelessly as the man took the girl into the bathroom and locked the door. Two other men held Sarah down as Hussein kept Muhammad at bay at gunpoint.

"Sir, you can't hurt her," Sarah begged. "She's only eight. Please!"

"Tell me where Sireen is and where your son is."

"I don't know a girl by that name. My son is at the hospital."

"Really? He hasn't been in the hospital for months now. You think we don't know about his secret clinics to help the traitors?" He stopped talking as a scream from the bathroom broke Sarah's heart. She pushed the soldier off her and stormed to the bathroom door. Inside, she could hear the sound of the soldier striking the poor girl again and again.

"Please stop!" she hollered through the door. "Please, she is only an innocent girl!"

Hussein and his men were clearly amused. Sarah began crying as she fell to the floor. She kept knocking on the door and praying out loud that God punish these men. Ten minutes later, the door swung open, and out stepped the soldier, muttering something to himself. In the bathroom, the girl's face was mangled and her clothing ripped. A hollow fear came to Sarah that the soldier had raped the girl, but she found relief when she saw that the child still wore her pants. The girl sobbed uncontrollably as Sarah took her in her arms.

"Don't cry," Hussein said to Sarah. "We would have done the same to you if you weren't too old." He laughed along with his men.

At that, Muhammad stood and shoved Hussein to the floor. "She is my wife, the mother of my boys, and my love. You will not insult her like that."

Hussein got up slowly, aided by two of his men. The other two grabbed Muhammad by the arms, threw him down, and pinned him to the floor. Sarah and Soso remained huddled in a corner as the two began to kick Muhammad, spit on him, and use racist and sectarian slurs.

In time, Hussein signaled for them to stop. He aimed his rifle at Muhammad's head. "Beg me for your life, you dog."

Muhammad remained silent.

Hussein's four men each held onto one of Muhammad's limbs as Hussein pressed his shoe against his face. The madman put his rifle aside and snatched a dagger from his handbag. He carried it cautiously like a precious child. Sarah whimpered as she watched Hussein rip her husband's clothes with the dagger until his chest was bare.

"Beg like the dog you are," Hussein ordered.

Sarah's heart soared and her chest ached as Muhammad remained silent.

The madman began to slash her husband's chest with the dagger as he grimaced in pain. Still, Muhammad kept his silence. Sarah could not quite see what was happening, but she could hear the sick sound of metal carving through flesh. It drove her to stand, to leave the quivering child behind, so she could see the torture her husband endured.

The knife gleamed in the soft light of the living room as Hussein carved into Muhammad's chest. As Sarah drew closer, she saw that her husband's tormentor was writing letters into his flesh. *Aleph... Lam... Aleph... Seen... Dal...* It was the name of Al-Assad.

Sarah wept and trembled as she watched in agony. "Please, leave him alone," she said, reaching out to touch Hussein's shoulder.

Muhammad looked at her with a scowl that said a million words, starting with, *I know what I'm doing. There's nothing they can do to humiliate me. Don't enable them.* It even said, *I love you and I love my boys.* She obeyed and watched silently as her husband submitted to the torture.

When he had finished, Hussein stabbed Muhammad deep in his abdomen three times before climbing off him. Sarah could feel each sharp stab penetrate her own heart. Two men grabbed Muhammad by his legs and dragged him outside the apartment. As she followed, Sarah began to get flashbacks from the Hama Massacre. She started panicking and breathing hard. She cried, shivered, and bit her hands.

Muhammad looked up at her, still scowling. "Om Khalid, pull yourself together. The boys need you." Blood spilled from his mouth. His head rippled against the stairs as the men dragged him down and out of the building.

One man stayed in the apartment, holding Sarah back. "Tell your son to turn himself in if he wants his father's body." With that, he left the apartment.

Sarah's heart wanted to shatter into a thousand pieces, but instead, she honored her husband's last wish and pulled herself together. She watched through the window as they dragged the father of her children through the street, bleeding from his chest, mouth, and the back of his head. A mob of young men rushed to him to try to intervene, but they were simple, unarmed civilians. The soldiers, a gang that had by now grown to ten, hunted them like doves. Perhaps ten young men fell down either dead or wounded. Meanwhile, the soldiers tied Muhammad to the back of their truck by his legs and paraded him through the neighborhood before dragging him into the dark, neglected alley across the street from Sarah's apartment.

By the time they stopped, Sarah had run into the street, close enough that she could see that her husband was breathing his last breaths. He was still conscious, but completely disoriented, thank God. Hussein placed his foot on Muhammad's chest and pointed his rifle at his face. "Where's your son?" he asked.

Muhammad smiled and ignored him.

"Where's Sireen?"

He continued to ignore him.

"Well, then you can go to hell. Any last requests?"

"Sami," Sarah heard her husband mumble. When he smiled, he revealed teeth red from his blood.

Hussein leaned closer, presenting his ear in a mocking fashion. "What?

What was that?"

"I want to see my son Sami," Muhammad said.

"Your son?" Hussein mocked. "With a wife like yours, how do you know he's your son?" He burst out laughing.

"My wife?" Muhammad said, his voice becoming clear once again. "She's a woman of honor. She's my love. She's—"

He could not finish as the bullet ripped through his forehead. Sarah, standing far behind, did not shed a tear, did not shiver, did not yell. She kept herself together as she returned to the apartment and firmly grabbed the hand of her new daughter. She found herself in a state of silent catatonia. She heard not the bullets in the background, but rather heard love songs from the eighties. She saw no blood and no fallen bodies on the streets. Instead, she relived her life with her beloved Mohammad.

She remembered when they had first met a couple of years after the massacre. She had just lost her family, her home, her lover, and her peace of mind. She was a psychological mess as she struggled through PTSD, anxiety disorders, depression, and panic attacks. He was there to hold her hand whenever the monsters in her mind attacked. He helped her stand back up on her feet and become functional again. Then they got married and had their first son, Khalid. She could visualize the day Khalid was born like it was only a week ago. She could smell his babyish aroma, and she could almost feel his tiny hands squeeze her finger. Warm tears snuck out of her eyes at the thought as she squeezed the hand of Atargatis, just to be sure she hadn't left her in one of the remote rooms of her imagination.

~~~

Waleed clenched his jaw as he realized that he and Omar would not be able to save the man who was shot in the neck. They had given him fluids, vasopressors, and even blood, but were unable to keep up with his blood loss and the dropping of his blood pressure. They gave him the last bag of A-positive blood that they had. Omar tried hard to fix the damage the bullet had caused to his carotid arteries, but with no use. When it was over, Waleed took the man's son aside and tried to console him.

He patted the boy on his back and hugged him. "He's been martyred. I'm so sorry. We couldn't save him."

"Can't you give him more blood?" the boy pled, tears of grief streaming down his face. "You can take mine."

"I'm sorry," Waleed said, his own eyes watering.

"What do I tell my four-year-old brother? How do I take care of him? Tell Baba to come back. He can't leave us." He ran to his father's dead body and began to yell, "Baba! Baba! You can't leave us alone! Baba!"

Waleed went to him. "There's nothing harder than losing your father. He's now a martyr. He's with God."

"Have you lost your father, too?" the boy asked, his cries slowing.

"No, but I can imagine how it must feel. Where's your little brother now?"

"He's at home alone. Should I go bring him?"

"Do you have any relatives here?"

"No, not here. My uncle lives in the village of Hola."

"All right. We'll try to help you and your little brother get there. Is it all right with you if we bury the martyr's body and pray on him today?" Waleed asked this despite anticipating dozens more bodies to be found on the streets throughout the day. He was getting worried about the spread of disease and rodents if the bodies were not buried in a timely manner.

The boy agreed, and soon the martyr was wrapped in the revolution flag and placed in a cheap wooden box filled with roses and jasmines. Dozens of strangers showed up for this flash funeral, in what had become a new Syrian tradition. The martyr was lifted on people's shoulders to the cemetery as the mourners sang songs of the revolution.

As anticipated, soon the soldiers arrived and began to shoot at the mourners, forcing them to disperse. Fortunately, this time no one was killed, but funerals had become particularly popular targets for regime snipers and soldiers. Future martyrs would carry past martyrs, or perhaps past martyrs somehow selected their successors. Either way, the train to heaven was loaded with martyrs multiple times a day.

When the shooting was done, Waleed and the mourners regrouped. The grieving young boy followed behind as the men carried his father all the way to his house, where his younger brother awaited. Waleed's heart sank when he saw that the four-year-old was thrilled by the celebratory funeral, clapping and singing along. He failed to understand that he would never see his father again. Solemn prayer hung in the air as the martyr was laid to rest in a newly established cemetery.

Later that afternoon, back at the hospital, Omar agreed to keep the two boys with him until they were able to transport them to their uncle in Hola.

Every hour, dozens of new trauma cases would come in through the doors, most of them gunshot wounds. Soon they ran out of supplies. By late evening, people started showing up with symptoms of severe gastroenteritis. All the underground clinics were saturated with patients. They were also understaffed and severely short on resources.

When there was no more to be done, Waleed took Sireen by the hand and invited her to join him in following Omar back to his house for dinner after a long day of work.

~~~

After a light meal, Sireen asked Omar's permission to go with Waleed onto the roof. They hadn't been there since March. Much had changed since them. They had changed as individuals; the people around them had changed; even the laws of nature had changed. She sat quietly beside him as they looked down on the city of Homs. Electricity was out in the wounded city. Bandages of darkness covered its wounds. A cold breeze pushed Sireen closer to him. They could hear crickets, gunshots, and small explosions in the background.

They held hands and stared at their beloved city without saying a word. Waleed looked at Sireen and slowly opened his mouth as if struggling to say something. What was he going to say? Perhaps "I love you," or "Are you scared?" or "You look beautiful." Sireen's heart raced. A few seconds later, he managed to say what was on his mind.

"Are you still hungry?" he asked, showing her a sandwich he had been hiding.

"Am I hungry?" she asked, smiling. "People are dying, I'm freezing from the cold, and you ask me if I'm hungry? You're ridiculous." Even so, she snatched the sandwich from his hand. She was indeed still hungry.

"You know *za'atar* is good for you. So eat it and be thankful. People used it as a medication in the past."

"Oh please, Waleed, be quiet. You're only saying that because za'atar and bread are the only things left in this neighborhood." She had been eating za'atar sandwiches all day long, and in a way, she was thankful. She was conscious of Waleed staring at her as she quietly nibbled the sandwich like a child.

"I finished the poem I started," he said.

She swallowed quickly. "Really? That's wonderful. Why don't you read it?"

He stood and walked to the edge of the roof. Sireen followed. He gave her a smart look as he came to stand beside the jasmine tree. She smiled, shook her head, and watched. She missed those old days as though her life had been frozen for the past ten months and only resumed this very moment.

"*The shine in your eyes . . .*" he read, pausing to look deep into her eyes.

"Like angels of the morning . . .
Stealing my heart into heaven
When my heartbeats rise . . .
With a touch of your fingers, my heart reaches cloud number seven
The unborn dream dies . . .
Like shadows from a sunset, on Earth there's no such thing as heaven
The angel then flies . . .
With a touch of reality, I lose sight of cloud number seven
My heart bleeds and cries . . .
A rage like insanity, as flames steal away my heaven
Promises and lies . . .
Your crime is that I loved you, chasing you to cloud number seven
A sea of hope dries . . .
The dream of dreamers dies, and clouds block all roads to heaven . . ."

He closed his eyes, took a deep breath, and sighed. His eyes glittered under the moonlight, or perhaps the moon glittered due to the shine in his eyes. If it wasn't for his light beard and mustache, she would have thought that his face was the moon itself. She pushed her hair back and looked away before his charms became too powerful for her broken soul to resist. He reached for her hand and held it tight as they both looked down at the old city quietly. She felt invincible and immortal, like a Greek goddess, or simply like a woman in love. If only they had met earlier, she wouldn't have wasted all those precious years with that despicable fiancé of hers.

The silence was beautiful. She closed her eyes and felt the warmth of his hand creep into her veins and melt her heart. She began to shiver, either from the cold or from the magnificence of the moment.

Then something changed. It was preceded by silence—the calm before a storm. As Sireen watched breathlessly, a rumbling force gathered in the distance. It surged through the sleeping city as if shaking it from beneath. Her feet trembled. Her bones shook. A strong force thrust her into Waleed's arms and pushed them both onto the floor of the roof. Only then did she hear the ear-splitting blast and see the white, blinding light.

"What just happened?" she asked in shock, her ears still ringing. They got up and rushed toward the other side of the building, where the noise had come from.

Smoke and fire were erupting from a distant neighborhood. They stared at the blazing fire spreading throughout the neighborhood as the attacking tanks quickly withdrew.

Omar appeared, carrying his baby nephew Hod-Hod on his shoulders. "What just happened?" he asked.

Sireen pointed toward the burning buildings without saying a word.

"Those bastards!" Omar said. "That's the Bab Tadmur neighborhood, probably. God knows how many people are dead or wounded. We need to get to work soon." He handed Hod-Hod to Sireen, who was delighted to carry the beautiful boy.

She watched as Omar checked his cell phone to see if the service was back. It wasn't. He opened the bird cage and got out one of his pigeons. "Sireen, you know this darling very well. This is my F-16." He kissed the pigeon and sent her toward the fire. "Fortunately, the government has no way of stopping our pigeon mail. Someone will send us back a message about the number of casualties and the supplies needed." He turned to Waleed. "For now, you and I need to get ready to pull an all-nighter like in the old days."

"You mean you're going to Bab Tadmur?" Sireen said, her eyes flashing to Waleed. "It's not safe."

"We have to," Omar replied. "It's only a matter of time before no place in Homs is safe, anyway. We need to help each other out and establish a strong alternative to government services." He pointed at Hod-Hod. "I need you to take care of these kids. There are lots of them today."

"Man, I haven't been home all day," Waleed complained. "I'm worried about my parents."

Omar did not break his incredulous stare.

With a sigh, Waleed relented and agreed to go. Sireen's heart sank, as she had hoped he would refuse. "I'll ask Khalid to join us and ask Sami to go home and check on Mama and Baba. Are they still downstairs?"

"Yes, they're playing with the kids. Go talk to them while I wait for my F-16 to come back."

Waleed quickly ran downstairs. Sireen did not follow this time. She watched him disappear as a heavy weight pressed on her chest. She closed her eyes and took a deep breath. "Omar, take care of him, please."

"You're telling me to take care of Waleed? This is the one person for whom I would take ten bullets and a hundred knives. He's not just my friend; he's much more. He's not a brother; he's much more. He's my soul mate. Don't tell me to take care of Waleed, Sireen. Never. You don't know him a quarter of the way that I know him."

Sireen was taken aback by Omar's sudden anger. "I'm sorry. I didn't mean to upset you. I'm just worried and exhausted."

Omar hung his head. "I apologize, too. We're all tired, but we cannot be tired yet. The road ahead is long, painful, and full of thorns."

"This peacefulness is killing us."

"I don't want to discuss this with you again. This revolution shall remain peaceful as a dove and pure as snow. That's the only way we can have any legitimacy."

"In whose eyes, Omar? In whose eyes? I saw what happened in Daraa, and I know it will happen in Homs and everywhere else. Those people don't understand the meaning of protests and sit-ins, or even hunger strikes. They are criminals. If you want any chance for freedom, you need to fight."

Omar turned his back on her. "Start your own revolution, then, and be as violent as you want. Thousands of martyrs have died for this peaceful revolution, and it has to remain this way so we can win. Besides, the free world won't sit and watch the regime slaughter us."

Just then, his bird appeared from out of the darkness, taking perch on the edge of the rooftop.

"Come here, darling," Omar said, holding out his finger to coax the bird over to him. "Oh no, you've been hurt, my dear. You're bleeding." He took a small letter off the pigeon's leg, then carried the bird downstairs to bandage its wounds.

Sireen remained on the rooftop, staring at the blazing fire. In time, when she could take it no more, she looked up at the sky and yelled in old Aramaic, "*Elahi, Elahi, lema sebaqtana?* My lord, my lord, why have you forsaken us?"

Chapter 23
Wrath of the Doves

"In one hand she holds a scepter, in the other a spindle. On her head she bears rays and a tower and she wears a grindle . . . On the surface of the statue is an overlay of gold and very costly gems, some of which are white, some the color of water, many have the hue of wine, and many are fiery."

So wrote the early Syrian novelist Lucian of Samosata in the second century A.D., referring to an ancient Syrian goddess. The city of Samosata was composed of native Syrians who spoke their Syrian Aramaic tongue and Greeks who had been imported since the time of Alexander the Great. Many educated Syrians like Lucian were forced to use Greek as their official tongue. This was a recurrent theme in Syrian history, when Latin became the official tongue and then Arabic. All those layers of languages were imposed atop the native Western Aramaic tongue of Syria, eventually giving birth to "Syrian Arabic."

Lucian shed light on the world's first half-human, half-fish creature long before it was incorporated into Roman mythology and American movies. Her name was Atargatis.

Atargatis was known to the Greeks and Romans as Dea Sura, or the goddess of Syria. Syrians knew her by her original name, Ataratheh. She was extremely important in Syrian culture during the first millennium B.C. She was to them what the Virgin Mary became when Syria turned to Christ. However, she was not quite the Virgin Mary. She was the goddess of nature, fertility, love, and war. She was very much a personification of Mother Nature with her beauty, her cruelty, her smoothness, and her might. It was a time in history when femininity was celebrated. She used lions to punish the wicked. She proclaimed doves to be sacred animals. She forbade Syrians from hunting them, until one day when she met a young Syrian hunter.

Atargatis, the glorious and powerful, discovered her weakness in the arms of that mortal Syrian man. Her powers dwindled on his lips, and her heart was crushed under his feet as the lines between mortals and gods blurred. The goddess of love and sexuality lost control of her own instincts and became pregnant. Her beloved man was her ultimate weakness and her greatest *threat. After bringing shame to herself and to the gods, she self-imposed her punishment by throwing herself in the Euphrates River and casting a spell to turn herself into a fish. However, her beauty was so intense that the spell wasn't strong enough to turn her into a full fish. She instead became mythology's first mermaid. As the story goes, she would have drowned in the Euphrates, had the fish of the river not saved her.*

After that, fish were declared sacred animals, and their killing was sure to bring the wrath of the half-fish, half-human goddess. It is to this day that some Syrian women will gasp at the sight of dead fish in an aquarium, given the bad omen it represents.

In many ways, the ancient Dea Sura was similar to the new lady of Syria, the Tumultus Sura [Syrian Uprising]. There was her obsession with beauty, peace, and doves; her resilience and her ownership of Syria's best men; her agony, her misery, and her sorrows; her immortality, her justice, and her imperfection. The revolution had at last filled that ancient Syrian yearning for a sacred feminine spirit worth dying for. However, too many sacred doves had been slaughtered, and the nation was left wondering when the wrath of the new lady of Syria would be unleashed upon the transgressors.

—*Syria: A History in Blood* by Celine Dubois

February 4, 2012
Deaths: 6,700

"Sireen, someone is outside looking for you," Sami said, barely lifting his eyes off the floor. "He says it's very important."

Normally, Sireen would have been frustrated at the lack of eye contact, but she couldn't blame Sami on this day. The news of his father's death had taken a heavy toll on him. He hadn't left the house since then, and had hardly eaten anything. Sami had a very special bond with his father and was still in denial about the whole situation. Strangely, he was grieving the least. His mother and two brothers, meanwhile, had been haunted by unpredictable crying spells for the previous two weeks. Their work at the underground clinics had come to a screeching stop. Much of the burden had fallen back on Omar, Sireen, and new volunteers.

"Did he tell you his name?" Sireen asked as she looked into Sarah's vanity mirror and brushed her hair with her fingers.

"He probably did. I can't remember. He had a thick Horani accent."

Sireen couldn't hide the broad smile on her face as she rushed to the door.

It must be Yousef, she thought. She opened the door, delighted to find that indeed it was him. She wanted to hug him and kiss him on the cheek, but she simply extended her hand. He placed his hand on his heart and smiled, a gentle gesture of refusal to shake hands common among the more conservative Muslims.

"I see it's getting worse," she joked. "You don't even shake hands now."

He smiled and furrowed his eyebrows. "How is my princess?"

She really missed him, she realized. It was a strange feeling she had for him. It wasn't that passionate love she had for Waleed, but it wasn't the brotherly love she had for Khalid, either. It was confusing, the way he affected her. She loved being in his presence. It made her feel safe and protected. Who could hurt her when she was with him? She sank into that feeling of serenity that she had dearly missed.

"I was asking how you're doing," he repeated.

"Oh, Yousef," she quailed. "It's been tough." She lowered her voice to a whisper. "They just lost their father. Regime thugs killed him. The situation at the clinic is deteriorating, as well. We're running out of basic medical supplies and food. There is no water or electricity."

"We've got sources that have informed us that the situation is about to get much worse in Homs. That's why we're here."

"We? Don't tell me you're armed."

He moved his neck to the side to reveal a rifle he was hiding inside his shirt. "The government forces are planning a huge massacre here. Iranian and Russian special forces are planning to turn Homs into another Grozny. This will be even worse than what happened in Daraa. Many of my men and I have been coming from Daraa to fight with the Farouq brigades here for some time."

"But the problem here is that no one supports an armed rebellion. They all want a peaceful revolution."

"Well, the activists can want whatever they want, but when our women and children start getting slaughtered by the regime's army, the Free Syrian Army cannot stand by and watch."

Sireen sighed. "But they're so much more powerful than you."

"They're not more powerful; they just have more weapons and air power. We have faith and a just cause. We fight for our freedom, while they fight for their slavery."

Sireen cast a glance over her shoulder to make sure no one was listening from inside the house. "I can't say this too loudly, but I totally support you. The doves of the revolution have accomplished their mission; it's now time for a true armed resistance. It's the only language this regime understands. The revolution must show its true might."

"I have something for you." Yousef smiled, bit his moustache, and reached into his shirt. It was a letter. Sireen's heart skipped a few beats. "It's from your parents. I was there at the Za'atary camp in Jordan two weeks ago."

She grabbed the letter and sniffed it.

Yousef laughed. "I don't think it smells like your mother anymore. Probably it just smells like me."

"How can I thank you, Yousef? This means the world to me."

"It's my duty, princess." He turned halfway, as if to leave. "There's one more thing I need from you before I go."

"Name it."

"There are two foreign journalists that we helped sneak into Syria. I'll give you their address. They're not too far. If you could talk to them and help them get a good story to spread the message of our revolution to their countries, it would help our cause . . . just in case there is still some country out there with a bit of conscience left." He handed her a piece of paper with the address on it, gave her a military salute, and walked away.

Sireen went back into the house, shut herself alone in the bedroom she shared with Sarah, and opened the letter from her parents.

> *Dear Soso,*
>
> *I was very happy to read your last letter, which your friend Yousef delivered to us. God bless him. We're glad to know that you are safe and cared for at Abu Khalid's house. Sarah, Om Khalid is a great friend of mine. She will be like your mother. Life here at the camp has not been easy, but we thank God for everything. We found out that our house was completely destroyed. The news was like a bullet in my flesh, but we are thankful for our safety and yours. Take care of yourself and keep praying.*
>
> *Love, Mama*

Sireen's eyes filled with tears as she kissed the letter softly. She wiped her tears and got up. "I'm going to the Khaldiyeh neighborhood," she said to the walls, figuring no one was with her in the room. "There are some people I need to meet."

"It's not safe for a woman to go out alone," Khalid said in a soft voice.

Sireen startled when she saw Khalid standing in the doorway. She had not heard him enter. Ever since his father's death, he'd had to deal with the extra burden of being the alpha male of the family, and had taken it upon himself to make sure everyone else was cared for and protected. This led to him skulking around the house like a ghost. "I'll come with you, if you must go."

"It's really not necessary. I think I'll be fine."

"No, I'm coming with you," he insisted as he put on his coat and walked to the door with her. "Where are we going?"

Sireen hesitated for a moment, wondering whether she should share the information with Khalid or trust him to join her in the mission Yousef had left with her. "There are some foreign journalists in the Khaldiyeh neighborhood.

They need help getting around, and they need an interpreter. Hopefully they can get our story out."

With a nod, Khalid stepped aside and let Sireen lead the way.

"Looks like we might be a bit late," he said as they walked through a small alley to avoid the government checkpoint at the end of the road. "The United Nations Security Council will meet today to vote again about Syria. We'll see if the Russians veto the resolution this time." He was clearly fuming with anger. He stopped abruptly and pulled Sireen toward the wall. "There's a sniper on that building," he said, looking over her shoulder. "Let's carefully take a left."

They traveled in much the same way for many blocks.

When they reached Khaldiyeh, they were greeted by several dead bodies scattered on the streets. This meant that there would soon be a funeral protest and more deaths and more funerals. Earlier that same day, the news was that dozens of people had been killed in a large funeral protest in Daraya in rural Damascus. Two days before that, hundreds were killed in large cross-country protests commemorating the thirtieth anniversary of the Hama Massacre. It was the very first public commemoration of that horrendous massacre in Syria. Protestors were dying by the hundreds, activists hunted like birds, one at a time. Numerous voices for the first time began to question the utility of keeping the revolution peaceful.

"We're here," Sireen said as she compared Yousef's note to the address on the dilapidated building looming before them. It was a tall structure with broken windows and peeling yellow paint. "Let's go up to the third floor."

"No, wait," Khalid said, holding out his arm to bar her entry. "We don't know who might have been watching us. Let's just sit at the entrance of the building for a few minutes, and then we'll go up. We don't want to risk the lives of the foreigners."

They sat on the staircase and observed the street for any signs of a potential spy or government agents.

"Do you know if the two boys made it safely to their uncle in Hola?" Sireen asked after a time.

"Yes, Abu Shehab delivered them to their uncle's doorstep. You know Abu Shehab, don't you?"

"Vaguely. I've heard of him. The guy who pirates movies, right?"

"Pirates movies? Oh, that was a lifetime ago. Now he's our main guy who disseminates videos from Homs to the rest of the world." Khalid smiled. "Nerds are crucial to our revolution."

Sireen didn't feel like laughing. "I'm worried about Atargatis," she said with deep concern. "She lost her parents, she was beaten by Assad's criminals, and we've been too busy with our own funerals that I don't know if moving her to a new place was a good idea."

"What can we do, Sireen? Our mother is in no position to take care of a child. She will be better cared for in Hola. The boys' uncle and his wife said they would be glad to support her as long as she needs."

"I just hope she'll be fine. She's been through too much for someone her age."

"Too much for someone of any age," Khalid said as he came to his feet. "I don't see anyone watching us. Let's go meet those journalists."

They climbed to the third floor. The apartment was the one next to the elevators, which had been turned into a distasteful ornament ever since electricity had fled the city of Homs. Khalid gently knocked on the door, and a beautiful blond lady in her late twenties answered.

"'Ello," she said with an anxious smile. It was clear that she wasn't sure who they were, but extended her hand nevertheless. Both Khalid and Sireen shook her hand.

"My name is Sireen. Yousef asked me to stop by and meet you."

"I am Celine Dubois," she said in a heavy French accent. "I am sorry. I don't speak any Arabic. I am from France. I came 'ere to report the story from inside Syria."

"Well, welcome to Syria," Sireen said. "I'm sorry it's under these circumstances, but thank you for caring about our story."

Celine stepped aside so Sireen and Khalid could enter. Inside the sparsely furnished apartment, Sireen saw piles of dirty plates, an unmade sleeper sofa, and a young, pallid man with greasy black hair.

"This is my friend David," Celine said. "He is also a journalist, but he's from England."

Sireen shook David's hand, and so did Khalid, who clearly didn't understand much of what was being said.

"How can we help you?" Sireen asked.

David asked permission to record the conversation. "Why don't you start by telling us about your view of this whole uprising? Is it more of a social awakening like Egypt and Tunisia, or more of an armed rebellion like Libya?"

Sireen waited for the reporter to get the camera running before she replied. She felt somewhat self-conscious about appearing on film, but the fear quickly faded when she considered the depth of the question presented to her. "The Syrian revolution is one like no other. It's one of those stories that will be glorified in history to the degree of mythical legend. It is the purest manifestation of a struggle between good and evil, peace and war, freedom and slavery. The people of Syria have had enough of being treated like slaves for this corrupt regime, and so they have demanded their basic human rights. The regime has so far unleashed a war on the men and women of Syria, but the people have not fought back. This is unprecedented in our very long history."

"Some are concerned that there are extremist elements that could make it to power if the revolution succeeds. What do you think?"

Sireen nodded thoughtfully. "So far, the revolution has been completely peaceful, completely democratic. We are here to fight for all Syrians, not for a specific religion or sect. However, I don't know how much longer people will be able to watch their sons killed and their daughters raped without responding. The world needs to step in. This is genocide. This is ethnic cleansing. It needs to be stopped."

David leaned forward and gave her a serious look. "What will happen if the world continues to ignore the cries for help coming from Syria?"

"The worst will happen," Sireen said with a sigh. "The peaceful revolution will mutate into an armed rebellion, which would then mutate into a civil war. This would not be a simple civil war like the one in Iraq. It would be a vortex that would absorb the entire Middle East. Lebanon, Turkey, Saudi Arabia, Iran, Jordan, and even Iraq, all would join. There would be chaos, and extremists would thrive. Moderates would vanish, and hundreds of thousands would perish."

David flashed a strange look at Celine, who frowned. He turned back to Sireen. "Don't you think there is some exaggeration in what you said?"

"Not at all. Every Syrian child knows this fact. This is Syria. It's the heart of the Middle East. When the heart is ill, the entire body crumbles. What I don't understand is why your intelligence agencies in the West don't know this."

The British journalist let the comment slide off him. He made a quick note on his pad and then returned to his line of questioning. "Do you think the people would support Western intervention in Syria?"

"Yes, absolutely. We need it as soon as possible, because if the free world doesn't step in to help, someone else will. That someone might not be a great fan of your country."

"Do you think you can win?" he asked, his gaze drifting to the window as the loud chants of protestors began to fill the air.

Sireen got up and went to the window, then signaled for the two journalists to come and watch. Thousands of protestors were gathered in the Khaldiyeh neighborhood, all of them carrying the flag of the revolution, flowers, and wooden boxes bearing their fallen martyrs. They had their hands on each other's shoulders as they moved from side to side, chanting songs of pain and sorrow.

"Look at them yourself and tell me," Sireen said. "Do those look like people who would ever give up? They are protesting at a funeral. What stronger message can you think of? Soon the soldiers will come and shoot at them."

The soldiers did eventually show up as they watched, but they weren't there to shoot down the protestors. They arrived in tanks and armored vehicles and began a shocking campaign of bombardment of the neighborhood. Bombs fell on the protestors, on buildings, and on playgrounds. The journalists took cover, trying to pull Sireen along with them, but she could not tear herself away from the horrors she saw below.

Bombs fell like rain, not discriminating between protestor and those minding their own business. The journalists were clearly terrified at the thought that a bomb could strike their building at any moment. Khalid and Sireen exchanged glances hardened by war, and kept watching. A bomb fell among the protestors, killing dozens instantly. Another hit the building on the opposite side of the street, completely shattering its eastern side. The protestors scattered in every direction, but the bombing continued.

Sireen saw panicked women carrying their infants and running aimlessly in the streets among bloodstains, bodies, limbs, and rubble from buildings. An unsettling odor eventually reached Sireen, wafting through the broken window. It was a heavy mixture of smoke, blood, and burning flesh.

A bomb eventually found its way to their building. Sireen wasn't sure whether it had hit above them or below them, but the entire apartment shook as though it were made of cardboard.

As the blast rippled through the building, Sireen went to Celine and huddled close to her, comforting her as she cried. When another bomb hit their building, the side of the ceiling facing the street began to collapse over them. Only then did Sireen feel fear. Khalid charged at them, throwing rubble off of them and pulling them free. Together, the four rushed to the door, but another bomb landed on the roof of the building, pushing everyone to the floor. The ceiling could no longer withstand the cruelty of the bombardment, and collapsed under the weight of its own guilt. Khalid threw himself on Sireen and Celine, protecting them with his body as the building began to collapse. Then there was darkness, screams, and utter silence.

～～～

Time passed. Perhaps it was a minute, or an hour, or a week. Sireen could see ghostlike figures floating above her and talking to her in a language she couldn't understand. Was this heaven? No, it looked too hellish to be heaven. There was a taste of blood and cement in her mouth, and when she took a handful of her hair, she saw that it had more gray in it than a woman of eighty years. Three manly figures lifted her up. One of them carried her in his arms like an infant and placed her on a stretcher. He was yelling and wrapping her with white tape and gauze. What was he doing? Was he mummifying her? He then gave her an injection that made her loopy.

She saw that Celine was also pulled from the rubble and placed on a stretcher beside her. She recognized her only because of the blond hair. The angry man then came back and began to wrap Celine in a similar fashion. His features were becoming more visible. She recognized him at last as Omar. She smiled before sinking into deep sleep.

～～～

Waleed gradually learned that the couple he helped resuscitate in the field was a pair of foreign journalists. He wanted desperately to finish with them so he could go help Omar take care of Khalid and Sireen, but the chaos was too rich for him to carve through. Khalid survived, but sustained a major blow to his spinal cord that would cost him movement and sensation from the waist down. Within the first hour, Waleed heard the grim statistic that four hundred people had died in the attack. The field hospitals were overwhelmed, and they were severely low on staff and resources. Medical students became doctors and art students became nurses to fill the deficits. Hundreds of activists spent the rest of the night trying to evacuate survivors from beneath the debris.

"We have no more morphine," Waleed yelled to Omar as the two of them worked so quickly over the bodies that their hands became a blur.

"Check if there's any left in the old syringes," Omar hollered. "This kid needs his leg amputated tonight."

"There is nothing, Omar. I'm telling you."

"Oh dear God, don't make me do this," Omar said as he went to a six-year-old boy crying in pain. He had sustained several fractures and lacerations, but worst of all was his gangrenous leg.

Waleed held the boy's hand as Omar stood over him.

"*Habibi*," Omar said, "Assad's dogs put something bad in your leg which needs to be removed." Tears flooded his eyes. "When we try to remove it, it will hurt you. So whenever you feel pain, I want you to recite something you know from the Quran. Do you know any Quran?"

The boy nodded vigorously, clenching his teeth as he tightened his grip on Waleed's hand.

Just as Omar reached for the saw, there came a harsh voice from the door.

"So this is your secret dog clinic?" it said. "Who's Omar?"

Waleed's first instinct was to step in front of Omar, hiding him, but Omar was clearly not intimidated.

"It's me," he said, striding around Waleed. "I'm Doctor Omar. How can I help you?"

"You can help me by coming with us. You are under arrest for treason and aiding traitors."

"All right, I will come with you," Omar said quietly. "But I need to operate on this boy's leg first. He will not survive otherwise."

The lead soldier came to the front, his face obscured by a black scarf, but his eyes cutting daggers into Omar. "Shut up before we shoot you and your boy. Are you coming, or do I need to explain myself again?"

Omar said nothing. Waleed drew a breath to protest, but his friend silenced him with a wave of his hand.

"Bring him," the leader said.

Two soldiers grabbed Omar by the arms and dragged him outside. They did not get far before they were interrupted by a strong voice from behind. "Let the doctor go."

"Put your weapon down before we shoot everyone in this clinic," the soldier threatened of the man who had spoken.

Waleed exited the clinic, awash in light and cold, to find a man he recognized standing outside with a half-dozen others. All of them held guns. Waleed struggled to remember the man's name, but then it came to him all at once. This was Yousef, the man who had saved Sireen. He stood bravely in the street outside the clinic, unthreatened by the soldier's bluff.

The soldier sneered and shot a patient in the head. Blood misted into the air. Everyone watching from the clinic gasped, but the soldier moved on to the next patient with a mechanical grace. Before the soldier could shoot again, Yousef and his men opened fire on the four soldiers, killing them all.

When it was over, Yousef approached Omar. "Don't operate on the boy yet. We're going to get you some morphine and whatever medicines you need from the government hospital. We can be back in fifteen minutes. Write down a list of what we need to get."

"You can't," Omar said. "There are guards that watch the pharmacy."

"Really?" Yousef said with a sarcastic smile as he looked at his rifle. "We will be back in fifteen minutes. I'll just get whatever I can find."

~~~

That night, the UN Security Council voted on a plan to force the Syrian government to stop its strikes on civilians. Russia and China vetoed the resolution again, further fueling the genocide in Syria and the rage in the hearts of Syrians. February 4, 2012, was the bloodiest day of the revolution yet. It brought back memories of the Hama Massacre of February 2, 1982, and it also served as a rude awakening for the proponents of the peaceful movement. The revolution was ready to change her white dress and take her boxing gloves off. The Free Syrian Army and the armed resistance were officially born.

Chapter 24
Siege on Baba Amro

In Arabic, the name Baba Amro means "the two doors of Amro." Like many of Syria's old cities, Homs featured seven gates that helped control movement and deter enemies in old times. The two doors of Amro were the eighth and ninth doors to the city of Homs.

According to scripture, Amro bin Maad Yakreb was a companion of the prophet Mohammad. Legends say that he had the might of one thousand men. A mosque in the center of the neighborhood commemorates this legendary fighter.

Over the years, the neighborhood grew and became one of the most densely populated areas in the city. On one end of the neighborhood stood the vegetable market, famous for its etteh (known as "snake cucumbers"), its green plums, and its fresh almonds. None of that existed after the siege began; no fruit or vegetable survived the blockade. Wheat was the most targeted trespasser, leaving the besieged people without bread.

On the other end of the neighborhood was the souk, which the regime had burned to the ground. Neglected ruins from all eras of history were scattered throughout its streets, between its houses, and over its hilltops.

—*Syria: A History in Blood* by Celine Dubois

February 18, 2012
Deaths: 7,800

"And if I touched the moon,
Would you be within my reach?
Let the world laugh at us . . .
Let the devils preach
So would you wait for me
In an ancient city under siege?
Even as blood replaces the sea
And drowns the mountains and the beach

Wait for me, love will win at the end
Along with liberty and freedom of speech
Let the world watch us from a distance
We do have a lot to teach
Close your eyes. Time will pass.
Blood will vanish like stains off glass"

Waleed read to a sleepy Sireen as he sat next to her bed, holding her hand. He knew that she was incredibly fortunate to survive the bombardment of Khaldiyeh and the collapse of the building. Some two hundred survivors were removed from under the rubble. The four hundred who died either bled to death or were buried alive. Both she and the foreign journalist named David remained at Omar's clinic, which had grown to be a real field hospital with proper medication since then. Sireen had a fracture in her left arm, a small fracture in her skull with minimal intracranial bleeding, multiple large bruises on her body, and a laceration on her left cheek.

Waleed had been staying with her in Baba Amro while Sami stayed at home to take care of their mother and the now-paralyzed Khalid. The French journalist Celine had sustained the least injuries, thanks to Khalid's heroic move. She decided to stay with Khalid in Bab Sebaa to help take care of him while working on what might be the story of her life. She submitted daily reports via satellite phone regarding the events she was witnessing. At the same time, she began writing a book about the history of Syria and the current conflict. One night over coffee, she shared with Waleed her tentative title: *Syria: A History in Blood.* Given her frail beauty and her French origins, Waleed never would have guessed that Celine would be such a tough and determined woman, but she surprised him and the rest of his family every day.

Shortly thereafter, Waleed found himself separated from the group occupying his home, as the siege on the various neighborhoods of Homs intensified. From the flow of bodies entering the clinic, it was clear that the siege was tightest around the rebellious neighborhood of Baba Amro. With the exception of wind, nothing was allowed to move in or out of the neighborhood. Thousands of government troops surrounded it and banned any food, water, gasoline, or medical supplies from entering the neighborhood.

Over the ensuing days, Waleed and everyone else at the clinic suffered from the water pipelines being destroyed, electricity shutting down, and the sewage system becoming clogged. Hundreds of bombs fell randomly every day. The destruction was indiscriminate. The besieged families of Baba Amro were hungry, cold, and scared. A picture emerged that the regime's message was to show them how helpless they were against its wrath. The objective was clearly to bring Baba Amro to her knees.

"Look who's here to visit!" Waleed shouted as he ran to Omar's two young nephews at the door of the clinic. "What are you two thugs doing here?" He laughed and lifted the boys into his arms. Shadi giggled while baby Hod-Hod donned his usual irritated face.

"She okay?" Hod-Hod asked as he pointed to Sireen.

"Yes, she's just sleeping. Let's go find your silly uncle." He carried the two boys to the adjacent room and threw them on their uncle's back. "Take. That's for you."

"I guess it's time for their injections!" Omar joked, looking at a syringe in his hand.

"No! No! I break your head!" Hod-Hod threatened.

The men laughed.

"How did you two get here?" Omar asked six-year-old Shadi.

"Baba brought us here so we don't stay alone at home."

"Where did Baba go?"

"He went to look for bread. We're hungry!"

"What about Mama and *Tete* [Grandmother]?"

"They went to wash our clothes at the well and haven't come back yet."

Omar's face became serious as he looked to Waleed. "Do we have any food left to give the kids?"

Mournfully, Waleed shook his head.

"All right, why don't you keep an eye on them while I prepare some more bags of normal saline? The bombing is likely to intensify today, and we're out of supplies. Where's the salt?"

"It's under the counter. The distilled water is there, as well." Waleed sighed. "We're out of antibiotics and analgesics."

"No you're not," a voice interjected from the doorway.

Waleed turned to see Yousef at the door with three of his men, all of them wearing grey pants, white shirts, sneakers, and the flag of the revolution around their necks. Two of them Waleed recognized as defected soldiers. Each bore a Kalashnikov on his shoulder, while Yousef and the fourth man carried a stolen shotgun each. On his head, Yousef alone wore a white Syrian shawl with black stripes as if to serve as some sort of placebo helmet. The men had two large boxes with them that they carefully placed near Omar's feet.

"Those are yours, doctor," Yousef said with a wink and a salute. "We're the Free Syrian Army, at your service."

Omar smiled ear to ear as his eyes glowed at the sight of the large amount of medical supplies in the boxes. He rushed forward and shook Yousef's hand with both his hands. "I'm Omar. This is great, sir. Did you steal them?"

"No, the government stole them. We simply returned them to their rightful owners." Yousef cocked his head to one side. "Are you going to judge us or what?"

"No, not at all, sir. We are in bad need of those supplies. I don't know how to thank you."

"Don't thank us yet. The revolution has barely begun. We will need your services more than you'll need ours." Yousef then looked at Waleed and offered to shake his hand. "You're a doctor, too, aren't you?"

Waleed shook his hand. "Yes. So, I see that you guys are only lightly armed. How are you going to fight an army armed with tanks and planes?"

"I don't know, but we'll work with what we've got. We have a weapon that they don't have." He pointed his index finger to the sky. "We should get going. How is Sireen doing, by the way?"

"She is fine," Waleed said, tensing at the mention of the woman whose affections the two men shared.

"We're old friends, you know," Yousef said. "I knew her from Daraa, and I know you, too. My men helped smuggle you out of Jasem City to Homs."

Waleed felt embarrassed, for he had not known that Yousef had been behind his rescue. "I don't know how to ever thank you for that." He lowered his gaze sheepishly. "Sireen was inside a building that collapsed, but she is doing much better now. Would you like to see her?"

When Yousef nodded, Waleed led him into the adjacent room, where Sireen was still asleep.

"She's exhausted," he said. "She had many bruises and fractures and has only just recovered from rhabdomyolysis."

Yousef raised an eyebrow in confusion.

"I'm sorry," Waleed said with a soft smile. "It's when someone's muscles break down and release toxic substances. She is recovered from it now. Let's leave her sleeping."

A guilty look crossed Yousef's face as he clenched his fists. "I promised her that I wouldn't let anyone hurt her. Why is the foreign journalist sleeping here, as well?" He pointed to David.

"They were in the building with her, but they're both fine. My brother wasn't so lucky. He was paralyzed in both his legs." Tears came to Waleed's eyes unexpectedly. At that moment, he realized how much he had been pushing away his feelings and delaying his inevitable confrontation with them. "They also killed my father, and they refuse to give us the body to bury unless both Sireen and I hand ourselves in or pay a ransom of half a million liras, which we don't have." He bent over and placed his hands over his knees, looking down so that his hair would hide his weeping eyes.

He felt Yousef's hand on his shoulder, then under his chin as he lifted it up. "Brother Waleed, your tears are precious. Don't cry. Men don't cry, no matter what happens."

"Yes, they do," a weak voice said. It was Sireen.

Waleed looked over just in time to see her trying to sit up. He and Yousef rushed to her side and sat on their knees next to her mattress. Waleed held her hand while Yousef simply stared at her, as if afraid to get too close.

"Everything hurts," she said, laughing softly. "Listen, Yousef. Baba Amro is a war zone by all standards. You need to get David out of here."

"The siege is extremely tight," Yousef said just as a large explosion shook the ground beneath them. When the noise died down, he continued. "We can only get a few people out at a time. I will get you and David out, and then we'll come back for the two kids. We'll try to evacuate the clinic of everyone except the doctors."

"I'm not going anywhere," Sireen said.

"Yes you are, darling," Waleed interjected. "You're only interrupting our work. Go back and check on my mother and on Khalid. He needs a lot of help. I wish he had a wheelchair, at least."

Sireen looked like she wanted to protest, at least until another bomb exploded, this one farther away.

"We should get moving," Yousef said. "Keep this with you." He handed his shotgun to Waleed.

"Don't you need it?" Sireen asked.

He tilted his head to one side, revealing the Kalashnikov hidden inside his shirt. Waleed felt the warmth of their smiles as he held the gun in both hands as he might an infant. Yousef signaled for his men to enter. Two of them carefully lifted Sireen while the other two woke David and carried him on their shoulders. Waleed turned his back on the scene in the hopes of making it easier for Sireen to leave without changing her mind.

As they departed the clinic, Yousef looked at Waleed and smiled. "Don't worry. We'll protect her with our lives. Use those bullets wisely. We're really short on ammunition."

Waleed nodded before turning back to the work facing him in the clinic. As he placed the shotgun beside the useless refrigerator, he saw that Omar was still busy emptying the boxes and organizing them.

"Hod-Hod, get that out of your mouth!" Omar hollered at his nephew. "It's a medicine."

"But I'm hungry!" the little boy whined.

"It's fine. Just wait. The *ammo* [uncle] from the Free Army will take you and feed you soon. Stop complaining and give me those medicines. Those are bad." He snatched the pill bottle from the child's hands before looking back at Waleed. "I can't leave the clinic. There are three wounded people who I need to suture soon. Do you mind going to our apartment and telling whoever is at home that we're sending the kids outside the neighborhood? If no one is there, just wait till someone gets home."

Waleed nodded, picked up the shotgun, and headed for the door.

"Be careful," Omar called after him. "There are bombs everywhere."

"I will," Waleed said over his shoulder. "No one dies before they're supposed to."

"Hey, in case something happens, what's your blood group?"

"I'm A-positive. What about you?"

"I'm O negative," Omar said as he shook his head. "Yes, that's my deep, dark secret. Anyone can drink from my blood."

The way from the clinic to Omar's apartment was only two hundred meters, but it felt like two hundred miles. Every step of the way, Waleed could hear bullets, bombs, and the noise of moving tanks. Every few seconds, the absolute darkness of the evening was disrupted by a bright light—not the kind of light that brings hope and joy, but the kind that brings death and destruction. Nevertheless, the flashes did help him find his way around in the dark.

Eventually, he reached Omar's apartment. No one was there, so he waited in the dark, cold apartment and stared out the window, waiting for someone to arrive. After more than half an hour of waiting patiently, he got bored and went up to the roof, just for old time's sake. He could see the building where the underground clinic resided, lit by a generator. Other than that, the city had sunk into a black swamp of darkness. The only lights were from the armed vehicles and the blasts of bombs. He knew that it was probably not wise to be up on a roof in such circumstances, but Waleed needed to breathe in the air of the city, even if it was polluted by smoke and gunpowder.

~~~

Sireen's journey was even more challenging. The entire neighborhood was completely surrounded by tanks and troops. Everything moving in or out of the neighborhood was either shot or shelled. The water supplies were bombed, all visible clinics and hospitals were flattened, and the civilian buildings were slowly eradicated one by one.

"They call this the scorched land policy," Yousef explained to an appalled Sireen.

It appeared that every area that the regime perceived as hostile was completely wiped off the map. As Sireen trundled along on her stretcher, carried by two of the five men, the frequency of the shelling intensified. Two of the other men carried David's stretcher while Yousef led. In this way, they moved to the eastern side of the neighborhood. Soon they stopped near a pile of dirt. The men began to push the dirt aside and uncovered a large tunnel.

"How did this get here?" Sireen asked.

"We dug it two weeks back," Yousef explained as he disappeared into the cavern.

After setting Sireen on the dusty ground, her two carriers jumped into the tunnel. The remaining two men lowered her down to the others before doing the same with David. When they had finished, they moved together through the tunnel.

"This tunnel connects Baba Amro to Bab Sebaa," Yousef said as they plodded forward through the dimly lit but remarkably wide tunnel. "There we will reunite you with Waleed's family."

"Is it safe there?" David asked.

"We have encountered gunshots there, as well," Yousef said sorrowfully. "But at least there has been no shelling for the past few days."

After emerging into the darkened streets of Bab Sebaa, they all rushed to Waleed's house. Yousef knocked on the door.

"Who is it?" came a frightened voice that Sireen recognized as Sami's.

"It's Yousef, with the Free Syrian Army. I have Sireen with me here."

Sami opened the door and asked the men to enter. Sireen was embarrassed to be seen carried by men in this way, so she closed her eyes and pretended to be asleep. They gently placed her on the sofa. Sarah rushed into the living room, her hair haphazardly covered with a shawl. Sami explained that their visitors were with the FSA, or the Free Syrian Army.

"How is my son doing?" the disheveled Sarah asked.

"He's doing great," Yousef replied. "You should be proud, for he is helping many people."

"How are the people in Baba Amro?"

"They're hungry, cold, and under constant shelling."

"Don't move," Sarah ordered as she went to her bedroom. Sireen opened her eyes just enough to see that Sarah had returned with some gold bracelets and necklaces, which she handed to Yousef. "Take these. Buy food and clothes for the people of Baba Amro. And if you have money left, buy yourself some ammunition. No one helped us in Hama, and no one will help us in Homs. We have only ourselves and God to depend on."

Yousef bowed his head. "I can't accept that, madam."

"You can and you will," Sarah insisted as she placed the baubles in his hand. "I only ask one favor in return. Please help us get a wheelchair for my son."

"I'm at your service, madam," Yousef replied.

Sireen had no doubt that her guardian angel would deliver.

"We have to go back and get more people out of Baba Amro, and more supplies into the neighborhood."

"May God and his prophet be with you," Sarah said. "May God send his angels to fight with you against those devils."

Over the ensuing days, Sireen would learn by word of mouth that dozens of FSA fighters had used those underground tunnels to sneak into Baba Amro and prevent the regime forces from performing a ground invasion of the neighborhood, an invasion that would have resulted in a horrific massacre. Others helped move things in and out of the neighborhood. As time wore on, the FSA's ammunition was running out. They received no help from the outside world. The free world condemned the regime, but did little more than wait for the massacre to happen. Sireen knew very well that there was no shortage of images or intelligence; there was simply a shortage of conscience.

The news traveled quickly from home to home as the bombing intensified, hitting schools and houses. Then one bomb found its way through the night like a cunning serpent, landing directly at the site of the field hospital,.

~~~

Omar could feel the ground shaking, the walls drifting apart, and the roof breaking like a biscuit under the force of the explosion. His first thought was to protect his nephews, but a big chunk of debris punched him in the stomach and knocked him down. The kids were screaming. *Good,* he thought. *That means they're alive.*

But when more fragments of the roof collapsed, everything got quiet. Omar's legs were buried under a pile of debris. He could see that he was bleeding from his abdomen. The roof didn't completely bury them, but half of it had been destroyed, and everything in the clinic was decimated.

"Shadi!" Omar called. "Shadi, can you hear me?" There was no reply. "Hod-Hod. Hadi!" When that, too, was met with no response, he began to cry. "We're going to be fine. We'll go home, and I will buy a PlayStation like I promised." He said this to the pile of debris lying over him as he tried to pull himself out of the rubble. The pressure on his abdomen made him bleed more. He was glad to feel some pain as he pulled his legs out. Eventually he was able to see his feet. They were covered in blood and dirt, but his sensation was intact and he was able to move his toes.

He crawled through what remained of the room. He could see someone's feet under another pile of rubble. He began to remove the debris until he could see the man's face. It was one of the three patients at his clinic. His face was smashed. He was dead. Omar's tears poured from his eyes just as blood poured from his stomach and legs.

"Shadi! Hod-Hod!" he yelled again as he moved more debris aside. He saw a hand. He removed more debris to reveal a man's arm. It was another patient, this one pulseless, as well.

Then he spotted a child's foot. From the size of it, it had to be Shadi's. Omar felt a rush of adrenaline as he quickly threw debris out of the way until only a few small pieces remained. He paused as the dreadful realization dawned on him. "Shadi!" he yelled as he lifted the child into his arms. "Shadi! It's *Khalo* [maternal uncle]! Answer me!"

The boy's body was cold and motionless. The pain of the moment masked Omar's physical pains as the tears streamed down his face. "Shadi, *habibi*. Shadi, please answer me." He stood with the body of his dead nephew and began reciting the opening *surah* of the Quran softly. When he had finished, he looked at the sky, visible now through the shattered roof, and began to scream. "God! God!" he roared. "Do something, please!"

"Khalo!" a weak voice said from another corner of the room. Omar placed the dead child on the ground and ran toward a large chunk of concrete where he thought the voice had come from. He rolled the chunk aside, finding Hod-Hod beneath, his arms hugging his legs. His left eye was bruised badly, and his right arm was bleeding profusely. His body was covered in blood, mostly from his arm. Omar reached into his pocket, where fortunately he had stored some surgical sutures. He lifted the child, hugged him tightly, and kissed him. "Hod-Hod, you're a big boy now, aren't you?"

He nodded, his lip quivering as if he were preparing to cry.

"We need to stop the bleeding in your arm, all right, baby?"

"Khalo, you also have blood."

"Yes, darling. We'll fix you and then me. Now you have to help me. As I try to stop the bleeding, you will feel some *wawa* [Syrian baby talk for pain].

Every time you feel it, I want you to say, '*Allahu Akbar*' [God is great] and it will get better. Okay?"

"No," Hod-Hod said, his face contorted in the anticipation of pain.

Omar tried to sound reassuring, but his voice quivered from his exhaustion and fear. "What are you doing, baby? You can't cry. You're a big boy now." He grabbed the child's arm and held pressure tightly. As he hummed softly, he used his other hand to begin suturing Hod-Hod's wound.

"*Allahu Akbar*!" Hod-Hod cried as he tried to withdraw.

"See how it helps? Keep saying it, darling." Omar looked the other way as he began to sob. Then he pulled himself together and continued suturing the wound.

Hod-Hod yelled, "*Allahu Akbar*!" continuously until he passed out.

He must have lost too much blood, Omar thought, ignoring the fact of his own blood drenching his shirt.

He went to the wall and grabbed an empty blood bag, attached it to his vein, and began filling it up with blood. He began to feel more lightheaded as he did so. Before he lost consciousness, he injected a bag full of his own blood into Hod-Hod's arm. At first, he squeezed it with his own hands, but as he got weaker, he placed a blood pressure cuff around it and allowed it to squeeze itself.

He examined his abdominal wound. It was deep. He felt a sharp pain and then a bowel movement composed entirely of blood. He moved closer to Hod-Hod and lay next to him, leaving behind a pool of blood that soaked his pants.

"My heart, I promise to avenge you." Severe explosions rollicked in the background. "What have you done to them? What has he done to them? People! Human beings! What did those children do to deserve this?" He cried some more, laid back, and let go of everything.

~~~

That night, protests erupted throughout Syria as the nation grew more outraged by the atrocities taking place in Homs. Damascus witnessed its largest protest to date. Dozens of people were shot dead there. Even Aleppo witnessed some protests in a new breakthrough for the revolutionary movement. The world continued to condemn Assad's criminal behavior as they silently watched the massacre unfold without lifting a finger.

Chapter 25

Adagio in D Minor

Volunteers joined the FSA by the hundreds as they traveled through the multiple sieges across the country. Those who survived the journey to Homs tried to enter the besieged neighborhood to protect its civilians from Assad's army. This Free Army proved to be a stubborn force of resistance that managed to deflect Assad's army from entering the neighborhood for more than three weeks.

However, eventually the smuggling tunnels were destroyed, sealing the neighborhood from the outside world. The fighters quickly ran out of ammunition. More importantly, no help was on the way. Unlike what had happened in Libya, NATO's Rasmussen made public statements to reassure the Assad regime that there would not be any intervention in Syria, no matter what. Saudi Arabia, Qatar, and Turkey were outraged by the regime's brutality, but felt powerless, given the lack of an international desire to help.

Assad's army flooded Baba Amro with tanks and armored vehicles. Almost every public building was leveled to the ground. Loyalist troops invaded the private buildings, killing everyone who remained alive and looting everything in the neighborhood, from gold and jewelry to clothes, underwear, and even apartment doors and windows. Dozens of women were raped prior to their murder, and some were paraded naked through the neighborhood prior to being shot.

Soon after the massacre was over, the United Nations met and agreed to assign the seasoned Kofi Annan as the UN envoy to address the "Syrian file." Mr. Annan didn't have a particularly impressive résumé when it came to stopping genocides in the past. He had failed to stop genocide in Bosnia, and he had failed in Rwanda.

Mr. Annan went back and forth like a pendulum between Moscow, Washington, and Tehran, trying to come up with some sort of political solution to the crisis. By the end of March, Assad himself visited Baba Amro to declare victory over the people of Syria.

"Life will return to normal in Baba Amro," he declared.

"Better than it was before." The words ignited a wave of rage
and fury throughout the country.
—*Syria: A History in Blood* by Celine Dubois

March 1, 2012
Deaths: 9,000

My heart used to beat inside my chest
Now I keep it in my hands all the time
Waiting for you to come and claim it
I want for it to no longer be mine
With all its pain and its agony
Help me forget, be my wine
Take my thoughts and feelings, too
Steal me away; it's not a crime
Come back to me quickly
Before we both run out of time
Love on this land can't be flawless
So don't wait for the stars to align

Sireen was impressed as she read the poem again. She had always loved
poetry, but she had never known that one day she would have poems written
just for her. She had been trapped in Baba Amro for weeks. The whole
neighborhood had been destroyed, and there were rumors that the field hospital
had been bombed, as well. She didn't want to think about the possibility that
something bad might have happened to Waleed. The situation in Bab Sebaa
was miserable at best, but it was in no way as bad as Baba Amro. Close to a
thousand people had died. The neighborhood reeked of death from every
corner. Hundreds of bodies were scattered in the streets, buried under rubble,
or cremated into nonexistence.

~~~

The field hospital was gone, as were Omar and his nephew Shadi. The
news tossed Waleed into an abyss of depression, rage, and frustration. Gone
was his best friend and his true soul mate. Gone were the deep talks and silly
jokes. Forever gone was the people's faith in a peaceful revolution. It wasn't
so much a desire for revenge, but rather a grim realization about the reality of
the situation. Omar's mother and sister were caught in crossfire and ended up
hiding in a shelter for women and children, which was later bombed by
Assad's army. They both passed away. Omar's brother-in-law had lied about
leaving the kids at the clinic to go find bread. He had instead gone to fight with
the Free Army and was among the dozens of fighters killed defending the

neighborhood. The family's only survivor was three-year-old Hod-Hod, who stayed with Waleed and his physician colleagues at all times as they rushed from one place to another, trying to help the wounded. For Waleed, this child was all that remained from the ashes of his best friend. He held on to him like he was his own son.

~~~

A group of four FSA fighters helped escort the journalist David out of Homs to Lebanon. One of them was killed along the way, and one was shot, but to them, getting the message out to the world was more important than their own lives. Celine, on the other hand, refused to leave Homs, instead asking Sarah to allow her to stay with them longer. She remained capable of communicating with correspondents in France via satellite phones that the Syrian government had no way of shutting down. Right from Waleed's living room, she spoke to the world media of the atrocities taking place at Baba Amro and Homs at large. Rumor had it that the Syrian regime was hunting for her like a mad, hungry dog.

Sireen had developed a close friendship with Celine over the past few weeks as they learned how to share all the aspects of life under siege. There is a sort of brotherhood that forms between men who serve as comrades in arms; this brotherhood quickly breaks apart once war is over. However, what is much more meaningful and long-lasting is the sisterhood that forms between women struggling to protect themselves and their loved ones at times of war.

Celine also helped look after Khalid as his wounds began to heal and as he made the adjustment to living in the wheelchair Yousef had secured for him. She often expressed her indebtedness to Khalid for saving her life that day. She had picked up enough Syrian Arabic words from him and Sireen, and he had picked up enough English and French words from her to be able to communicate somewhat over the past month. In spite of all the tragedies surrounding them, Celine and Khalid carried out broken conversations that Sireen would have found hilarious under other circumstances.

"*Merci* for helping me from the building," Celine said slowly, using many hand gestures.

"No merci, *ala wajeb* [my duty]," Khalid replied with a big smile as he patted himself on the head, a common Syrian gesture of respect.

Sireen watched admiringly as Celine moved closer to him, sat on her knees, and placed her arm over his legs. She looked down at his feet and then lifted her gaze toward his eyes. Her green eyes were flooded with tears. "*Je suis désolée* [I am sorry]." She placed her head on his paralyzed knees, crying as he sat in his wheelchair and repeated, "*Je suis désolée.*"

A tear fell over Sireen's cheek as Khalid held his breath, and in a breach of Syrian custom, placed his hand on Celine's golden hair and began to pat her head. "It's okay," he managed to say in his heavily accented English. "It's okay."

Watching from a distance, Sireen wasn't sure whether to laugh or continue crying. She pulled herself together and went to Celine, smiling. "Trust me," she said in English, "anytime this guy gets a chance to jump on top of a French woman, he doesn't hesitate."

They both laughed and hugged as Khalid smiled, clueless about the English she had used.

"Thank you, Sireen," Celine said. "You've been a great sister to me."

"No, honey, thank you. You could have left us like everyone else did, but you chose to stay with us and tell the world our story. Thank you."

"I'm so sorry about the way the world has abandoned you. We spend millions of dollars on endangered species and to save the rainforests, and we do nothing about a nation being exterminated slowly. I'm so ashamed." Celine continued to cry.

"Don't be ashamed," Sireen said, wiping a tear from her friend's cheek. "It's not your fault at all. Besides, the world can't sit and watch indefinitely until the entire Syrian nation is destroyed."

"*Oui*? Trust me, they can. They watched as the Holocaust took place, and they will watch as the Syrian genocide happens. They say the world changed after World War Two, but it really hasn't. This is your war, Sireen; yours alone. This is your revolution, and it is a great one. It's like the French Revolution. It will change history. I know what I'm saying."

Sireen smiled. "Guess what?" she said joyfully, suddenly remembering the reason she had intruded on Celine and Khalid in the first place. "The Free Army just distributed bread and oranges to our building. We've got four loaves of bread and five oranges for us! I know you're starving." She rose to her feet. "I'll go call Om Khalid and Sami."

"Sami is not here," Sarah told Sireen in Arabic as she walked out of her room. "He's been gone for two days now."

"Where did he go?" Sireen asked, surprised that she hadn't noticed him missing.

"He's where he's supposed to be," Sarah said as her eyes began to water. "He went to fight for his country and his people in Baba Amro. He even took his guitar."

"What?" Khalid asked, appearing shocked.

"As you heard. He went to Baba Amro two days ago, and if you hadn't had an accident, I would have sent you, too. Your father didn't die for nothing. My father and mother didn't die for nothing." She sobbed. "This land is our land, and those people are our people. If you don't fight for them, who will?"

~~~

Sami was one of the last fighters to be able to sneak into Baba Amro through the underground tunnels before Assad's army blew them up. He was given the last available Kalashnikov and received a two-hour crash course in using it by a member of the FSA, a man who called himself Nezar. He was a bizarre fighter, this Nezar. On the battlefield, he proved fierce, physically fit, and he was an artist with an AK-47. However, in a previous life, he had been a graphic designer and a guitarist like Sami. He always had an iPod plugged into his ears or a guitar hanging from his shoulder as he moved around from one battlefield to another. Most notably, he was always fully dressed for battle, his shirts well-ironed, his shoes polished to a high shine, and his slacks always pressed. He had three shirts that he alternated between each day: white, light brown, and baby blue. He also had two black suits, a pair of black shoes, and a golden tie that he would never leave the house without wearing. Had it not been for the setting, one might have assumed he was about to attend a wedding, perhaps even his own. He never seemed concerned about the mockery of his co-fighters, many of whom were dressed in undershirts and flip-flops.

"I'm out of ammunition, Nezar," Sami told his friend and self-assigned boss.

"I think we're all out of ammunition," Nezar replied stoically. "Here are two bullets for you. I'll keep three for myself."

"What do we do now? Is there more ammunition on the way?"

"No," Nezar replied as he loaded his AK-47. He pushed his weapon through a hole in the wall, placed his sunglasses over his head, and looked through another hole. Quickly he took two shots. "One Assad thug down. One bullet left." He dusted off his pants with his free hand.

"What do we do when the ammunition runs out?"

"Do whatever you want. I'm joining the Northern front. I'm going to Idleb, and from there, I will join the battle for Aleppo. They're much better armed there."

"What are you talking about? Aleppo barely has a protest movement. We need to fight for Homs now. This is the heart of the revolution."

"We're out of ammunition. No outside help is one the way. There's nothing left to do here. The guys are digging a tunnel out of Baba Amro. We need to evacuate as many families as possible, and then we need to get the hell out of here."

"I'm not going anywhere. I'm fighting for my city."

"With what?"

Sami clenched his teeth. "With my bare hands, if I have to. I will not wait here while strangers burn our homes and rape our women."

"Go find your brother, then, while I go talk to the fighters to see what they're planning." Nezar ordered him around like a father talking to his son. "Take you guitar as well. I'll steal it back from you later. I still have to teach you my favorite piece." He added as he gently placed the guitar on Sami's shoulder.

"What is it called?" Sami asked, smiling boyishly.

"'Sunshine Adagio in D Minor.' Now stop wasting time and go."

Sami obeyed without question, leaving at once. He ran to the new location where his brother and a few other doctors and nurses had set up another field hospital. When he arrived, he found no one there except Waleed and three dead bodies that he clearly had been trying to resuscitate. Around them stood the remains of buildings and the ghost of a neighborhood once thriving with life.

"Waleed!" Sami yelled as he ran to his brother

"Hello, brother. It's getting bad here. I'm really only counting the dead. I'm out of medical supplies. I don't even have sutures."

A huge explosion rocked the neighborhood, causing Sami and Waleed to duck.

"What was that?" Waleed said. "It sounded different."

Within seconds, a huge layer of black smoke became visible in the sky, casting a thick coat of black clouds over the neighborhood. Sami's first thought was that the regime had decided to block even sunlight from entering the neighborhood, lest it bring some measure of joy or vitamins to the residents. *If they could block air from our lungs, they wouldn't hesitate to do that, either,* he thought.

"I think they blew up the oil pipeline," Waleed said angrily. "We really need to evacuate people before they suffocate. Are they done digging the new tunnel yet?"

"Shh!" Sami said, placing a finger over his lips. "You hear that? The tanks are entering the neighborhood. They know we're out of ammunition!"

"I hear it. How close are they?"

"Very close," Sami replied, trying to hide his fear as he pointed to the tanks and troops already visible in the smoke-shrouded square behind them.

He grabbed his brother and pulled him away, running as fast as he could from the tanks. He ran faster than he had ever run before, faster than his racing heart, and faster than his fleeting thoughts, but not faster than the four bullets that slammed into their backs: one in Waleed's, two in Sami's, and one in the guitar he carried, generating a wave of melancholic chords.

Sami felt as if someone had lit him on fire as he fell face first into a pile of rubble. He struggled only for a moment before he gave up trying to rise. With the last of his strength, he picked his head up and rolled it to the other side so he could see his brother one last time in case he lost consciousness.

~~~

Waleed reached for Sami's face and gave him three gentle slaps. "Sami, stay with me. Keep your eyes open."

Sami opened his eyes, his sweat trickling into them as he smiled. "I'm here. I'm all right."

They held hands and remained on the ground. Waleed pressed his thumb over Sami's thumb like they used to do when they were kids. Sami smiled.

"Your pulse is getting weak, brother," Waleed said, trying to keep himself together.

"They're coming," Sami sputtered a laugh. "Leave without me or I'll tell Baba."

"I can't get up," Waleed said, laughing and crying at the same time.

A tank blasted a nearby building, covering the two brothers with debris. The layer of rubble and the black smoke covering the sky turned their daylight into a dark night.

Two pairs of shoes appeared at the level of Waleed's gaze—one pair of sneakers and one pair of black polished shoes. A man knelt before him, shoving the rubble aside and lifting Sami like an infant.

"It's Nezar," the man said. "Don't bleed over my suit, and stop drooling on my tie. It's Pierre Cardin."

Sami smiled.

The owner of the sneakers bent down and showed his face. It was Yousef. Waleed felt ashamed as Yousef slung him over his shoulder. They quickly made their way to the remains of an old allied building. The man who called himself Nezar placed Sami on the ground and tried to stop his bleeding. He removed his golden tie and wrapped it around Sami's back.

Watching closely, Waleed offered his advice. "Just tie it around the place that's bleeding the most." He closed his eyes again as the pain overwhelmed him.

In spite of his agony, Sami managed to forge a smile. His blue eyes were pouring tears like an angry sky. "Nezar, I always loved the D minor. I wish I could have heard you play, but the guitar is broken and I don't think I will—"

"Shh," Nezar ordered as he pressed his finger against Sami's lips. "We both live, or we both die. I think we'll live."

~~~

"What are you doing?" Yousef yelled. "There's no time! We need to get to the tunnel before they destroy it."

"He won't survive through the tunnel," Nezar said as he looked Sami over. "He's bleeding too much!"

Yousef kept walking with Waleed slung over his shoulder. "Just carry him and come before we all get killed!"

"I'm not leaving him. You can go."

Waleed opened his eyes and whispered to Yousef. "Where's baby Hod-Hod?"

Yousef shifted Waleed's weight on his shoulder and whispered back. "He's already been evacuated. Go back to sleep. I need to keep you alive or she'll kill me." He looked back at Nezar and yelled one more time. "Don't be stubborn. Carry him and come right away, even if he bleeds."

Up ahead, Yousef spotted a tank heading off their alley. He began to run as fast as he could, carrying Waleed on his back.

The tank took a shot through the alley, destroying the wall of a building. Two large rocks fell on top of Nezar. One hit him in the head, knocking him unconscious. Sami was still bleeding and gasping for air. He began to drag himself towards Nezar leaving behind a trail of blood and a broken guitar. He lifted Nezar's head of the ground with both his hands and closed his eyes. He could hear the melody of their harmoniously beating hearts. The tank continued to shoot viciously through the alley and buried them under a blanket of stone and debris. The two men remained motionless in a river of their mixing blood. There was a peculiar comfort in that unyielding cuddle of death.

Yousef and Waleed made it to the tunnel and were able to safely get out of Baba Amro before Assad's army took it under occupation. True to Yousef's word, baby Hod-Hod had been evacuated by the Free Army, along with hundreds of men, women, and children prior to the destruction of the last tunnel.

~~~

To further humiliate the survivors of Baba Amro, the loyalists of the province of Homs established a market that they called the "Souk of Sunnis." This was basically a marketplace where they sold the looted goods that had belonged to the residents of Baba Amro. The mothers of Baba Amro went there to buy photo albums of their dead children. Sons and daughters went to buy the quilts of their dead mothers and the watches of their dead fathers. Lovers went there to buy memories of a lost beloved. The prices were not based on regular supply and demand mathematics, but rather on the perceived emotional value of an item.

Waleed, still wincing from the bullet that had ripped into his lower back a few weeks earlier, found himself limping through that market on one occasion. It was a walk of shame and humiliation. Around him hung pictures of once happy families, wedding rings, and even women's lingerie. In accordance with his mother's wish, he was looking for something that belonged to his brother Sami. He walked back and forth in the market, but with no luck.

"What are you looking for?" asked a man with a large moustache.

"I'm just looking around," Waleed said glumly.

"Was it a man or a woman?"

"A man."

"Was he your age?"

"A few years younger," Waleed replied as if it wasn't his dead brother he was talking about.

"Come over to this corner," the vile entrepreneur said eagerly as he guided Waleed to an area full of men's clothes. There was nothing that belonged to his brother, but something else caught his eye: a golden tie and the remains of a guitar.

"How much is that tie, the yellow one with blood stains on it?" Waleed asked. "And the broken guitar next to it."

"Those? They're pretty dirty. I'll sell them to you for five hundred liras."

"All right," Waleed said, reaching for his pocket.

"Wait. How was he related to you?"

"He was my younger brother," Waleed said, hoping to get some sympathy.

"In that case, make it a thousand. Take it or leave it."

The blood boiled in Waleed's veins. "I'll take it."

Chapter 26

Hola Massacre

It had been over a year since the uprising first began. Massacres and ethnic cleansing had become part of the new Syrian routine. The angels of death were overworked. Every possible way to die had been done and redone. Every day, tears turned into blood, and blood turned into more tears. But there was no stopping now, at least not until the battle for freedom was completely won.

Almost every country and political entity had its own vision of what an ideal resolution would look like on this extremely strategic piece of land. Iran's regime had the most vivid image of all. Neglecting the rights and needs of its people, Iran's dream of a Shiite crescent had become the obsession of its policy. It was able to completely dominate Iraq, Lebanon, and Syria and had already set its gaze on Bahrain and the oil-rich countries of the Arabian Gulf, but one small miscalculation threatened to bring the entire project crumbling down before their eyes: the Syrian Revolution.

For this reason, Iran viewed the Syrian Revolution as a serious threat that had to be crushed no matter the cost. It aided the Syrian regime with everything it needed to accomplish this mission, and gave orders to Hezbollah and the Iraqi regime to make Assad's survival their main priority.

As more images of Hezbollah's involvement in the Syrian Genocide surfaced, the image of Hezbollah in the Arab mind was changed forever. What hurt the Syrians most was that it was those very Hezbollah fighters whom they had sheltered during its war with Israel who had now turned their guns on them. Their ugly sectarian colors were at last revealed.

—*Syria: A History in Blood* by Celine Dubois

May 25, 2012
Deaths: 12,100

"Just a little more," Celine told Khalid in a French-sounding Syrian Arabic as she fed him a spoonful of hot soup. She knelt beside his wheelchair in the men's bedroom, a room that Sireen had told her used to be packed full of sleeping men each night. Now there was only Khalid.

"I swear I don't have much appetite," he replied before sipping the soup off the spoon.

Celine smiled, her heart fluttering at the sight of her savior eating. "Just a little more before your mother comes."

He smiled back. "You're starting to talk Syrian better than me."

"You're not learning French, so I had to learn Arabic. Sireen helped me." She filled another spoon with soup and fed it to Khalid.

"I did learn some French," he objected as he played with his mustache.

Celine sat down on the floor next to one of the wheels of his chair and placed her elbow on Khalid's knee. She looked at his glittering eyes and asked in her funny French-Syrian, "Like what? Tell me."

"*Je t'aime*," he said, sounding like he really meant it.

She had been pondering her feelings for him for some time. At the words, her reply came pouring out of her. "*Je t'aime aussi.*"

She looked deeply into his dark brown eyes for a time, seeing herself reflected back. Her body warmed from the inside out.

"In France," she said in French, hoping he wouldn't understand, "this is the point where we kiss."

"This is not France," he replied in perfect French, shocking her. Then he switched to Syrian Arabic. "Here it is love, then marriage, and then the kiss, or else my mother will shoot us both."

They both laughed.

A devious smile crossed his face. "But my mother is not here right now."

She giggled.

He leaned forward and pressed his forehead against hers. "When this is all over, are you going back to France?"

"Only if you come with me."

"I can't leave this land. My soul is stuck to it. Unless you want a paralyzed man who also has no soul."

"Then I will stay here with you, and maybe we'll adopt 'od-'od." She kissed him gently on his lips.

"It's Hod-Hod," he teased. "What about your work?"

"My work is here. I have my book to finish. And besides, I'm a journalist. There will always be a story to cover here." She paused and pulled away.

"What's wrong, darling?"

"I'm going with Yousef to Aleppo."

He furrowed his brow. "Why are you going to Aleppo?"

"He is joining the Free Army there. The battle for Aleppo will be crucial. I need to cover it. Is that all right with you?"

Khalid sighed deeply. "I wish I could come with you, but . . ." He pointed to his wheelchair.

She hushed him and kissed him again.

He went on anyway. "I will miss you a lot."

"I will miss you, too, my darling. But we're both doing this for Syria. She gave me you, and I have to give her something back."

"If only you were the president of some Western country," Khalid said, grumbling. "Syria would have been free a long time ago." The admiration brightened his eyes.

"No one will spend their dollars or Euros for Syria. We have to fight for her ourselves."

"We?" Khalid laughed. "You're not Syrian."

"No, but I'm human. Today, every true human being should be Syrian."

~~~

Miss Amal pondered how the day, May 25, 2012, marked little Atargatis's ninth birthday. Ever since she had arrived from Om Khalid's home in Homs, Atargatis had been living with her new family at the small, quiet village of Hola, away from all the bombings and shootings. After witnessing the slaughter of several people, including her parents, and after enduring the trauma of a savage beating, she desperately needed safe haven. The village of Hola was that perfect getaway. She had been living with the two younger boys, nicknamed Hamody and Abody, their uncle, and his wife. The family had no kids of their own, but they took care of the three children as if they were their own. They all attended a small elementary school, the only one in the village. After graduating from sixth grade, students had to go to a neighboring town to get their middle school and high school education. Every day, Atargatis would walk her two younger "brothers" to school and drop them off at their assigned classrooms. Miss Amal and some of Atargatis's other teachers were concerned about her mental well-being, so Miss Amal had arranged for her guardians to stop by for a chat later that afternoon.

"All right, class," Miss Amal said to her students. "I want each of you to pick one sheet of colored paper. We're going to write a letter to someone you love, and I'll mail it to them." Miss Amal watched with admiring eyes as the kids rushed to pick their favorite colored sheets. Pink and blue were the first colors to run out, as always, followed by red and green.

"Tooti," Miss Amal called out, using the pet name she had created for Atargatis to make it easier for the other kids to remember her name, "which color do you want?"

"*Anseh* [Miss], I will take whatever is left," she replied without enthusiasm.

Miss Amal sighed, worried about what a child's lack of interest in color might mean for the poor girl, but didn't press the issue. "All right. Who do you want to write a letter to?"

The girl scowled. "To Bashar Al-Assad. I want to ask him why he killed Baba and Mama."

The teacher's heart sank. "Darling, this letter has to be to someone you love, not to that monster."

"All right, *Anseh.*"

"So tell me, who do you love?"

"They're all dead, *Anseh,*" Atargatis said. She began to cry.

Miss Amal held back her tears as she hugged little Atargatis. "If you could spend one day with anyone in the world, whom would you spend it with?"

"Sireen," the girl said quickly. "She's the beautiful lady I met in Homs. She was so nice and warm."

"All right, then. Let's write a letter for this nice lady. Here's a bright mauve sheet and some markers. Which colored markers do you want?"

This time, the girl replied with eager interest. "The green one, the white one, the black one, and the red one."

Miss Amal laughed. "Normally you get only two, but for you, Tooti, it's fine."

"Thank you, *Anseh.*"

Atargatis took the red marker first and began to write. Miss Amal watched over her shoulder.

> *Dear Sireen,*
>   *I am now living in Hola. It's very green and beautiful. We have a small pond with fish in it. I love playing with the fish. My mother once told me that she named me after a mermaid that used to love fish. You should come visit me here. Hamody and Abody are so annoying. I wish they were girls instead. The only boys I like are the ones in the Free Army. When I grow up, I will marry someone from the Free Army. No, I will join the Free Army and be the first girl-commander of the Free Army. You should do that, too. I miss you. I love you. I hope you reply to my letter. Also when you reply, please send me a picture of you. I want to make my hair like yours, but I need a picture.*
>
>   *Atargatis*

She concluded her letter, and then used all four markers to draw the flag of the revolution below her name with red hearts around it. Miss Amal went around and distributed envelopes. Then she taught the kids how to write a mailing address.

Half an hour later, a tall man arrived. He wore a visitor's tag on his shirt and a rifle on his back. He shook hands with Miss Amal, then hugged her, causing the kids to giggle.

"Class," Miss Amal said, "this is my husband, Uncle Ameen. He will collect your letters and send them for you. Is this how we greet visitors?"

The kids all stood and yelled in a cacophonous manner. "Good morning, Uncle Ameen!"

Miss Amal was amused. She thought she would take advantage of the moment to impress her husband. She pointed to the blackboard and asked the kids to recite the poem they had learned the day before. When the children had finished, she and her husband applauded them. Then she calmed them down and asked them to take their seats. Ameen went around to collect the letters and shake hands with the kids.

"Uncle, are you really going to deliver those letters?" Atargatis asked suspiciously.

"Of course, dear," Ameen replied as he bent down to the troubled young girl's level.

"Well, I don't know if this is the correct address." She looked at him gravely. "But I really want this letter delivered to Sireen."

"Of course," he replied, smiling.

From that one moment, Miss Amal loved her husband more than she ever thought possible.

"Are you with the Free Army?" Tooti asked.

"Yes," he whispered.

The girl lunged forward and hugged him.

Smiling, Ameen assured her that he would meet her request. "I'll make sure this letter gets delivered."

With that, he carried the bag of letters to the door. Miss Amal followed him into the hallway, keeping her voice low as they spoke.

"I heard some loud explosions this morning. What's happening?"

"They bombed the outskirts of the village. They threatened to bomb the entire village if we don't withdraw."

"What are you going to do?"

"We're going to withdraw. We're only twenty, and we can't risk hundreds of civilian lives."

Miss Amal laid her hand on her husband's chest. "Are you sure this is a good idea?"

"We have no choice. We'll withdraw for a few days and then come back to guard the village. We just have to wait for the tanks to get bored and leave." He moved close and kissed her on the cheek. "I'll miss you."

The students, having gotten out of their seats to watch, giggled again.

"I'll miss you, too. Please stay safe."

"Do you need anything before I leave, darling?"

"I've ordered ice cream for all my kids. If you could pay Abu Ahmad the money before you leave."

He shook his head and laughed. Miss Amal heard Tooti laugh from behind her, as well.

"Don't leave the school and don't send your students home without their parents," he said as he walked out. She closed the door and went to the window to watch him walk away.

Over the next hour, the bombings intensified. The students began to panic. Everyone in the school was instructed to gather in the gymnasium, since they had no bomb shelters.

Tooti's foster mother, Hayat, arrived. Miss Amal saw her and ran up to her.

"Don't worry. This is just a precaution until the bombings stop. They're far away from the school."

She then asked the school principal to join them for the discussion while the madness calmed down. The four ladies headed to the principal's office and locked the door.

"Madam Hayat, we are worried about Atargatis," the principal said. "Miss Amal, why don't you show her the drawings?"

Miss Amal handed her a folder full of drawings. Hayat went through the drawings as Miss Amal stood next to her shoulder, watching as well. The first one was a drawing of a dead boy in a coffin full of flowers with the initials "S. R." on top. The second one pictured a dead girl in a glass coffin with a bouquet in her hands, the initials "L. S." hovering above. The remaining five drawings were very similar.

"As you see," Miss Amal said to Hayat, "all her drawings are of dead kids."

"Well, Miss Amal, she's been through things that no child, or adult in fact, can handle."

"You see those initials on top, Madam Hayat?"

"Yes, what about them?"

Miss Amal leveled a steady gaze on her company. "They are the initials of her classmates."

Hayat looked genuinely surprised. "Oh my lord! The poor child! What do you suggest we do?"

~~~

Meanwhile, the students and teachers waited patiently for the principal's orders to resume classes. The kids were beginning to get noisy, so science teacher Mona turned on the television and put on a cartoon to calm everyone down. After succeeding at controlling the chaos, the five teachers sat down at a wooden picnic table in the corner of the gymnasium and began to talk about the news that government tanks had surrounded the city. Sounds of battle had been heard even here in the village, and everyone feared that the tanks might head their way.

"I don't think the FSA can stop the tanks if they come," said Alisar, the math teacher. "There are very few of them here."

Mona felt her face grow warm. "I heard the FSA is withdrawing from the city as the government requested."

"Maybe that's why the explosions stopped. I think the FSA withdrew from this area already. My husband said he saw many men with strange accents entering the village because they knew the FSA was withdrawing."

"I don't have a good feeling about this," Mona said.

A heavy beating on the gymnasium door interrupted their conversation. Alisar was the first to rise in answer. "Who is it?" she asked cautiously.

"Open the door!" a voice yelled.

"Sir, only teachers and students are allowed here. I cannot open."

"Open before we break it."

"Oh my God!" Mona said, panicking. "What do we do? Where's the principal?"

"Quick!" another teacher said as she flew to the back door. "We need to evacuate everyone through the back door." She opened the door wide and instructed the students to run outside quickly.

"Can't we finish the episode?" whined a first-grader.

"No, dear," Mona replied. "We need to leave now."

~~~

Atargatis rushed to find her two "brothers." The banging on the door got stronger. She found Hamody and grabbed him by the arm. "Where is Abody?"

"I don't know," the boy replied. "He's with the kindergarten students, I guess."

"Fine," Atargatis said as she approached the back exit. "Do as the teachers say and run home."

"But I don't know the way home."

"Listen to me!" she yelled again. "You're six. You're not a baby! I need you to run to the ice cream place and find someone named Uncle Ameen! Do you understand? If you don't do this, we will all die and it will be your fault! I will haunt you every day!"

"Stop yelling at me!" the boy said as she pushed him into the stampede of children trying to run for their lives. He ran away while she went back to find Abody.

She had taken only a few steps across the gymnasium floor when the main door burst open, and a large group of men dressed in villager clothes rushed in. They had no guns or rifles, just knives. One of them charged to the backdoor and locked it. Another one locked the main door and guarded it. The kids began to scream and run around in a frenzy.

"All right, kids!" one man yelled. "Everybody sit down now!"

Atargatis lost her breath as she sat on command.

~~~

Mona could feel her knees shaking. "Kids, sit down like the gentleman over here said."

The kids sat down.

"Such bad manners!" another man said. "You make me sick."

"Sir, welcome to our gymnasium," Mona went on. "If you want, I can go call the school principal to welcome you."

The men laughed.

"She already did," said one man as he looked at his knife, which was dripping with blood.

Mona stared at the knife, petrified. The accents of the men were certainly foreign to the village, and she felt certain that they were the regime's killer gangs, or the *Shabeeha.*

"So here's the deal," the man with the bloody knife told Mona. "We're here for blood. Either the teachers die or the students die. Unfortunately for the kids, the teachers will decide."

"Sir, you don't have to do this," Mona begged. "We're all Syrians."

"You thought you could protest in the streets against our rule and get away with it?" the thug said with a sneer. "You thought you could defeat our regime and not pay for it?"

"Sir, we have nothing to do with this. We're just teachers, and those are just innocent kids. Please leave us alone."

The man grew furious. He grabbed Mona by her hair, stabbed her throat, and left her on the floor bleeding and gasping for air. Panic reigned again. Both teachers and students began to scream as the students gathered behind their teachers.

As Mona lay dying, she stared up at the men and the hungry look of slaughter on their faces. They looked as if they were possessed by Jinn. By now, each man held a hostage in his hands, either a woman or a child, with a knife at their victim's throat. As her warm blood pooled beside her outstretched arms, she noted for the first time that their foreheads bore sectarian phrases written in a rough scrawl. *Avenge our Bashar!* they said, and *Avenge Hafez!*

One man screamed the same as he slashed the throat of a second-grader. Another men followed suit, throwing his hostage on the floor with a cut throat before snatching his next victim by the hair. Mona tried to cry out, but her voice stuck in her throat as the blood trickled from her mouth.

~~~

"Stop crying," Atargatis whispered to Abody. "Shut up before you attract their attention." She covered his mouth and hid with him under a desk in the corner of the vast gym. "Stop crying. You're not a baby. You're four!"

He stopped crying, but did something even more annoying to Atargatis.

"Oh great," she said with a sigh. "Now you're peeing."

Atargatis pushed her hands tightly on her brother's lips and began to cry silently at the sound of the screams from her teachers and schoolmates. A river of angelic blood flowed under the feet of the *Shabeeha* all the way to the desk where she hid with her foster brother.

"It's not blood," Atargatis lied when she felt Abody begin to squirm. "It's just tomato juice."

"I think there are more pigs over there," came the voice of one man as he pointed toward the desk where Atargatis had come to hide. "Get out of there, you pigs!"

Atargatis and Abody remained frozen.

"Listen," she whispered to her brother. "They're going to kill us. But do not worry. It only hurts for a little while, but then we'll go to heaven with the angels."

"I don't want to die," Abody said, crying.

"You know . . . when we go to heaven, there are entire rivers made of chocolate and ice cream." She tried to hide her own fearful tears. "They are going to ask you to say something, but you can't say it. Instead, you have to say that there is no God but God. Then you will go to heaven. All right?"

"Okay," Abody said, sniffling.

The men lifted the desk violently, and Atargatis felt herself hauled to her feet.

"Don't forget to say it," she told her brother with a smile as they dragged them apart.

He nodded.

Just as Atargatis braced for death, the main door swung open. There appeared a tall man with a visitor tag on his shirt and a big gun cradles in his arms. He looked around as he roared like a furious lion.

"What have you done here, you bastards?"

Immediately Atargatis recognized Ameen, Miss Amal's husband and her latest savior. He aimed at the man holding Atargatis and riddled him with bullets too numerous to count. Atargatis felt her captor fall away as if blown over by a stiff wind.

The other men panicked and began running toward the back door. The man holding Abody let go of him and ran for his life. Ameen kept shooting at him until his gun ran dry. The other men got away.

Atargatis gathered Abody and led him to Uncle Ameen. The dozen or so surviving children followed them, piling in behind Ameen for protection, fear lining every face.

Once the gym had cleared, Ameen hugged as many of them as he could. "It's all fine. You're safe, my darlings. You're safe. I'm sorry. Please forgive me. I shouldn't have ever left. I'm so sorry."

Then someone snuck up from behind him. Atargatis was relieved to see that it was Hamody. He toppled into her embrace.

"Good job," she said to Hamoody. "You saved our lives."

Atargatis was glad to have escaped the ordeal with her foster brothers, but as she surveyed the scene, she realized that her foster mother, the principal, and Miss Amal were all dead. Miss Amal clutched a mauve-colored sheet of paper in her hand. Seeing that the paper bore writing, Atargatis took it from her teacher and brought it to Ameen.

"Uncle Ameen, this is for you," she said, choking back tears.

He opened it and read it aloud with tears flooding his eyes.

Ameen,

My husband and the love of my life. A group of Shabeeha have entered our school. They have blocked all possible exists, and it's only a matter of time before they find us. I don't know if they'll kill me or not, but if they do, I want you to stay strong. I know how much you love me, and God knows how much I love you, but I want you to love Syria even more. Give her everything you have. I haven't told you this, but I am pregnant. Take care of my mother and your parents. Fall in love again and have many children. I love you. I love you more than I ever knew I could love a person.

Amal

He squeezed the letter in his hand as he held Atargatis tight and began to cry on her shoulder. She patted him on the head and played with his hair. Then she pulled away.

"Don't cry, Uncle," she said. "You're not a baby. Go fight."

~~~

The news of the massacre reached Sireen as she and Waleed prepared food for the family.

"What was the name of the village again?" she asked the fighter who had come to tell them about the terrible scene.

"Hola. It's not too far away. About fifty school children were massacred."

"Oh no!" Sireen said, feeling as if the weight of the entire revolution had just dropped on her shoulders. It was as if the earth had begun to move under her feet. All she could think to do was sit.

Waleed came up behind her and rubbed her shoulders.

It occurred to her all at once. She opened her eyes and stood. "Atargatis!" she yelled. "Atargatis, my little friend!" She fell back once more, shocked at how low the regime and the entire world had sunk. "Atargatis!" she yelled once more, as if calling on the ancient powers of Syria to wake up and avenge them once and for all.

The massacre continued. Children as young as three were killed without mercy. Their screams, tears, and pleadings fell on the dead hearts of their murderers and the deaf ears of the world. One after the other, they were slaughtered like little angels that had somehow fallen into the devil's lair. With every child slaughtered, a guardian angel died, and a part of human decency died, reducing humanity to its true driving forces: power and money.

It wasn't the Shabeeha alone who killed those children; it was the silence of mankind that served as their invisible accomplice. Forty-seven children were massacred that day, and thirty-four women. Across the village, 108 people died. The remaining residents fled the village. The UN condemned, Europe condemned, the US condemned, and yet little was done to stop more villages from facing the same fate.

—*Syria: A History in Blood* by Celine Dubois

Chapter 27

Battle for Aleppo

Lord of heaven and Earth:
The Earth was not, you created it
The light of day was not, you created it
The morning light you had not yet made exist . . .

Those were the pleas inscribed on a tablet by a Syrian man in the city of Ebla as the Akkadian king Naram-Sis ordered his army to destroy Ebla and Aleppo in the twenty-third century B.C. After fighting for almost a decade, the Syrians were able to take back their land from Naram's grandfather, the ruthless Akkadian ruler, Sargon. Decades later, Naram-Sis was able to reoccupy Syria. He ordered that the cities of Ebla and Aleppo, both symbols of Syrian pride, be burned to ashes.

Aleppo, which means "white" in Aramaic, was turned red by Naram. He then declared himself a god. Revolts broke out throughout the Middle East, including Syria, leading to the entire disintegration of the Akkadian empire.

The pleas were written using the world's earliest Semitic language, Eblaite. This was the language in which humanity first learned how to write. Back then, Syria gave the world the gift of writing, and to return the favor, the world gave her genocide.
—*Syria: A History in Blood* by Celine Dubois

July 19, 2012
Deaths: 20,000

"A white dress? A ring? A wedding? Can you afford any of those?" Sarah said from the computer screen. Ever since satellite internet services were smuggled into Syria with the help of allies, the government had been struggling to bring about complete internet shutdowns in rebellion hotspots.

"Mother, we don't need any of this," Khalid replied through the Skype connection.

"I knew that you going with them to Aleppo was a bad idea." Sarah shook her head.

Khalid scoffed, unsure why his mother would so object to this idea. "Why? You've wanted me to get married since I was born. She's a wonderful woman. She's very educated, well-mannered, and she loves Syria."

Sarah fell silent for a moment. "All right," she said finally. "You can marry her. But my grandkids have to be Muslims."

"Of course," Khalid said with a broad smile. "Thank you, Mother. We'll get married as soon as we get back to Homs."

"No." She shook her head adamantly. "If you're thinking about it, then get married while you're in Aleppo. I don't trust European women. I don't want you falling into sin."

Khalid laughed. "All right, we'll get married in Aleppo, and then we'll have another wedding party when we get back to Homs." A feeling deep inside him suggested that they would never be reunited in Homs, but he smiled all the same.

The Skype conversation ended shortly after, and Khalid was hardly able to hide his joy from the rest of the guys with whom he had been staying. He charged into the living room, where he found them all fixated on the television screen with even broader smiles on their faces.

"*Allahu Akbar!*" one of the men yelled as he leaned back against a pillow with his eyes glued to the screen.

Khalid came around to see what they were watching, finding Al Jazeera blaring over the airwaves. The reporter was saying something about the rebel forces making significant advances in Damascus over the past four days. The Free Army had taken the fight into Assad's backyard in the capital. They made advances in the rebellious neighborhoods of Midan and Tadamon. They made even more advances in areas of rural Damascus, particularly Daraya. To make things even worse for the Syrian regime, fighters from the Free Army had detonated a bomb at the capital's National Security Building, killing Assad's brother-in-law, the notorious Asef Shawkat, the interior minister, and the defense minister. The next day, July 19, the news was confirmed by the regime itself.

"*Allahu Akbar! Allahu Akbar!*" the fighters hollered in joy as they clapped and exchanged hugs.

The joy the scene brought Khalid nearly made him forget about the strides he had just made with his mother.

Only Yousef remained calm. "Calm down, men," he said. "Let's watch the rest of the news."

Khalid found a seat on the floor next to the couch. The next segment on the news mentioned that another UN resolution to end the violence in Syria was proposed to the UN Security Council and vetoed again by both Russia and China. However, this time no one in Syria was disappointed. They did not expect much from the international community at that point, and they had already grown self-dependent.

"The battle of Damascus has begun!" one of the fighters declared so loudly that it startled Khalid.

"We should all head there," another said. "That's where the final battle will take place."

"The battle has not yet begun," Yousef said as he pulled off his boots. "We never meant for it to begin so quickly."

"What are you saying?" one fighter asked, echoing the question in Khalid's mind.

"I'm saying we are not ready to fight in Damascus yet. That's not the point of those operations. Now we are fighting the battle of Aleppo."

Khalid thought the rest of the fighters looked as confused as he felt.

"Everything will make sense when it's supposed to," Yousef said. "I just want you to realize that the coming few weeks are going to be difficult. This will be a heavy battle. I know many of you are not from Aleppo, and you are eager to fight for your own city, but right now, we are here to fight for Aleppo. I'm from Daraa." He pointed at the fighter next to him.

"Me?" the man said. "I'm from Aleppo."

Yousef pointed to the next fighter.

"I'm from Rastan."

"I'm from Douma."

"Der-El-Zor."

"Hola," the last fighter replied with sadness in his eyes.

Yousef walked up to him and patted him on the shoulder. "What's your name, brother?"

"Ameen."

"Did you lose anyone in the massacre?"

"My wife. My village."

"Your wife is a martyr. We can't bring her back. Your village, we will bring back. I promise." Fire flamed in his eyes.

Ameen hugged him, looking grateful and sad. He then came to Khalid and asked loudly, "So, what do we do with this brave Homsi man?"

"Well," Khalid said as he rubbed the wheels of his wheelchair, "here's what you will do. At the end of this week, find me an imam or a sheikh who can marry me to the woman I love, because I'm not waiting till the revolution ends. I already can't walk; I don't want to lose other abilities."

The joke roused a burst of laughter from the group.

"All right, we'll do that." Yousef scratched his head as his smile began to fade. "Why don't we all get some sleep? I'll wake you all at dawn. We'll pray and then head out to battle." He took his shirt off, turned off the light, and slept on a pillow on the floor.

Everyone did the same, except Khalid.

"Hey, you," Khalid whispered as he knocked on the door of the adjacent room. It was the only room that had a bed in it.

"Who is it?" came the reply.

"It's me, *mon amour*," he said in his broken French. He heard her shuffling around inside, presumably putting on decent clothes, before she opened the door.

"You heard the news from Damascus?" she asked, excited.

"Of course. It's great news, but Yousef doesn't think the battle of Damascus has begun yet."

"Of course not. This is the opening show for the battle of Aleppo."

He smiled. "God, you sound exactly like him. I don't understand you."

"Well, let me explain."

"No, no. Let's not. There's something else I want to tell you. Could I come in?"

Celine looked behind her as if assessing the situation. "No, let's just stay here. People would talk."

"You have become too Syrian." He laughed. "Celine, I want to admit something to you."

She crossed her arms and raised an eyebrow.

"You know when I jumped on top of you when the building collapsed, I didn't do so because I'm a good guy. I did so because I had fallen in love with you from the very first minute that our eyes met. When you said you were going to Aleppo, I couldn't imagine life without you, even for a day. I've never loved anyone like this before, and I don't think I ever will."

Celine closed her eyes, a tear escaping over her cheek. "Khalid . . ."

"Let me finish," he said as he held her hand. He reached for his pocket and took out a golden ring with a shining crystal on top. "This gold is fake gold," he said as he placed it on her finger. "This diamond is fake diamond." He brought her hand close to his lips and kissed it. Then he placed her hand on his chest and said, "But this heart is a real heart, and it's yours. Celine, would you be my wife?"

"*Eh, oui*, yes," she answered in every language she knew, "and if I knew any other languages to say it in, I would. Yes, I will be your wife, your lover, your sister in arms, and the mother of your children. Yes. Yes. Yes." She sobbed happily as she threw herself on his chest and held him close.

For a moment, even Aleppo herself smiled, for there was nothing she enjoyed more than pure love and white dresses. It was a fleeting smile that would precede the river of blood and tears to come, but nevertheless, at that point in time, the world seemed like a beautiful place.

~~~

Panic had set in among regime forces and supporters as the rebellion rocked the very heart of the country. Assad's army began bombing the rebellious neighborhoods and committing numerous massacres in and around the capital. The regime also withdrew some of their forces from the heavily guarded Aleppo and the Syrian-Israeli border to better occupy the capital. The rebels were blocked from advancing further into Damascus, but they achieved their objective: the regime's chain of forces surrounding Aleppo had been broken.

This was the rebels' chance to advance into Syria's largest city and main economic center. Their plan was to move from the rural areas of Aleppo and advance into the city. The first area of the city they chose to liberate was Salahuddin, so named for the Muslim leader who fought against the crusaders in Syria and other places.

On the night of July 19, thousands of rebels of the Free Army moved from the northern and eastern countryside and battled Assad's forces in the neighborhood of Salahuddin. The regime brought tanks and, empowered by the UN's paralysis, also mobilized its air force. Yousef and his fighters joined that battle the next day.

~~~

"They want to destroy that building to prevent us from placing snipers on top," Yousef told two younger fighters standing beside him in the apartment building entryway in which he had taken cover. "Both of you go ask the residents to evacuate the building and flee immediately."

Bullets, bombs, and missiles landed throughout the neighborhood indiscriminately. *This isn't a war zone,* Yousef thought. *This is hell.* The residents of the building began to flee as Yousef and dozens of Free Army fighters created a "protected corridor" for them.

One woman dropped dead, then a boy, then a fighter. Yousef spotted the sniper who had shot them, stood up from behind four bags of cement, and returned fire. The sniper's body rolled and fell from the rooftop.

"Yousef, look!" Ameen called from his position on the other side of the corridor. "There are helicopters and fighter jets on the way. What do we do about them?"

Yousef cast a desperate look at the sky. "Not much we can do. We keep advancing. That's what our commander said."

"I didn't think that bastard would bring his air force," Ameen yelled as the fighters advanced further into the neighborhood.

"Why not? Who's going to stop him?"

"Damn it, I hate the world's politics," Ameen said as he shot two regime soldiers. "So there won't be a no-fly-zone for us like in Libya, will there?"

"They had oil; we don't," Yousef replied as a missile landed only meters away from him. He was thrown to the ground from the force of the impact. A strange desperation washed over him. Then an idea flashed in his mind. "Ameen, quick, I need you to lift me up on your shoulders as high as you can." He got the words out just as a helicopter fired another missile at a civilian building.

Ameen ran up to him and helped him step over his shoulders. "I'm holding your feet, but my shoulders are about to break, so do whatever you're trying to do quickly."

"The world can block us from acquiring anti-aircraft missiles, but they cannot stop us from bringing down aircrafts." Yousef took a deep breath, aimed at the helicopter and began to shoot.

The helicopter wheeled around, leveling its weapons system on him.

"I'm out of ammunition," Yousef said. "Give me your AK."

The Free Army fighters around him kept advancing deeper into the neighborhood, helping secure the areas and evacuate civilians. The explosions all around him faded into a Zen-like silence within his mind; all he could hear was his own breaths and the beats of his heart. He saw the face of his dead mother nodding and smiling. He remembered his city burning up in flames. He remembered how he had shot the government soldier while saving Sireen months ago. The soldier had placed a rifle close to his head and said, "This is for trying to help that whore." The soldiers back then were not used to being met by resistance from the peaceful protestors, so it had taken him by surprise when Yousef kicked the soldier in the abdomen, pulled the rifle out of his hand, and said, "She is not a whore." When the soldier had produced a second gun from his jacket, Yousef was faster. He had shot him and whispered, "Go to Hafez [Assad's father]."

Now, as he sat perched atop Ameen's shoulders, Yousef leveled his gaze on the helicopter as it prepared to fire. He took a deep breath and whispered, "Go to Hafez." He shot only once, right at the gas tank of the helicopter, but his aim was true.

The aircraft seized at first, whirring awkwardly in the air before exploding in a spectacular blaze. Even from this distance, even as Ameen fell under the weight of Yousef, the freedom fighter could feel the heat.

~~~

"This is Celine Dubois," she said in French as she reported live through her satellite phone. "I am at the city center of Aleppo right now. The Free Army has pushed the regime's army all the way back to this point using only their light arms and determination. The world powers, including the EU and the US, continue to refuse to give any arms to the rebel forces. The civilian toll has been devastating over the past few days."

She was interrupted by a harsh male voice.

"You cannot be at the front lines! Do you see any journalists here?"

She turned to see Yousef ordering her behind him with a wave of his hand.

"Stay behind and report from there," he barked. "If anything happens to you, he'll kill me."

Celine laughed, rolled her eyes, and followed the orders. She wore a helmet and a big shirt that bore the word PRESS, but she knew that wouldn't help her if a missile landed on her head.

She went on reporting. "I apologize. I had to move back for my own safety. The rebel forces are continuing to advance in the city center, and have now reached the gates of the Old City, which is a globally famous site. Those on the ground pray that the regime will not use its helicopters to destroy this important piece of human heritage."

~~~

By the next day, the rebels had taken control of the area and had begun advancing to Saif-Al-Dawla neighborhood, which in Arabic means "The sword of the nation." A group of Free Syrian army fighters began advancing east and captured the Helweniyeh area. By the end of the week, the FSA had advanced all the way into the city center as they pushed away Assad's soldiers, tanks, and air force in defiance of all odds. By July 24, the battles were raging in the very center of the city.

The regime didn't only use helicopters; they used fighter jets—all without triggering any meaningful objection from the international community. Thousands of Assad's troops came from all around the country to fight in Aleppo, in what Assad himself called "the mother of all battles." Despite heavy bombardment from both land and air, the Free Army was able to capture most of the city center by July 27. The Free Army continued to push deeper and deeper into Aleppo over the next couple of weeks, and soon had seized control of over 60% of the city. This was in part because of their recent successes at smuggling in better arms over the Syrian-Turkish border with help from their Qatari and Saudi allies. Independent media and cameramen were able to enter Syria in reasonable numbers at the rebel-controlled areas.

~~~

"This is Celine Dubois reporting live from the periphery of the Hanano military base in Aleppo." She looked at the camera confidently. "The Free Army has taken over one of the most important military bases in the city and liberated four hundred prisoners taken hostage during the time of the peaceful protests."

~~~

Several brigades of the FSA had besieged the base from several angles. Tanks, helicopters, and fighter jets failed to deter the fighters from advancing. Ten fighters moved on the base, nine of them shooting continuously, while the other held a loudspeaker calling for those soldiers willing to defect to do so immediately.

"We do not need to fight one another," he said. "We do not need to kill each other. We are one nation. Join our cause of freedom. Are you satisfied living as slaves for a mad dictator and his corrupt family? Stand up for the honor of your nation and your people. Defect and join us."

The message did not fall on deaf ears. Soon gunshots could be heard from within the military base as some soldiers tried to defect. One brigade of the Free Army used that opportunity to advance further and enter into the base. Dozens of fighters died in the process.

~~~

"Remember, we are not here to liberate the Hanano base today," Yousef reminded his men. "We are here to achieve two objectives and withdraw." He held up two of his fingers, both of them caked in dirt and blood. "We are here to liberate the prisoners and to acquire weapons. We cannot afford to run out of weapons. Once we receive the orders, we will proceed to find the prisoners. Another brigade will try to acquire new weapons."

~~~

Soon the orders came down to attack. More than a hundred fighters entered the military base and began searching for the prisoners and hostages. Time slowed as bullets pierced the flesh of men fighting on two very different sides. Dozens of Free Army fighters and regime soldiers lost their lives, but the rebels kept pushing on until they found the underground dungeon where hundreds of civilians had resided since the days before the conflict. The prisoners rushed to the metal bars that separated them from freedom. They couldn't believe that someone had come to their rescue. There were dozens of prisoners clustered into each prison cell. They barely had any room to sit down, let alone sleep. They looked severely malnourished, bruised, and lifeless.

The Free Army fighters broke the prison doors, and hundreds of innocent people began to run for their freedom with tears in their eyes. Many had been subjected to so much torture that they couldn't run away and had to be carried by the fighters, while many more had been dead for days inside their cells. The other brigade was able to get their hands on large quantities of ammunition, AK-47s, and most importantly, several RPGs. The rebels withdrew from the base the next day with a promise to return to liberate it when they were better prepared.

The overjoyed prisoners reunited with their families. Those that were too far from home took shelter in rebel-protected areas.

~~~

"Is it all right if I interview you, sir?" Celine asked one prisoner now staying with Yousef and his men. The two of them sat in a dusty room furnished with only two wooden chairs. Outside the empty window frame, the war raged on.

"Yes," replied the pale, cachectic man.

"I'm Celine. I'm a French journalist. What's your name?"

"Yasin."

"Where are you from, Mr. Yasin?"

"I'm from the north of Aleppo."

"For how long were you a prisoner?"

"About five months."

"How were you arrested?"

"I was participating in a peaceful protest against the regime. Soldiers showed up and began to shoot at us. They killed a lot of people. I was shot in my leg and couldn't run away, so they arrested me."

"What happened after that? Were you treated?"

Yasin shook his head. "No, I wasn't treated. They threw me into a cell with ten other men. I was bleeding, but fortunately one of the prisoners was a doctor. He helped me as much as he could. The other guys squeezed closer to give me room to extend my leg. We were left without food or water for days at a time, and we didn't have a bathroom." He began to cry. "We were treated worse than animals."

Celine offered him a tissue and a heartening smile. "We can take a break if you want."

The man's face hardened with determination. "No. I want the world to know. Twice or three times a day, they would take us to a room and blindfold us. Then the soldiers would beat us with metal rods and leather whips for hours. They would spit on us and use the most offensive words. After that, they would force open our eyes and let us stare at each other covered in blood. When I first got there, I was still bleeding from my wound. One of the men begged them not to beat me. They said they would agree under the condition that he took twice the amount of torture. He agreed." Yasin paused and dried his tears with a tissue.

"What happened to him?"

"They were mad at his courage. They castrated him. They did that to many other men, as well. They also made him swallow an electric stick and kept shocking him until he began bleeding from his mouth. When they finished, they beat him and beat him . . ." His voice broke.

"Did they kill him?"

"Yes," he said with great difficulty.

"How many prisoners died under torture there?"

"At least fifty."

"Did they rape any of the men?"

He looked around in shame. "Forgive me, but I don't wish to answer that."

"I'm sorry. Please forgive *me*. I have asked you too many questions. I'm sure it's extremely difficult for you." She decided to shift to another topic. "Are you going back home?"

Yasin shrugged. "I have no one left there. I'm staying here. Once I get my strength back, I will join those fighting for our dignity." His eyes grew dark. "Promise me you will deliver the message to the world. The world must know what's happening to the people of Syria. We cannot suffer in silence."

"I promise. Thank you very much for all your help."

The broken prisoner stood, shook hands with her, and opened the splintered wooden door separating Celine's makeshift interview room from the place where the men made plans. Yousef was on the other side. They passed each other, heading in opposite directions.

"Did you interview him?" Yousef asked her.

"Yes. It's so heartbreaking." She let go of the tears she had been holding back for almost an hour.

"That's why we're fighting, sister. Listen, I'm sorry I yelled at you in front of the men a few days ago. I just didn't want you to be in danger."

"Don't worry. I understand." She wiped away her tears.

Yousef bowed his head. "I've been meaning to tell you . . . one of our fighters was an imam. He said he's willing to marry you to Khalid whenever you're ready. I think now is a good time, before the fighting gets more intense."

"Tell him next Friday. I need a few days to find a dress."

He smiled. "I didn't think you wanted a wedding party, but if so, we'll throw you the best wedding party in the history of Aleppo."

"In eight thousand years?" she asked wryly.

"In a million years," he quipped.

She looked at him with a new appreciation. "What about you, Yousef?"

"What about me?"

"Don't you have any special girl in your life?"

"Do you want the truth or its cousin?"

Celine laughed. "I've never heard that expression before. No, I want the truth."

"I've been in love with a girl for more than a year. She is the most beautiful and the most sensitive woman I have ever met. I love her with all my heart."

"So what are you waiting for?"

Yousef frowned. "She's with someone else. She loves him a great deal. I would never take that away from her."

"You have amazing manners. So what's your plan?"

"My plan is to keep fighting for my country," he replied stoically. "Hopefully I'll get the honor of martyrdom and won't have to deal with this situation at all."

Her lips quivered with sorrow as she failed to think of something to say.

"Enough of this, sister," he said, batting his hand at the air. "I need to go plan your wedding." He winked and exited the room.

~~~

Fighters across the country were inspired by the success of the Free Army in Aleppo, and began to better organize themselves. The cease-fire—a cease-fire which never really took root in the first place—was officially declared dead when Kofi Annan resigned from his mission as the UN-appointed peace envoy to Syria.

The Assad regime escalated its killing rate to somewhere between one hundred and two hundred murders per day. Several Hola-style massacres were repeated in other villages, towns, and suburbs. A massacre in the rebellious town of Daraya in rural Damascus left at least four hundred people dead. Government TV channels interviewed bleeding children and dying women on the streets to rally the morale of their base and remind the Syrian people that they were still in control.

Meanwhile, the world watched the ongoing slaughter on their television screens only for a moment before simply changing the channel.

—Syria: A History in Blood by Celine Dubois

Chapter 28
Demons of the Sky

September 26, 2012
Deaths: 30,200

Your eyes are two rivers of sorrow
Two rivers of music that carried me
To a time before time
Two rivers of music that got lost
And then, my lady, they lost me

I love you a thousand times
So go away tomorrow
Because I have nothing for you
But your eyes and my sorrow

—Nizar Qabbani

She had to admit that the two of them looked beautiful in white: she and the city of Aleppo. They both had tears in their eyes: the tears of joy and the tears of pain. She gazed through the blond hair covering her eyes and through the thick lens of tears, and there he was in his black suit. There he was, handsome as ever, brave as ever, and happy like never before. His body was confined to his wheelchair, but he looked as if his soul could not only walk, but could fly across the aisle to carry her home to his heart.

Two fighters preceded him, dressed in traditional Syrian clothing. They performed a traditional sword dance as the gathering sang wedding songs and ancient blessings.

"*Shinnig Leleh, Shinnig Leleh.* God help him tonight. From this night, his family will be born . . ."

The Syrian accent then got too heavy for Celine to follow, so she simply stared at her husband-to-be with love and passion. She never expected it to be this way. She always assumed that she would marry a French doctor or lawyer in a five-star hotel, not a Syrian freedom fighter in war-torn Aleppo. But how could she have predicted the way love would fall upon her from the sky? Perhaps that was the beauty of it, that was its magical charm. She could hear explosions and jet planes as he approached her at the head of the ruined square, but she had never felt this safe before. She was with him; he was with her. The whole world faded into irrelevance. All she ever wanted and cared about was right there in front of her. Two other fighters pushed his wheelchair and sang along, altering the traditional blessings for the occasion.

"Peace on you, peace on you, oh people of Paris and Sham [Damascus]."

As he got closer, she sat in the chair provided.

The imam arrived with two witnesses. He, too, sat, facing them, brushing his long, thick beard aside so it hung beside his knees. "Do you speak Arabic?" he asked Celine.

"Yes, sir, but only Syrian Arabic, not classical."

"It's all right. Just repeat after me. I, Seeleen Doobwa."

"I, Celine Dubois," she repeated with a smirk.

"Offer you myself in marriage."

"Offer you myself in marriage," she repeated.

"In accordance with the instructions of the Holy Quran and the Holy Prophet."

She repeated.

"I pledge, in honesty and with sincerity, to be your faithful wife," he said at last.

She repeated the words intently as she stared at Khalid to her right.

"Excellent!" the imam said. "Your classical Arabic needs some work. Now your turn," he said to Khalid. "Are you ready?"

Khalid's face grew red as he beamed. "Yes, sir."

"I pledge, in honesty and sincerity, to be for you a faithful and helpful husband."

"I pledge, in honesty and sincerity, to be for you a faithful and helpful husband." Khalid seemed unable to look away from her as he spoke.

The imam then smiled and said, "You can kiss the bride at home. This is not Paris."

"Of course, sir," Khalid said, laughing, but he did reach out and offer his hand anyway.

She took it, blushing, wanting so much more.

They held the reception in a small café long since abandoned. Yousef appeared at the doorway, carrying his beloved AK-47 in his right hand, and in his left, a plate of *awameh*, a very sweet Syrian dessert that translates literally to "floaters." He passed the dessert around to the fighters before handing the rest to Khalid. He kissed him on both cheeks and embraced him.

Then, despite the disapproval of both the imam and Yousef, the men put on some music and began to dance and clap. Celine's cameraman, Bernard, got out his camera and began creating a wedding album that she would one day dearly cherish.

In this way, two hours passed without tears, without blood, and without the cries of death. Those fleeting moments of joy were short-lived dreams. Peace of mind had become a rare delicacy, and like a forbidden fruit, it was quickly snatched out of their hands.

A devastating nearby explosion caused the earth beneath their feet to dance and shake as if it were invited to the reception. Two windows shattered, and the door was slammed shut. Celine latched on to Khalid's arm. The fighters all stood up at once and prepared their weapons—not just their AK-47s, but also their newly acquired RPGs. This wasn't a missile or a regular bomb; it carried the sound of demons falling from the skies.

"Did the sky just fall?" Celine asked Yousef in fear.

"I don't know what that was," he replied. "I've never heard anything like that before." He rushed outside with his men.

"*Mon cheri*," Celine said to Khalid sorrowfully, "I think we need to get to work or we'll lose all this footage." She gave him a seductive look. "Don't fall asleep before I return."

"I don't think that would be possible," he replied, smiling.

"Bernard, let's go," she told her cameraman in French.

"But you're wearing a wedding dress!" he objected.

"And you're wearing a bow tie. Let's get to work, darling."

"At least put on your helmet."

"No! It'll spoil my hair." She blew a kiss to her new husband and rushed out with Bernard.

The explosion had occurred much further away than they had thought; it was perhaps two blocks from where they had set up the reception. But when they found it, the destruction was complete. An entire civilian building had been rendered a mass graveyard. Dozens of families were buried under layers of broken concrete, stone, and dirt. No one was calling for help.

Yousef's men and dozens of other FSA fighters rushed to the site and began removing the layers of rubble in the hope of finding survivors. Celine stood back, looking for a shot that would best capture the devastation.

"Are we on?" she asked her cameraman.

"Just a few more minutes," he said. "I'll start recording the damage until we can get satellite."

"*Oui, oui.*"

"I've never seen such destruction," she heard Yousef say to one of the brigade leaders. "It's like a comet fell from the sky." He pointed here and there at the smoldering rubble. "This was not just a missile."

"No," the leader agreed. "It had to be multiple. But I don't see any missile remains."

"Grozny," Celine offered. "This must be a new technique. Something the Russians must have used in Grozny."

"Something like what?" Yousef asked angrily. "Where are the remains of the missiles?"

Celine looked back at Bernard to make sure he was capturing the scene. He nodded silently and gave a thumbs-up.

"What are those?" *the* leader asked, pointing toward three broken boxes. He moved closer to them and sniffed. "It smells like TNT."

"Those must have been boxes full of TNT that they simply threw on top of the building."

Just then, a MiG Russian-made fighter jet roared over the site.

"It's a trap!" Yousef hollered. "They're killing civilians to create traps for us. They knew we would come to rescue the victims."

"Everyone evacuate the site immediately and halt your rescue efforts!" the brigade leader ordered.

"But sir, I found a survivor!" one of his men said.

"It's up to you," he called back as he climbed out of the rubble. "I cannot command you to die. Everyone else leave the site. We cannot lose sixty fighters in one attack. Off the site now and disperse!"

Bernard chose this moment to inform Celine that they had achieved a satellite link.

With the camera rolling, Celine didn't hesitate. "This is Celine Dubois reporting live from Aleppo. As you can see, numerous families have been buried under the rubble of this building which was bombed by the Assad regime. In spite of this unprecedented brutality against a civilian population, the world continues to refuse application of a no-fly zone to protect Syrian families. Behind me, numerous fighters from the Free Syrian Army are trying to find survivors."

She turned her head and saw only three fighters left at the site. Everyone else stood behind other buildings, taking cover. She looked up just in time to see a MiG approaching. A terrible feeling ran down her spine.

~~~

"Sir, the journalists!" Yousef suddenly remembered.

"What journalists?" the brigade leader hollered. "Why are there civilians with us?"

"Let's go bring them! Let's go!"

They both ran back to the destroyed site. Celine was talking to the camera and pointing toward the sky at the approaching MiG. Neither she nor her cameraman appeared particularly alarmed. She ignored Yousef's calls and kept talking. A few seconds later, the leader of the brigade reached her, snatched her into his arms, and began to run, ignoring her objections. Yousef grabbed the camera and the cameraman's hand and pulled him along behind.

When the MiG reached its destination, its bay doors opened and it dropped a large box. Two of the remaining three FSA fighters on the site took off in a sprint. The last one remained, still trying to remove the survivor.

"Move out!" Yousef called to him.

"I have his hand!" the fighter screamed back. "I'm not leaving him!"

A box loaded with TNT landed a few meters away from the brave fighter, creating a devastating explosion. The blast was so strong that it knocked Yousef off his feet, causing him to drop Celine awkwardly on the ground.

Quickly he regained his balance and brought her to her feet. Looking back, he could see that there was no hope that the brave soldier had survived. The blast came with such force that rubble continued to rocket in all directions. The other two fighters were struck by flying stones and fell dead as they fled.

~~~

"What was that?" Celine asked. Her white dress was covered with dirt. She could feel a fresh bruise blooming on her cheek. She looked at Yousef and the brigade leader and thanked them for not leaving her behind.

"It's our duty, madam," the brigade leader said. "I'm Khalid, with the Free Syrian Army."

"You're Khalid, too?" she asked, surprised. "My husband has that name. How poetic that a man with that name should be my savior. It was our wedding today. I don't usually walk around in a wedding dress."

He returned her bright smile.

The smoke from the blast was acrid and black. It wafted in airy waves over the broken concrete jungle in which they found themselves. In the distance, the jet could be heard receding, perhaps circling around. Celine saw that several Free Army soldiers had been the injured by the blast. Three were killed. A team of physician volunteers rushed to the site to help the injured. Khalid ordered a group of fighters to enter all the civilian buildings in the neighborhood and evacuate them.

"The jets will be back," he said. "They were simply testing whether there would be an international response to their death boxes." He glared at the sky. "It seems that the great powers have given the green light for them to continue. They will be back. They will destroy every liberated area as a punishment. We need to begin evacuating civilians out of large buildings to safer areas. As long as we don't have a no-fly zone, no place is immune from those death boxes."

"So what do we do?" Yousef asked.

Khalid took a deep breath and frowned. "There's only one thing we can do. We create our own no-fly zone." He pulled out a map of the city, which he kept folded in his pocket, and flattened it on a jagged rock beside him. "We need to attack the air bases and acquire more of the anti-aircraft weapons no one seems willing to provide for us. You see, only your fingernail can scratch your own skin. Don't wait for anyone to come to the rescue. This is our revolution, and we will win."

~~~

An Arabic proverb says, "Every person gets a share of his name," and perhaps that applied well to the leader of this particular battalion of the FSA. He was named after another much more prominent Khalid.

The year was 634 A.D. Khalid ibn Al-Waleed had just struck a major defeat to the Persians in Iraq, establishing a cascade of events which would eventually lead to the collapse of the Persian Empire altogether. Empowered by their victory, the Muslim armies turned their gaze westward to Syria.

After months of decisive battling, Khalid defeated the Byzantines and eventually captured both Damascus and Homs, a victory well celebrated by the locals of Syria.

—*Syria: A History in Blood* by Celine Dubois

~~~

Celine supposed that she should not have been surprised to meet two Khalids during her short stay. As she tried to walk, she realized that she had sprained her ankle. She continued to walk carefully toward the café where she had left her small wedding party. The guests had all gone to help evacuate civilians, and the imam left to help in the burial rituals of the people buried under their own roofs. Her wheelchair-bound husband was the only one left behind.

Awkwardly she continued to limp toward him. Her dress was no longer white, and she knew that her hair had become chaos. She could hear a MiG approaching from a distance. She stopped and looked behind her to find that it was heading right for her. She quickly sat, placed her hands over her head, and shut her eyes tight. The MiG passed over her, its roar deafening, so loud it rattled her bones. She exhaled in relief as the jet disappeared without leaving its fiery death behind.

The relief was short lived. A gift box from hell dropped from the sky. Celine's soul died as the box made its way toward the building where she had last seen her husband.

"*Non! Non! Mon Dieu!* Khalid!" she screamed as she began running toward the café, ignoring the pain in her ankle.

A Free Army fighter grabbed her and pushed her to the ground before she could advance any further. The box fell right on top of the café. Another box, this one unseen, dropped on the adjacent building, destroying it completely as the MiG passed out of sight.

"Noooo!" Celine screamed. She pushed the fighter away and got up again. The pain in her ankle was too intense. She fell back down. She squeezed the dirt into her fists and wet the land with her tears. Unable to walk, she began to crawl to the café, only there was no café left. All that remained was rubble made of stone and flesh. The nearby building had fallen over the café like a domino.

"Khalid!" she screamed when she reached the site. She tossed the rubble around frantically. "Khalid, *habibi!*" she moaned from the marrow of her bones as she collapsed on the rubble. She wiped the dirt on her face as if searching for any remains of his scent. Desperately, she scanned the area for Yousef, the only man she knew capable of performing miracles.

~~~

Yousef watched the ill-fated bride from a distance, rage building as he realized what had happened. The MiG returned, carrying more boxes. He closed his eyes, his blood hot in his veins. He grabbed an RPG and disappeared into a building that he had just helped evacuate. Soon he appeared on the rooftop. As if accepting the challenge, the pilot brought his MiG to bear on him.

He had no training in using RPGs, but Yousef was angrier than a wounded lion.

"Celine!" he called.

She looked up from the rubble.

"This one is for you!" He fired, hitting the jet in the wing before it could drop more boxes of TNT.

The jet rolled out of control, making an emergency landing in a nearby square. Yousef watched in grim victory from the rooftop as the pilot tried to escape. The Free Army quickly captured him. Two fighters twisted his arms and forced him down on his knees.

~~~

Khalid strode to the captured pilot. "What's your name?"

"Murad," the pilot said, panting.

Khalid grabbed his hair and sneered in his face. "How could you do this? How could you bury entire families in their own homes?"

The pilot smirked. "We're determined to exterminate you from this land."

"Exterminate whom?" Khalid yelled in amazement. "You think you can kill twenty million people?"

"If we have to, we will. Who's going to stop us? You?"

"Why are you doing this? We're all Syrian. We've been together for thousands of years. You're destroying the very fabric of our country so that an immature man can stay in power and so that his wife can continue to buy Chinese silk and African diamonds. Is it worth it?"

"The Syrian Arab Army gave you a choice. Al-Assad, or we burn the land."

Khalid sighed deeply. "I promise you that we will not watch quietly as your army kills our women and children. I promise to keep you alive so you can witness the day that we march into the presidential palace in Damascus and drag your president into the streets." He pointed his finger in the pilot's face. "I promise!"

"Can I break his bones at least?" one fighter asked.

"No. He's now our prisoner, and that's not how we treat our prisoners. We cannot become the enemy we're fighting."

"Yes, sir," the fighter replied.

Hearing a shuffling from behind, Khalid turned to see Celine limping toward them.

She stood gingerly on both feet as she glared down at the pilot. "What are you?" she hissed.

He ignored her and looked the other way.

"She's talking to you," Khalid warned.

"Go away, blond woman," the pilot said with a scowl. "Go breastfeed your kids."

"My kids?" she said. She looked down at the high heels she was carrying in her hands.

Khalid thought about intervening, but decided to let the woman go.

She smacked the pilot with her heels, again and again, crying and yelling at him in French.

"Stop her!" the pilot pled. "Stop this mad woman!"

When the shoes broke, she threw them away, grabbed his hair with both her hands, and spat on him. She released him and began to sob. By the time she was finished, the pilot bore multiple bruises and was bleeding from his head.

Khalid knelt down beside her and took her into his arms. "Freedom is not cheap. There's a tax we have to pay."

"I promise you, it will be a high tax," the pilot interjected.

Celine got up, wiped the tears off her cheeks, lifted her dress, and kicked him hard in the face, knocking him unconscious. "I'm sorry," she said to Khalid. "I know you said not to hurt him."

"I said that to my men," Khalid told her, smiling. "You're not one of my men." He pushed her hair back. Her face was awash in color and tears.

"Do you accept women in the Free Army?" she asked.

"You?" he said. "Of course. Power to you, Zenobia." He embraced her tightly.

Over four hundred Syrians died that day, but the one he regretted most was the man with whom he shared a name.

Chapter 29

Shame

In 267 A.D., Syrian king Odainat of Palmyra had just died. His wife, Bat-Zabbai, was twenty-seven years old. That was her Aramaic name, but later, Greek historians referred to her with her more famous name: Queen Zenobia. In addition to her Syrian-Aramaic tongue, Zenobia was also fluent in the old Egyptian, Greek, and Latin languages. Alarmed by the growing Persian threat from the East, and tired of growing Roman corruption on her own land, Zenobia and her army gently pushed the Romans out of Palmyra.

Using her charms and her fluency in ancient Egyptian, Zenobia convinced Timagenes of Egypt to help them "liberate" Egypt from the Roman grip. Zenobia's army, along with Timagenes's men, violently took over Egypt, sending a chilling message to Rome by beheading the Roman prefect of Egypt, Tenagino Probus. The warrior queen then headed back to her native land and liberated all of Syria from Roman rule. Along the way, she also conquered Anatolia and Palestine.

The Roman Emperor Aurelian was outraged. In 273 A.D., a massive Roman army arrived in Syria. They easily crushed the rebellious forces, then went ahead and destroyed the city of Palmyra. The people of Palmyra and their queen fled to Homs. Aurelian besieged Homs and eventually reoccupied it, killing hundreds of Syrians who refused to surrender. Eventually he captured their queen, as well.

Zenobia was taken to Emperor Aurelian in Rome. There, she was chained with chains of gold and made to march in the emperor's scheduled victory parade. Refusing to be humiliated, Queen Zenobia chose to starve herself to death instead.

Two thousand years later, Homs was besieged again. The people were hungry and cold, but they refused to bow down. Both the protest movement and the armed rebellion were alive, and fear was dead forever. For weeks, the regime continued to shower the people of Syria with missiles and TNT boxes, destroying large areas of Aleppo, Homs, and rural Damascus. They wanted to not only exterminate the people of Syria, but to erase all memory of

that nation except from history books, much like the ancient nations of Babylon and Sumer.
—*Syria: A History in Blood* by Celine Dubois

November 6, 2012
Deaths: 41,500

<>

Every day was a struggle to survive for Sireen, Waleed, and his mother. Daily bombardment, the lack of the basic necessities of life, and the chains of the past losses had taken a grave toll on them. The recurrent visits of the angel of death to Sarah's family made Sireen feel that death was himself a resident in the home. More and more, Sarah began talking like she was ready for her turn to go. Life simply had become unbearable for her.

"I'll go get the door," Sireen said to Sarah when she heard the knock.

Sarah nodded and went back to reading the Quran.

At the door, there stood a tall, well-built man with an AK-47. He looked like he was from the Free Army. He wore a woolen hat. His face was reddened from the cold.

"Hello, brother," Sireen said. "Can I help you?"

"Miss, is your name Sireen?"

"Yes, why?"

"I have two letters for you," the soldier explained as he dug into the satchel slung over his shoulder. "I took over the mail delivery after Yousef departed for Aleppo."

"Where are the letters from?"

"One is from Jordan and one is from Hola," he replied as he handed her the letters.

"Hola?" Sireen said, her heart skipping. "Oh, thank God! She's alive! Atargatis is alive." She stuffed the letters under her arm and shook the soldier's hand. "Thank you very much. Please come in and rest a bit."

The soldier pursed his lips as if battling whether to accept the invitation. "Thank you, Miss, but I need to stay down and help guard the building."

"When do you head back to Jordan?"

"In a week. Is there anything I can do for you in the meantime?"

"Yes. I need to send a letter to my mother at the Za'atari camp."

"Sure. Just come down and find me downstairs anytime before next week."

After he had gone, Sireen read the letter sent to her from her little friend in Hola. It brought her great joy and made her smile for what felt like the first time in weeks. She loved the innocence and honesty in it, but most of all, she loved the fact that the little girl was still alive. She folded the letter and elegantly placed it in her drawer. Then she opened the letter from her mother and began to read it.

    Dear Sireen,

    My precious daughter, paper and ink cannot convey how much your father and I miss you. You are all we think about all day and all night. I don't want to imagine how difficult life in Homs must be. I just pray that God will send his angels to guard you, protect you, and comfort you.

    There is something I wanted to talk to you about. Only God knows when we will be able to go back to our Syria, and only God knows when we will reunite again, if ever. It was always my dream to see you as a bride one day. If your destiny comes and you meet the man of your dreams, marry him. Don't wait for the war to be over. Show Assad's bastards that, even in the midst of war and genocide, love prevails. Find someone who values you and will be there for you even in the most difficult hour. Return his love, honor him, and send me pictures.

    My darling baby girl, you've grown to become a better woman than I ever dared dream. We couldn't be prouder of you. Forgive us if we ever stood in your way. Forgive us if we ever forced you to do anything against your will. Forgive us if we ever made you cry. We did the best we could. Sometimes it wasn't the best decision, but it was always motivated by our deep love for you.

    Sireen, I'm not going to lie to you. The situation here is miserable. The refugees here call this camp "the death camp." The food and water are just barely enough to keep us alive. We live in tents that fly away with every strong wind and fall apart with every rain. The children here are freezing in the cold. Two died. But worst of all, my beloved daughter, is the feeling of shame—the feeling of being a burden on others. For thousands of years, Syria welcomed those who fled persecution from all over the world. Today, we walk around other people's land, eat their food, breathe their air, and look down in shame.

    Sometimes men come to our camps to find cheap wives. Sometimes they bargain with women about their honor. Our doctors work as nurses, our teachers as cleaners, and our lawyers collect trash. They're saying that the number of Syrian refugees in neighboring countries is way over half a million, and I hear it's even worse in Lebanon than here. I can't imagine how that could be true. Humanity has died, my dear. Oh, my heart aches for my nation, but the world's heart aches not. The world has a heart of stone. I wish I had a heart like that, so the hurting would stop.

    I love you. Your father loves you. May God bless you and be with you.

Mama

Sireen's tears dropped like rain on the letter. She kissed it and read it again. She grabbed a blank sheet of paper and a pen, lay on her bed, and began to write. At first, she wanted to tell her mother that everything was fine, but she decided to tell her the truth instead. She told her how insanely difficult the past few months had been. She told her about her love for Waleed and the suffering of his mother. She told her about Omar's family and about baby Hod-Hod. She even told her about Celine and Khalid. She explained that her ex-fiancé Hussein was still hunting for her. "The shame should not lie on your shoulder, Mother," she wrote. "It should lie where it belongs: on the shoulders of those who have the power to do something about it but choose not to. The shame, Mother, is on the Arab League. The shame is on the United Nations and the so-called Free World."

She cried as she drafted the letter, but in the end, she felt much better. She folded the letter and placed it in an envelope, put on her jacket, and walked downstairs. She found the fighter-mailman sitting at the front entrance of the building with an *arguileh* [hookah] in one hand and an AK-47 in the other. Sireen greeted him and began to chat to him about how important this letter was for her.

~~~

From behind a nearby building, a regime spy observed the interaction between the familiar-looking woman and the mailman. He quickly checked his cell phone for a picture of the "general's girl" and realized that this was indeed her. He watched her go back into the building before quickly running to please his general with the good news.

~~~

Sireen returned home to sit next to Waleed, who was busy cleaning his Kalashnikov. Sarah had gone to sleep after performing her daily routine of staring into space silently for hours. Sireen got her measuring tape and began taking measurements of Waleed's shoulders and waist while he tried to push her away and continue playing with his rifle. She wrote down the measurements and began entertaining herself by cutting pieces of colored fabric.

"Here they come again," Waleed said. "The planes. They bombed a building with a missile this morning. Did you hear it?"

"I heard it and felt it," Sireen said as she made a long cut in the thick fabric.

"It's sad that we no longer panic when we hear them."

"Oh well." She sighed. "I guess it's amazing what people can adjust to."

An explosion rippled, shaking the windowpane.

"Here it goes again," Waleed said. "It's getting closer to us. God be with us. This is really beyond human bearing."

"The strikes haven't stopped since the morning. Are they trying to invade the neighborhood?"

"No doubt about it." Waleed shook his head. "The men will try to hinder them as much as possible." He fell silent for a moment, looking tense. "I've been meaning to tell you . . . I've completed my training with the Free Army. I'll be joining them officially tomorrow."

Sireen stopped what she was doing and looked up at him. "You know how much I worry about you, but if every woman prevented her beloved from fighting for his country, no one would fight. So go fight, and may God be with you."

He went to her, kneeling down before the coffee table to look her in the eye. "I feel that lately I've been neglecting you. I'm sorry."

She waved the scissors. "Don't be silly. We're at war. The rules of everything change during war—even the rules of love."

"We just need to be patient. God will not abandon us."

"You think we'll win in the end?" she asked, wrinkling her nose.

"Of course. If we don't win, then it's not yet the end."

She smiled and went back to working on the fabric. "What's all this talk about chemical weapons on the news? You think he'll hit us with chemical weapons?"

"He's already hit us with white phosphorus and cluster bombs. I don't see what would stop him."

"If he does, maybe that will wake up other countries to come and help us."

Waleed grumbled. "If we keep waiting for help, we'll die in the waiting. We need to get this idea out of our heads. No one cares. So forget help from the outside. Instead, ask what you can do to help in the revolution. As long as God is with us, we don't need anyone else."

~~~

The shelling in Bab Sebaa intensified. Many of the residents began to panic. The Free Army asked the women, children, and elderly to evacuate the neighborhood while they tried to deter Assad's forces from performing a Baba Amro-like massacre. Soon the shower of missiles turned into a storm of TNT boxes. The civilians fled through tunnels protected by the FSA. Multiple attempts by the regime's tanks and troops to occupy the neighborhood failed due to the fierce resistance of the freedom fighters.

It was Waleed's first day as a fighter-doctor and not just a field doctor. He was part of a team assigned to prevent tanks from entering the neighborhood. Using simple AK-47s, handguns, and a scarce supply of RPGs, Waleed's brigade succeeded in paralyzing the tanks—until Assad's loyalists came up with a Satanic plan.

~~~

"*Khale*, I'm very worried," Sireen told Sarah as she paced the table. "I don't think Waleed received enough training to be thrown onto the battlefield like that."

"Pray upon the Prophet," Sarah said tersely before she continued reading the Quran.

"He's all I have left."

"Me, too." A tear trickled down Sarah's cheek. "They're all gone. Oh Lord, I do not object to your wisdom."

Sireen hugged her. "He'll never leave you, and I'll never leave you. You are the crown of our heads." She kissed Sarah on the forehead.

When Sarah pulled back, her eyes looked lucid for the first time in weeks. "If anything happens to me, take care of him."

"Don't say that. May God keep all evil away from you."

Sarah's face contorted with sadness. "My son will never find a girl that cares about him like you do, and I will never find a daughter that I care about like I do with you. What are you two waiting for?"

Sireen looked away. "It's not the right time. Our people are dying. We can't be celebrating."

Sarah came to her feet, placing both hands on Sireen's shoulders. "We can't stop living, my daughter, even in times of war. I have a nice piece of white fabric that I'd love to use on a dress. What do you say?"

Doubt and excitement warred in Sireen's mind for only an instant before she felt certain that she agreed with her hostess. "I say, whatever pleases you," she replied, smiling.

"You know that I gave up all my jewelry to the Free Army to buy weapons."

"Of course."

Sarah, almost looking like her old self, held up a finger. "I kept two pieces."

"Oh yeah? What are they?"

"My wedding ring and a diamond ring that I've been saving for Khalid's bride." Her voice broke as she looked haunted by sorrow once more. After a moment of struggling with the sadness, she collected herself and continued. "Now I want to give it to Waleed's bride. I think you'll love it."

The two women hugged, holding each other for a time, until Sireen felt a tugging on her shirt and pulled away from Sarah. It was Hod-Hod. The boy had woken from his nap and was demanding to be fed. Sireen glanced at Sarah, who shook her head regretfully. They were almost out of everything.

"All right," Sireen said. "I'll go make you a sugar sandwich, darling."

"We're out of bread, dear," Sarah whispered in her ear.

Sireen felt great sadness for the poor child. "Hod-Hod, who's *habibi* [my beloved]?"

"Me, me, me!" Hod-Hod chirped.

"All right. You know how I said you're not allowed to snack on the sugar cubes?"

"Yeah?" he said with his eyes wide open.

"Well, today is an exception. You can have as many sugar cubes as you want."

The boy ran ecstatically to the kitchen while the two women exchanged looks of misery.

~~~

Waleed had received only basic instructions on how to use RPGs to deter regime tanks from advancing, yet there he stood with an AK-47 in his hand and an RPG slung over his shoulder. He had helped the Free Army block several attempts to invade the neighborhood by land. The tanks had disappeared for some time while the air strikes continued using missiles and TNT. Then the tanks returned. When he saw them, Waleed grew determined to teach the regime that no amount of firepower was strong enough to stop the Free Syrian Army from protecting the lives and dignity of their people.

Unfortunately, as Waleed would soon learn, the regime's tanks had spent their time away strategizing on the major weakness they had observed in the FSA's lines.

"They're coming back!" yelled Ghaith, one of the commanders of Waleed's brigade. He was a squat, barrel-chested former dentist who had become an excellent military strategist. "Snipers to the rooftops! RPGs come forward!" He settled his steely gaze on Waleed. "Doctor, we might need you. Do you feel prepared for this?"

"I've never been more prepared," Waleed replied as he began adjusting his RPG.

It was almost night. With the darkness, the air strikes came to a screeching halt. The tanks moved rapidly closer to the neighborhood. The fighters were all in their assigned positions and holding their fire until orders came down. Ghaith was the only one in the brigade equipped with night vision gear. As the tanks approached, his confident authority and fearless voice turned to astonishment at what he saw. He dropped his RPG and looked at his men with tears in his eyes. Waleed had never seen him with tears in his eyes.

"Retreat!" Gaith screamed.

"Shame on us if we retreat a single meter!" one fighter yelled

"Death! Death! Death, not humiliation!" the fighters yelled after him.

Ghaith moved to the fighter next to him and handed him the night vision gear.

The soldier climbed to the top of a nearby wall like a proud lion and looked. "Oh God of the universe!" the soldier roared. "Oh God of Syria! Oh God of Syria!" He looked down at the fighters. "Hold your fire!"

"What's happening?" Waleed asked Ghaith.

Ghaith looked at him, having calmed down. "Pay attention to me, men," he said to the group. "I have no time to explain. Snipers, hold your positions and fire at the Assad soldiers, but not at the tanks. RPGs, I have no use for you. Those with RPGs, take your weapons and evacuate the civilian buildings immediately and distribute the families to the three safe neighborhoods."

The men followed orders. Many men, including Waleed, rushed to evacuate civilians through the tunnels to safer areas. Those who remained were determined to give the evacuation process as much time as possible, and to fight until the last man. Soon after Waleed returned from his mission, the tanks had come within striking distance of the neighborhood. They began to fire indiscriminately. Waleed and the others climbed the walls and rooftops to find better angles. At last, Waleed caught his first sight of the tanks. Through the darkness, he could scarcely see what was different about them, but in time, he saw that they bore moving objects around their midsections.

"What on earth is wrapped around those front tanks?" he asked Ghaith, who had joined him on his rooftop.

"Our children," Ghaith whispered. "Aim at the soldiers!" he yelled to his men. "Avoid the tanks!"

The tanks advanced further to the immediate borders of the neighborhood. Waleed and his comrades were outraged by what they saw. The four front tanks were wrapped with huge iron chains. Embedded within the chains were dozens of Syrian children kidnapped from other neighborhoods. Waleed imagined the devil bowing down in shame at the horror of the idea. He pictured Adolf Hitler smiling in his grave, Stalin crying tears of joy, and Hafez Al-Assad telling the world of the damned with pride, "Yes, this is my son."

The tanks had gotten close enough for Waleed to look into the terrified eyes of the children. The war machines fired death at both the fighters and the inhabitants of the neighborhood. One by one, the AK-47s dropped to the ground like dead birds. The first tank entered into the neighborhood and began to throw its hate in a circular manner. It was outfitted with five children, four boys and one girl. The children screamed and cried, piercing through the hearts of the fighters like gunshots.

Waleed watched as one of his fellow fighters collapsed to his knees from revulsion. After firing off one last round at an enemy sniper, Waleed looked through his scope to see if he could identify the soldier kneeling in the tank's path. It was Taym, a brave fighter he had only met three days prior. Taym had been a teacher, as Waleed recalled. The former teacher looked up as the second tank, carrying more children, entered the neighborhood. He stood, his body tensing as if preparing to run.

~~~

"*Ammo* [Uncle]!" one of the children, a boy of three or four, shouted at Taym. "*Ammooo!*" His arms and torso chained tightly to the tank's hull, the boy wiggled his legs in the air.

Taym could take the sight of this no more. He threw away his rifle and reached for his belt, producing a knife. He looked to the sky one last time, hoping for NATO planes to arrive. When it was clear that no miracle would come, he sprinted for the tank and leapt onto the web of chains binding the children. As the boy that had called him *Ammo* cried, he cut at the chains with his knife, pried them with his hands, and gnashed them with his teeth. For all his efforts, he was unable to even move them.

"Make him stop!" the boy cried. "I want Mama."

Taym placed his left hand on the boy's head and scolded him. "I don't want to see you crying. You understand? You're not a girl. I'll make him stop. My name is Taym. What's yours?"

"Dodi," the boy hollered over the rumbling of the tank.

The former teacher lost his grip for a moment, falling several inches before getting another hold on the chains. "That's your baby name. What's your real name?"

The boy sniffled. "Dawod."

"All right, Dawod. I want you to keep kicking the tank with your feet as I try to stop it. Clear?"

Determination surged in Taym's heart as the boy nodded obediently. Even as he climbed to the top of the tank, a few of his fellow fighters threw down their AK-47s and RPGs and joined him. The metal chains made it easier to climb the devil's machines. In short order, Taym found himself joined by dozens of fighters as they mounted the tops of the moving tanks. There were at least twenty tanks assaulting the neighborhood, by then, and not one of them was without a freedom fighter standing on its hull. The chaos did not stop the tanks from firing nonstop at their civilian targets.

Taym at last found the lock holding the chains together. He tried to open it; he tried to break it; but nothing seemed to work. He turned to prying at the vehicle's hatch, but it was no use. The rumble of the tank was almost unbearable as he crawled to the front and broke the driver's optic scope with his knife. That did not stop the tank from continuing to fire, but it did slow it down. The explosive report of the canon rang in Taym's ears.

Despite the awesome destructive power of the machine, Taym's hope was renewed. He carefully climbed to the top of the tank's main gun and slid his arm into its opening. He closed his eyes, held his balance, and looked the other way. He was sure that he was committing suicide, but had no idea what else to do.

The tank stopped firing. Its hatch opened, and a soldier's head peaked out cautiously. His helmet was covered in blood. "I defected," he whispered.

"There is no God but God," Taym yelled joyfully as the defector disappeared back into the tank. "God is Great!"

In a moment, the defector returned with keys. "Here, take these."

Keys in hand, Taym waved to some nearby fighters to join him. The fighters gathered around the tank, each next to a child. Taym rushed to the lock and freed the chain. The children fell into the arms of the fighters. Each grabbed a child and began to run. Meanwhile, the defector turned his tank's main gun on the other tanks.

A state of bewilderment seemed to seize the enemy soldiers. From the roof of the tank, Taym yelled at the top of his lungs, "Shame on you! Do any of you have a speck of honor left? You come here to kill the women and children of your country? You come here hiding behind the bodies of little children? Do any of you have any manhood left in you? Have you no shame? Have you no hearts? Are you blind to where your leader is taking us all?"

At that, another tank defected, carrying its chained children away from the conflict. Then another tank, this one already relieved of its children, defected and headed in another direction. The rest of the tanks moved back and forth in confusion. It looked to Taym like everyone was waiting for orders from higher authorities to help solve the crisis.

Two other tanks defected, one of them still bearing children. The five defected tanks circumscribed the rest in a pentagon. The fighters relieved each tank of their chains, the kids falling into the waiting arms of the soldiers below. No further defections occurred.

At last, one of the loyalist tanks fired at one of the defected tanks, blowing it up, along with the soldiers inside and the fighter on top. Within seconds, a defected tank fired at a loyalist tank barren of children, blowing it up. The balance was re-established. No one made any more moves. For Taym, time froze.

~~~

The fighters leapt from their tanks and reorganized themselves. Assad's soldiers waited outside the neighborhood, wondering what was taking the tanks so long.

Ghaith called on his men to grab their weapons and take their positions again. They gathered around the entrances of the neighborhood, behind walls, and on the roofs of houses. Ghaith handed his RPG to one of the fighters, his AK-47 to another, took off his shirt, and walked bare-chested toward the enemy. The fighters observed from behind as the enemy leveled their weapons on the defiant rebel leader.

Ghaith glared at them with confidence. "Assad's soldiers of the Syrian Arab Army!" he yelled at the top of his lungs. "I have come to you carrying no weapons. The men of the Free Syrian Army have AK-47s and some RPGs. You have better weapons, but unlike you, my men do not know what fear is. They love dying for their country and for their honor, and they will fight as long as there is air in their lungs." He paused, looking around as if waiting for his words to sink in. "If you choose to defect," he continued, "you are welcome to our neighborhood. You will be our brothers, and we will continue the fight together. If you choose to continue fighting on the side of a madman who has betrayed everything Syrian, then you may not step one step into this honorable neighborhood, for we will kill every last one of you. I am a messenger. This is my message. This is my promise."

With that, he raised his finger to the sky. Half a heartbeat later, hundreds of bullets rippled through the night, riddling his body. Such was his resolve that he remained standing long after he should have fallen.

The fighters of the Free Army were outraged, opening fire at the Syrian Arab Army of Assad. The two groups began a costly battle that succeeded in giving the civilians more time to evacuate. Defections within Assad's army further complicated the situation. News about the chaotic course of events at Bab Sebaa went up the chain of command as the regime scrambled to find a solution. Meanwhile, the Free Army continued to evacuate the civilian buildings one after the other.

~~~

Waleed went from apartment to apartment in his building, knocking on each door and asking the people inside to head to the tunnels immediately. Then he went into his own apartment, where Sireen, Hod-Hod, and his mother were waiting for him. "I have no time to explain," he told them. "We're evacuating the neighborhood. Pack only what's most valuable and wait for me downstairs."

"I need some time to pack a proper bag," his mother objected.

"Mother! There is no time. I will go tell the others. You have to be down in five minutes at the most."

With that, he left them, continuing on his mission.

~~~

Sireen helped Sarah grab a few things at random and throw them into two large bags. With Hod-Hod in tow, they carried the bags and headed downstairs, where Waleed was already waiting anxiously. A large group of families marched through the street, carrying their luggage, their children, and their uncertainty. Many looked back to get a final glimpse of their cherished homes as they traveled surrounded by fighters from the Free Army.

For Sireen, this felt like one of the most difficult moments of the Syrian tragedy. Her people had endured pain, death, and hunger, but nothing compared to the harshness and disgrace of leaving their neighbors, their dreams, and their memories behind as they marched toward the lands of others in search of safety. The shame was unbearable, the torment everlasting.

"Oh God!" Sarah said suddenly. "Waleed, I have to go back."

Waleed stopped long enough to glare at his mother before continuing the march. "What? Mother, no. No one is going back."

"I will go back. I forgot something important."

"What did you forget?" he asked angrily.

"None of your business. I'm going back." She turned around before he could object.

"Mother, this is nonsense," he said, breaking file and chasing after her.

"I'm not moving a single step if you don't let me go," she said as she sat in the street like a child having a temper tantrum.

Even Hod-Hod looked surprised.

Sireen's heart went out to the old woman, even though she knew she was putting their lives in danger. "What did you forget?" she asked softly as she leaned over her.

"The ring and the dress," Sarah whispered in her ear. "They're under my bed."

"What?" Sireen said, stepping back, surprised. "You made it already? I thought you were just planning."

"Well, I didn't want to get this reaction from you, so I didn't tell you."

Sireen sighed, looking at her beloved in a way meant to soften his anger. "All right. Why don't you take Hod-Hod and follow the crowd? I'll go with Waleed and bring the stuff. Deal?"

"Oh thank you, sweetheart," Sarah said, rising at once.

"Mother, this is ridiculous," Waleed repeated.

"Shut up. Ever since your father died, you have been showing no respect."

To Sireen, it seemed that Sarah had hit a nerve with her son, for he hung his head and complied without question. Taking his hand, she led him back the way they had come. The gunfire from the east drew ever closer.

~~~

The chaos between the tanks continued. Only one of them had true purpose.

"Is this the address he gave us?" Hussein asked one of his men.

"Yes, sir."

"Well, well," the general said with a smirk. "Look who's here."

He watched as Sireen and Waleed ran toward the building and entered.

"Should we fire, sir?" the tank operator asked.

"No, you idiot. Get me my box of toys and follow me."

The four men did as their commanding officer instructed. The moment he swung the hatch open, Hussein could hear the children strapped to the hull begging to be freed.

"Someone shut those rats up!" he ordered one of his men as he walked toward the building.

Five gunshots followed, bringing silence to each of the children in turn. When it was over, the soldiers followed Hussein, carrying his boxes of toys.

~~~

"What are we looking for?" Waleed asked as he stood with Sireen in the room she shared with his mother.

"Under the bed, there's a white dress," Sireen said as she disappeared into the hall. "Just get it, and I'll explain later."

Waleed went to his knees and found the dress immediately. It was white, he noticed. *Strange,* he thought.

"She also said there's a ring box," Sireen said anxiously as she returned empty handed.

"I don't see it," Waleed said, scanning the room.

He went from room to room as Sireen searched for it under the bed, on the bed, and between the bed sheets. It wasn't there.

"She must have forgotten where she put it," Waleed said. "We should get going now."

"I'll carry the dress," she said, taking the heavy frock in her arms and leading the way out. "Let's go."

Sireen kept a sharp eye as they descended the stairs and rushed outside the building. They stopped immediately when they heard the rumble of an idling engine, and Sireen spotted the nose of a tank that was stopped just around the corner. Before she could react, she heard a voice that brought a hundred ugly memories flooding back to her mind. The nausea roiled in her stomach.

"Not so fast, Romeo and Juliet," Hussein said as his men flashed four rifles in their direction.

Sireen looked around. The sidewalk and street were deserted. She turned back to Hussein. "What do you want from me?" she said with a fury so desperate it made her feel weak. "Leave me alone!"

Hussein laughed. "You know what I love about Romeo and Juliet? They both die at the end." He looked to his men as if expecting them to join in the joke, and scowled when they only looked at each other and grinned uncertainly. "But I'm a gentle soul, so no one has to die here today."

"Good," Sireen said as she carefully placed the dress on a wood-slatted bench. "Then we're done."

"Well, I have to say, my love, that I'm doing you a great favor. And I'm not accustomed to doing favors without expecting something in return. What would you say, Sireen? For old time's sake . . ."

"I never loved anything about you," Sireen said through her teeth. "You're a criminal. You shouldn't be with a woman; you should be in a cage."

"Let's get to the point here," Hussein said sternly. "I want a little something." He walked toward her and raised his arm to touch her. "Take off your shirt, darling."

Sireen took a step back, causing Hussein to laugh wildly. She realized that her ex-fiancé, though admired and respected in Assad's army, had let his obsession with her take over his mind.

"Come now," Hussein said. "Just a little flash, if you please."

Waleed lunged forward, grabbed Hussein's arm, twisted him to his knees, and kicked him in the abdomen.

"If you touch a hair on her head," Waleed snarled, "I will kill you."

Hussein wrenched himself free with another unsettling burst of laughter. "All right, I see what you're doing. You want to play a game." He looked at his men and nodded.

Two ran at Waleed, grappling with him and forcing him to his knees. Sireen watched helplessly as Hussein pointed his rifle at Waleed's head, then between his eyes, and then shoved the barrel into his mouth.

"I can't shoot you," Hussein said. "That's boring." He turned to his men. "Bring me the box."

It seemed to Sireen that the men moved slower to Hussein's commands than they had before. Even so, they delivered their general a small wooden box carried by two iron handles.

"Let's see," Hussein said melodically. "Where are the handcuffs? Oh, here they are." He grabbed two sets of handcuffs and ordered his men to bind each of Waleed's arms to a metal bar of an apartment window with his back facing the street. When it was done, Hussein took off his belt, "No, I'm not going to rape him," he said to Sireen with a broad smile. "I've been saving that for you, my love."

"Shut your mouth, you honor-less bastard," Waleed yelled, his arms taut.

"Now how do we get rid of his T-shirt?" Hussein asked of no one in particular.

Sireen could take no more of this. She ran at Hussein and shoved him. To her revulsion, he barely flinched. He pointed to one of his men and motioned for him to hold her back.

"Look what else I have," he said to her as he dug around in the box. "A dagger." He pulled out a long, shiny knife and flashed it at Sireen before striding over to cut off Waleed's shirt. "You know, this is a special dagger. It's been saturated with poison. One stab, and your Romeo will be gone to his God. Should I do it, or will you behave?"

"Don't do it," Sireen quailed. "What do you want from me?"

Hussein grinned. "Well, for a start, I'd like you to take off that shirt like I asked. It doesn't suit you all that much."

"Sireen!" Waleed yelled. "I would rather die than have you do this. Do you understand?"

"I'm not going to do it, Hussein," she challenged.

A wild look crossed Hussein's eyes. He snatched out his belt and started whipping Waleed until blood dripped from his back.

Overcome with passion for Waleed's pain, Sireen reached down to grab the hem of her shirt.

"Don't do it!" Waleed pled. "He can take my life, but I won't let him take your honor."

"You don't think I'll actually stab him with the dagger," Hussein said, cocking his head to one side. "Or maybe you think I'm bluffing about the poison."

She shook her head, her tears falling freely.

"Well, let me show you a little something." Hussein ordered his men to line up against the side of the building. "Where are you from, son?" he asked the first man.

The man wore a troubled expression. "Safita, sir."

"Oh, Safita. Good people there. Good people." He moved on to the next one. "What about you?"

"Kafranbel, sir."

"Kafranbel!" And the next. "And you?"

"I'm from the South of Lebanon."

"Oh, wonderful!" Hussein said. "Our great friends from Hezbollah fighting here with us."

Sireen bit her lip as the four soldiers traded anxious glances. Hussein looked from face to face before nodding in the direction of the man from Kafranbel. "Hold him."

The other soldiers immediately grabbed their comrade and pushed him to his knees.

"Please, sir, I didn't do anything," the man from Kafranbel begged.

"You know there are many cities and towns in this country that I utterly despise," Hussein said as he grabbed the man by his hair and placed the dagger close to his neck. "Kafranbel tops them all. I hate every last artist son of a whore who lives there. We will soon turn it into a potato field, I promise you."

"But, sir," the soldier said, "I'm with you."

"I saw you praying last night," Hussein accused, looking wildly from man to man as if seeking confirmation.

"No, sir," the man from Kafranbel insisted. "I never pray. It must have been someone else you saw."

"You, from Safita," Hussein said. "Did you see him praying or not?"

Hesitantly, the man nodded.

"No, sir," the man from Kafranbel said. "It must have been someone else."

Hussein stabbed the dagger into the right side of the soldier's chest. The soldier screamed in pain before tumbling into hyperventilation.

"Now we leave it in for a few seconds," Hussein said, glaring back at Sireen with hunger in his eyes. Less than a minute later, he pulled out the dagger, which was dripping blood.

The soldier's muscles started to loosen and he became more flaccid. He was clearly struggling to breathe.

"At a high enough concentration," Hussein said proudly, "simply breathing this substance can kill." He shrugged. "This dagger is useless now. Give me a fresh one."

One of his men rushed to the wooden box as Hussein tossed the bloody dagger aside. When he had his fresh knife, he began running the flat side of it across Waleed's bare back as he smiled at Sireen.

"Stop!" Sireen said. "Please stop!" She burst out crying as she removed her shirt. She looked down, trying to cover her body with her black hair as she crossed her arms over her chest. When she could bear it no more, she shut her eyes firmly to avoid seeing her own body.

"Sireen, no!" Waleed sobbed. "Don't let them kill me twice."

"Good girl," Hussein mocked. "Now come closer."

She dragged herself slowly toward him, burdened by the weight of her own shame. The whole time, she walked with her eyes glued to the ground before stopping just a few feet away from him.

"Come closer," Hussein said in a deep voice.

Sireen refused, shaking her head without saying a word.

Hussein smiled wickedly and stepped to her. His eyes lingered on her flesh for a time before he lifted her chin up and tried to kiss her lips. She turned her head to the right, away from Waleed so she didn't have to see how he looked as she submitted. Hussein began kissing her neck.

"No!" Waleed screamed, pulling hard on his handcuffs. "I will break the world over your head, you bastard!"

With a laugh, Hussein stopped kissing her long enough to glance at Waleed. He slid his arms around Sireen, placing his hands on her back and pressing them into her. She held her breath and grimaced. She pushed his hands away gently. He resisted. They struggled awkwardly in this way for a moment before a miracle came to spare her.

Hussein's phone rang. Never had the sound given Sireen such hope. But then, just as quickly as the hope came, it was dashed away as Hussein cut off the call and began fumbling with her once more. The phone rang again. Again he shut it off. It rang a third time, and for a third time, he ignored it. Then one of his soldier's phones came to life. Hussein pulled away from Sireen, looking annoyed as the soldier answered the call.

"He's here, sir," the soldier said as he stared at Hussein. The soldier's eyes widened. "We need to evacuate? What happened?" Slowly, his expression melted to frustration. "Hold on . . ." He held the phone away from his ear so he could speak to his commanding officer. "Sir, there have been defections among the tanks. We need to evacuate the area. The air force wants to flatten it."

"To hell with the air force!" Hussein spat. "Tell them I'm busy."

"Sir, these are presidential orders."

Hussein growled, glaring at Sireen for a moment before tearing himself away from her. She felt unchained the instant she was free of his touch.

"Take your stupid friend here," Hussein said, pointing at each soldier in turn. "Get in the tank and leave. I'll follow you when I'm ready."

"But—"

"*Now!*" Hussein screamed.

"All right, sir," the soldier said.

When the men had loaded up, the tank rolled away, carrying its adornment of small, lifeless bodies along for the ride.

"Much better," Hussein said with an oily smile. "Now it's just the three of us. Just like I always pictured it." He pulled Sireen back into his fidgety embrace.

"I swear that you will pay with your blood for this," Waleed threatened.

"I will pay with my seed," the general said, barking with laughter. He pressed firmly on Sireen's shoulders. "Get down, you whore. You thought you could make a mockery out of me with your lover? I will show you what such things cost."

"Don't do what he says!" Waleed yelled.

All resistance having left her, Sireen slowly went to her knees without speaking. She looked down as he pushed himself closer to her face. His shoes were covered in mud and blood. She heard the sound of his pants unzipping.

"Come on, baby," he grunted. "You know what I want, don't you?"

She dared not look up. For a moment, she squinted her eyes closed. But then, upon opening them again, she noticed something new on the sidewalk. A few inches to the left of Hussein's shoes rested a dagger covered in blood.

"Yes," she said softly as she looked up at him. As she had hoped, his eyes were closed. She also saw that his hands were empty. In his anticipation of pleasure, he had discarded the other dagger. Quickly she reached for the bloody dagger with her right hand, then slowly stood.

"What?" he said, opening his eyes to stare at her in surprise.

"That's not how I like it done," she said playfully. Careful to hide the dagger from sight, she wrapped her arms around his shoulders and placed her lips close to his.

"Ah . . ." He closed his eyes and eased his lips forward.

"This is how I like it done," she said as she thrust the dagger into his back with all her strength. She locked eyes with him, clenching her jaw as she buried the dagger as deeply into his flesh as she could manage. She did it for the blood dripping off Waleed's back; she did it so that the soul of Waleed's father could rest in peace; and she did it to avenge herself from the shame of being forced to strip outside on a cold November day.

Hussein cried out in pain, arching his back to escape the knife. "You whore!" he screamed as he grabbed her by the shoulders.

She kneed him in the groin and shoved him to the ground, where he twisted and turned, moaning. She reached down and snatched his rifle. "Give me the keys to the handcuffs before I shoot you."

There was an animal madness in Hussein's eyes. "I swear I'll cut off your limbs with a chainsaw and feed them to dogs while you watch. We've done it before."

"I'm sure you've done worse," Sireen said. "This is really not helping your case to stay alive right now. Give me the keys or I'll shoot you."

"I will cut off his genitals. I swear, you whore."

"I'm sure you've done that to people, too." She cocked her head to one side. "Wait. I see the problem. You think I'm bluffing." She pointed the rifle at his foot and shot it without flinching.

He screamed and yanked back his foot as blood sprayed.

"This is the last time I say it. Give me the keys."

He reached for his pocket and threw the keys to the ground. "Take them, you *whore*." By now, he had begun to spit the word he so favored as if he thought it could still save him, as if it could still break her.

"Don't move, or I swear I'll kill you," she said. "Don't test me."

Sireen took the keys, grabbed her shirt off the ground, and walked backward to Waleed, never taking her eyes off Hussein. She gasped when she saw the blood on her love's back out of the corner of her eye. He was very quiet as she unlocked the handcuffs and began wiping the blood off his back with her T-shirt. The threads were drenched before she could finish. When Waleed turned and lowered his arms, they both avoided making eye contact.

"Let's leave," he said.

She nodded, and they began to walk away.

"Hey, you!" Hussein yelled.

They turned back.

"You should have seen him," Hussein said to Waleed.

"What do you mean?" he asked, sounding exhausted. "I should have seen who?"

Hussein grinned even as he grimaced from the pain of his wounds. "You should have seen him pleading for his life like a dog." He snorted through a bout of laughter. "He begged us to take his wife for our pleasure, if only we would let him live."

Waleed's face darkened. "You mean my father."

"Who else could I mean?"

"My father would never say that."

"He moaned like a whore as I wrote Bashar's holy name on his chest with my knife."

Before Sireen could stop him, Waleed went to Hussein and began to punch him. Through it all, Hussein chuckled. Waleed dragged him to the window of the nearby building and handcuffed one of his hands to the bars.

"Let's see how much mercy your people show you when they destroy our neighborhood," Waleed said. Then he joined Sireen in a sidelong embrace.

As they gathered themselves, they cried for a time—tears of anger, tears of love, tears of sorrow, and tears of joy all joining into one long sob. When they had finished, she snatched up the white dress and used it to cover as much of her body as she could manage. Huddling together, they hobbled in the direction of the escape tunnel.

~~~

The air force arrived, showing the regime's paranoia by bombing all the tanks indiscriminately. When the deed was done, they began showering the civilian buildings with boxes of TNT. The noise was deafening as the night sky blazed with lights and the smell of smoke permeated the air.

Sireen held tight to Waleed as they reached the underground tunnel and looked back one more time at their burning neighborhood. Several boxes of TNT had just dropped on their building. She watched with a hollow sort of sadness as it crumbled to the ground. It wasn't the building she would mourn, but rather the memories she had shared there with Waleed's family.

They held hands and stood in silence beneath a large olive tree decorated with three independence flags. Her skin trembled at his touch as he pulled down one of the flags and wrapped it around her.

"Thank you," she whispered, looking down in shame.

He took another of the flags and wrapped it around his bleeding torso. "Could you please grab the last flag?" he asked. "My back hurts. I don't want them burning it or stepping on it."

"Of course, *ya omri* [my life]."

She tried to reach it a few times, but could not reach. She placed the dress on the ground and tried again, but failed. She turned to Waleed, embarrassed, but what she saw washed her shame away in an instant. He had bent down on one knee and was holding an open box bearing a beautiful ring of white gold, diamond, and turquoise.

"I found this under the bed," he said, smiling. "Will you marry me?"

Everything faded: the bombs, the bullets, and the death falling from the sky. She felt that saying yes would not be a strong enough acceptance of the offer. If only the clouds could spell *yes* and rain *yes* all over the city. If only spring would arrive and bloom *yes* in every jasmine flower and on every plum tree. If only the moon could shine *yes* and the stars align to read *yes*.

"Yes," she said softly as he slid the ring around her finger.

She could not take her eyes off him as he picked her up and carried her into the smoke-filled tunnel. The flags they wore pressed together as they vanished into the darkness and the unknown beyond. For the first time in her life, Sireen did not fear, but rather, loved the unknown.

Chapter 30
Red Lines and Bread Lines

The rate at which the Syrian Genocide unfolded defied all acceptable international standards. Even the most conservative estimates placed the number of dead at 60,000 and projected it to climb to 100,000 in a matter of months. The number of refugees in neighboring countries approached a million, while the number of those displaced within the country was at least three times as high.

The West kept drawing lines in the sand for the Assad regime that he simply walked over each time with no consequences. At first, Syrians assumed that the use of the air force against civilians would trigger a response. It didn't. Then they thought that the use of the Scud ballistic missiles against schools and hospitals would trigger a response. It didn't. Then at last, a new "red line" was drawn for the regime, and that was the use of chemical weapons against civilians.

The Assad regime turned its attention to destroying crops, burning wheat storage sites, and leveling bakeries. The goal of this latest scheme was to create a great famine in Syria. Indeed, the shortage of bread and food grew alarming by December. Bread lines stretched for miles at a time, with only enough bread for the first half-mile of people. The hungry citizens started taking turns at which families got to eat each day. The famine became ever more real, but this one was different than any other famine in history, because the starving people of Syria had too much dignity and too much pride to even look hungry. Society did not disintegrate, as Assad had predicted, but instead, it revealed a proud sense of Syrian-ness not seen in the country in a thousand years.

Meanwhile, loyalist regions like Tartous enjoyed the luxuries of extra wheat, no cuts in the electricity, and the best dishes of Syrian cuisine. The people lived a life of excess, driving the best cars and staying in fancy villas. Regime loyalists began flocking to beach resorts to avoid the headaches of war while their army tried to crush the rebellion. The contrast was stark and painful, the difference between heaven and hell. It was no wonder that Assad and his loyalists thought that he was a god.

—*Syria: A History in Blood* by Celine Dubois

December 23, 2012
Deaths: 60,400

Sireen had followed Waleed for days, along with the rest of their neighborhood. It was no easy exodus, as they had to spend numerous nights sleeping on the cold, rainy streets. They marched from neighborhood to neighborhood, absorbing as many citizens as possible.

There were hardships. Hod-Hod caught the flu, and Sarah's knees were the size of soccer balls, but they kept marching in silence. They were cold, hungry, and many were wounded. Their exodus came to an end when they reached the distant neighborhood of Der Baalbeh, named after the ancient Syrian rain god. The people of the neighborhood offered them food, water, and places to stay.

"How is he doing?" Sarah asked as she looked at the boy cradled in Sireen's arms.

"He still has a fever," Sireen said, clutching the wet towel to Hod-Hod's head.

"The poor soul. He's too young to tolerate this."

"This is too much for an adult, let alone a child. He's lost so much weight."

"*May he bury my heart,*" Sarah said, fanning herself with her hand.

"You know, *Khale*, this boy will one day be a great man."

She looked to the heavens. "*Inshallah*. Hardship makes great men."

They plodded on for a few more steps before Sireen finally found the courage to say something that had been bothering her for days. "I'm very sorry that I got the dress all dirty."

"The wedding dress?" Sarah asked, her eyebrows raised. "Oh, I took care of that. It looks better than before. I added blue beads to it to protect you from the evil eye."

"You're sounding like Om Zaki," Sireen said, laughing.

For the first time in ages, Sarah joined in the laugh. "I haven't laughed in so long. May God grant you happiness. I've also made a beautiful white shirt and black pants for Waleed."

"Could I see them?"

"No, darling. They'll lose their brilliance."

"I made him something, too," Sireen admitted sheepishly. "It's like a vest."

"Show me! Let's see if I've taught you something."

Sireen handed Hod-Hod to her future mother-in-law and fell back in the procession of people until she found the wagon where she had stashed the vest. When she had it in hand, she jogged back to Sarah's position in the line. The vest was black with three red buttons and the flag of the revolution sewn to its left breast, right over his heart.

"What do you think?" she asked anxiously.

Sarah stuck out her lower lip. "It's not bad. You're getting better than me."

"*The eye is never higher than the eyebrow*," Sireen quipped.

"Oh, darling," Sarah said with a sigh, "let's have this wedding soon. What's the date today?"

"December sixteenth."

The old woman clapped her hands happily. "Let's have it a week from today. We'll tell our new neighbors, too. Hopefully Hod-Hod will be better by then. We all need something happy to look forward to. Enough sorrow. What do you say, darling?"

Sireen beamed. "I say yes."

"Habibti!" Sarah said and hugged her with joy.

Over the next week, Der Baalbeh placed its sorrows on hold, dried her tears, and got ready to celebrate love. It was amazing how the neighbors clung to any excuse to be happy in spite of their misfortunes. Happiness, like sadness, proved an inherent function of the human brain. When they found a suitable place for the wedding, the women of the neighborhood quickly distributed the tasks of cooking, preparing the wedding hall, and helping the bride with her hair and makeup. Om Zaki took care of all the metaphysical aspects of the wedding. The biggest fight erupted over who would get to take care of the neighborhood's superstar, Hod-Hod, during that week. The men went on with their daily tasks of securing the borders of the neighborhood from Assad's *Shabeeha* and fixing electricity lines and phone lines destroyed by the regime's war machine.

~~~

"Hello?" Sireen said into the phone. "Can you hear me?"

"I hear you," came the reply. "Is this Sireen?"

"Yes, how are you, Celine, my darling?"

"It's so good to hear your voice! I'm doing well. How are things in Homs?"

"They're very bad, I'm afraid."

"I know, dear. It's not much better here in Aleppo."

"Are you going to stay there?"

There was a sigh from the other end of the line. "Yes. My husband died here. At least I have his grave to visit. Many don't even have a body to cry over. Besides, I'm preparing *un reportage* about the women joining the Free Army."

"No way! Are they?"

"Yes, and I hear they're even better than the men."

Sireen started to choke up as she thought about her friend's loss. She wasn't sure she could bear to endure the same. "I'm so sorry that I couldn't be there for you when it happened."

"We've all lost precious things, my darling. We have to fight this battle till the end. This is not about Syria. It's a battle to save the face of humanity."

Sireen's heart raced as she remembered the reason she had called.

"Celine?"

"Oui?"

"I'm getting married in a few days."

"Oh! *Mabrook* [Congratulations]! *Mabrook!*"

"I know you can't come here to join us, but I wanted you to know that we will be thinking of you as if you were here."

"I'm so happy, my darling. I really am."

"I promise you we'll host another party for everybody after the revolution."

"Can I tell Yousef?"

"Yes, of course. Why not?"

There was a long pause from the other end of the line. "It's just that I think he . . . what am I saying? Tell me about the dress!"

"Women will be women even if they join the Free Army," Sireen said with a laugh.

Celine chuckled in reply.

They talked for a few more minutes before the phone service finally died.

Later that day, when service returned, Sireen was also able to call little Atargatis and tell her of the news. The young girl was euphoric. She screamed in joy over the phone. From the warm reception she was receiving all around, Sireen wished that she could call her mother, as well, but she had no way of finding her contact information.

~~~

That week at Der Baalbeh was the happiest week Sireen had known in months, perhaps years. The day before the wedding, she went to talk to Waleed as he sat with three other men from the Free Army, all of them occupying plastic chairs as they drank tea and smoked *arguileh*. Each held an AK-47. One man carried an RPG.

"You're really working hard, I see," Sireen mocked.

"You must be Waleed's bride," said the man with the RPG at his side.

"Not yet," she corrected. "I'm simply Sireen for now." An uncontrollable smile came to her lips. "I hope to see you all at the wedding tomorrow. The women have worked hard to prepare some good meals."

"I'm Ahmad," the man said as he looked out of the corner of his eye at Waleed. It seemed to Sireen that he was unsure whether her future husband would approve of the introduction. Of course, Waleed was secure enough in their relationship that he would never disapprove.

"We were just talking about what to get you as a wedding gift from the Free Army at Der Baalbeh," Ahmad said.

"You are doing enough for us already," Sireen insisted. "Your presence will be a great gift."

"Is someone making you a wedding cake?"

Sireen frowned. "We really don't have the ingredients. We're trying to work around the siege."

Ahmad raised a finger to the air. "Then that will be it. I'll get you the best wedding cake you've seen in your life."

"Really? How?"

"I'm from a town near Hama. I haven't been there in months, and I miss my mother and my fiancée terribly. I've been waiting for an excuse to go see them. My mother works at a bakery there, and I swear to the God of the heavens that we make the best cakes and most delicious bread in all of Syria. I'll get you a three-story cake that will have all of Der Baalbeh talking."

Sireen giggled as she thought about her new friend carrying a three-tiered wedding cake through a war zone. "Oh, brother Ahmad, that is so kind of you, but it's really not necessary."

"No, it's done," he said with a dismissive wave. "A man is his word. I won't take it back. I swear by my moustache." He twirled his moustache just then, causing Sireen to laugh once more and Waleed to grin with pride.

"It's really too risky to travel now. It's really fine."

"Waleed, talk to your bride! I told her a man is his word."

"Let him do whatever he wants, Sireen," Waleed said with a gruff smirk.

Sireen looked at Ahmad with wide eyes. "Thank you so much. Really."

"I'll head there tonight and will be back with the cake before your wedding. What time will you start?"

"Probably late—around eight in the evening."

"I'll be back at seven with the cake, or I'm shaving this moustache."

Sireen laughed. "So what's the name of your town?"

"Halfaya. The Free Army has recently liberated it. Have you heard of it?"

"Of course," she said.

An awkward silence followed, leaving Sireen to pick up the pieces and change tack. "Waleed, could I talk to you for a second?"

The two walked away from the rest of the men and climbed up an isolated green hill overlooking the neighborhood. She could see and hear smoke and explosions coming from nearby neighborhoods, but Assad's army had failed at breaching Der Baalbeh. All prior attempts to invade the neighborhood had failed, and Assad's forces had given up. The weather was cold and windy as Sireen found herself standing beside the love of her life, surrounded by a thicket of sugarcane plants alive with birds by the dozens. The birds had also learned to migrate away from regime loyalists and seek asylum with the revolutionaries.

"Sireen, look over there!" Waleed said suddenly. "You see that pigeon?"

"Which one? I see a lot of them?"

"It's F-16!" Waleed said in disbelief. "That's Omar's pigeon that brought you all my love poems." He grabbed one of the sugarcanes and began to wave it in a way that she had seen Omar do before.

"You're insane," she said with a grin.

The pigeon left the flock and flew toward him. Sireen's mouth hung open in amazement as the pigeon landed on Waleed's shoulder. He took the pigeon in his arms and hugged it gently before passing it to Sireen, who stroked its feathers as the two of them sat down on the hilltop. She and Waleed chewed on sugarcane, even feeding some to the bird as they gazed at the setting sun. As dusk settled in, Sireen grabbed a handful of lipsticks and make up from her bag and used them to paint the pigeon's right wing with the colors of the revolutionary flag.

"I can't believe we'll be getting married without Omar in attendance," Waleed said sadly.

"I know," Sireen said. "But they will all be with us: Omar, your father, Khalid, and Sami. Martyrs don't die."

"You must really miss your parents, too."

"Yes. Not having my mother at my wedding is something I never imagined would happen, but I have you." She took his hand. "We have each other. That's all I need right now."

"You will always have me, my love."

"You are everything I need, Waleed. You are my lover, my father, and my mother. I can give up anything, but not you."

"God, how I love you." His eyes fluttered as he searched for words that seemed to elude him. "It's not even love; it's something much deeper than love. I love this revolution that brought us closer, I even love the misery that we shared together."

She demurred, unable to look him in the eye for fear of how it would break her inhibitions. "Are you nervous about tomorrow?" she asked, trying to change the subject as quickly as she could.

"Not at all. My greatest dream is coming true. Why would that make me nervous?"

"You're not afraid of commitment?"

"I could never love any other person the way I love you, so why worry? The only thing that could come even close is my love for Syria. You're not jealous of her, are you?"

F-16 kept moving its head left and right as if trying to follow the conversation.

"Sometimes." She smiled. "What if she takes you away from me?"

"Darling, Syria doesn't take. She only gives. Look, she gave us sugarcane." They both smiled.

When it grew too dark to see one another, the young couple rose and went home, Waleed carrying his pigeon friend with him all the way. Later, the younger women took Sireen for a bachelorette party outside the neighborhood, where they spent the night singing and dancing—any excuse to be happy.

~~~

"Ladies, wake up, wake up!" one of the women from the party yelled. "It's morning."

Sireen was the first to wake. Slowly she realized that it was Lamees, her self-appointed wedding planner, rousing them. "Oh, Lamees," she whined. "It's still early."

"Wake up, or I'll pour water on you," the girl threatened. "Sireen, we've heated a lot of water for you on coal since there's no electricity. Go shower before it gets cold."

Sireen obeyed. She pulled herself to the shower, not wanting to upset her wedding manager's balance so early in the day. By the time she was done, all the girls were wide awake and excited to begin the tasks Lamees had assigned them.

"All right, ladies," Sireen said. "Are you ready?"

"Yes!" they replied in unison, startling Sireen.

"Maya, you will do the manicure, and Reema will do the pedicure," Lamees instructed. "Jana, could you put some music on? Is it a funeral or a wedding that we're going to?"

Everyone followed her instructions. There was an atmosphere of fleeting joy, a bubble of happiness floating on a river of sorrow. It was clear that every woman in the room wanted to believe that they were normal ladies living a normal life. It was as if they all saw themselves in Sireen. They wanted to make sure she was happy so that they could have hope for happiness for themselves.

As they tended to their labor, they used coal to heat water, batteries to operate the radio, and mirrors for extra lighting. When they went to fit the dress on Sireen, they found that it was perfect. It was a long, strapless white dress with shiny blue beads scattered across the waist, "to protect her from the evil eye," as Sarah had put it. The girls donated a pearl necklace and blue earrings made of glass as a wedding gift. The day could not have been more perfect in Sireen's eyes.

Then the music stopped, and the radio news anchor said the two words that every Syrian feared the most: "Breaking news."

The announcer continued: "Assad loyalists have committed yet another massacre."

Every girl stopped what she was doing and listened silently, hoping that the massacre hadn't occurred somewhere they recognized.

"Two hundred to three hundred people were killed instantly after regime fighter jets bombed a bakery north of Hama," the announcer continued.

Sireen's heart dropped, and her eyes opened wide as she whispered to herself, "No . . . no . . ."

"Several hours ago, regime forces killed hundreds of civilians at a bakery. The actions have failed to trigger any international response or a comment on the incident so far. This is the fourth time that a bakery was targeted in the country in the past two weeks. Destroying eateries appears to be a new strategy by Assad loyalists, designed to crush our blessed revolution. Our reporter will take you live to the town of Halfaya north of Hama . . ."

Sireen got up from her chair, placed her hands on her mouth, and then knelt on the floor, wrinkling the white dress. When the weight of what she had just learned hit her fully, she threw herself on the floor, crying. "It's my fault! It's my fault!" she said repeatedly. She could not stop thinking about Ahmad and the way he twirled his mustache. He was a man of his word, but even his word could not withstand the regime's missiles.

It was clear that none of the other girls understood what was happening or why Sireen had reacted in this way, so they just kept listening to the story.

The announcer's voice became grim as he continued. "Regime loyalists said, and I quote, that they were trying to 'provide those complaining of famine a little meat to mix with their bread.'"

Jana cried out in anguish. Maya lifted Sireen up and began crying herself. Soon, all eight girls were in tears, even Lamees. The wedding preparation had indeed turned into a funeral.

After a time, Lamees had had enough. "Everyone pull yourselves together! I don't want to see one more tear!"

Silence fell as the girls collected themselves.

"Who here has lost a father?"

Three girls, including Lamees, raised their hands.

"Who lost a mother?"

Two girls raised their hands.

"Who lost a brother or a sister?"

Five girls, including Lamees, raised their hands.

"Who lost a lover?"

Two girls raised their hands.

"Who has been raped?"

One girl raised her hand in tears.

"Who lost a friend?"

Everyone raised their hands.

"You see?" Lamees said, sticking out her chin. "Look at us. We've all lost people dearer to our hearts than our own souls. We've all cried endless nights. We've all been through the pain, cold, and humiliation. Those bastards have killed our loved ones. They took away everything from us. We have no food, no water, and no electricity. Some of us got raped, and many of us are targets for kidnapping, rape, and murder simply because of what we believe.

"You know why they do all this?" she continued, looking at them fiercely. "You know why? Because they want to take from us the one thing that we haven't given them yet: our hope. Now look at yourselves weeping on the floor like widows. Do those look like the faces of women determined to win this war, no matter the cost? Are you the daughters, sisters, and lovers of men of the Free Army? Our men are out there facing bullets with their bare chests, and what do we do? We sit here and weep! Aren't you the granddaughters of Zenobia? Maybe we can't use guns and rifles, but our job is to look the devils in the eye and not blink or bow. Now one of our men in the Free Army is expecting a bride today. Are we going to help her get ready or not?"

By the time Lamees finished, she was red in the face and out of breath, but her speech had achieved its intended end. The girls had washed their faces and were back in business. The music returned as they tackled the sensitive missions of hair and makeup for their beautiful bride. By the time they finished, it was already seven in the evening, and the girls hadn't yet started on their own hair and makeup. Panic set in. Dresses were tossed around and makeup wars erupted. The collective conclusion was that there was no way they would be ready on time.

~~~

Meanwhile, in the neighborhood, one of the backyards was transformed into a ceremony hall decorated with dozens of colored light bulbs powered by a small generator. Many middle-aged women ran around, placing various Syrian dishes on the tables and arranging the seats. Several men from the Free Army helped Waleed get ready by giving him embarrassing wedding night advice. Half of them decided to attend the wedding, while the other half remained in their positions, guarding the neighborhood. The news of Ahmad's death in Halfaya came as a shock to all of them, but they pushed it aside and decided to give Der Baalbeh the one happy night it had been hoping for.

The clock struck eight. A heavy fog covered the neighborhood, and for the first time in two years, it began to snow lightly. Waleed could hear no gunshots or bombings in the background, only music. The guests had arrived, and Waleed and his friends from the FSA had gathered at the mosque, but the girls and the bride were nowhere to be found. The imam talked to the men about marriage, about the war, and how to manage the two simultaneously. The men carried Waleed on their shoulders according to Syrian tradition, singing folk songs and revolution songs at the same time. There were so many flags on their shoulders that the whole scene looked more like a protest. They paraded the groom proudly through the neighborhood until they reached the ceremony hall. There they were told to wait because the bride was not ready yet, and it was considered very bad luck for the groom to enter before the bride.

Upon learning that his future wife was not yet ready for him, Waleed began to get nervous for the first time. He wondered whether she was late because she was having second thoughts. Of course, his nerves weren't helped when Om Zaki kept everyone on edge with her predictions of doom and omens of imminent trouble. Through all this, Waleed did his best to wait patiently with his men. The wait was so long that even his brigade leader had time to make it back before the start of the ceremony. The leader kissed Waleed on the cheeks and gave him a watch as a gift.

Still the girls were nowhere to be found. Despite the chill in the air, Waleed began to break out in a sweat. Some of the others appeared to notice, for a gentle ribbing of Waleed commenced among those present at the doors of the ceremony hall.

The good feelings were shattered when a military plane approached the wedding site uninvited. Waleed held his breath as he watched, along with everyone else. It passed over the area a few times, then disappeared without shooting missiles or sending gifts of TNT.

Maybe the pilot grew a conscience on my wedding day, Waleed thought. Then, without another passing thought on the matter, he returned to worrying about Sireen.

~~~

The girls were at last ready, half an hour late. They had all paused when Sireen cried out for silence. She had heard the military plane overhead before she saw it. Together the women rushed outside, half made-up and scared. Sireen could hardly see the plane through the fog, but it was gone not long after they stepped outside. When no explosions followed, they all held hands with the bride in the center and began reciting Syrian wedding blessings.

Lamees began. "*Aweeha!* Oh girls of Syria, gather in grace. *Aweeha*, oh night get longer and longer. *Aweeha*, oh sun never show your face!"

"*Lele lele leesh!*" all the ladies repeated in accordance with the ancient custom.

Sireen beamed, hardly able to believe that this was all happening to her. She had participated in circles like this before, but never had she stood in the center—and even in her wildest dreams as a girl, she could not have imagined the opportunity to stand in this place in advance of marrying such a wonderful man.

"*Aweeha!*" Jana said, her thin lips parting into a smile as she led the next chant. "Fill the plates with pears, I told. *Aweeha*, and whoever takes our girl. *Aweeha* should fill her plate with diamonds and gold!"

"*Lele lele leesh!*"

Maya followed, her long black hair flowing in the wind. "*Aweeha!* Waleed is one. *Aweeha!* Sireen is two, oh my! *Aweeha*, get some blue beads. *Aweeha*, to push away the evil eye!"

"*Lele lele leesh!*"

They were interrupted by the sound of a thud. Something had fallen on the ground, but it was too foggy to see.

"Wait," Sireen said as she walked toward the fallen object. It was a bird—a white pigeon, in fact. She went to her knees and lifted up the fallen pigeon. It still bore the colors of the Syrian independence flag on its wings. Sireen's heart sank. "Oh, F-16," she said, a tear coming to her eye. She had thought the bird was dead, so when it twitched in her hands, she was startled.

The women all jumped back with a collective whimper. Sireen calmed them by holding out her hand. The poor bird seemed to be struggling to breathe. It took a few heavy breaths before turning its head to one side and sputtering into stillness. Omar's beloved bird was dead, and Sireen could sense that this meant something. It was as if F-16 had come to deliver one last message from her beloved.

She looked at the girls, her eyes filled with tears. "You all should wait here. Don't leave this place. I will be right back."

"What's going on?" Lamees asked.

"I don't know, but I have a very bad feeling. Take the girls and go inside."

"Don't be gone for too long."

Sireen froze, holding her hand out to drive home her point. "Listen, no matter what happens, don't follow me until I come back and ask you to leave. You've got seven lives in your hands, so trust me. I know what I'm saying."

Lamees nodded in reassurance.

Sireen ran barefoot to the wedding hall, her throat seizing with the dread she felt. When she arrived, she found six men lying on the ground outside the ceremony hall, all of them motionless.

"Oh, God! No!" She went from man to man, shaking them each in turn. "Can you hear me? Can you hear me?"

Her voice grew faint as she wept. She could feel the mascara zigzagging down her cheeks as she prodded the bodies one at a time, looking for any signs of life. There was no blood, no bruises, and no gunshot wounds—just silent death. Desperately she searched for Waleed, realizing only a moment of relief when she could not find him.

Then she saw it. The doorway to the hallway stood wide open.

"Waleed!" she called. "Waleed! Waleed!"

Inside, the colored light bulbs flickered. The food had been set on all the tables and remained untouched. The guests had all arrived. No one moved.

"No!" she yelled from the marrow of her bones. "No!"

Most of the guests were slumped in their chairs, but some had fallen to the floor. All were silent and motionless. No one said any wedding blessings. No one sang wedding songs. No one threw rice and rose petals on the bride as she entered.

Then she heard agonized grunts from her right. She rushed toward the sound and found Om Zaki lying prone on the polished marble floor, the old woman trying desperately to lift her head.

"Are you all right?" Sireen asked.

"The garlic," she mumbled. "The garlic." With those words, she took her last breath.

"Om Zaki, answer me! Om Zaki!" It was no use. Indeed there was an odd smell like garlic. Sireen began to feel lightheaded, but she stood and went out through the back door in search of Waleed. She kept calling his name as she ran down the street. Corpses of dead pigeons and dead cats were scattered everywhere.

"Waleeed!" she yelled again before collapsing to the ground.

~~~

Waleed watched his beautiful bride from the top of a four-story building. He was unable to stand, so he knelt, his legs folded under him, and grasped the edge of the rooftop. He wanted to call out to Sireen, but he remained silent. He knew that if she saw him, she would come up and try to save him. He wanted her to get out of the area as soon as possible, but he didn't know how to make that happen.

Only he and four others had managed to run up to a high place before losing their muscle control and ability to breathe. But it was no victory. His mother had already stopped breathing, and so had two others. Only he and Hod-Hod remained alive.

With the last fleeting vision of Sireen in his mind, Waleed pushed back from the edge of the roof and lowered himself to lie facing Hod-Hod. He reached out a trembling hand to touch the boy's cheek. "We're going to see your mommy and daddy and *Ammo* Omar soon," he whispered with great difficulty. "They will be so happy to see us."

A smile crossed Hod-Hod's face as he stopped breathing.

Gently Waleed closed the child's eyes and began to cry. The only muscles he could move voluntarily were those in his arms and face. He could see that his skin was flushed. His head throbbed painfully. The task of breathing was becoming more exhausting. He lifted himself up to get one last glimpse at his beloved, but she was gone. The thought that she had escaped brought him warm relief that washed all the pain away.

He turned onto his back and began to recite verses from the Quran. In time, he began to hallucinate. First he heard a woman's voice repeating something in the distance. Then, as it drew closer, he realized that it was Sireen's voice. He shook his head in disbelief when a blurry woman in a white dress emerged from the fog that grew thicker around him. The woman looked just like Sireen. She sat down next to him and kissed his hand. He couldn't understand what she was saying, but she was the prettiest thing he had ever seen. If this was the angel of death, then she was the most beautiful angel he could have asked for.

When he tried to speak, he found that he couldn't. He wanted to reach out and touch her face, but his hands wouldn't move. He could still see her when he stopped breathing. Her lips got closer to his and then kissed him. That was the last thing he saw.

~~~

Sireen kept counting: two breaths and then ten chest compressions. She kept repeating the routine maniacally.

"Waleed, don't leave me," she begged. "Waleed!"

Two breaths, ten chest compressions.

"Waleed! Answer me, *habibi*. Answer, my darling."

She was sweating, exhausted, and dizzy. She tried again. Then once more. When he didn't respond, she finally gave up, her muscles failing her. She fell onto his chest, weeping into him. She held his hand, kissed it, then lay down beside him and waited for life to come back to her beloved or for death to take her to him.

"They used chemical weapons, Waleed," she whispered. "Now the world will step in to help us. They said it was a red line. Waleed, we're free at last." She sucked in a breath, her lungs wheezing. "Waleed? Syria will be free soon, and our children will be born free. You'll open a clinic, or we can publish your poems and use the money to build a new house. Your mom and Hod-Hod can live with us, too." With the last of her strength, she lifted her head to look at her would-be husband. "We'll have children of our own. If it's a girl, we'll call her Nagham, after all the songs and poems you wrote for me. If it's a boy, we'll call him Khalid. That way his name will be Khalid ibn Waleed. He will be a hero, like his father. He will be so handsome . . ."

She paused as her breathing grew more labored and her head began to hurt. She placed her head on his chest again, closed her eyes, and fell asleep.

~~~

The fog kept them hidden from the eyes of the world while the snow fell. Each snowflake was like an angel's frozen tear. Silence echoed through the neighborhood.

Later that day, Western leaders condemned the attack on the Halfaya bakery. Iran and Russia watched in silent approval. As for the chemical attack on Der Baalbeh, it was forgotten. The red lines were erased and redrawn, and numerous similar attacks occurred thereafter. The world listened as the silent Syrian melody kept playing over and over. No one tried to change the tune.

The Free Army grew more determined every day. Qatar, Saudi Arabia, and Turkey were the only countries that agreed to provide some degree of assistance to the freedom fighters. Yousef continued to fight with the Free Army, and eventually decided to go back to Daraa after it was clear that the battle in the north was heading toward a victory for the resistance.

Celine stayed in Aleppo, and through her book, the love story of Waleed and Sireen remained alive in every breeze that blew the ashes of war over Homs and every raindrop and snowflake that kissed the wounds of Syria.

The revolution continued . . .

About the Author

Anas A. Ismael is a Syrian-Canadian physician, poet, and writer. He lives in the United States, where he continues to practice medicine. Most of his earlier publications were either poems or scientific papers. He began writing his first novel in the spring of 2011, when the Syrian revolution first began. He has a particular interest in ancient history and human rights issues. His dream is to practice medicine in a new Syria, which is free, democratic, just, and at peace with itself and its neighbors.

5366876R00155

Printed in Great Britain
by Amazon.co.uk, Ltd.,
Marston Gate.